HE-MEN, BAG MEN, & NYMPHOS

OCK
er

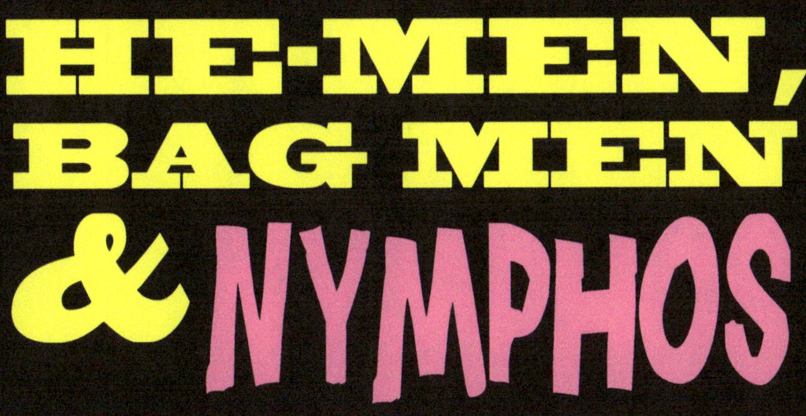

HE-MEN, BAG MEN & NYMPHOS

COLOR EDITION

WALTER KAYLIN

EDITED BY **ROBERT DEIS** & **WYATT DOYLE**

MensPulpMags.com

#new texture

Men's Adventure Magazines [MAMs]

A bona fide publishing phenomenon that emerged in the 1950s and thrived through the 1970s, the tropes and aesthetic established by **men's adventure magazines (MAMs)** have proven so durable and have been absorbed so totally into the American consciousness that even decades after their demise, MAMs remain an incontestable—if invisible—hand behind key events and directions in entertainment and popular culture.

Incorporating the colorful, eye-catching cover paintings and pulse-pounding action/adventure fiction of pre-World War II pulp fiction magazines, MAMs added non-fiction adventures to the mix, and blurred the line between the two by frequently claiming the outrageous, high-octane fiction was *also* true, even when such claims were implausible, preposterous, or demonstrably false. This blend quickly became standard for the genre, and pulp "fact" ran side by side with pulp fiction.

The MAM formula cannily incorporated aspects of other popular magazines that appealed to the working-class readership they targeted, including racy "bachelor" and pin-up mags, outdoor and travel periodicals, true crime and detective magazines, and celebrity scandal rags.

The format was adopted by multiple publishers, who produced magazines of varying quality. All told, more than 160 different periodicals fit the classification. Some lasted decades, others, only a few issues—or just one. While the more lurid varieties (sometimes called "sweats" or "sweat mags") often draw the most attention (and criticism), the range and quality of MAM content is more varied than is generally understood.

Though dismissed in their time as downmarket, lowbrow entertainment, the magazines were an enduring success, enjoyed by millions of readers over three decades. MAMs published popular writers of the day, and artwork by many of the era's top illustration artists. The terse, hard-boiled intensity of the writing and the dynamic, explosive, and racy illustration art—on their covers and in their pages—are essential to their appeal, then and now. The potency of these words and images remains undiminished; their excesses still spark gobsmacked wonder, and their artistry inspires fascination on its own terms.

CONTENTS

"The Exterminators"
Written as Roland Empey
For Men Only, April 1972
Illustration by Samson Pollen

THE RIGHT MAN FOR THE JOB

Comments on the New Edition
by Wyatt Doyle

LIKE THE magazines whose readers devoured his work nearly as fast as he could hammer it out, Walter Kaylin is gone. Kaylin and men's adventure magazines (MAMs) both—gone, and irreplaceable.

Though Kaylin's career writing for MAMs didn't line up precisely with the years those mags filled newsstands, it came close. Collector-historians define the MAM era as starting in the late 1940s and ending in the mid-1970s. This collection is chronologically ordered, opening with an appearance under his own name in the June 1956 issue of *Men*, and closing with his contribution (as "Roland Empey") to *For Men Only*, August 1975. It's a mere slice of one gifted writer's contributions to three-plus decades of MAMs, in 15 hard-charging steps (16, in the new expanded hardcover).

KAYLIN stories are fast reads. Ever emphasizing forward momentum, each line propels the reader into the next. The stories' breathless urgency and unstoppable velocity sometimes knock the reader off-balance, perhaps preventing them from challenging their veracity or realism. Indeed, from the first line, the reader often finds himself plunked straight into the white-hot cauldron of conflict, like a paratrooper dropped into battle. Reading his work, it's easy and even irresistible to imagine Kaylin feverishly pounding typewriter keys, swept up in flights of his enviable imagination.

It's a hallmark of Kaylin's stories (and much MAM fiction) to begin in the middle and work backward before speeding to an explosive—and generally quite final—conclusion. These reshuffled structures keep the stories lean, and respect readers' impatience to get to the good stuff. There's not a lot of room for reflection in a Kaylin yarn.

Where another writer might employ terse, tight exclamations to communicate speed and punch, Kaylin tends to go the other way, composing snaking (at times unwieldy) sentences that send violent and

"We Stopped India's Greatest Elephant Rampage"
Written as Roland Empey
Illustration by Earl Norem
Male, July 1971

dramatic events rumbling through his plots like armored tanks over rough terrain.

The approach is no less effective when describing more intimate physical conflict. The rabbit punches of other writers' short sentences have less in common with a real-world punch-up than Kaylin's weighted, bumpy approach. In Kaylin fistfights, there are no easy knockouts; only brutal slugfests.

It's immersive, and combined with complicated, everything-*plus*-the-kitchen-sink plotting, readers tend to share anxious states of mind comparable to Kaylin's overpowered protagonists. Even at their most extreme, the stories afford no time for skepticism.

That multi-car pile-up approach to plotting can be reflected in story titles, with many reading like grocery lists of tough, hard-boiled plot elements: "He Shared Their Food, Their Guns and Their Women" (*Male*, June 1959); "The Helicopter Hero and the 100 Ladies of 'Undress' Atoll" (*Men*, September 1959); "The Black Lace Blonde, the Yank Jungle Fighter and the Chicom Plot to Grab the Mid-Pacific" (*Men*, July 1966). MAMs' most consistent approach was to overwhelm the reader, and like the mags' graphic and extreme approach to illustration art, story titles were constructed to make for eye-grabbing cover headlines and stuff tables of contents with the promise of excitement.

He was an intensely physical writer, with rich descriptive gifts and a sense of movement that does not quit, to the point where his endings can sometimes feel like afterthoughts; some stories halt more than conclude. With Kaylin, the journey can count more than the destination.

That's not to say he didn't know and appreciate the values of killer endings, silence, or slow burns, particularly when employed as counterpoints to unspeakable savagery. Stories like "Emperor Blaine of 'Sweet Woman' Reef," "The Helicopter Hero and the 100 Ladies of 'Undress' Atoll," "The Nymph Who Leads an African Death Army," and "The Black Lace Blonde, The Yank Jungle Fighter, and the Chicom Plot to Grab the Mid-Pacific" all begin with humor and playfulness that encourage the reader to drop their guard just ahead of the nightmarish turns that soon follow.

KAYLIN had an innate understanding of the highly specific needs of MAM fiction, and his work in the field across decades would help define the unique genre. But that once-in-a-career symbiosis came at a price: For decades, those musty, obscure magazines—most now well over half a century old, with copies hard to come by—have provided the sole portal to the majority of Kaylin's prodigious output. (In his interview with Bob Deis, Kaylin offhandedly estimated his tally at near a thousand stories in MAMs, and that casual figure might well be close.)

Our priorities for this collection were to present a selection of some of Kaylin's most memorable stories, while also covering as many MAM obsessions and sub-genres as could reasonably fit between covers. You'll read Kaylin takes on hard-boiled crime ("Snow-Job From a Redhead"), Westerns ("The Cruel Gun Brothers"), dark historical fiction ("The Terrible Reward of 'Far East Harry' Wax"), tropical adventure ("Emperor Blaine of 'Sweet Woman' Reef," "The Helicopter Hero and the 100 Ladies of 'Undress' Atoll"), revolutionary battle ("The Nymph Who Leads an African Death Army"), alarmist non-fiction ("The Army's Terrifying Death Bugs and Loony Gas"), a WWII "death trek" saga ("The Yank Who Survived the 300-Mile Death Trek From Stalingrad"), reality-based survival ("... 108-Hour Mid-Ocean Ordeal ... 500 Dead ... 300 Still Afloat ..."), varied approaches to international espionage and intrigue ("Meet Our Terms or We Destroy 500 Million People," "The Black Lace Blonde, the Yank Jungle Fighter and the Chicom Plot to Grab the Mid-Pacific," "Surf Pack Assassins"), bogus biography ("Detective William Clive: Is He the Real James Bond?"), gangsters ("My Bloody Life as a Mafia Bag Man"), humorous tall tales with a wartime theme and a sexy bent ("They Call Him Father Italy"), and, in the new expanded hardcover edition, a highly unconventional animal attack story ("Cry of the Killer Cat"). Even so, we still couldn't squeeze in everything we wanted to, and we continue to uncover new-to-us Kaylin treasures in Deis' vast MAM archives. (Hungry for more?

"Trapped in Mexico's 'Cave of Giant Rats'"
Written as Roland Empey
Illustration by Mort Künstler
Male, July 1973

You'll find additional Kaylin stories in the Men's Adventure Library collections *Weasels Ripped My Flesh!* and *I Watched Them Eat Me Alive.*)

OUR INITIAL edition of this collection suffered from spotty distribution, making it less accessible to readers of what would become our acclaimed, multi-volume Men's Adventure Library series. We also didn't issue a hardcover, as has since become standard for the Library. We're glad to put those issues right with these new, color editions, which include supplementary illustrations and commentary that further illuminate the range and quantity of Kaylin's work in MAMs.

We've kept most of the book's introductory material unchanged from that initial edition. Although we lost Kaylin in 2017, four years after this collection first saw print (then Bruce Jay Friedman in 2020), we've chosen to reprint the original commentaries and encomia more or less as they were first published, rich with enthusiasm and optimism for the project at hand.

A little over a decade on, with multiple editions of this collection on shelves, our initial exploration of the imagination, invention, and talents of Walter Kaylin is at an end, for now. Your own journey is likely only just beginning. Enjoy the ride—and keep your left up. ✳

[2024]

INTRODUCTION

by Robert Deis

WHEN Wyatt Doyle and I were putting together our first anthology of stories from vintage MAMs, *Weasels Ripped My Flesh!*, we discussed what we might publish as a follow-up.

It didn't take long to decide.

We both came to the same conclusion. We wanted to publish the first-ever anthology of stories by the man other, better-known writers who worked for MAMs in the 1950s and 1960s considered to be one of the best men's adventure writers of them all. The guy writers like Mario Puzo and Bruce Jay Friedman (his colleagues at Martin Goodman's Magazine Management Company) referred to as "the great Walter Kaylin."

I originally tracked down and contacted Walter in 2010, to do an interview with him for my blog about MAMs, MensPulpMags.com. At the time, he was 89 years old and living with his beloved wife Peggy in Old Lyme, Connecticut.

After several conversations, I made a deal with Walter to buy publication rights to a number of his classic men's adventure magazine stories, with an eye toward bringing them back into print. I didn't know exactly when or if that might actually happen, but I knew I wanted to do it.

Since then, Peggy has passed away. And, as I write this, Walter is in a nursing home.

Not long ago, Walter's daughters Jennifer and Lucy graciously arranged for me to talk with him there by phone, so I could tell him that Wyatt and I would soon be issuing our long-planned collection of his MAM stories.

Walter was delighted to hear it.

"Trapped in the Bayou's Pit of a Million Snakes"
Written as Roland Empey
Illustration by Bob Larkin
***Male*, January 1974**

***This tense, squirmy tale of relentless snake terror is a highlight of our Men's Adventure Library collection,* I Watched Them Eat Me Alive.**

Soon after that, he sent me a wonderful letter he typed with
an old standard typewriter. For me, it will be a long-treasured
piece of memorabilia.

Walter once used such a manual typewriter to pound out stories for
Male, Stag, Man's World, Men, True Action, For Men Only and other men's
adventure magazines.

In fact, from the '50s to the '70s, he wrote several hundred stories
for those magazines. And he wrote almost every kind of story they
featured, from Westerns, war stories and exotic adventure yarns to spy
stories, crime thrillers and exposés.

Most were published under his own name. More than a hundred
were credited to his pseudonym Roland Empey.

Some of the men's adventure stories Walter wrote were credited
to a third pen name, David Mars. That one was typically used for his
exposé-style stories.

Walter was so prolific—and so good—that it was common for two of his stories to appear in the same issue of a men's adventure magazine, credited under two different names. That way the editors could make even more use of Walter's incredible output and fertile imagination, without the readers ever knowing their favorite writer Walter Kaylin was also their favorite writers Roland Empey and David Mars.

It was also common for stories by Walter to appear in two different men's adventure magazines published in the same month.

For example, this collection includes Bruce Jay Friedman's favorite yarn by Walter, from the September 1959 *Male* ("Emperor Blaine of 'Sweet Woman' Reef"), another story from that same issue credited to Roland Empey ("The Terrible Reward of 'Far East Harry' Wax")—*and* a Kaylin story that appeared that same month, in the September 1959 issue of *Men* ("The Helicopter Hero and the 100 Ladies of 'Undress' Atoll").

All three of those stories, and others in this collection, show that Walter was a master at depicting intriguing and unusual characters, exotic locales, and gritty, often jaw-droppingly gruesome violence.

Walter could also write gripping, fact-based stories about historical events, like "… 108-Hour Mid-Ocean Ordeal … 500 Dead … 300 Still Afloat …" (which tells the tale of the *USS Indianapolis*, a true story that fans of the movie *Jaws* will recognize).

He could even write humorous pieces, like "They Call Him Father Italy," and science fiction, like "Meet Our Terms or We Destroy 500 Million People"—two of the other classic Kaylin stories we selected for this volume.

Once it's published, I hope to be able visit Walter in Connecticut. I would love to personally hand him a copy and say: "Thank you, Walter. Thank you for writing so many amazing stories. Thank you for allowing us to reprint some of them, so people today can discover why you have rightly been called "the great Walter Kaylin."

In case I don't get the chance to say that to Walter in person, I'm saying it here. *

[2013]

"A TEACHER, A DREAMER, A CHARMER AND A SCHEMER"

by Jennifer Kaylin and Lucy Kaylin

WE BOTH remember the dark day we learned that Wilt Chamberlain was taller than our father. We weren't as young as you might think. To say that our father stands tall in our lives would be an understatement. A teacher, a dreamer, a charmer and a schemer, he is a larger-than-life character—one who, for us, brings new meaning to the expression "shock and awe."

He is a history buff, a jazz lover (Charlie Parker, Louis Armstrong, Billie Holiday, Miles Davis, John Coltrane), a lionizer of sports greats (Lou Gehrig, Babe Ruth, Kareem Abdul-Jabbar, Muhammad Ali). But most of all, he is passionate about good writing, as admiring of the well-crafted story as others are of a mint Rolls. His favorite authors, Faulkner, Conrad, Hemingway, Bellow, Marquez, and Simenon, led him to his chosen profession. Our father never wanted to be anything other than a writer.

A Jewish guy from the Bronx, he was the second son of a schoolteacher and a homemaker whose signature dish was pineapple upside-down cake. After graduating from William and Mary College and serving as a member of the signal corps in World War II, he began his career as a conventional writer, producing ad copy for J. Walter Thompson and working briefly at *Woman's Day*. But his heart was always in fiction, the more muscular and hairy-chested the better. When he landed in the world of pulp magazines, he knew he'd found the fraternity of writers he wanted to join. As part of a stable that included Mario Puzo and Joseph Heller, presided over by Bruce Jay Friedman, he pumped out stories about the sexual conquests and derring-do of he-men with take-no-prisoners relish.

To hear our father tell it, those years were as lean as they were fun: By day, he lived so close to the bone he would ritually pawn his typewriter for quick cash, then retrieve it just in time to save it from being sold. He was a regular blood donor—back in the day when you got paid for it. He and his buddies made a science of figuring out which midtown hotels were hosting events, the kind that had open bars and ample buffets.

Eventually he married a lovely Vassar-educated shiksa, a social worker, and had two daughters (us). For an edgy striver who double-dated with the noir crime photographer Weegee, and belted back bourbon at Manhattan jazz clubs until the stools went up on the tables, family life was an adjustment. His third month as a father, in October of 1956, he and fellow scribe Alex Austin skipped out of work early so they could hunker down in a neighborhood bar to watch game 5 of the World Series. Don Larsen, a journeyman pitcher, was on the mound, but to everyone's amazement he kept throwing strikes or pitches that led to easy outs; no Dodgers got on base. The two AWOL wordsmiths agreed to go back to the office as soon as Larsen gave up a hit, but as we know from the history books, that never happened, and our father punted on work that day. Our mother, home with an infant, wondered about his whereabouts as well.

A few years later, Dad was ready to leave New York and raise his kids somewhere small and safe. Hardly basketball-hoop-in-the-driveway people, our parents chose a cottage on a windswept stretch of beach in Old Lyme, Connecticut. Dad's office, on the first floor, just off the kitchen, is where most of the stories in this volume were written.

The walls of the house were wafer-thin, which meant that most nights we fell asleep to the sound of him tapping on his Royal manual typewriter, the bell chiming soothingly as he reached the end of the carriage. As kids, when we asked him what his job was, he'd tell us he wrote "adventure stories," which we took to mean he wrote about safaris and ocean voyages. Many a night, after dinner, he'd head to his office and declare, "This one will write itself." We came to learn that meant he was in for a long night.

But he had a ball writing those stories—reflexively blocking our view of the page with his left arm when we entered his office. (Similarly, when he took the latest issue of *Male* or *For Men Only* from the mailbox, he'd press it to his chest, lest we catch a glimpse of the buxom bikini-clad blonde holding a knife between her teeth on the cover.)

Eventually, the pulps disappeared, replaced by *Playboy, Hustler* and the like. By the '70s, our dad was exclusively committed to trying to write that Great American Novel of his dreams. He published two novels, but the Big One never happened. Yet he still talks about story

A snap of Walter Kaylin (center) and family, circa 2013.

ideas he's working on, and hardly a day goes by that he doesn't pull up
to his typewriter and try to tell a great story. Now in his nineties, he
is fascinated by politics and world affairs, is an avid reader of *The New
York Times* and is as vigorous a conversationalist as ever.

The fact that he still has fans out there, enough of them to warrant
the publication of this terrific volume, is a fitting finish to a storied
career dedicated to the art of rollicking good fun as executed by one of
the greatest practitioners the genre has ever seen. ✳

[2013]

"SEAMLESS, OUTRAGEOUS, AND WONDERFUL"
Bruce Jay Friedman Remembers Walter Kaylin

BRUCE *Jay Friedman (1930–2020) was a critically acclaimed novelist, playwright and screenwriter. He was the author of bestselling novels (*Stern, A Mother's Kisses*), popular plays (*Scuba Duba, Steambath*), and screenplays for hit movies (*Splash, Stir Crazy*).*

But prior to mainstream success, Friedman was a men's magazine editor for nearly a decade, from 1954 to 1965. Hired as an editor for the Magazine Management company by legendary publisher Martin Goodman (founder of Marvel Comics), Friedman took the reins on Mag Management's Playboy *competitor,* Swank, *and served as editor of several of the company's flagship men's adventure magazines, including* Men, Man's World, True Action, *and* Male.

He also had a knack for hiring writers who could churn out hard charging, frequently over-the-top stories—writers like Walter Kaylin and Mario Puzo, who went on to greater success as author of The Godfather.

Both Friedman and Puzo singled out Walter Kaylin as one of the best MAM writers of all. Friedman elaborated on his admiration for Kaylin in this conversation with Robert Deis from April 2013.

THERE were two people whose stories I really looked forward to. One was Mario Puzo, the other was Walter Kaylin. And there was a competition of a kind to win my favor. I think Mario wanted to be the favored son, and he always kept an eye on Walter. I may have even played the game a little, by sometimes telling him a bit too strenuously how much I enjoyed a Kaylin story.

"You know, Walter didn't even look like us. I mean, he looked like a divinity student. He was always buttoned up. He didn't wear a jacket but he wore a crisp shirt and tie. The rest of us at Magazine Management were sort of a scruffy-looking lot. But not Walter. He looked like he could have been an official at some Baptist Church. He was a very attractive man, a handsome man.

"Mario, Walter and I and other writers at Magazine Management, we all did our other work at night—our 'serious' work. Everyone was moonlighting. We did our magazine work very professionally, and then we went off and Mario wrote *The Godfather* and I wrote my books, and there was an assumption that Walter did the same. And we assumed that, if his work was this good in the adventure category, God knows how good it would be when he attended to his serious work.

"I think part of what made his stories effective was that they were informed. They were the product of a guy who read quite a bit, not just the classics, but obscure books that none of us would ever read, often to do research for the stories he did, which were seamless and outrageous and wonderful.

"There are a few pieces I still remember. One was about the guy who rode around on the island on the shoulders of his second-in-command ["Emperor Blaine of 'Sweet Woman' Reef," pg. 75]. I think that idea may be in *The Arabian Nights* somewhere. I have a funny feeling it was an echo of an old *Arabian Nights* story. [1]

"I remember another one, he had a guy fighting in the Far East, who led a bunch of warriors and in the course of the fighting his arm was injured. He showed it to the doctor, who told him what had to be done, and he said very impatiently, 'Well, just take it off as soon as possible. I want to get back. Just rip it off.' He wanted to get back to his men he was leading. That stuck with me. The casual way in which he gave up his arm."

I USUALLY talked with them one-on-one, focusing on what each writer's strength was. I knew what I wanted, somewhat based on past sales and somewhat based on my own head. I couldn't write those stories, but I could tell writers like Walter and Mario *how* I wanted them to be written. It was sort of fun. I did quite a bit of reading myself. And a lot of it was just me thinking this stuff up, variations on certain basic stories we did. I had different categories, and I would think up variations. Like 'sin town' stories. You know: *So-and-so is a sleepy little town with teenagers and their ice cream cones, but beneath the surface ....*

"The truth is, I was really the quarterback. Sometimes a story would come from something I'd seen in *The New York Times* and I would just sort of extrapolate from that. Sometimes Walter brought it to me, some version of it, and between the two of us we'd come up with the bare bones, and then I let him do whatever he wanted. Off Walter would go and a week later come back with this classic little work. He rarely —if ever—disappointed.

––––––––––––––––

1   *According to legend, there was a class of warriors in Iran and Iraq in the 9th to 12th centuries, called the Ayyars, or Ayyarun, who rode into battle on the backs of human servants.*

"Emperor Blaine of 'Sweet Woman' Reef"
Illustration by Al Rossi
Male, September 1959

"Walter was a very withdrawn, controlled guy, at least outwardly. You felt like you'd won an award when you got a smile out of him. The biggest reaction I could get from him was when we'd have our little talk and I'd suggest a piece for him to write, he'd give a kind of a snuffle, sort of an exhalation of breath. And that was it, pretty much. And then of course, the stories would come in. They were special. And they were a special treat for *me*. You would think buying all those stories I bought for four magazines, it would become sort of rote and reflexive. But not when it came to a Kaylin story. I always looked forward to reading one of his stories, or one of Mario Puzo's, with particular pleasure. And I was always rewarded.

"I don't think most readers knew most of our so-called true stories were made up. I think they took a story for what we said it was. We never worried too much about it. There's that one example I mentioned in my article "Even the Rhinos Were Nymphos" [included in *Weasels Ripped My Flesh!*], where at one point we had run out of major battles to feature in stories. So, Mario and I made one up. It was a battle that was close to Anzio and just as fierce. Nobody would have ever heard of it. It was a completely mythical battle, which Mario wrote about in great detail and nobody ever questioned it. Until one guy—I still remember! —wrote in and corrected us about the tank tread. We had the wrong tank tread on one of our tanks that were going in against the Germans. That's about it. Almost no one ever really questioned that stuff.

"I didn't realize how much fun I was having back then."

WALTER was staff, and did earn a salary. But nobody at Magazine Management just existed on their salary. It was all about how much you could pile up in freelance work; they also got paid for stories they brought in as freelance submissions. I did the best I could for those guys. I was paying about three hundred bucks a story, which today would be like three thousand.

"Book bonuses were about thirty thousand words and paid about five hundred bucks. One of Mario's stories was so good I went in and got Goodman to raise him up to seven or eight hundred dollars, or something like that. It was precedent setting. But Goodman went along with it.

"Sometimes staff would help out as Associate Editors—writing headlines, subheads, story blurbs. Mario really resisted it. When I would ask him to write a blurb or subtitle for some story that he didn't write, he really would get upset. He would say years afterward that blurbs drove him crazy. He felt he never could master them. It got him terribly frustrated. And I would send him back to try it again, and you wouldn't want to see his face when he had to go back and write another one.

I'M DELIGHTED you're doing this. He really deserves a tribute. I think of him as a treasure that never really got exploited properly. We wanted him to go further. Here you had him sitting next to Mario Puzo, and you could argue that Walter had more ability in a way. Probably a better sentence writer; certainly had as much imagination. Yet, Mario became this iconic figure and Walter didn't. So there is some sense of disappointment built into that.

"I don't remember much more, except how much I loved his stories." *

Edited by Wyatt Doyle
[2013]

"THE TYPEWRITER IS AS FAR AS I WENT"

A Conversation With Walter Kaylin

Intrigued by admiring talk of Walter Kaylin by several notable veterans of the Magazine Management company (former MM editor Bruce Jay Friedman, novelists Mario Puzo and John Bowers, MM associate editor Mel Shestack), Bob Deis set to tracking down the then-elusive men's adventure mag writer. Thanks to Walter's daughter, O, The Oprah Magazine editor-in-chief Lucy Kaylin, Bob was able to speak with Kaylin at some length about his life and career.

Bob conducted these April 2010 conversations for publication on his MensPulpMags.com site. When Walter said he never went online, Bob asked if he could fax over a printout of the post. Kaylin replied, "I don't have a fax. I don't go in for any of that stuff. The typewriter is as far as I went."

I was born in the Bronx in 1921. I read some good literature when I was a kid. I read *King Solomon's Mines* by H. Rider Haggard. I remember H. Rider Haggard in particular because I thought he was one of the best. I think he only wrote about four or five books but they were all very, very good. I think they edged on to literature; they were better than pulp by a great deal. I also read all of Zane Grey. I like cowboy stories very much, and I thought Zane Grey was the best that there was.

"If you ask a good writer 'Who influenced you?' you very rarely have the writer say they were influenced by someone they read when they were 8 or 9 years old. But I think that a lot of writers are very influenced by those things that happened years and years ago. They mention Tolstoy and they mention Chekhov, but the fact of the matter is that they were influenced by things they read when they were children. So to this day, I think that I was influenced by H. Rider Haggard.

"I was a miserable student. When it came time to go to college, I couldn't get in anyplace. Somehow or another, someone in my family applied for me, and on the basis of their applications, I wound up going to William and Mary College. I got out in 1942 and went into the Army. I was in the War and got out in the late '40s.

"I wanted to be a writer, in great part, because I saw it was about the only thing I could do. I thought I would enjoy it.

"I had some interesting jobs in New York. I worked briefly for J. Walter Thompson, the advertising agency. I went to see the guy who was in charge of writing the radio copy for the ads run during the baseball games, the New York Yankee games when Mel Allen was announcing, Mel Allen and Russ Hodges. I said I would like to try writing some commercials, and they said go ahead and do it. And back then you would do eleven commercials, one for each inning and one for before and after the game."

I GOT a job with *Woman's Day* magazine. I just called them up. Someone said I should come in, and I went. We talked two or three minutes and I was given the job. I got a kind of general writer's job. I was rewriting and I was writing captions and I was writing blurbs and things of that sort. I was very surprised by the fact that I was getting paid for this— and getting paid, it seemed to me, pretty well. I think I made $7,500 a year, which seemed like a ton of money at that time—and for me it was. It was an office full of women. All women. On the whole floor, I was the only man.

"I did some commentary on food. Of course they were wild about food; the entire thing was food! It was interesting. The lady who was the head of the food department saw me writing at my desk one time and she realized I was writing something that hadn't the slightest thing to do with *Woman's Day*. Very shortly thereafter, I got fired—and for good reason! I shouldn't have been there in the first place, because I didn't like it.

"I had difficulties at home, so I went to California, to Los Angeles. I was living in California and having an awful time. The whole idea was that I would just keep writing and writing and writing. But I did very badly. I was selling stories to magazines in Canada. I wrote something for a magazine called *The Standard* and others of that sort, where you could get $75 or $100 for a story. I was doing a lot of that stuff.

"I was taking on a bunch of junky jobs, one after the other, and sending articles through the mail. One day I came home and there was a letter in the box saying I had just had a story accepted by *The Saturday Evening Post*. That was a very, very big thing to happen. I was paid $850 and it was a great deal more money than I even knew existed.

"I wrote the story as 'Much Ado About Islands,' because a character in the story gets involved with the writing of Shakespeare. But the editors sent a note saying they were changing the title to 'The Lady on the Island.' They explained to me that the writers do not know what sells a magazine; that's *their* business, and their title would be better than the title I had.

"It was picked as one of the best stories of the year in the *Post.*"

ON THE basis of that story, I thought I'd go home to New York and live with my parents, who I hadn't seen for a long time. I went back east and have been back here ever since. When I came home I went to a party, and at the party I saw this very nice looking girl who I got interested in and subsequently married.

"I got more freelancing work and I also had several jobs. Some of them I can't remember because I can't stand remembering them. Then I started to work with Martin Goodman's company, Magazine Management. "

I WAS looking for a job where I'd only have to work for a few hours a day, and they said, if you want to work here, there's a full-time job for you. That's how I went into Magazine Management; I got a job there just because I was looking for a job.

"Most of the time I was writing for the men's adventure magazines, I was writing for Bruce Jay Friedman, who was a wonderful editor. Very, very good. After I had been there a short time, Bruce and I made a nice connection. One day I suggested a story to him, and he said I should go ahead and do it. He liked it. Then I did a few more, and then I really poured them out. Pretty soon I just quit the magazine and put all my time into writing the stories [as a freelancer]. I would have one story as Walter Kaylin, and if I had two of them I'd [also] be Roland Empey. I didn't pick the name; I assume it was Bruce who did, or somebody in his office. Sometimes I had three [stories in one issue]; the other name I used was David Mars.

"Writing these men's adventure magazine stories, I kept going and going and I found that I was writing something I liked. It didn't bother me a bit that I was writing what some people would view as sheer trash. It didn't bother me for a second. I had a lot of fun.

"You know, you push your trash as far as possible. I mean, you got a guy who's gonna get into a fight with three or four people and he's gotta beat them all. And then you think, *maybe I should try* six *people ...* You go as far as you could go, to see what would be acceptable by your own standards.

"I used to write them pretty fast. Not as fast as someone like Mario [Puzo]. Mario was a speed demon. But I would write at a good pace and I was having a good time.

"I would send in outlines, usually ten or twelve outlines of stories I wanted to do. And then Bruce would tell me which ones I should do. If I wanted, he would send me the money before I even wrote them, because he had a lot of confidence in me. It always turned out very well. We had an extremely good relationship and he was a swell guy to work with. I liked him a great deal.

"The thing about Bruce was that he was very well contained. He

never got upset or excited. He knew exactly what he wanted, and he
managed to get it from the guys he worked with. He was just a very
good guy. While I was working for him, he brought out his very first
book [*Stern*]. Then he went on to write a couple of plays and developed
a pretty nice career.

"Mario Puzo was one of the world's nicest guys. He was a lovely,
lovely fellow. Everybody loved him. But I didn't hang out with
[Magazine Management guys]. I knew them, and when I was in the
office we would sit around and talk. But I rarely met with them outside
the office."

Another Time, Another Woman (1963, Gold Medal) was a suspense
novel, a paperback. It was pretty cheesy, but I got $2,500 for it. And
$2,500 was a lot of money when you were getting $300 for writing a
story, so I was very pleased with that."

I was a very big reader. I read *Argosy*, but mainly I read books. As a
writer for those magazines, I was going back to Dashiell Hammett,
who wrote *The Thin Man*. I thought Hammett was a very good writer.
Detective stories that also had an adventure element, and they were
quite funny. I think Dashiell Hammett was a genuinely good writer.

"Then Raymond Chandler came into the scene. I always thought he
was very overrated.

"Mickey Spillane ... No, that was not for me. I liked hard-boiled
detectives, but I liked to feel that it could be happening. That stuff
of Spillane's didn't mean anything to me. But Spillane did work for
Magazine Management before I was there.

"I was very fond back then and continue to be fond of adventure
stories, especially the good ones. Some of the people who wrote them
were very good writers. Interestingly enough, a lot of these things
like I was writing were based on the writing of very good writers, like
Joseph Conrad. He was probably the best all-around adventure story
writer who ever lived, although his stuff was very, very serious.

"I would steal ideas from Conrad and from other writers as well. I
was very taken with a novel Conrad wrote called *Typhoon*, a marvelous
story. It took place in the South China Sea, but *Typhoon* can be [set] any
place there's a body of water and there are people hit by a storm. So I
did variations on that. Sometimes I had it in the Congo and sometimes
I had in Hudson's Bay; it could be any place. I made variations of his
theme and put it in many other places, but essentially it was the same
story. A lot of the stories we'd do were done that way. If I could steal
something—that's an ugly term, but it's really what it comes down
to—I would take their stuff, to a small degree.

"They're just things I kept in my head because I liked them so
much. I was a nut for adventure stories. Another writer that impressed
me very much who I got a lot out of was Jack London. *White Fang...* I

read a lot of his stuff. He was a very good writer, a wonderful adventure story writer. He really knew how to write them.

"Mainly it was imagination, but I would have something to guide me. I'm a big newspaper reader, because I like to know what's going on in the world. I read a lot of that stuff, maybe without intending to get anything out of it. But you could read something in the newspaper and get a story out of it, just switch it around to someplace else. Stuff was written that way. I don't know that anybody [at Magazine Management] ever wrote anything that was pure imagination. There's a germ of truth in all these things—sometimes not much more than a germ!

"You know I must have written about a thousand of them. And a lot of them I don't remember at all. I'm an old guy and I've forgotten an awful lot. I've forgotten stuff that happened yesterday! The fact that I don't remember something from 40 or 50 years ago is not surprising.

"I do remember 'Emperor Blaine of "Sweet Woman" Reef'. That was a pretty funny idea. I just thought that maybe the idea of one guy riding around on another guy's back would be of interest to the guys who read those stories. The primary audience for these things was young GIs, who wanted stories with action, violence and ridiculous sex and so forth and so on. So you had to put all of that kind of stuff into it. You had to come up with ideas by thinking along those lines. What would those readers like? That had to be your viewpoint all the time: *What would they like?* In the men's adventure magazines, what we would do is push it as far as possible and see if you could get away with it, in terms of what was acceptable to that audience.

"Incidentally, are you familiar with the notion that there are three ways of writing these stories, three writing principles? It's very interesting.

"The first one is *man against man.* An example of that is the shoot 'em up in Dodge City, the two guys meeting at high noon.

"The second one is *man against nature.* That's the animal story and the survival story.

"The toughest one is *man against himself.* That's the psychological story or novel. Only a small percent of the men's adventure magazine stories were man against himself stories. But that's one of the reasons why Conrad was considered such a remarkable writer. That's what *Lord Jim* was all about."

I WAS starting to run out of steam because I was repeating myself too much. And my girls were getting into school and I started getting jobs. I never did quite establish myself [as a writer]. All the time that I was writing, I frequently had a regular job, because I needed the money.

"I worked for a company in Waterford, Connecticut that was a direct mail operation. I worked for them for about 7 or 8 years, which was hard going because I hated it so much.

"I think around that time I was writing *The Power Forward* (1979, Atheneum). Another writer had just published a book about football—*North Dallas Forty*—and that was successful. And my agent said publishers were looking for a basketball book because the football book had done so very well. So they thought they could do something with a basketball book. But the book did badly. I wrote a very bad book by my standards—or by anybody's standards. It's a terrible book.

"I went into jobs and out of jobs and trying other things—while still writing, which I'm still doing.

"I'm partway into writing a book right now that I think has great possibilities, but I gotta write the damn thing. It's about a kid from the age of three, four months. The kid lives in the Bronx and he is taken care of by a Black woman from Rwanda. His real mother is not interested in him, so the woman from Rwanda takes care of him until he is two. By his 20s, he hates his mother and she hates him. He makes contact again with the woman from Rwanda and she persuades him she is the mother he needs. What constitutes a mother is what I'm getting at. I'm having a good time with that, and I'm having a hard time. It's a tough thing to write."

At the time that I left, the story was going around that the men's adventure stories were finished. *Men* and *Male* and *True Action* and all those, they went out of business. Eventually Martin Goodman's whole company went out of business.

"I don't think there's any market for those things anymore, is there? I mean as a regular thing, like writing a story a month. I'm under the impression that there's no more market for those stories. Maybe there is.

"I looked in my closet, and I find that I have seven *Male* magazines from back then. I'm looking at the covers right now, and they look good to me.

"We invented a lot of stuff. Bruce used to have fun kidding about the way that Mario Puzo used to invent entire battles and wars. He said Mario would write a war story and the whole war never really happened—he went that far with it. I think the better writers did that kind of a thing. You just went as far as you could. I really think the idea was to just have a lot of fun at what you were doing, and you had to know that what you were doing was really pretty funny.

"I enjoyed reading the stories. So when I got into writing adventure stories, I was having a good time. And I enjoyed them right up until the very end." ✳

Edited by Wyatt Doyle
[2013]

"Betrayal on 'Nude Redhead' Beach"
Written as Roland Empey
Illustration by Samson Pollen
Man's World, February 1967

the couch and she turned around
and settled into a corner of it
to keep some distance between us.

"Why don't you get rid of
that monster?" she said. "He
gives me the creeps."

She was talking about the
Robot, and the fact that he
gave her the creeps just proved
she was normal. He had the flat,
dead face of an item turned out
by machines. His eyes were cold
as marbles pressed into dough.
His insides went with the surface. He could beat a man insane
or take it himself, and it didn't
mean a thing to him.

"He's useful," I said. "Some
things he does just about perfectly."

"Don't tell me about them,"
she said quickly. "Let me use my
imagination. Incidentally, this
is the fifth or sixth time this
meeting has taken place. What's
it all about?"

"About the price of eggs in
Mexico City," I said.

"SNOW-JOB FROM A REDHEAD"

Men, June 1956
COVER ARTIST: JOHN KULLER

The police ran into a brick wall.

All they had was the knife I had picked up

in Italy when I was fighting across Europe.

SNOW-JOB
FROM A
REDHEAD

by Walter Kaylin

It was late in the afternoon when Simmons called. Long distance. He had just crossed over, dirtied up to look like a wetback.

"Fred, he got away from me," he panted. "He was ready for it. Almost put my eye out with that big ring he wears. He'll be up there in about two hours."

"That's great," I said. "That's just great. Does he still have the bull?"

"He's got it wrapped up in a pile of clothes. Fred, you going to take him yourself?"

"Well, what else can I do since you loused it up? Sure, I'm going to take him. Didn't I work out the whole thing? Why should I have to keep splitting with Paulie and the Robot?"

"All right, don't get sore, Fred. I'm just telling you to watch yourself. And, look, Fred. I'm sorry. I'm sorry as—."

I hung up on him. What's an apology *(Continued on page 62)*

Illustration by **Don Neiser**

IT WAS late in the afternoon when Simmons called. Long distance. He had just crossed over, dirtied up to look like a wetback.

"Fred, he got away from me," he panted. "He was ready for it. Almost put my eye out with that big ring he wears. He'll be up there in about two hours."

"That's great," I said. "That's just great. Does he still have the bull?"

"He's got it wrapped up in a pile of clothes. Fred, you going to take him yourself?"

"Well, what else can I do since you loused it up? Sure, I'm going to take him. Didn't I work out the whole thing? Why should I have to keep splitting with Paulie and the Robot?"

"All right, don't get sore, Fred. I'm just telling you to watch yourself. And, look, Fred. I'm sorry. I'm sorry as—"

I hung up on him. What's an apology worth in cold cash? Not a damn thing.

Two hours later I was parked across the street from Tessie Roman's rooming house. I didn't have long to wait. Carlos showed up in about ten minutes. He was wearing blue jeans, a work jacket, and carried the small bundle of clothes you'd expect a wetback to have. I gave him a couple of minutes to get in, saw the light go on in an upstairs room, then got out of the car and went across after him.

Getting upstairs without being seen was easy enough. I just peeked into the sitting room, saw that Tessie was lying on the couch looking the other way, then walked past the door and upstairs.

"Who is it?" Carlos asked quickly when I knocked. No trace of an accent, he'd spent most of his life in the States. "Who's there?"

"It's Fred, Carlos. Open up."

He opened the door and I slipped inside. He had taken off his jacket and undershirt. His face and chest were wet and the water was running in the basin.

"What's the idea?" he asked. "I just got here. I didn't even call up yet."

"Just nervous, I guess," I said. "How did it go?"

"There was some trouble." He went back to the basin and splashed water on his face. There was a cracked mirror on the wall in front of him. He never stopped looking at me in it. "Someone tried something. He looked familiar. He looked a little like a guy you used to run with."

"You're imagining things," I said. "Here, dry off."

I tossed him a towel. He caught it, but looked uncertain about using it. Then suddenly he grinned and said, "Okay, so I'm suspicious," and lifted it to his face. It gave me the second I needed. I had the knife stuck into his side before he knew it, my free arm tightening around his throat to keep him from hollering out. He tried to pull free, but I rode his back to the bed and went down on top of him. Then I pulled the knife out and slid it in again. When I had done it twice more he stopped moving, and I got up off of him. He slid back a little till he was squatting on the floor, with his head turned against the side of the bed.

I found the bundle of clothes in a bottom bureau drawer. I untied them, took the bull out, tied them up again and put them back.

You'd have taken the thing for a book end. It was about eight inches long and five high; black all over except for the horns which were gleaming white.

I put it under my coat, realizing the big bulge it made there, and left the room. I didn't like that part of it, carrying the thing around, but there was no choice. I closed the door and it locked automatically. That was that.

I went downstairs. Tessie was still lying on the couch, but reading a magazine now. I could see the top of her red hair, then her bare feet at the farther end. I went past the door and outside, crossed the street and got into the car.

Twenty minutes later, I was in the basement of my apartment house. The thing was a jumble of bikes, carriages, discarded furniture and trunks. One of the trunks was mine, a solid job with the name Homer R. Wilson stenciled on it. If there was any Homer R. Wilson, I never knew him. I unlocked it, put the bull inside, and locked it up again. Then I went upstairs.

You think you're working things right, but you never know. There was blood on my trousers, blood on one hand. I'd been too excited to even realize it. I needed a drink, but there was too much work to be done first. I cut the buttons and zipper off the trousers, burned the material in the bathtub and flushed the scorched remnants down the toilet. I put the buttons and zipper into a paper bag, making a mental note to dispose of it some distance from the house, preferably in an ash can soon to be picked up. Then I scrubbed my hands clean. After that I had the drink. When it was gone, I phoned Paulie.

"Any word?" I asked. "It's getting pretty late."

"That's what I was thinking."

"Maybe he's had some trouble. Maybe we'd better go check."

"Pick me up. We'll get the Robot and go on over there."

We rang the outside bell this time. Tessie opened it and let us in. She was a tall woman of about 30, good looking but with something in her face that told you to go slow, don't look for trouble. She looked as though she thought people wanted to take advantage of her, which obviously was the case. She had the sort of look to interest an ambitious man. It did the job on me, all right.

"Your friend is upstairs," she said. "Left front room. What took you so long? He's been here over an hour."

"He was supposed to call," Paulie said. "Maybe something's wrong. Let's go, Freddie."

"You go ahead," I said. "I want to make some time with Tess. I don't get much of a chance."

He went upstairs with the Robot and I followed her into the sitting room. We sat down on the couch and she turned around and settled into a corner of it to keep some distance between us.

"Why don't you get rid of that monster?" she said. "He gives me the creeps."

She was talking about the Robot, and the fact that he gave her the creeps just proved she was normal. He had the flat, dead face of an item turned out by machines. His eyes were cold as marbles pressed into dough. His insides went with the surface. He could beat a man insane or take it himself, and it didn't mean a thing to him.

"He's useful," I said. "Some things he does just about perfectly."

"Don't tell me about them," she said quickly. "Let me use my imagination. Incidentally, this is the fifth or sixth time this meeting has taken place. What's it all about?"

"About the price of eggs in Mexico City," I said. "The guy upstairs is an authority. Look—how about if we drive out to Hollywood tomorrow night? We can do some dancing or listen to some jazz music or—"

"Forget it," she said, getting up. "You're not my type, Freddie. I don't know what you do for a living, but I have a feeling the police wouldn't approve. A girl can get nervous—"

Then Paulie and the Robot were back with us, Paulie all tensed up. They had been knocking on Carlos' door, but hadn't received any answer. Tessie got her passkey and we all went upstairs.

"That's funny," she said. "I didn't hear him go out."

SHE OPENED the door. We went in. He was sitting on the floor with his face against the bed. His side was a mess. No one had to take his pulse to know whether or not he was dead.

"Oh, my God!" Tessie said. Her face was white as paste. "I'll have to call the police. My God, it's horrible!"

"Yes, you'll have to call the police," Paulie said, but he held her by the arm. "You don't have to mention our coming to see him, though. What would it accomplish? What would be gained?"

"Don't be silly," Tessie said. "I can't keep back a thing like that!"

"Let's you and I go downstairs and talk for a few minutes," he said patiently. "If after that you still want to tell them about our visit, I won't try to stop you. You two," talking over his shoulder, "look around. It's undoubtedly gone, but look around anyway."

After they had gone downstairs, the Robot and I went through the room. I made sure he was the one who found the clothes bundle. When we had gone over the place well enough to know the bull couldn't be there, we went downstairs. They were just finishing their conversation.

"Well?" Paulie asked.

"No dice," I said. "Maybe something went wrong on the other side. Maybe he didn't even bring it with him."

"Maybe," Paulie said, "maybe not. In any case, it is quite a loss. However, one thing has worked out well. Miss Roman has agreed to handle the police without involving us. We've worked out an agreement."

"All right, that's enough talk," Tessie said nervously. "You'd better get going now. Remember, if any of my roomers see you going out of here it's all off."

"We'll be careful," Paulie promised.

"You, too," she said and touched my arm. "I'm sorry about before. Call me up."

"Now you're talking."

We got out without being seen. My car was across the street. Paulie and I got into the front seat, the Robot in the back.

"Well, that's that," Paulie said as we started off. "We're out in the street."

"What kind of agreement did you make with her?" I asked.

"Money." He shrugged. "There's something in it for her if she keeps us out."

The rear-view mirror was off and I reached out to adjust it. For a second all it caught was the Robot's face from the back seat. His eyes were dead as stones and watching me....

The police ran up against a brick wall. All they had was the knife, and that wasn't traceable. I had picked it up in Italy during the war. The handle was wooden and badly beaten up. They'd never get a print off it. Despite having so little to go on, though, they knew the right people to question about Carlos, and one was me.

"You never knew the guy?" Rogers asked me—a big brute of a cop, Rogers, big red face, hands like boxing gloves. "We've heard you knew him well."

"Just by sight," I said. "Used to give him the time of day, but that was years ago. Don't remember the last time I saw him."

"I guess you wouldn't know the line of work he's in, either, would you, Freddie?"

"Not me, Cap."

"Same thing you're in, Freddie."

"No kidding. And what's that, Cap?"

"Happy dust, Freddie. You know all about happy dust, don't you? Those little white grains?"

"You're off-base this time, Cap. I'm a sporting type fellow. My income comes from Santa Anita."

"Well, that's better than claiming to be a Bible salesman. Freddie, you ever hear of a little carry-all called the black bull?"

"Don't follow you, Cap. Never was in the poultry business."

"Poultry?"

"See what I mean, Cap? I don't know a thing. Strictly a mutton-head."

"One day you'll have a different kind of head," he promised, grabbing the front of my shirt, his face going red enough to explode. "The thing's hollow inside and it's been used to transport heroin from Mexico into the States."

"My head, Cap?"

He flung me away from him. I took it, grinning at him and straightening my tie. Sure, he knew about Paulie and me and the Robot. Sure, he knew where Carlos fitted in. But he didn't even have enough evidence to get me for double parking. I was clean as April showers and we both knew it.

Rogers turned me loose around supper time, so I decided to take Tessie up on that invitation to call. How about dinner? Fine, she said. How about if we go out to Hollywood and examine some of the bright lights? Fine. The police had been questioning her most of the day and she could use a few laughs.

We ate at The Brown Derby, caught a show at the Mocambo, listened to some jazz music at Sardi's and the Rumpus Room, and wound up dancing at the Palladium. She looked beautiful. I mean, on a trip like that you're going to see half a dozen actresses and maybe 50 who want to be, but Tess was one-two out of the whole crowd.

Driving back, she leaned her head on my shoulder, and when we were in front of her place I kissed her.

"Fresh," she said, but she was smiling. "It's been a lovely night, Freddie."

"Listen, what is it with you?" I asked her. "A beautiful girl like you, why do you waste your time running a dump like this?"

"I inherited it," she said. "It used to be my father's. It's paid for, the income isn't bad and the work is easy. Why shouldn't I stay with it?"

"Because you could do better."

"Where, how and with whom?"

"I could tell you all about it," I said carefully. "Supposing we go inside for a little bit and talk."

"It's too late," she laughed. "Let's make it another time."

"That a promise?"

"Try me."

"Tomorrow night?"

"All right."

I went around the car to help her out, then walked up to the door with her. She took the key out of her purse and smiled at me. I kissed her and she kissed me back, then smiled again and went inside.

My PLANS were to wait till some of the excitement had died down before getting rid of the stuff. That was going to be a risky business, but I had an idea how to do it. Our handler always paid us a flat $18,000 for it. We split that three ways. He retailed it for maybe three times that amount, but that was okay because he ran a risk in every sale he made.

My idea simply was to offer him the stuff for $15,000—an extra three for him —in exchange for his promise to keep it quiet, keep it from Paulie and the Robot. Hell, it's a way of doing business. Why wouldn't he say yes? But I wanted to wait a little before getting in touch with him. Besides, I was keeping pretty busy trying to get somewhere with Tess.

I was trying because we continued saying good night at the front door. Either it was too late, or she was too tired, or she had to get up early the next day. I played it like a little gentleman the first couple of times, but a man can take just so much.

"You're not playing me for some sort of patsy, are you?" I finally asked one night.

"What do you mean?"

We had spent the day down at Laguna Beach. I'm not much for swimming, but it had been worth the trip just to see her in a white swimming suit and catch the envious looks of the crowd down there. Later, we'd had dinner in a seafood place, then gone dancing, and driven back to town. Now, we were outside her door and she was explaining that it was late and it had been a big day.

"You know what I mean," I said, knowing I sounded ugly but not caring much. "I'm getting a little tired of this perpetual stall."

She looked at me before saying anything. She looked lovely enough to make me feel weak.

"Yes, Freddie," she said, looking straight at me. "I know what you mean. I was going to ask you in tonight, honestly, only I just didn't know if I could do it without you thinking—well, you know, thinking things. Please come in, Freddie. I want you to."

I'd thought a hundred times that I'd move in like a shot when I got the chance, and all I did was stand there like a hoople. "You mean it?"

"Yes," she said, "I mean it."

We went into her sitting room. She made us drinks and we sat down on the couch. She took off her shoes and put her feet on a little table in front of us. Just seeing her relaxed like that almost made the nights I'd waited worthwhile.

"I guess I have been a little mean to you, Freddie," she smiled. "That wasn't very nice, was it?"

"That's all right," I said, and my voice sounded hoarse and strange to me. I put my arm around her and drew her head down on my shoulder. "It's just that I've got it for you so bad, it's been driving me a little nuts."

"You're sweet," she said. Then: "How bad do you have it for me, Freddie?"

"Bad enough to want to get you out of this dump, for one thing."

"Well, that's very nice, but how? My entire income comes from this house. What would I do for money?"

"Supposing," I began, then got up and walked away from her. I felt jumpy and excited and this great new plan was forming in my head. "Supposing I could get my hands on $15,000. Bang! Just like that! One lump sum. Just supposing, I say. Would you give up this place—put it on the market—and go off on a trip with me? Maybe Europe or South America or the Bahamas, something like that?"

"It sounds lovely, Freddie," she said and smiled. "But where would you ever get that kind of money? Everyone knows you're a spender. Nine out of every ten dollars you get your hands on wind up in some bookmaker's pocket."

"I can get it," I said. "Take my word for it. I can get it."

"Don't be angry, Freddie," she said, still smiling, "but I think you're dreaming a little. You don't have to talk like that to impress me. So what if you can't get $15,000? There's nothing disgraceful about that. Lots of people can't and they're not as nice as you."

"But, I can," I insisted angrily. "Just say yes and I'll do it. Look, Tess, you know how I feel about you. What do you say?"

"I wouldn't want to take the chance of being stranded in some place like Rio de Janeiro," she said. "I'd have to be sure. Where's the $15,000 coming from, Freddie?"

"The black bull."

I hadn't meant to tell her, but the way she had been picking at me I didn't have any choice. It just came out. She leaned forward, no longer smiling. She looked frightened.

"The police have been after me all week about that," she said. "Freddie, you're kidding, aren't you?"

"No," I said, deciding I may as well go all the way with it now. "I've got it."

"That means you killed that man?"

"Yes, I killed him. The whole idea was mine to begin with and I got tired of splitting the take. I wouldn't be telling you this, Tess, except for the way I feel about you, I know I can trust you. Now, how about that trip?"

"Oh, Freddie, I am sorry," she said and her eyes were wide with fear. "At the beginning I didn't care about you, now it's different." She gasped: *"Freddie!"*

THEN I knew what she had led me into. I didn't move. There was no reason to. I just stood there watching her. Then something smashed into the side of my face and I went down tasting blood and seeing the Robot's flat, dead face moving in and over me.

"How's it going, Fred boy?" Paulie grinned from behind him. "Still a pushover for a good-looking girl. When are you going to learn, buddy? Maybe now, huh? Maybe it's really a break for you that the Robot's going to give you a little lesson."

The Robot was slipping on a glove. It was the sort fighters use to work on the big bag. There was a metal slug sewed into it across the inside of the fingers. I had seen him use it before.

"I don't have to watch this," Tess said quickly getting up. She looked sick. "There was nothing said about that in our agreement."

"Stay," Paulie said, grabbing her arm. He wasn't hurting her, just holding her. "You're a partner, now."

She stopped trying to twist away from him. She smiled. "You can give me back my arm, now," she said. "I can see you're right."

"Smart girl."

He grinned and let her go. His eyes went all over her. She took it smiling, handed it back to him. They were talking to each other without saying a word. I wondered what he'd be saying when she handed him over to Rogers. It was as plain as neon lights. I mean, she wasn't the kind to go getting sociable just for the hell of it.

"All right," he said suddenly.

Then the Robot pulled me up off the floor and began the lesson. ✱

"He Shared Their Food, Their Guns and Their Women"
Male, June 1959
Illustration by Samson Pollen

her eyes didn't leave his. "I told you right from the beginning I wouldn't do that. What gives you an idea like that, anyway? You want to watch?"

"Don't get fresh with me," Grantly shouted, taking a step toward her and raising his hand. "If I tell you to do something, by God -"

"No," the girl said, pulling a knife out from under the blanket. It was an incredible weapon, the handle hardly more than the width of her hand, but the blade well over a foot long and razor-sharp along both edges. "I won't do that."

"Don't get yourself cut up on my account, Grantly," Ringgold said. "I'm a little particular along that line anyway."

Howard Cole chewed thoughtfully on his lower lip, but lifted a hand quickly as Barney stepped toward the girl. He dropped it without touching his brother, though. Barney had

"THE CRUEL GUN BROTHERS"

True Action, July 1959
COVER ARTIST: MORT KÜNSTLER

THE CRUEL GUN BROTHERS

**They gunned the old man down, relaxed, celebrated, forgot all their troubles—
forgot a couple of Cole boys riding their way with two holsters full of murder**

By Walter Kaylin

A PAIR of cowpunchers were helping Deputy Sheriff John Winters build a well that August morning in 1875. The three men were behind Winters' house in Mason, Texas, a town flat and hard as a pool table, but the color of prairie dust. When Barney Cole rode up, one of the punchers was digging 40 feet down while Winters and the other were up above talking.

"Am I heading right for San Antone?" Cole asked.

"Hundred miles," Winters said briefly pointing southeast.

"Thanks," Cole said and at the moment the man in the well called up to the others to pull him out. The two men began tugging on the rope and when they had him more than halfway up it occurred to Winters that the rider behind them hadn't moved. Stilling his hands on the rope, he sent a careful look back over his shoulder to find Cole grinning at him with a gun in each hand.

"What's the trouble?" the puncher pulling with him asked as Winters stopped. "Ain't I tired, too?"

"Look there," Winters said. The cowboy turned his head sighing, "Oh, God," at what he saw.

"Name's Cole," the gunman said, a dark-skinned, blue-eyed man, heavyset, not much more than twenty. "If they ask you who sent you where you're going, just tell them it was Tim Harrington's boy, Barney."

His first shot went into Winters' face above his lifted shoulder and his second killed the puncher, entering the side of his head. Inside the hole, the man being pulled up fell 30 feet and howled in pain as something snapped in his leg. He had heard voices and the shots, but hadn't been able to make anything out of what had happened. Lying at the bottom of the hole he cursed the two men for dropping him and stopped only when he saw Cole's unfamiliar face looking down at him.

"You don't sound happy down there," Cole said. "What you need is some company."

"Who are you?" the puncher asked anxiously. "What are you doing? What the—?"

He threw an arm over his head as a limp body appeared over him, head and hanging arms slipping slowly into the shaft. His upraised arm probably stopped him from getting killed, but it couldn't save him entirely. The dead cowboy being lowered down toward him weighed close to two hundred and when Cole gave him the final shove, his falling body knocked the man beneath him senseless.

With the voice from the well silenced, Cole brought his attention back to Winters. The deputy lay on his back semi-conscious and moaning in pain, blood from the wound in his cheek forming a puddle on the ground. Cole stood over him, a foot on each side of his body, and drew a buffalo skinner's knife from his belt. Then he scalped him, fired the four remaining shots from one gun into his face, and threw his body into the well on top of the two men already down it.

"I hope you're not crowded down there, Winters," he said as he mounted again, "because Pete Braden's going to be joining you real soon."

As he came back around the front of the house, a half dozen men were standing in the street with drawn guns. Cole grinned in his good natured way and rode through them in no particular hurry. He had stuck one gun back in his belt, but still carried the other. There seemed no point in asking him what all the shooting had been about. They watched in silence while he rode out of town, then ran around behind the house to see what he had accomplished.

Three miles west of (Continued on page 72)

CROSSFIRE—Craig was caught between the two gun-slingers when Grantly shoved him through the door, then opened up

Illustrated by George Eisenberg

Illustration by **George Eisenberg**

A PAIR of cowpunchers were helping Deputy Sheriff John Winters build a well that August morning in 1875. The three men were behind Winters' house in Mason, Texas, a town flat and hard as a pool table but the color of prairie dust. When Barney Cole rode up, one of the punchers was digging 40 feet down while Winters and the other were up above talking.

"Am I heading right for San Antone?" Cole asked.

"Hundred miles," Winters said, briefly pointing southeast.

"Thanks," Cole said and at the moment the man in the well called up to the others to pull him out. The two men began tugging on the rope and when they had him more than halfway up, it occurred to Winters that the rider behind them hadn't moved. Stilling his hands on the rope, he sent a careful look back over his shoulder to find Cole grinning at him with a gun in each hand.

"What's the trouble?" the puncher pulling with him asked as Winters stopped. "Ain't I tired, too?"

"Look there," Winters said. The cowboy turned his head, sighing "Oh God," at what he saw.

"Name's Cole," the gunman said, a dark-skinned, blue-eyed man, heavyset, not much more than twenty. "If they ask you who sent you where you're going, just tell them it was Tim Harrington's boy, Barney."

His first shot went into Winters' face above his lifted shoulder and his second killed the puncher, entering the side of his head. Inside the hole, the man being pulled up fell 30 feet and howled in pain as something snapped in his leg. He had heard voices and the shots, but hadn't been able to make anything out of what had happened. Lying at the bottom of the hole he cursed the two men for dropping him and stopped only when he saw Cole's unfamiliar face looking down at him.

"You don't sound happy down there," Cole said. "What you need is some company."

"Who are you?" the puncher asked anxiously. "What are you doing? What the—?"

He threw an arm over his head as a limp body appeared over him, head and hanging arms slipping slowly into the shaft. His upraised arm probably stopped him from getting killed, but it couldn't save him entirely. The dead cowboy being lowered down toward him weighed close to two hundred and when Cole gave him the final shove, his falling body knocked the man beneath him senseless.

With the voice from the well silenced, Cole brought his attention back to Winters. The deputy lay on his back, semi-conscious and moaning in pain, blood from the wound in his cheek forming a puddle on the ground. Cole stood over him, a foot on each side of his body, and drew a buffalo skinner's knife from his belt. Then he scalped him, fired the four remaining shots from one gun into his face, and threw his body into the well on top of the two men already down it.

"I hope you're not crowded down there, Winters," he said as he mounted again, "because Pete Braden's going to be joining you real soon."

As he came back around the front of the house, a half-dozen men were standing in the street with drawn guns. Cole grinned in his good-natured way and rode through them in no particular hurry. He had stuck one gun back in his belt but still carried the other. There seemed no point in asking him what all the shooting had been about. They watched in silence while he rode out of town, then ran around behind the house to see what he had accomplished.

Three miles west of Mason, Cole came to Olney's store. Olney's was a plank bar, a pair of round tables for poker, and Olney himself, a fat, balding man who wore carpet slippers and couldn't keep a shirt in his pants. Five men stood at the bar as Cole entered, four of them well-known hard cases named George Grantly, the brothers Mose and John Burnside, and John Ringgold. The fifth was with them, but somehow removed, too, a somber man who took no part in their conversation, nor much apparent interest in his drink, either. This was Howard Cole, a taller version of his younger brother, but with the same blue eyes and Indian-dark skin. The five had been waiting for Barney. At his entrance, they left the bar to join him, and at something he said, they started for the door.

"Just a second there," Olney said with one hand reaching around behind him to where he kept his shotgun. "Who's paying?"

"Don't shoot us with that thing or there won't be enough left of us to bury," Howard Cole said, taking a step back toward the bar and putting a hand in his pocket. "A man can forget—"

"I'm paying," Barney said loudly and pitched Winters' scalp in an underhand motion onto the bar. Olney jumped away from it as though it were a snake and the others looked at it in startled silence. Grantly was the first to come out of it, his powerful body bending almost double as he pounded his knee, his mouth above the thick blond beard opening in a great roaring laugh. The Burnsides chuckled, shaking their heads good-naturedly at each other, and Ringgold smiled indulgently as though at a boy's prank. Only Howard Cole didn't seem to see much fun in it.

"All right, the drinks were on me," Olney said, breathing heavily. "Now, get that goddamn thing off my bar."

Barney laughed, put the scalp back in his pocket and led the others outside. As they prepared to mount, Howard took his brother's arm.

"I thought the idea was you were going to just go down there and look things over," he said, his eyes hard and accusing. "We weren't going to move against either Winters or Braden until we had them both together. Then we'd get both of them at once and that would be the end of it."

"Well, we got Winters," Barney grinned, patting his pocket, "and Braden will be just as easy. I ain't so sure it should just be the two of them, anyway. Wasn't there a lot more than two of them there when Tim was killed?"

"Half of Texas was there when Tim was killed," Howard said. "Ain't that a little too much for us to be taking on?"

"Not if they all come this easy," Barney said, patting his pocket again. He swung into the saddle and looked down at his brother. "Come on, let's go, Howard. Sometimes these things don't work out exactly the way you want."

"You should have done it the way we said we would, and even if you didn't you ought to be able to kill a man without mangling him up that way," Howard said, seeing Barney's face go even darker than usual. "All right, you go ahead and I'll be along. I want to pay Olney for those drinks."

He went back into the store and put some coins on the bar. Olney looked at him curiously.

"Wasn't that Barney Cole that used to be with the Rangers?" he asked. "One of the boys that old Tim Harrington brought up?"

"That's right," Howard said.

"Well, that was a crazy thing to do, putting that hair on the bar," Olney said, "but it don't surprise me now that I know who he is. They say he used to have some kind of fits where he'd fall down; and I remember three-four years ago when he was just a boy, he brought Hoffman, the saddle-maker, some strips of hide to be made into a quirt. Hoffman saw right away it was Indian hide and ran him out with a gun, but the boy just laughed like he was never going to stop."

"Be careful with that kind of talk," Howard said, "or I'll bring my brother back in here to show you his toy mouse again."

HE WENT outside and got on his horse. The others were all mounted and waiting for him. Grantly and the Burnside brothers looked as though they had suddenly stopped talking when he came out. Ringgold was bored and Barney was sullen.

"Maybe we can go now," Barney said pulling his horse's head savagely. "What were you doing in there, telling him he don't have to worry about me as long as you're along to see I'm a good boy?"

"That what the boys been telling you?" Howard asked. "No, all I was doing was paying him for what we drank."

"The hell that's all you—"

"Let's get going, gents, let's get going," Grantly shouted riding in between them. "You never been out to my place or you wouldn't be wasting time this way. You ask John and Mose there if it ain't going to be worth the ride."

"Well, it ain't been before, but it's sure worth trying again," Mose howled, a lanky boy in overalls and the scraggly beginnings of a beard. "How do, Miss Eulalie. Sweet Mose is come a-knocking."

THE MASON County War was essentially a problem in cattle. The law was unable to cope with the rustling that went on, and finally a band of vigilantes was formed to bring it under control. Sheriff Abe Craig didn't approve, but his deputy, John Winters, a new man in the county, was anxious to cooperate with the vigilantes. One of his first acts was to arrest a ranch foreman named Tim Harrington on suspicion of stealing cattle for his employer.

While Harrington was being transported from the ranch to the jail in Mason, he and Winters were suddenly surrounded by vigilantes in blackened faces. Harrington begged Winters for a chance to flee or a gun to defend himself with, but his pleas were denied. A shot from the crowd knocked him off his horse and as he lay on the ground badly wounded, he recognized the leader of the vigilantes despite his blackened face and spoke to him by name, suggesting they quit "this foolishness before it goes too far." The vigilante leader answered, "I've blowed my coffee and now I'm going to drink it," and shot Harrington dead. Then he dismounted and tried to pull an expensive ring off the dead man's finger. When he was unable to, he cut the finger off with a knife and took it along with him wrapped in a bandana. There hadn't been much doubt in Mason as to who was leading the vigilantes, but when Henry Braden was seen wearing Harrington's ring, everyone was sure.

THE KILLING of Harrington didn't end the rustling, but it did set up the situation that brought the Cole brothers onstage to play their violent roles. Their parents had been killed and they had been taken by Indians in a raid when they were boys. For three years they lived with the Indians, abused and mistreated in ways that were to mark Barney for the rest of his life.

The man who took care of the Cole boys after they were freed was Tim Harrington. He fed them, clothed them, saw Barney through a severe attack of typhoid fever, and generally watched over them as though they were his own sons. When Barney turned eighteen, both boys joined the Texas Rangers and distinguished themselves fighting Cherokee at the battle of Loss Valley in 1874.

The day they heard of Harrington's murder, the brothers quit the Rangers and came back to Mason. Their original plan was to kill Winters and Braden, whom they had been told were the two significant figures in Harrington's death. But such projects have a way of mushrooming. The death of one innocent puncher and the crippling of another accompanied Barney's murder of Winters. As they left Olney's Store and headed for Grantly's log house that same day, other atrocities were inevitably in the cards.

From Olney's, they rode west for about two hours. The flat plain gave way to a heavy thicket and then they were in the back country, country outside the law, where a man's only responsibility was to his clan and where the disputed ownership of a cow or horse could start a blood feud that would last for years. Grantly had lived there all his life and such a feud had taken six of his brothers and caused two more to leave that part of the country because the odds had tilted too sharply against them. After their leaving, Grantly had made peace with the Mallorys, arguing that he couldn't very well do them any damage by himself and begging them not to make him go, too. Against the judgment of some, they had permitted him to stay.

It was late in the afternoon when they reached his log house. They unsaddled the horses in the corral and then went into the house. A girl of about 16 was sitting on an unmade bunk sewing a patch on a pair of trousers, her bare feet curled under her, her elbows propped against her knees. Her face was expressionless as she watched the men file in, the intermingling of Indian, Mexican and Negro blood apparent in her features and color. This was Eulalie Fenn, who had lived with a dozen different men and been thrown out by each when they had been made sufficiently infuriated by her indifference and inability to be impressed. There was no response in Eulalie, only the promise of one in her slow, dark-eyed glances and the pressing of her bosom against her man's shirt.

"Well, how long are you going to sit there?" Grantly demanded, the Burnsides grinning and winking at each other behind him. "Can't you see I brung some friends? Go rustle us up some grub and then—"

"What?" she said as he stopped. "And then what?"

"Hell, you know what," he said loudly. "I told you they're all friends of mine."

"I wouldn't care if they was your mother," the girl said putting the pants aside. She shifted her position to slip her feet into moccasins on the floor, but her eyes didn't leave his. "I told you right from the beginning I wouldn't do that. What gives you an idea like that, anyway? You want to watch?"

"Don't get fresh with me," Grantly shouted, taking a step toward her and raising his hand. "If I tell you to do something, by God—"

"No," the girl said, pulling a knife out from under the blanket. It was an incredible weapon, the handle hardly more than the width of her hand, but the blade well over a foot long and razor-sharp along both edges. "I won't do that."

"Don't get yourself cut up on my account, Grantly," Ringgold said. "I'm a little particular along that line anyway."

Howard Cole chewed thoughtfully on his lower lip, but lifted a hand quickly as Barney stepped toward the girl. He dropped it without touching his brother, though. Barney had stepped in front of Grantly a foot away from the point of the girl's knife.

"We ain't so bad," he said making his face go solemn. "Look what we brung you."

He tossed the scalp, and it hit her body and fell to the floor. The Burnsides laughed, but looked unhappy when she kicked it aside and began to back toward the door, the knife still in front of her.

"Make her stay, George," Mose pleaded. "Can't you make her stay?"

"I'll cut anyone that tries," she said. "I'm going to have to borrow one of your horses, George. I'll see you get it back."

"You ain't taking one of my horses," Grantly said positively. "Everyone here will testify I'm saying you can't and if you do it's horse stealing. You know what they do to horse stealers around here."

"You can take my horse," Howard Cole said. "I'll use one of Grantly's till I get it back. He won't mind. Come on, I'll put you up on it."

He went outside with the girl, threw a blanket over his horse's back and helped her up.

"That man's crazy, ain't he?" she said in a low voice. "That man with the scalp."

"He's my brother," Howard said. "Listen, I'm going to walk up here a little ways with you. I want to ask you something."

He walked beside her horse till they were out of earshot of the cabin, then stopped.

"I guess you know Grantly pretty good," he said. "What does he want from us? What's he being so friendly about, lining up with us and everything?"

"Don't you know?" she said leaning forward with her arms on the horse's neck and watching him curiously.

"At first I thought he was going to want us to help him rustle some cattle, but now I'm not so sure. That's his line of work, isn't it?"

"Yes, but that isn't what he wants with you. He's going to want you to help him wipe out the Mallorys. That's why he's getting a gang together. Those two boys are his cousins and he's paying the other one money."

"Ringgold?"

"That's right. He's just a man with a gun. This won't be the first time he was paid to kill people."

"Listen, wait here, will you?" Howard said. "I've got to get Barney out of there."

He ran back to the house and pushed the door open. Four of them had been talking; Ringgold was putting dents in his hat. They all looked up as he came in. Then Ringgold went back to what he'd been doing, his face wearing the bored look of a man who's been playing too long among children.

"Get your horse, Barney," Howard said. "We're leaving."

"What?"

"We're leaving, I said. I didn't quit the Rangers to help Grantly in his personal fight with the Mallorys. That's what he—"

"Who said anything like that?" Grantly shouted, rushing across the room. "I'll bet it was that witch. By God, I always thought she was a liar and I'll be damned if that don't prove it."

"She ain't lying," Howard said flatly. "You coming, Barney?"

"No, I'm staying," the other said sullenly. "You're acting too damn funny for me lately. George is going to help me get Braden and some of the others and then if there's something he wants—"

"Some of the others?"

"That's right," Barney said, nodding rapidly. "That's right. It was more than just Winters and Braden that did it, wasn't it?"

"You settle pretty easy, don't you, Howard?" Grantly said. "Old Tim's dead and as far as you're concerned—"

HOWARD'S left hand drove the wind out of him. He gasped, and as his face came forward, Howard smashed a revolver butt over his ear. He fell to all fours, then sank back on his haunches and remained that way, his hands on his hips and blood leaking slowly down the side of his head. The Burnsides came forward, but stopped as Howard waved his gun at them.

"That was a damn fool thing to do, Cole," Grantly said. "A man's got to have some friends in a place like this."

"You coming, Barney?" Howard said.

"No, I'm staying," his brother said, bending over to help Grantly up. "I don't know what's coming over you, Howard."

"All right, you can stay if you want, but just remember this: We came down here to get Winters and Braden. You've gotten Winters. I'll get Braden. That ought to take care of it. You go back to our Ranger camp and stay there till I join you. Whatever you do don't get in too deep with this bunch or it will be the other way around and the Rangers will have to come looking for you."

"You're lucky Grantly ain't me, Cole," Ringgold said as Howard backed toward the door. "It don't look good for someone to hit you that way. I wouldn't let anyone do that to me."

"I know," Howard said. "I'll remember."

He went back outside, picked up his saddle and led one of Grantly's horses to where Eulalie was waiting. There he saddled and mounted.

"You know where Henry Braden lives?" he asked.

"I don't want to be there if you're going to kill him," she said. "I can't afford that kind of trouble."

"I'm not going to kill him," Howard said. "I just want to get a confession out of him and turn him over to the Rangers."

"Well, I think I can find his place for you."

THEY RODE back toward Mason, but circled the town and came out two miles beyond it. A mile further than that, they dismounted, tied their horses to a tree and went the rest of the way on foot. It was night now and no moon overhead, but Howard had no trouble making out Braden's house, squat and flat against the side of a hill, when the girl pointed it out to him. Extending out in front of it, a quarter of a mile on every side, was his pasture land.

"After what happened to Winters today, he's probably expecting visitors," Howard said softly. "The idea of trying to sneak up on him don't make me too happy, but maybe I can get him to come out here. You got that knife?"

She did.

They went into Braden's pasture and 50 yards inside it, Howard struck a match and dropped it. As the grass caught, he fanned the small flame with his hat until a breeze came up suddenly and did the rest of the job. In a moment the original flame had split in two to form a pair of racing red snakes crackling jaggedly through the grass, but they had made hardly any distance at all before the door of the house opened and a man came running down the hill. Howard and Eulalie sank to the ground and it wasn't until he had stamped out the flames that Howard spoke to him.

"Braden."

"I knew you were there," he said bitterly turning around, a stocky middle-aged man with a heavy mustache. "Fires don't start by themselves, only what could I do? A man can't sit on his porch and watch his land go up in smoke. What do you want anyway?"

"What do you think I want?" Howard said covering him with a revolver and motioning him to unbuckle his gun belt. "You killed Tim Harrington, didn't you? Well, I'm Howard Cole. You know what Tim was to me."

"He was rustling my cattle and everybody else's around here," Braden said heatedly. "What's a man supposed to do? Hell, I knew Tim for twenty years. You think I wanted to do that? Besides, if it comes down to that, why put it all on me? It was a vigilante action. Everybody's got the same responsibility in—"

"How about that ring of Tim's?" Howard asked, and when the other didn't answer: "Come on, we'll go up to the house."

It was just two rooms and Braden lived alone in it. When they were inside, Howard took the knife from Eulalie and told Braden to put his hands flat on the kitchen table. Harrington's ring was on the middle finger of his right hand.

"Jesus, wasn't enough done today?" Braden said. "Winters and those two punchers, one of them probably crippled for—"

"It sounds like we had an even bigger day than I knew about," Howard said, shaking his head. "Maybe this will finish it. I'm taking you to the Rangers, Braden, and suggesting they send some men up here. They're needed. But before I do I'm taking Tim's ring back and I'm taking it the way you took it from him."

"You wouldn't do that, Cole," Braden said, his face going white as Howard handed Eulalie his gun.

"Jesus, Tim was dead. It's not the same—*Jesus!*"

He howled and his head went back, then came forward face down on the table. Howard removed the ring from his finger and dropped a bandana on Braden's mutilated hand. Then he took his gun back from

Eulalie and handed her the knife.

"You're all right, Braden," he said impatiently. "What's something like that compared to getting shot? You know damn well when people hear about it they'll say I wasn't a good boy to old Tim for letting you off so easy. Well, come on, let's go. We've got some riding to do."

They went outside and Braden muttered "You lying bugger" when he saw the five mounted men waiting for them. They stopped at the edge of the porch and Howard went down the three steps to the ground, leaving Braden and the girl behind him.

"I'm taking him to the Rangers, Barney," he said. "Let's let them—"

"I thought you'd get an idea like that," his brother shouted. "Well, I say no. I was Tim's boy, too, and I'm telling you no. We'll take care of him right here."

"Barney—"

"Talk to me about it, Cole," Ringgold said. "I been wondering about you and me all night."

Then Howard went for his gun, knowing the moment he saw the other move that he was too slow. Ringgold's shot numbed his arm and as he bent to retrieve the fallen gun with his other hand, a horse moved bulkily toward him, looking immense as a mountain from his crouching position, and a gun butt came down on the top of his head, knocking him out and he fell heavily, his head on his chest.

HE CAME to lying on the ground with Henry Braden's dead body swinging from a branch over him. His head throbbed, but it was only when he tried to stand up that he discovered one arm wouldn't work. Ringgold's bullet had shattered it below the elbow. He wondered why he hadn't been killed and decided it must have been Ringgold's way of showing his contempt for a man he had discovered wasn't even in his class as a gunman. He went into the kitchen, doused his head in cold water, then looked at the arm. A bone had been shattered, but the bullet hadn't entered. He wrapped a bandana around it, using his teeth and free hand to knot it, then came outside again, passing under Braden's body and walking to where he and Eulalie had left the horses. They were both still there. He got on one and led the other, retracing the circle Eulalie had led him on and heading back to the log house. He didn't think about what had happened.

Dawn was coming up as he came out around the other side of Mason. A half hour later he was passing Olney's Store, and three hours after that he was at the backwoods, with the sun blazing overhead and clouds of smoke far ahead of him. They lay just above the tree tops as though resting on them and looked like shapeless bladders being slowly filled out from underneath. He rode into the thicket, and an hour later figured he must be a mile from the log house. He dismounted, tied the horses to a tree and went the rest of the way on foot. When he could see the house, he drew his gun with his left hand and sat down to watch. When after ten minutes he hadn't seen or heard anyone, he got up and ran down to it and pushed the door open with his gun.

Eulalie stood facing him, naked and with her arms over her head. Ropes ran from her wrists to nails in one of the roof logs. Her face and body were lumped and bruised and she was gleaming wet with perspiration.

"George finally got to watch," she whispered, closing her eyes as he began to cut the ropes. "Everyone had their chances. God, how I hurt. Your brother almost killed me. Kicking, hitting— He's so crazy, he can do anything. They finally stopped him so I'd be alive when they came back."

"Where did they go?"

"After the Mallorys."

SHE SAGGED and would have fallen, but he grabbed her arm and held her. She shook her head and said she'd be all right and when he let go, she was able to walk to where her clothes lay in a pile and start putting them on.

"I saw smoke as I came up," Howard said. "That could mean they found them."

"There was some shooting earlier, too. They— Listen."

They could hear horses coming. Howard waved the girl back, then went to the front corner that would face into the door as it opened.

The horses came to a stop outside and Howard drew his gun. They heard men's voices, Grantly saying "Easy, Abe." The door opened and a tall man with a star on his vest entered. Grantly was behind him with a gun in his hand and Barney Cole behind him.

"How did you—" Grantly started, seeing Eulalie. Then he whirled, swinging his gun, but Howard shot twice, putting both of them into his chest and Grantly fell, spinning and landing full length on his back.

"Hold it, Barney," Howard shouted and his brother stopped with his hand on the butt of his gun, but didn't try to pull it out of his belt. The man with the star stepped quickly to his side and took his gun. His eyes on Howard's, Barney made no effort to stop him. Eulalie came from her corner and stood looking down at Grantly. Slow-spreading smears were beginning to redden the front of his shirt.

"I'm Abe Craig," the tall man said, talking to Howard, but covering Barney with the gun he had taken from him. "You're Howard Cole, aren't you?"

"That's right."

"Well, I can't figure where you stand in all this, but you sure showed up at the right time. I don't know what these two would have done next. They slaughtered the Mallorys this morning. I never saw anything like it. Burned their houses and barns. Shot them when they tried to come out. Killed their stock. We had a posse in there looking for this one," nodding at Barney, "but we got there too late to do much. We managed to kill the Burnside brothers and some of us were chasing Ringgold when I got separated from them and I don't know if they ever caught up with him or not. Then I ran into these two and Grantly got the drop on me and they brought me back here. God, it was awful in there. Listen, Cole, I'm grateful for what you done here, but you know I've got to take this boy with me. First Winters and those two cowboys yesterday and now this. I know he's your brother, but I've got to take him."

"Don't let him, Howard," Barney said. "You know what they'll do to me in Mason. Besides, what I did there was for Tim. They'll lynch me, Howard. You know they will. They will, won't they, Mr. Craig?"

"He'll have to come with me, Cole," Craig said. "There's no other way."

"You were such a patient man, George," Eulalie said thoughtfully, slipping her foot beneath the side of Grantly's face and lifting it so that his dead eyes looked into her own. "You waited and waited and finally you got what—"

SHE jumped backwards as Howard's gun went off, her hands rising as though to shield her face.

"My God," she said. "Your own brother."

"There was no other way," Howard said. He crouched next to Barney's body. The shot had entered his heart and killed him instantly. Howard touched his brother's face and looked up at Craig. "There was no other way, was there?" He whispered. "No other way."

"I guess not," Craig said. "But your own brother. My God, what a thing to have to do." ✳

Harry Wax rose to his feet and ran toward the cannon. His cry was taken up by Mii Djun and Dei Bhan, and then from all over the area the knife-wielding Mongols swung onto their horses and charged. The Chinese went to their knees trying desperately to get their rifles into action, but the Mongols were on them too fast. Abusing their horses cruelly, they drove them right in among the riflemen and men were kicked, stamped upon and died beneath frantic hooves. This early success seemed to inflame the Mongols still further. Many left their horses' backs to burst into clusters of the Chinese, their thin-bladed knives working like buggy whips against the faces and bodies of those about them. The knives lacked the weight necessary to decapitate a man, but whipped back and forth as though they were giant straight razors, they be-

"THE TERRIBLE REWARD OF 'FAR EAST HARRY' WAX"

— WRITING AS ROLAND EMPEY —

Male, September 1959

COVER ARTIST: MORT KÜNSTLER

THE TERRIBLE REWARD OF "FAR EAST HARRY" WAX

By ROLAND EMPEY

▶ Harry Wax was a natural with small arms and a hand-to-hand fighter of awesome skill and fury. He was a big man with a fighter's tough, battered face, and the bristling conviction of an Old Testament prophet. Some claim he was too big for his time, his visions too bold for this century's canvas. Five centuries earlier he might have made himself a warrior king, an emperor, even a Khan. But in 1923, when Harry Wax stood looking at the Great Bell of Urga, it was not easy to fight your way to the head of a kingdom.

The Great Bell of Urga had been long neglected.

China had never seen such a warrior, but he stayed for one night with an Eurasian woman and woke up in a bell, his sound moaning through the Orient

It hung over the mausoleum of Tamerlane on a wooded hill, a mile east of the dusty, time-forgotten city of Urga, and birds nested in its pocked and broken dome, while rats and other small animals scurried about the great pile of rubble below.

Fifteen feet across at its broadest diameter, the Great Bell is generally considered the most remarkable iron-smithing achievement of the Middle Ages; but Tamerlane (1336-1405), the most lordly of the Mongol Khans, had it built without a clapper, and would use one of his captives instead, lowering him, head down, into the great domed cavity and smashing his body from one side to the other, so that the people would hear and realize the massive, earth-shaking power of their Khan.

"Put me in charge of your army, and you'll hear the Bell ring again," Harry Wax said, when he reached Urga in 1923. "The Chinese under Hsu are coming at you from one side and White Russians under Sternberg on the other. They'll chew you up between them if you don't get yourself organized. Put me in charge and I'll use the pair of them for clappers, and ring Tamerlane's Bell till they hear it around the world."

"I would not like to see that barbaric custom started again." Hutuktu ("The Living Buddha") sighed, in response to Wax' suggestion. "Besides, when one has such powerful neighbors it is sometimes best to be allied with one or the other. I am not at all convinced that we must fight them both."

Although the accepted civil leader of that ancient country, Hutuktu was a contemplative monk, a thoughtful, scholarly man whose shaved head looked as though it had been sandpapered. He had received Wax in a tiny room in the 3000-year-old monastery of Jhadina in the Falaria Mountains.

"You have to fight them both if you want to survive," Wax said. "Let either one in and it's all over. Hsu wants to annex Mongolia for China and Sternberg wants to make it a new Czarist Russia now that the Reds have thrown them out of the old one."

"But each of them opposes the Communists and we do, too," Hutuktu said in his melancholy way. "Why should we not all work together to defeat them? They would like to take over Mongolia, too, you know."

"I know, I know," Wax said impatiently. "And in the long run they're going to be tougher to keep out than either of the other two. That's why you've got to get organized in a hurry. Look, I'm telling you I'm the man for the job. You've got two invading armies approaching Urga and you've got to make up your mind fast. What are you waiting for?"

"I must think about it and pray," Hutuktu said. "I will let you know."

The Chinese were 100 miles closer than the invading Russians and when they reached the foothills on the far side of the Falarias, Hutuktu sent word to the Mongolian leaders that they should put themselves under the command of Harry Wax. They had no difficulty finding him. Everyone in Urga knew he had taken (Continued on page 44)

THE HUMAN CLAPPER drifted and turned, not touching the giant bronze walls. Then the bellringers pulled harder . . .
Art by GIL COHEN

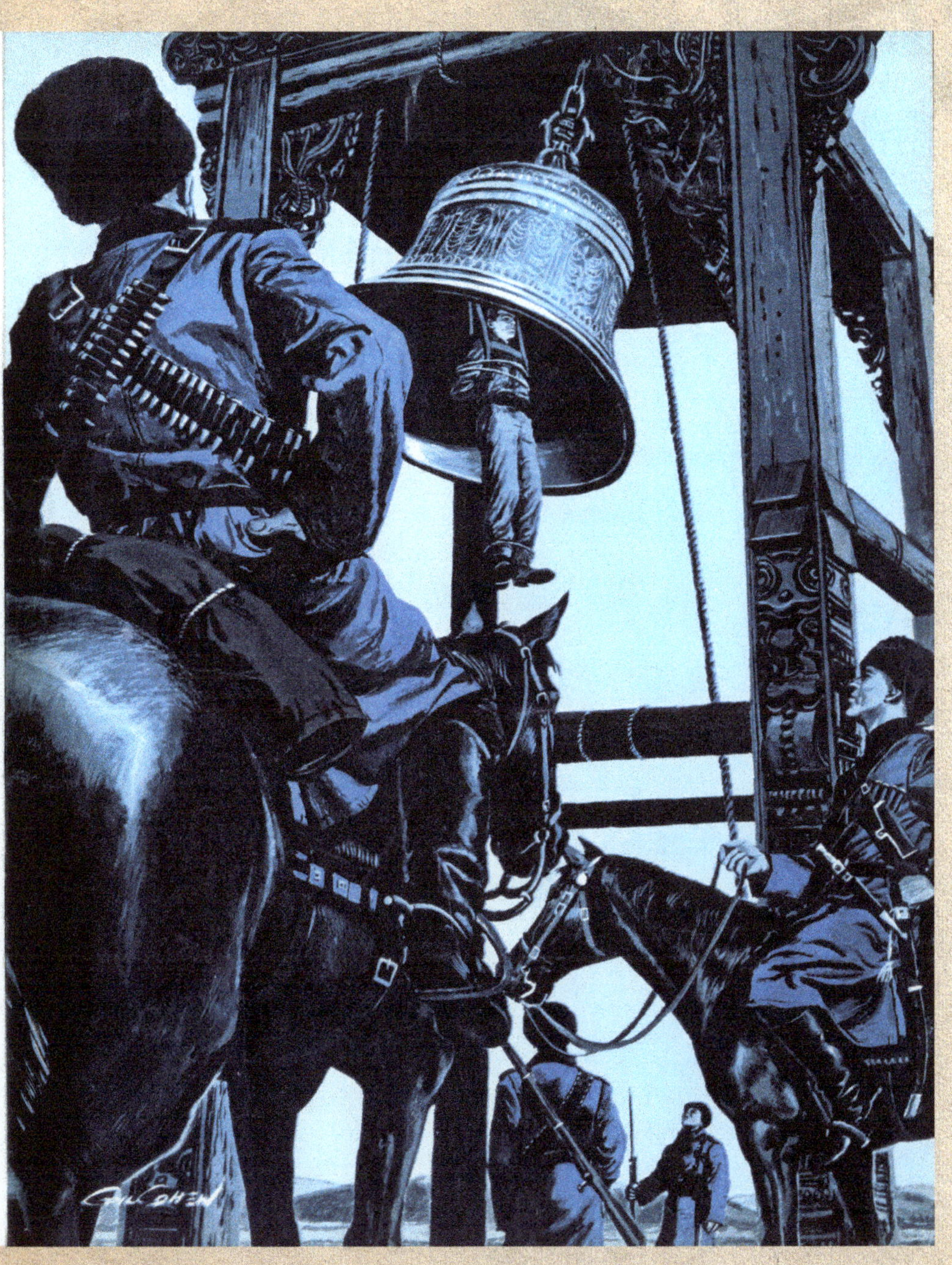

Illustration by Gil Cohen

HARRY Wax was a natural with small arms and a hand-to-hand fighter of awesome skill and fury. He was a big man with a fighter's tough, battered face and the bristling conviction of an Old Testament prophet. Some claim he was too big for his time, his visions too bold for this century's canvas. Five centuries earlier he might have made himself a warrior king, an emperor, even a Khan. But in 1923, when Harry Wax stood looking at the Great Bell of Urga, it was not easy to fight your way to the head of a kingdom.

The Great Bell of Urga had been long neglected. It hung over the mausoleum of Tamerlane on a wooded hill, a mile east of the dusty, time-forgotten city of Urga, and birds nested in its pocked and broken dome, while rats and other small animals scurried about the great pile of rubble below.

Fifteen feet across at its broadest diameter, the Great Bell is generally considered the most remarkable iron-smithing achievement of the Middle Ages; but Tamerlane (1336–1405), the most lordly of the Mongol Khans, had it built without a clapper, and would use one of his captives instead, lowering him, head down, into the great domed cavity and smashing his body from one side to the other, so that the people would hear and realize the massive, earth-shaking power of their Khan.

"Put me in charge of your army, and you'll hear the Bell ring again," Harry Wax said, when he reached Urga in 1923. "The Chinese under Hsu are coming at you from one side and White Russians under Sternberg on the other. They'll chew you up between them if you don't get yourself organized. Put me in charge and I'll use the pair of them for clappers, and ring Tamerlane's Bell till they hear it around the world."

"I would not like to see that barbaric custom started again," Hutuktu ("The Living Buddha") sighed, in response to Wax's suggestion. "Besides, when one has such powerful neighbors it is sometimes best to be allied with one or the other. I am not at all convinced that we must fight them both."

Although the accepted civil leader of that ancient country, Hutuktu was a contemplative monk, a thoughtful, scholarly man whose shaved head looked as though it had been sandpapered. He had received Wax in a tiny room in the 3000-year-old monastery of Jhadina in the Falaria Mountains.

"You have to fight them both if you want to survive," Wax said. "Let either one in and it's all over. Hsu wants to annex Mongolia for

China and Sternberg wants to make it a new Czarist Russia now that the Reds have thrown them out of the old one."

"But each of them opposes the Communists and we do, too," Hutuktu said in his melancholy way. "Why should we not all work together to defeat them? They would like to take over Mongolia, too, you know."

"I know, I know," Wax said impatiently. "And in the long run they're going to be tougher to keep out than either of the other two. That's why you've got to get organized in a hurry. Look, I'm telling you I'm the man for the job. You've got two invading armies approaching Urga and you've got to make up your mind fast. What are you waiting for?"

"I must think about it and pray," Hutuktu said. "I will let you know."

The Chinese were 100 miles closer than the invading Russians and when they reached the foothills on the far side of the Falarias, Hutuktu sent word to the Mongolian leaders that they should put themselves under the command of Harry Wax. They had no difficulty finding him. Everyone in Urga knew he had taken a room and girl in the sprawling, yellow-stone establishment of Foma Mnyori. Some even suggested that Foma herself was helping him speed the days along while he waited for word from Hutuktu. Others said this was nonsense. The black-haired Eurasian, cynical and amused in facial expression, but tantalizing in her sweet-breasted loveliness, had long let it be known that she was not to be used as her girls were. Why would she make an exception for a great, broken-faced brute like Harry Wax?

But that was all guess and conjecture. The fact is that when the men who came for him saw Wax, he was standing in a doorway wearing just a pair of soiled trousers, while behind him, a girl crouched naked on the bed he had just left—a small, dark-skinned girl, sweat-shiny and compact as a pony, her eyes heavy-lidded and cruel in their catlike calm.

Now, without a glance at her or even bothering to claim his clothes, he rushed from the building with the Mongol soldiers, to leap astride the horse being held for him. Then, in that brief moment before his bare heels were to pound urgently at the beast's sides and the yellow dust was to puff up and form swirling clouds about its hooves, Foma Mnyori appeared before her doors.

"There will be a great feast when you return," she screamed, and the soldiers were astonished at her impassioned tone and the expression of blazing triumph in her face, a beautiful face but rarely anything but good-natured and bored. "Repel the invaders and return as Asia's savior."

HE PULLED the horse up on its hind legs and shook a fist at her in the manner of Buffalo Bill acknowledging the applause at his Wild West Show. Then he thumped the animal with his heels and it went forward as though discharged by a great gun. The soldiers who had come for him rode on both sides and in a little over an hour they were at the sprawling encampment where the descendants of those who rode with the Khans waited. Tough, hard-bodied men. Slant-eyed, watchful, small by Western standards, but grotesque in the width of their shoulders and the knotted lumps that muscled their arms and legs.

At Wax's order, they streamed after him into the Falarias mounted on short-legged Mongolian ponies trained to work along those steep slopes and rocky defiles like flies maneuvering on a wall. His instructions were simple and direct. Perhaps that gives a clue to his peculiar genius. He sensed that the Mongols were too eager to get going to be able to absorb any complex battle plan. He scattered them through the hills and led them toward the peaks under orders to avoid the trails and cuts along which the Chinese would be coming. Scouts were already out and would send back word when the main force of the invaders was seen. Then the Mongols would stop their advance at whatever point it had reached and take cover or improvise it. In time, word would reach them from Harry Wax that they should attack. That's all there was to it.

"This is a plan you came halfway around the world to bring us?" Mii Djun grinned, a gray, grizzled fighting man much admired by the others for the frightening strength in his enormous hands. "I must sign my name with an X and have never been a hundred miles from Urga, but such a plan as this I could have made myself."

"Stop complaining, old man," said Dei Bhan, his grandson, a carbon copy of Mii Djun at 19. "Will it not be better than riding down rabbits and deer in the desert?"

"Do not advise me in these or other matters," the other said amiably. "It would not distress me to break you over my knee and send you back to your mother, my daughter, in several pieces."

"You could have done it when I was six, old man," the boy said. "Today I could put you in my hat and never even know you were there."

They rode on each side of Wax, insulting each other as though it were some sort of contest, and a little behind and spread out on either side of them, the rest of the Mongols advanced upward through the thick, dry growth of the Falarias toward the unseen invader climbing on the far side. When they were 200 yards below the ridge called Kubla's Comb because of the regularly spaced trails leading down from it, a scout returned to say the Chinese would be coming over it in less than an hour. Word went to the men from Wax that they should get under cover, keep quiet and try to keep their horses quiet, too.

Forty minutes later the heavy, black length of a cannon barrel rose above the ridge to be followed almost immediately by the foot soldiers of Hsu's army, tiny, ant-like creatures swarming down the teeth of the Comb with, here and there among them, an officer on an enormous horse. One hundred pulled and guided the cannon, an ancient weapon that had been used in the Boxer Rebellion a quarter of a century earlier. For perhaps 100 yards they were permitted to advance unmolested, an all-engulfing tide of men, pouring down the Falarias toward Urga. Then, bare-chested and howling, Harry Wax rose to his feet and ran toward the cannon. His cry was taken up by Mii Djun and Dei Bhan and then from all over the area the knife-wielding Mongols swung onto their horses and charged. The Chinese went to their knees trying desperately to get their rifles into action, but the Mongols were on them too fast. Abusing their horses cruelly, they drove them right in among the riflemen, and men were kicked, stamped upon and died beneath frantic hooves. This early success seemed to inflame the Mongols still further. Many left their horses' backs to burst into clusters of the Chinese, their thin-bladed knives working like buggy whips against the faces and bodies of those about them. The knives lacked the weight necessary to decapitate a man, but whipped back and forth as though they were giant straight razors, they became viciously punishing weapons.

At the top of their wild charge, Wax had gone directly toward the cannon and an officer riding a little behind and to the side of it. The animal was milk-white, the squat, fat-faced rider so cold and remote in appearance that he seemed a hand-carved idol tied to the horse's back rather than a human being riding it. Wax had correctly taken him for General Hsu. Now, as he scrambled toward him, Mii Djun, Dei Bhan and other Mongols at his back, a wing of the Chinese advance cut in from an edge of the ridge to intercept him. But the running Mongols split them like an axe cleaving a wooden shield, and then Wax had reached Hsu and was bringing up his knife into the belly of the general's horse. The beast's scream tore a hole in the din of the fighting. Blood poured from its body as though a stopper had been removed. It reared and bolted and General Hsu slipped off its back, his face frozen, with Death gliding toward him.

At the last moment he attempted to draw his revolver, but before he could, Harry Wax was on top of him and conducting a successful search for soft spots to insert a knife. Dead almost instantly, the general rolled 25 feet down the slope just as Mii Djun, Dei Bhan and the others with them fell on those controlling the cannon from the rear.

The huge, ungainly weapon suddenly found itself rolling free and as though to celebrate that independence, took on greater speed, passing with one wheel over the General's chest, and plunged madly down the slope through and over knots of struggling men to come at last to a shivering crash against a great pile of gray rock.

With the death of their general and the demolition of their cannon, the Chinese conceded that it wasn't their day. Many fled. Others threw down their weapons and waited stolidly for whatever fate their ill-advised invasion would bring. They had been told the Mongols would not fight, that their "Living Buddha" would not permit it; also, that they were a weary, decadent people who could be easily brushed aside even if they should choose to resist. In both respects they were misinformed. Although outnumbering the Mongols four to one, they were to have a third of their army destroyed and the remainder brought back to Urga as captives. And as they trudged along, many remembered what they had heard of the Khans and stole quick glances at the big, burly man who led the Mongols, wondering if perhaps another Tamerlane had appeared to drench all Asia in blood.

The feast that Foma Mnyori prepared was in many respects a duplicate of those that celebrated Tamerlane's greatest victories. The dishes were succulent, each platter supporting a mountain of fowl, wild pig, steaming rice, sweet potato and fruit of many sizes and colors. The wine, liquor and the potent Mongolian *dahss* flowed as though from a bottomless reservoir. A number of Chinese captives served their conquerors and were kicked or otherwise thrashed for anything less than perfection.

Foma Mnyori's prostitutes had been increased to five times their regular number and made themselves freely available to savage herdsmen they would have previously spurned as being beneath them. Songs were sung, stories of the afternoon's fighting told and re-told. Men lurched drunkenly about and staggered, greedy-lipped, from one laughing girl to the next. The old man, Mii Djun, fell on the floor in a stupor and was roused when a naked girl put her forefinger in his ear to explore it with a dagger-pointed nail. He rose to all fours, bleary-eyed and grinning vacantly, and the girl sat on his back and rode him about the room, controlling his direction with her hands on his ears until they reached an open door through which she took him and pushed it shut.

CLAD IN a robe of shimmering silk that Foma Mnyori had somehow obtained for him, Harry Wax dominated that bacchanal with his great bull-like voice and furious energy—a detonation, an explosion, an eruption of sound, will and strength. He roared. He howled. He drank more *dahss* than any other two men and heard himself referred to as "surely, a Khan of Khans." A captive displeased him; Wax slammed a loaded platter of food down on his head. A Mongol began to paw Foma Mnyori; it failed to ruffle the Eurasian's composure, but Wax knocked the man unconscious by driving a hand to his heart. He recited verses of his own composition, and one has since taken on a peculiar irony:

> *Hot sands of Asia*
> *Be his tomb.*
> *The first he's known*
> *Since his mother's womb.*

He kept the dark-skinned, cat-eyed prostitute with him most of the time and handled her as though he were a monstrous' child and she his sturdiest doll. He fed her with his hands, forcing the food into her mouth until she could take in no more and darted her head to his chest to bite him. He pulled her away and held her upside down between his legs and tickled the soles of her feet with his tongue. She kicked a leg free and blood poured from his smashed lips where her heel had caught him. He lifted her erect and threw her onto a table and began to clap his hands for her to dance. Others took it up until the whole building shook and the girl, her eyes narrowed to slits, her clothes falling away from her as she danced, executed a series of sinuous, supple, all-but-boneless twists and maneuvers that had the assembled Mongols exclaiming in astonishment and dismay—dismay that such a talented body should be forbidden to them by Wax's stronger claim.

It was while the girl was dancing that the emissary from Hutuktu arrived. Like the Living Buddha himself, he was a monk, a shaved and sad-eyed soul plainly distressed by the scope and intensity of the celebration. He spoke briefly to Harry Wax conveying to him Hutuktu's wish that the two get together immediately to discuss how best to meet the White Russian advance. While he spoke, Foma Mnyori came to stand close by, then nod approvingly at Wax's answer.

"I'll meet Sternberg's advance the same way I met Hsu's," he said poking the monk's chest with a heavy forefinger. "Tell Hutuktu to attend to the praying and I'll take care of the rest. No, I won't go and talk to him. He'll just waste my time with a lot of blather about maybe we shouldn't fight them at all. Maybe we should just invite them in. Praying is Hutuktu's business. Mine is fighting. If we each stay in our own territory, we ought to do all right."

Before the monk could respond, Wax returned to the table. The prostitute danced to the edge of it to face him, her feet wide apart. He took her on his shoulders, then went the well-remembered way to their room. She sat facing behind him and held her hands on the back of his head to press his face against her belly.

The Mongol assault on General Sternberg's White Russians is generally considered to be the most unorthodox military maneuver of the 20th century. Five hundred years earlier, it would not have had such a reaction. It is now accepted that Wax learned his tactic from reading about the Khans. Genghis, in particular, achieved great success by sweeping the people of captured villages along before his army, then hurling them against those that tried to resist him.

When Wax and his Mongols rode out to meet the Russians, the captured Chinese were brought along. And when the two armies drew within sight of each other across the frozen Azyribian plains, the Chinese, some armed and some not, were funneled through the Mongol ranks and out before them and then sent charging forward.

Their situation was helpless. Behind them were men with knives and whips and their own captured guns. They streamed hopeless and confused across the Plain and the Russians slaughtered them as easily as though they were a stampede of sheep. But immediately behind them came the Mongols and Wax's objective had been attained, that being to reach the Russians for hand-to-hand fighting. Without the Chinese in front of them, the Mongols could have been cut down by Sternberg's heavier firepower at long range.

As HE had with General Hsu, Harry Wax looked immediately for the enemy commander. But this time he was not to be so successful. Unlike the ragged Chinese horde, the Russians were a real army—organized, disciplined and led by a bitter, battle-toughened veteran of the battle against Lenin's forces.

General Sternberg was not nearly so available to Wax's charge as General Hsu had been. He was in a protected position, directing the withdrawal. Because withdrawal it had to be. There was no stopping the Mongols, no defeating them. But neither was there to be a total defeat such as that inflicted on the Chinese the day before. The Russians died by the hundreds, those in the front ranks simply being ridden down and hacked to pieces. Harry Wax, with Mii Djun and Dei Bhan at his sides, sped through them like a machine-driven scythe, charging directly into rifle-armed men and destroying them with his own rifle or knife before they could get a shot off.

But at the rear, the withdrawal went on—swiftly, efficiently, and although Wax and the Mongols outdid themselves in their speed of slaughter, they could not manage it fast enough to reach Sternberg's secondary defenders and disrupt the retreat.

At last the field was theirs. The Russians were in flight. Behind them lay the dead heart of their army and ton upon ton of supplies and equipment. These were gathered up and taken back to Urga by the victorious Mongols. Before them raced a messenger, carrying news of the victory to Hutuktu. He was a simple man, that Mongol peasant, and one with no concept of reverence. He burst into the Living Buddha's cell-like room in the monastery of Jhadina just as he would have into a saloon or brothel. The result was that he found Hutuktu deep in conversation with Foma Mnyori. He gave his report in the presence of the Eurasian. Later he accompanied her back toward Urga, but failed to complete the trip.

"My horse is limping," Foma Mnyori said to him when they had gone a short distance.

He dismounted, checked the hooves. While he was crouched over examining the beast's uninjured member, the Eurasian thrust her knife into the back of his neck.

"That doesn't come easy to me," she said unhappily. "But you would tell Wax you saw me with Hutuktu. It would not be well for him to know that."

By the time Wax returned to Urga, the prostitute with whom he had spent most of his time since being there had gone. In her place was Foma Mnyori.

"The poor girl's mother is dying," she smiled. "I hope I will be as pleasing to you."

She quickly demonstrated to Wax that he had incurred no loss. Less impassioned, perhaps, than her predecessor, she was infinitely more versatile. She could change her personality from one hour to the next and her lovemaking techniques with it. She could move with ease from a role of remote and all but inaccessible goddess to one of a furry, purring kitten. Her lack of predictability delighted Wax, as did her familiarity with poetry and other cultural subjects.

THERE had been a time when he seriously considered going into seclusion and devoting the rest of his life to writing poetry. But his physical nature wouldn't permit it, and at 19 he had embarked on his career as a soldier of fortune, a career that was to reach its hideous climax in Mongolia. But regardless of their treacherous outcome, he probably regretted no moment of those days he spent with Foma Mnyori. As they spent them, they were hardly days at all, but rather a timeless lovemaking on every level of personal union.

They loved each other with their bodies and minds and at moments of greatest ecstasy imagined that they had souls and loved with them, too. And when at length the comrades of Wax's two battles would no longer be sent away (they had been trying to get him to come to them for 24 hours) but burst into their room, the regrouped forces of General Sternberg were at the gates of the city.

"You have destroyed yourself and us along with you," Mii Djun said bitterly. "You could have been the Khan of all Asia and we would have ridden behind you into Moscow itself. Now there is nothing for us to do but die and my only prayer is that the Russians do not overlook or ignore you."

They ran outside then, and from every part of the city the Mongols came on their short-legged horses, but the Russians had already entered from two sides and buildings were beginning to collapse before their guns and torches. Now the element of surprise was in their favor and they did not fail to exploit it. Like Africa's plague of the red ants, they poured through the city devouring everything in their paths. Every man, woman and child they saw was slain and the desperate attacks of the disorganized Mongols were broken on the ever-advancing juggernaut.

Mii Djun and his grandson died within moments of each other and Harry Wax stood over their crumpled bodies and fought like one demented. Orders had been given to take him alive and half a dozen men died in the attempt. But finally he was swarmed under by a human wave, and when he was hauled to his feet, blood poured from his mouth and a vacant eye socket and his hands had been tied behind him. Then he was roped to an officer's saddle and made to march in the midst of the taunting Russians the mile to Tamerlane's mausoleum. Hutuktu was there, sad-faced and averting his eyes, and Foma Mnyori came, too, along with others who had come out of hiding when the fighting stopped.

A dozen men took him to the top of the Great Bell and ropes were fixed to his ankles. When this had been done, General Sternberg—a squat, balding man on a black horse—spoke quietly to an officer next to him. This man shouted an order to those on the Bell. Hands were put on the prisoner, but he was heard to roar that he needed no help. Then he took two quick steps and disappeared into the hole at the top of the Bell.

The men with him went to their knees, then lay flat with their hands in the hole holding the ropes they had attached to his ankles. They were seen to be working, straining. Soldiers rushed into the building to look up at the body hanging above them. It had begun to move, to swing. Farther and farther it flew, the arms hanging straight down, blood from his face flecking those beneath. Then a great roar went up and the heavy body smashed into a side of the Bell, producing no earth-shaking peal, but only the lusterless sound of a dead weight against cracked metal. Now, like a ball leaving a wall, it swung to the other side to be smashed again.

For perhaps five minutes it went on and no one kept count of the number of times the body of Harry Wax banged into a side of the Bell. There can be no question that he died long before they stopped. When they dropped him, there was no whole bone left in his body.

The intrigue and double dealing that accompanied Mongolia's entrance into the Soviet system are still a source of awe and wonder to historians. It is accepted now that Hutuktu, fearful of Harry Wax's ambition and rapidly growing power, invited General Sternberg to bring his troops to Urga. Their arrangement included the provision that after the Russians had subdued the city, Hutuktu would continue to be the actual head of government. Sternberg assented.

It is also accepted that Foma Mnyori was given and readily took on the role of Wax's mistress so that she could keep him out of the way while the Russians were moving in. She was probably more successful at this than had been expected. It could hardly have been hoped that she could keep him away from his men until the Russians were actually entering the city. But even had Wax gone into action hours earlier, his failure to set up a satisfactory system of scouts and outposts would have made a Mongol victory unlikely. For these failures, Foma Mnyori could claim complete credit. So delighted was Wax to be with her that he simply neglected to take precautions. In strength and energy he might have been a Khan. In shrewdness and tough judgment, he fell considerably short. Whatever Foma Mnyori was to be paid for her efforts has never been discovered. It is of no significance. Her real payment came later.

Three weeks after their entrance into Urga, the Russians ravaged the country. Village after village was destroyed, the people driven off or killed. In vain did Hutuktu try to stop it, reminding Sternberg that by their agreement he was still ruler and did not wish his people to be thus abused. His pleas were laughed at or ignored and the Russians went steadily ahead with their plan to bring the entire country under their control.

THEN ON the 24th day of the Russian occupation, the Mongols in Urga rose against the garrison there. Their leader was Foma Mnyori. Calling on them to strike in the name of their dead leader, Harry Wax, she infused in those who had fought with him earlier a desire for revenge so strong and demanding that the Russians could not contain or resist it. Their garrison was slaughtered to a man. Heads were hacked off and thrown into the streets of Urga like over-ripe cabbages. Bodies were heaped into piles and burned. General Sternberg followed Harry Wax into the Great Bell and was smashed against its sides until he resembled nothing human. Word of the Urga uprising spread quickly throughout the country and was followed immediately by others. Blood ran in the streets and blackened the earth and Hutuktu squatted in his room at Jhadina and prayed for an end to the horror.

On the eighth day following the uprising, peace was restored and the final mask was removed. On that day Foma Mnyori ordered a flag to be flown over Urga. Her triumphant troops, heart and soul behind the Eurasian for her inspired leadership against the Russians, cheered lustily as it rose above them. If they understood little of what had happened, Hutuktu saw and did.

The flag was red. Mongolia was passing into the hands of the Soviets. It had been Foma Mnyori's mission all along. She had been sent to Mongolia originally on assignment from Lenin and her job had been accomplished. A week after she raised the red flag over Urga, a full commissariat staff arrived from Moscow and she was recalled. One of the first acts of the new regime was to take away the Great Bell and melt it down for scrap.

Foma Mnyori was to make one more brief appearance on history's stage. In the struggle for power between Trotsky and Stalin, she sided with the former. She was tried as a traitor to the Revolution in 1932 and executed. This was eight years before Trotsky himself was assassinated in Mexico.

As for Harry Wax, that would-be Khan of Khans, the pawn she used in her remarkable coup—his remains lie in the Falarias close to where Tamerlane's mausoleum still stands. A white stone marks the spot. On it are words of his own creation:

> *Hot sands of Asia*
> *Be his tomb.*
> *The first he's known*
> *Since his mother's womb.* ✳

said brokenly. "This creature will kill us all."

"Albie, we done enough," Jens said backing away, his lips white and trembling with fear. "We done -"

"Do I have to do everything myself?" The cry was a soul-freezing mixture of rage and torment. "Ain't there no one to stop asking questions and just do my bidding? By God, I'll kill and kill and kill and kill and never stop killing if people don't do what I say. I'll beat you dummies till the blood runs out of your eyes. I'll tie every man on this godforsaken island to a tree and he'll bark like a dog for me to throw him a bone. And the women - the women! They'll lay on their bellies like snakes and crawl into holes when they see me coming. If one of them sticks its head up I'll kick it till it splits open. I'll trample - I'll crush - I'll -"

Now his fury was so great he

TRUE BOOKLENGTH

MALE

THE SEA NYMPH

IND.

SEPT.

25¢

All during its desperate WWII flight from the British, through mutiny, mayhem and madness, Elsa Schweppe, cunning, beautiful, sailed aboard the S.S. Ergenstrasse, proving that wars were won in bed...

N. Y. HERALD TRIBUNE: "Bang-up action from cover to cover..."

RECKLESS COMMANDO RAID ON TOBRUK

"WE'RE BRINGING BACK A GERMAN GENERAL"

"EMPEROR BLAINE OF 'SWEET WOMAN' REEF"

Male, September 1959

COVER ARTIST: Mort Künstler

He came ashore at Tuara, a cocky, bitter man, riding another man's shoulders. Within hours he'd hung a native and had jabbed his rifle deep into the bosom of an island empire

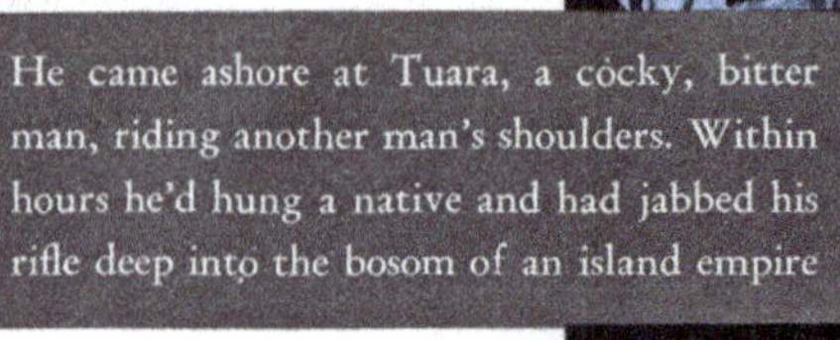

By WALTER KAYLIN

On a warm August night, the British merchantman, *Pharoah Queen,* was in southern waters carrying trade goods from Liverpool to Samoa. A slight breeze was blowing and a full moon floated at the stern like a child's white balloon.

At a little after three in the morning, the *Pharoah Queen* passed within five miles of the Island of Tuara and two naked men appeared silently at the rail on the port side. Working swiftly and with no words exchanged, they knotted two ropes to adjacent stanchions and lowered them into the water. Then, supporting a sea chest between them, they descended the ropes and entered the water without any splash to announce their departure.

In anticipation of its trip, the chest had been corked on the inside and was literally unsinkable. The men clung to ropes that were passed about it and paddled for shore. An hour later they were on Tuara's beach.

THEY presented an interesting contrast, those two who were about to write one of the darkest chapters in the often-violent history of the South Seas. Gundar Jens was a blond, blue-eyed giant, muscled like a gladiator and with the gentle expression of a cow that has just calved. Albie Blaine was half-a-foot shorter, thin to the point of emaciation, snap-mouthed as a woman's purse and with an enormous, lidless eye circled by a mottled snake tattooed on his chest.

When they had rested for a while, Blaine opened the sea chest and took from it a pair of rubber-soled shoes, a pair of khaki trousers and a black stovepipe hat. He put these on, first coiling a length of rope inside the hat,

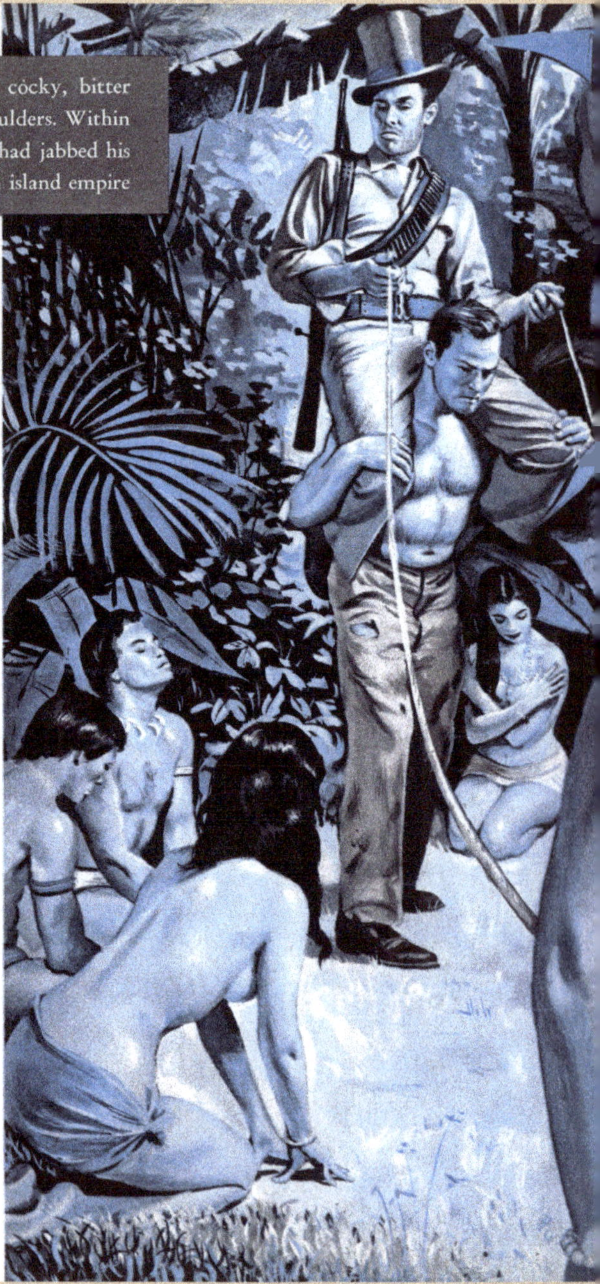

"DON'T ANSWER ME BACK," Albie howled, "or I'll tie every man and woman on this island to a tree and make 'em bark like dogs"

Art by AL ROSSI

Illustrations by Al Rossi

ON A warm August night, the British merchantman, *Pharaoh Queen,* was in southern waters carrying trade goods from Liverpool to Samoa. A slight breeze was blowing and a full moon floated at the stern like a child's white balloon.

At a little after three in the morning, the *Pharaoh Queen* passed within five miles of the Island of Tuara and two naked men appeared silently at the rail on the port side. Working swiftly and with no words exchanged, they knotted two ropes to adjacent stanchions and lowered them into the water. Then, supporting a sea chest between them, they descended the ropes and entered the water without any splash to announce their departure.

In anticipation of its trip, the chest had been corked on the inside and was literally unsinkable. The men clung to ropes that were passed about it and paddled for shore. An hour later they were on Tuara's beach.

THEY PRESENTED an interesting contrast, those two who were about to write one of the darkest chapters in the often-violent history of the South Seas. Gundar Jens was a blond, blue-eyed giant, muscled like a gladiator and with the gentle expression of a cow that has just calved. Albie Blaine was half-a-foot shorter, thin to the point of emaciation, snap-mouthed as a woman's purse and with an enormous, lidless eye circled by a mottled snake tattooed on his chest.

When they had rested for a while, Blaine opened the sea chest and took from it a pair of rubber-soled shoes, a pair of khaki trousers and a black stovepipe hat. He put these on, first coiling a length of rope inside the hat, and addressed himself to the blond man still lying on his back with his hands beneath his head.

"I can see from the look on your fat face you got wrong ideas about what we're going to do here," he said. "Well, this is a good time to get rid of them."

He kicked his companion in the ribs, receiving a howl of rage and indignation in response. Jens sat up as though intending to regain his feet, but was promptly put flat on his back again by another kick, this one to the side of his head. He made several more attempts to rise, but each ended the same discouraging way. Blaine was moving about and landing as easily as a skilled boxer punishing the big bag.

"A French hand off the old *Palmer Town* taught me this in '04," he said. "I wouldn't keep trying to get up if I was you, Jens. I could do this to Jim Jeffries himself without him being able to lay a hand on me. Just take it stoical like an Indian and maybe we won't have to go through it again."

A few minutes more of futile resistance convinced Jens that Blaine's suggestion was sound and he stopped trying to get up, but instead curled himself into a ball and tried to cover up his more vulnerable parts. Blaine kicked him a few more times, got no response, either vocal or physical, and went to the sea chest again to return with a jar of foul-smelling salve and a bottle of whiskey.

"Better for lumps and bruises than anything you'll ever buy in a drugstore," he said handing the salve to Jens and taking a drink of the whiskey. "Learned how to make it from a Kanaka snake charmer I met in Espiritu Santo when I was there with the *John B. Rutledge* in '01. Here, stop looking at me like a sick dog. You ain't going to get any of this whiskey, and you may as well know it right now. Just smear yourself with some of this salve and then put on your clothes and we'll be going."

"I'm beginning to wish I'd stayed on the *Queen,*" Jens said unhappily, as he began applying the salve. "They wouldn't have gave me more than three months for selling the mate's clothes. What did you mean about me having wrong ideas?"

"You were counting on waltzing around with these girls here," Blaine said. "And don't tell me you weren't. I been watching you and writing down records. Singapore, Lui Choi, Antsien, Liverpool, Marseilles, Papeete, Pago Pago … you ran with the girls in all those places and some others, too. I got it all written down."

"Well, what else am I supposed to do when I get off ship?" Jens asked in amazement. "Knit my old mother a shawl?"

"Don't get smart with me," Blaine said, and kicked him so hard Jens had to struggle for breath and seemed about to be sick. "Some day I'll lay one of them in there where it will do some real damage and then you'll really have something to sweat about. Here, put your clothes on and let's go. The natives are waiting for us to come put a little healthy morality in their empty lives."

WHILE Jens began dressing, Blaine took two rifles and two cartridge belts out of the chest. He looped one of the belts over his shoulder, slipped a cartridge into the gun and jammed the end of it into Jens' ribs. The blond man gave him a look of sheer terror.

"You big creeps sing big with the girls, but you ain't all that much anywhere else, are you?" Blaine said, sitting down on the chest and running a rag over the barrel of the gun. "Here, put on that belt and take that other gun, but don't put no bullets in it unless I tell you. Stupid as you are, you might get a funny idea."

Jens did as he was told, and soon the two men were walking along the beach. Close by a dog barked, and across the water they could see the first blush of the rising sun. As they walked, Blaine told Jens about Peter Flint, the first white man to set foot on Tuara.

One of Captain Cook's officers, Flint had been put ashore on Tuara with four men in 1778 to take it over for the Crown. But he had his difficulties right from the beginning. The natives were hostile and uncooperative. They could do very little against Flint's guns, but they tried, and it was necessary for him to treat them very harshly before they accepted his rule. His methods included cutting out a man's eye or tongue, and even minor infractions of his laws were handled that way.

"But he made his mistake when he started sleeping with the women," Blaine said. "Study your history and you'll see it's the same thing wrecks it for a man every time: Women. Now, you see why I told you about keeping out of them brothels?"

Evidently, the natives stood it for several months. Then one day, they seized Flint and his men, buried them in beach sand up to their necks and damaged their faces in the ways they had been taught. Totally mutilated and still imprisoned in the sand, the men were kept alive for hours until the high tide swept in and they were mercifully drowned.

After that, it wasn't until 100 years later that white men came to Tuara again. Then Yankee traders found it, paid a few visits, and forgot about it. There was nothing to trade for on the island and no one wanted to buy anything. The natives were no longer wild, but incredibly lazy and strangely childlike.

"Inbreeding was what done it," Blaine said. "That and the syphilis Flint gave their women and that they've been passing along ever since. Today, in 19-oh-eight, they're worse than ever before. Oh, I guess you'd say they look healthy enough, but except for the royal family you hardly ever see one that's lived past 30 or that has the intelligence of six years old." As he spoke, they had begun passing round, thatched huts out of which people came to run and dance about them. As Blaine had said, they looked healthy enough—the men bronzed and strongly built, the women slim-waisted, but sweetly formed at the breasts and with long, sturdy legs tapering down to slender ankles. Yet, Jens couldn't help noticing that their happy smiles were the smiles of children frolicking along about their teachers. Blaine spoke to two of the men, telling them to go back and get the sea chest. They trotted off as though delighted to have been selected.

By the time they reached the main concentration of huts, they were accompanied by well over 100 natives and now dozens more came pouring out to see them. They exclaimed in wonder over Jens' blond hair and Blaine's stovepipe hat, but it was the great tattooed eye that most fascinated them. Each had to run and peer into it as though expecting it to blink, although, having no lids, it obviously couldn't.

"Martin Flint, the current king," Blaine said suddenly, and nodded at a man who had just appeared in the doorway of the largest hut. As they approached, the king suddenly darted forward shouting "Off, off," and stamped his feet on the ground, at which the natives all fled, laughing merrily and resembling nothing so much as an enormous litter of playful puppies. As the two white men reached the king, they saw immediately how markedly he differed from his subjects. For one thing, he could have been as much as 40. And for another, there was a look of adult intelligence on his face, even shrewdness. He motioned them to enter his hut and a moment later they were seated.

"My name is Blaine and this is my assistant, Mr. Jens," Blaine said without any preliminaries. He took a drink of whiskey and put the bottle on the floor where Jens looked at it wistfully. "We come here special to help you get this place into shape. That's nice seeing all them women running around without enough dress on them to cover their navel, ain't it?"

"WHERE DID you come from and who sent you?" Martin Flint asked uneasily. "What do you intend doing here? Certainly you realize my people are quite incapable of taking a place in a modern society. Years of brother mating with sister, plus the disease our common ancestor Peter Flint willed us have so weakened—"

"The Prime Minister don't think that's the case," Blaine said, taking another drink and belching loudly. "That's right, the Prime Minister. That's who sent us. He wants us to crack down on some of this immorality around here and get the place into the twentieth century. We got a couple of blacksnake whips coming in our trunk and from now on they're going to be smacking it out day and night. Me and Mr. Jens is going to take care of that end of it personally, and you watch and see how quick some of these people start learning about what's right and what ain't. I got the schedule all down on a little list here. So many licks for sleeping with somebody more than once a month. So many licks for sleeping with somebody before you're 20. So many—say, this your daughter?"

"Yes, this is Audrey," her father said as a young woman entered the hut. The king's face was troubled. He tried unsuccessfully to catch Jens' eye. "Perhaps some corrective measures are necessary, but I don't think your program is a sound one for my people. The only severe punishment should be reserved for anyone who despoils my daughter. If Princess Audrey has a child by one of these poor souls before I can make a suitable arrangement with someone from Samoa or one of the other islands—that is what we have done ever since the time of Peter Flint— it would be the end of the royal line."

The young woman discussed differed from the average Tuaran girl in the same way that her father differed from the men. There was intelligence, even a hint of cunning, in a face of startling beauty. The eyes were black and enormous, the mouth soft-lipped and red as crushed roses. The hair tumbled in fragrant clouds about her face and shoulders. She was generously proportioned at the hips and breasts, but rounded and softly molded in both areas.

"Come here with me a minute, I want to show you something," Blaine said to Jens.

He took the bottle of whiskey with him and the two men went outside and around behind the hut. Some of the natives tried to go with them, but Blaine shooed them away. When 50 yards and a clump of trees separated them from the king's hut, Blaine said: "All right, get down on your hands and knees and we'll get it over in a hurry?"

"What's that?" Jens said thinking he had heard incorrectly. "What—"

"You heard me the first time," Blaine said, knocking his assistant down by kicking him in the groin. "I don't want to waste any more time on this than I have to."

"But, Albie—" Jens gasped, and was discouraged from further protest by a kick that caught him full in the mouth.

"Take it like an Indian," Blaine said. "Be stoical."

Jens obediently curled up to make himself as small as possible and Blaine walked around him kicking at his exposed portions and explaining it was for his own good. Occasionally, he interrupted the explanation to take a drink.

"Didn't I see the way you were looking at Princess Audrey?" he demanded. "You want to wind up like old Peter Flint with just your head sticking out of the sand and not much left of it to be sticking? That's what I'm putting down on the schedule for anybody that violates the Virgin Princess. All right, we'll go back now and don't let me see you making no more mistakes like that."

He threw away the empty bottle and they returned to the hut to find their sea chest had been delivered in their absence. Blaine opened it and took out two blacksnake whips and another bottle of whiskey.

"We'll set up a couple of posts right in front of your hut here and get to work," he said. "One is for the men and one for the women. We'll start off by giving them all a couple of wallops so they'll understand."

"It won't accomplish anything," Martin Flint said. "At least 30 of our people have gone off into the jungle where they are living an even looser life than they do here. If we do as you suggest, it will only cause others to go off and join them."

"Then the first thing we got to do is make them see there's no point in that," Blaine said. He opened the bottle, took a long pull and wiped his arm across his mouth. "You tell me where to find these people and me and my assistant here will go look into the matter."

Martin Flint and his daughter exchanged a look, but neither said anything. Blaine took another drink, then leaned across the table and slapped the king's face.

"You said you didn't know what would happen to these dummies if the royal line died out," he said. "Keep on not telling me where them others are and we'll find out right now. In case you don't know what this thing is, it's a gun and what it does is put holes in people, even kings and especially their daughters. Here, maybe you think I'm making that up."

He poked the gun between the girl's breasts and held it there with one hand. He put the bottle to his mouth with the other and took it away with whiskey spilling down his chin.

"Well, we're going to be setting up a hell of a draught through there, ain't we?" he shouted, bending over to sight along the rifle as though his target were half a mile away instead of across the table. "This thing will make a hole big enough to stick your head in."

"Jesus, don't do nothing crazy, Albie," Jens muttered.

"Here, you been wanting a drink, you fat-faced loon," Blaine said. He took a mouthful of whiskey and spat it into the blond man's face. "Now, don't say I never gave you nothing. All right, somebody say one, two, three, and when they get to three I'll put a tunnel in there big enough you could ride a horse through it. All right, I'm waiting. All right, I'll do my own counting. One, two—"

"There's a clearing about a mile from here," Martin Flint said. "You have to go straight out from the back of the hut to get to it. The people who left us sometimes gather there."

"I'm going to write up a good report on you for the Prime Minister," Blaine said. "He likes a man that cooperates. Here's that list on who gets what for doing what. Read it to the populace and when me and Jens get back we'll start handing out them licks. I didn't write it in yet but you can tell them that anyone violating the Virgin Princess gets the same thing Peter Flint got. All right, come on, Jens. We'll go learn these people about the error of their ways."

They went out around the back of the hut. The foliage was very thick and the smell of the jungle growth so sweet and strong it was almost overpowering. Small animals darted through the underbrush and occasionally they saw brightly colored snakes slipping through the leaves on the trees.

In about half an hour they heard voices, and a few minutes later climbed a clump of rock to look down at a semi-clearing, the grass knee-high. Here, mother-naked all, two dozen Tuarans frolicked in the innocent ways of the utterly primitive. Some ran about in childish games laughing in excitement and delight. Some bit into the luscious fruits that grew in profusion all about them. And others, unconcerned as healthy rabbits, were occupied in still other ways. Blaine lay down on top of the rock with just his head poked over the edge of it and motioned Jens to do the same.

"All right, you start on the left there and I'll start on the right," he said, and took a series of gulps from the bottle he'd brought along. "Work fast; get as many as you can."

"You mean shoot them?" Jens said, horrified. "Albie, I've never shot anybody in my life. Why them? What did they ever—?"

"Don't argue with me, you fat-faced coot," Blaine said, jamming the end of his rifle against Jens' ear and sighting along it. "I can waste a few of these things on you and still have enough to take care of every dummy on this goddam island. Now, you just take care of that girl with the big rump over there or it's one, two, three and out for you, stupid. One, two—"

Jens shot and the girl fell face down in the grass with a hole in the back of her head. A second later Blaine killed one at the other edge of the clearing. Then for the next five minutes the two men continued to fire at the people who ran back and forth before them, screaming in fear and confusion. So limited were they in intelligence or ability to reason, that few made any attempt to hide but simply raced about like panicky mice until they were shot down.

WHEN THE men went down to the clearing they found several still alive, although wounded. These were quickly dispatched. They also found one man who hadn't been hurt at all. He was lying in the grass with his hands over his face and sobbing. Blaine pulled him to his feet and made him walk in front of them as they started back to the village.

"Why did we do it, Albie?" Jens kept muttering. "All them poor people just tumbling around in the grass and having such a good time. Why did we have to do it?"

"For the same reason you got to stop a baby from crawling around a roof by itself," Blaine said. "Didn't you hear what Flint said back there? These people have lost all track of themselves. They don't know who's who anymore." He drank again and threw the empty bottle back over his head. "No more of this walking for me, Jens," he announced. "Give me a boost up on your shoulders."

"But, Albie—" Jens stood there helpless.

"Do what I say," he screamed, and smashed out with his rifle to knock the other down, then leaped at him with a volley of kicks that left Jens bleeding at the face and almost senseless. "Ain't I the emperor?" he howled, dragging him to his knees, then lifting himself onto his shoulders. "Don't everybody have to do what I say? Then get up and walk, you filthy fool, or I'll take your heart out in my hand and make you watch while I eat it."

The Tuaran had stopped his sobbing while this was going on to watch it with interest. But now he started it up again as they continued on toward the village. They arrived to find the king and Princess Audrey standing before their hut with hundreds of the Tuarans murmuring in bewilderment all about them.

"Well, that takes care of that little problem," Blaine said when he had gotten down from Jens' shoulders. He staggered and almost fell, but righted himself and ran lopsidedly into the king's hut.

"Where are the others?" Princess Audrey said, as she and her father went swiftly to Jens' side. "Is this man the only one you found?"

"Dead," Jens whispered and tears filled his eyes and began to run down his cheeks. "He killed them all."

"No," Martin Flint sighed and sank to his knees, his hand to his heart. "Not even such monster—"

"He?" his daughter pointed at Jens. "He? He? He? What about you? What are you doing?"

"He made me," Jens wept. "I was afraid he'd kill me if—"

"All right, let's take care of this bird, now," Blaine roared, bursting out of the hut with another bottle of whiskey in his hand. "Here, we'll use this tree right here."

He took the rope out of his hat, handed it to Jens and pointed at the Tuaran they had brought back.

"One end over the bottom limb of that tree," he said, weaving about with his gun in one hand and the bottle lifted to his mouth with the other. "The other around his neck."

"Lord, deliver us," Martin Flint said brokenly. "This creature will kill us all."

"Albie, we done enough," Jens said backing away, his lips white and trembling with fear. "We done—"

"Do I have to do everything myself?" The cry was a soul-freezing mixture of rage and torment. "Ain't there no one to stop asking questions and just do my bidding? By God, I'll kill and kill and kill and kill and never stop killing if people don't do what I say. I'll beat you dummies till the blood runs out of your eyes. I'll tie every man on this godforsaken island to a tree and he'll bark like a dog for me to throw him a bone. And the women—*the women!* They'll lay on their bellies like snakes and crawl into holes when they see me coming. If one of them sticks its head up, I'll kick it till it splits open. I'll trample—I'll crush— I'll—"

Now his fury was so great he could no longer speak. He waved his arms over his head, the gun still in one hand, the bottle in the other. His body shook. Hoarse animal sounds issued from the throat. Suddenly, he darted into the terrified crowd, seized an unresisting man by the hair and flung him to the ground on his hands and knees.

"Ain't I human?" he said, sitting down on him. "Don't I need my rest the same as anyone else? All right, now you just go ahead and hang that fellow, Jens. You saw what he done, the same as me. It was immoral."

"I can't do it, Albie," the blond man said and his face worked as though he needed to vomit but had nothing to bring up. "I already done enough."

"Here, you been under a strain, Jens," Blaine said, going to him and holding out the bottle. "You ain't had nothing to eat all day and it's making you nervous. You just take a drink of this and you'll be okay."

"I don't want a drink, Albie," Jens whined. "The way I feel I'd never be able to hold it—"

"Give it a try," Blaine encouraged him, and shoved the gun into his ribs. "Take about eight inches of that bottle and you'll feel like a new man. If you don't want to be a new man, just say the word and I'll fix it so this one don't get to be no older."

JENS BEGAN drinking and when he seemed about to stop, Blaine reached up to keep the bottle from leaving his mouth. Jens drank some more, lost his footing and fell to his knees, but Blaine continued to pour the whiskey into him. When he took the bottle away, Jens fell over on his side panting, as though he had been running all day.

"What's the matter, don't you never take a drink in them houses you're always running around to?" Blaine said. "Get up and hang this fellow like I told you. We got other things to get to."

"I'll need another drink, Albie," Jens said faintly. "I wouldn't want to even know what I was doing."

"I always knowed you was a greedy dog," Blaine said and poured some whiskey on the ground. "All right, there's your drink and you'd better have it because wasting whiskey's against my religion. Go ahead or you want me to shovel it into you?"

Jens put his face against the ground where the whiskey had been poured and Blaine stepped on his head. "Ain't I the emperor?" he said. "Don't everyone have to do what I say? Ain't we doing all this for their own good? You think it's easy bringing civilization to backward people? All right, now you go ahead and hang this fellow and I'll say a few words so there won't be no confusion about what we're trying to do here."

He returned to the waiting Tuaran and sat down on him again. Jens got up and began to knot the rope about the neck of the man they had brought back. Blaine paid no attention to him, but took another drink and then spoke to the waiting crowd.

"The big problem here is overpopulation," he said. "That's the first thing we got to do something about. Survival of the fittest, that's your answer. Me and Darwin talked it all out when he come off the *Beagle*. So all day tomorrow I'm going to be hunting and what I'm going to be hunting for is those that ain't fit enough to survive and if I find you, that's what it will mean. Anybody left by tomorrow night is going to be part of the permanent population here. Maybe that ain't the most scientific way of doing it, but you got to adjust your methods to the particular situation."

He stopped as the crowd groaned and shifted its attention away from him. Jens had put a rock under the feet of the Tuaran he was to hang and had just kicked it out. As he pulled on the other end of the rope, settling back so that his own weight was on it, the dangling man was unable to reach the ground with his feet. Blaine walked over to look up into his face.

"Well, you'll be in the history books one day, old sport," he said. "A doughty warrior in the fight for something or other. It depends on what they figure out." He turned around to face the crowd again.

"All right, now go and be fit," he shouted. "First thing in the morning I'm coming looking for you, and anyone I find, that's the end of *that* branch of the family tree."

He fired his gun into the air and the Tuarans fled, screaming in terror. In a matter of moments, the area before the king's hut was deserted except for the king and his daughter, Blaine and Jens, and the dead Tuaran just being lowered to the ground.

"All right, now Jens will tie up you two and then I'll do the same for him," Blaine said. "Everybody get a good sleep. We got a big day tomorrow. And don't nobody think he can try nothing while I'm getting my shut-eye. Maybe these eyes over here are going to be closed, but this one"—touching his chest—"never stops watching."

The next morning Jens announced he wasn't taking part in the hunt. He had done all he was going to. He wasn't going to kill anyone else or help Blaine to. He had made up his mind. There wasn't a thing Blaine could do that would make him.

"The worst you can do is kill me, Albie," he said. "After all I've done I deserve it, anyway. But I'm not helping you kill those people. I don't care what."

He had spent the night lying on the ground tied between two trees, his arms straight back over his head. He made his announcement of non-participation as Blaine was untying him. Blaine immediately re-tied the knots, then went back to the hut and returned with one of the whips.

Martin Flint and the Princess Audrey had already been untied and had been listening to Jens' speech in hopes it would persuade Blaine to change his mind. When they saw it hadn't, they walked away so as not to have to watch.

"Stop talking about me killing you," Blaine said. "I only want you at my side in the struggle to uplift their heathen souls."

He lifted the whip high and brought it down just under Jens' chin. The prostrate man screamed soundlessly and Blaine hit him again a little lower down.

"An Arab slaver I met in Zanzibar back in '96 showed me this one," he said. "He had some pretty tough boys to handle, but they always promised to be good by the time he got down to their belly."

WHILE he was talking, he had continued working the whip down Jens' body and when the blond man finally got some voice into his scream it was to say he had changed his mind, he'd go on that hunt after all.

Half an hour later they were on their way, Blaine riding on Jens' shoulders and driving the king and Princess Audrey ahead of him with ropes around their necks. He held the ends of their ropes and the whip in one hand and the rifle in the other and every now and then he would have Jens pass up the bottle so he could take a drink.

The blond man seemed past despair. He plodded on, dull-eyed as an ox, and stopped, started and made the appropriate turns in response to the thumps of Blaine's heels against his ribs. His face was bruised as though he had put it in the way of a rock slide. His clothes were wet with blood.

When they had gone two hours, they still had not seen any of the Tuarans. As could have been expected, the huts were deserted, but even in the jungle they saw no one. Blaine called a halt, signaled Jens to go to his knees, and dismounted. Jens sank face down on the ground and his body shook as though he had a fever.

"All right, where did they go?" Blaine asked Martin Flint. "They can't all have flown away. They're hiding someplace."

"Perhaps they *have* flown away," the king of Tuara said. "I hope and pray they were able to."

"Well, the odds are against it," Blaine said, and called back to Jens over his shoulder. "Tell her highness here what I learned from that old Arab in Zanzibar.

Jens told the king what would be done to him if he didn't tell Blaine what he wanted to know. Martin Flint went very pale, but said he would endure even that before telling where his people had gone. Blaine explained that it wasn't the king he intended working over. It was the Princess Audrey.

"There are a group of joining caves down near the water in that direction," Martin Flint said in a low voice. "In the old days the people used to hide there when pirates came. They may be there now."

"If they ain't, I'll take and hang you to a tree by your tongue," Blaine said. "How many ways in and out are there?"

"Two."

He put on both cartridge belts, running them across his body from each shoulder to the opposite hip. He held one of the rifles to the back of Jens' neck and poked him with it.

"Who's the emperor?" he said. "I want to be sure you don't forget while I'm gone."

"You're the emperor," Jens said listlessly. "Everybody has to do what you say. You're the emperor."

"Now you got it," Blaine said approvingly. "All right, now the three of you just stay here nice and quiet till I come back. Don't do no wandering around. Remember, the big eye is watching you all the time."

He took both rifles and the bottle of whiskey and started off at a trot in the direction Martin Flint had indicated. In about 40 minutes he came out of the jungle and saw the caves close to the water's edge. They ran under a rock roof for about 200 yards with an opening at each end.

As he came close he heard the murmur of many troubled voices inside and he began quickly to pile brush and branchwood at one of the openings toward which a gentle breeze was blowing. They heard him and the voices grew silent, but there was no sound to suggest they were doing anything but waiting.

When he had the opening almost completely covered, he set fire to what he had piled there, climbed to the roof over the caves and ran along it toward the other opening. Here he sat down with one rifle in his lap and the other beside him, took a long drink from the bottle and waited.

The first to come out under him were a man and woman running hand in hand. He put the bottle down and shot them both high in the back. The man died instantly, but the woman began to crawl on her hands and knees and he shot her again.

Next a man ran out, stopping when he saw the two dead ones in front of him and turning around. Blaine shot him in the face. Then they streamed out in screaming panic as the wind swept the smoke in thickening clouds into their cave, and Blaine worked the rifle as fast as he could, switching to the other when it became too hot.

The shooting further increased their panic and some ran back into the caves and Blaine let them go so he could concentrate on those trying to escape into the jungle. There was no way he could miss and by the time the last of those who were to make it had reached the jungle, bodies lay sprawled on the ground beneath him. Of these almost 20

PRINCESS AUDREY taunted him from the blue water: "Come for the rifle.

were still alive, although too badly wounded to run, and he climbed down to kill them by smashing their heads with the butt of his rifle.

They took it like voiceless sheep, watching with sorrowful eyes as he moved from one to the next. Then he sat down on a rock facing the cave from which came the fear-maddened screams of those still trapped inside. A man staggered out and he shot him. Several minutes later two others crawled out of the smoke-filled opening directly at him.

When they were 10 feet away he shot them both, then sat waiting for more, but they were to be the last. The screams became fainter and finally stopped altogether.

"Well, now we know who's fit and who ain't," he said, backing away from the black smoke funneling out at him. "At least for today."

HE CLIMBED back up to the roof over the caves to get the whiskey, then came down carrying it and both rifles and began to run along the beach. The day was warm and sunny, the water a sparkling blue. When he had been running several minutes, he stopped suddenly, drank all that was left in the bottle and threw it away. Then he took his clothes off, put both rifles down and ran into the water. For some minutes he bounced about in the waves shouting exuberantly and falling on purpose so they could rush over him. He would have stayed longer, but he saw someone coming along the beach and ran out to get the rifles. He got to them just seconds before Princess Audrey would have.

"What the hell are you doing here?" he said shrilly, trying to hide his nakedness. "Didn't I tell you to stay there?"

"How does it hurt if I bathe here?" she said slipping out of her garment and facing him naked. She lay down at his feet and looked up at him, unsmiling. "What are you afraid of? You're as much my emperor as you are that man Jens'."

He reached for the barrel of one of the rifles and stuck it between her breasts. He prodded her with it, but

continued to watch her suspiciously. She put her hands on the barrel of the rifle as though to keep him from taking it away.

"Who's the emperor?" he said, making a final checkup.

"You are," she said. "Everybody has to do what you say. Now, stop being afraid and come make me your queen."

He was to remember later, briefly, the sweet taste of her mouth, the fragrance of her hair as it pillowed his face, and the single blinding moment when he was truly the emperor. Then came the pain as her fingers reached deep into the wings of his back, and the pain of slow unconsciousness raced through his entire body.

"You're hurting me," he gasped, "hurting me…hurting…"

THE FINGERS twisted and probed below his neck and he felt as though he were being drawn into a pool of black ink. "I should have known …"

He woke to the sound of voices, many of them laughing. It sounded like a picnic. For the first time since being on Tuara, he heard children. *They must keep them all together someplace,* he thought. *I never thought to look for them.* There was a peculiar pressure on his body. He tried to move, but couldn't.

"You awake, Albie?"

Jens was sitting facing him, yet far above him, too. He had to look up to see his face, moving just his eyes because he couldn't tilt his head back. Behind Jens, towering over him because they were standing, were Martin Flint and the Princess Audrey. Behind them and all along the beach the Tuarans laughed and ran excitedly about, playing their childish games.

"What the hell, Jens?" he said trying to figure why everyone was at such a peculiar angle to him. Then he tried to move again and couldn't and realized what they had done.

"Your own idea, Albie," Jens said and stuck a knife in the sand in front of his face, its thin blade sharper than any razor's. "You were the one who said what to do to anyone who violated the Virgin Princess."

"Jesus, Jens," he said in hurt tones. "Ain't I the emperor?"

"Meet the new emperor, Albie," Jens said tapping the knife. His hand advanced crab-like along the sand to fasten on the lower part of Blaine's face, forcing him to open his mouth. "They're going to hold me until a ship comes and then they're going to send me to Samoa and try me for murder," he said. "But they say I got to do this first. Not that I mind."

Blaine tried to say "Jens" again, but the knife was in his mouth and he couldn't even scream until it was withdrawn. Then he did scream, but the sound was strangely inhuman, and the Tuarans came to watch while Jens went on with the job.

When he was finished they sat down in two facing banks, with none of them between the screaming, lump-like object on the sand and the water. As the surf began to move higher up the beach, those closest to the water's edge moved with it until finally they were even with Blaine, then behind him, at which point the screams stopped and they were able to go on with their games. *

ALONG with death trek and survival stories, yarns about tough cops who had embarked on county cleanups were surefire; also guaranteed to please were pieces that had anything to do with islands—storming them, hiding out on them, buying them at bargain rates, becoming GI king of them. (My favorite, written by the great **Walter Kaylin**, had to do with a seaman who took charge of one and went about ruling it while sitting on the shoulders of a weird little chum with whom he had washed ashore.)"

Bruce Jay Friedman
from "Even the Rhinos Were Nymphos"

"Even the Rhinos Were Nymphos" was first published in the Oct. 9, 1975 issue of Rolling Stone, *later reprinted in the book of the same name published by the University of Chicago Press, 2001 and in* Weasels Ripped My Flesh! *published by New Texture, 2013, 2024.*

the girl in. Pennant was the captain of the Chapman, a big man with rimless glasses, a head like a cannonball and a body thick and squared off as a safe. He sat on a rickety chair, tilted back against the shack, while Dunlap, the Chapman's chief engineer, was inside with the girl.

"Hand over a five-spot and you're next, Sultan," Pennant said as the blond man got out of the jeep.

"I'm asking about the kid," Root said. "What does she get out of it?"

"My fist in her ear if she asks as many questions as you do," Pennant said. "You worry too much. Well, what do you say, Sultan?"

"I got one arm twisting the other to make me say no," Root said, crouching beside his shipment and playing a flashlight over it to see that everything he ordered was there. "No time.

"THE HELICOPTER HERO AND THE 100 LADIES OF 'UNDRESS' ATOLL"

Men, September 1959
COVER ARTIST: JAMES BAMA

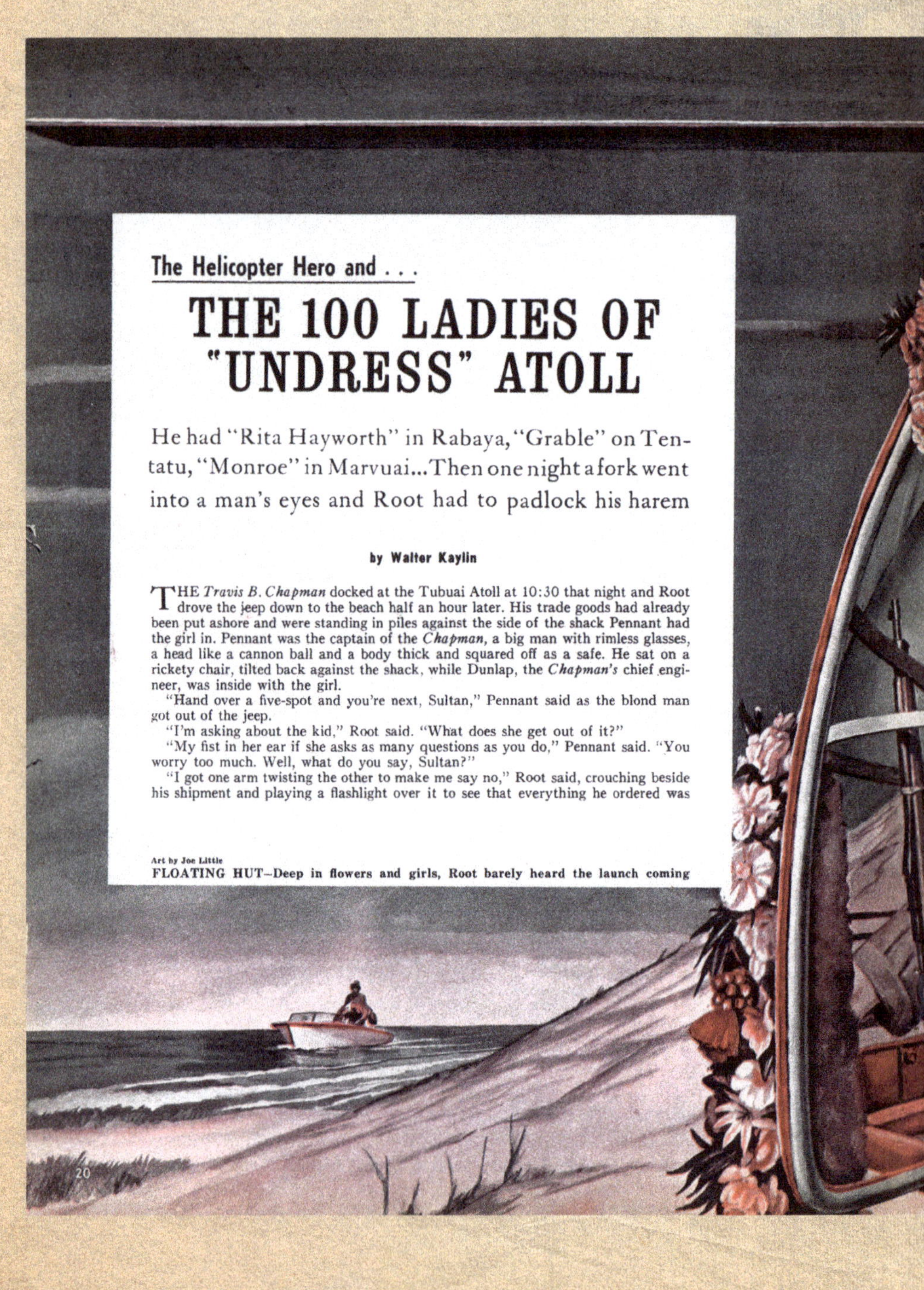

THE 100 LADIES OF "UNDRESS" ATOLL

He had "Rita Hayworth" in Rabaya, "Grable" on Tentatu, "Monroe" in Marvuai...Then one night a fork went into a man's eyes and Root had to padlock his harem

by Walter Kaylin

THE *Travis B. Chapman* docked at the Tubuai Atoll at 10:30 that night and Root drove the jeep down to the beach half an hour later. His trade goods had already been put ashore and were standing in piles against the side of the shack Pennant had the girl in. Pennant was the captain of the *Chapman*, a big man with rimless glasses, a head like a cannon ball and a body thick and squared off as a safe. He sat on a rickety chair, tilted back against the shack, while Dunlap, the *Chapman's* chief engineer, was inside with the girl.

"Hand over a five-spot and you're next, Sultan," Pennant said as the blond man got out of the jeep.

"I'm asking about the kid," Root said. "What does she get out of it?"

"My fist in her ear if she asks as many questions as you do," Pennant said. "You worry too much. Well, what do you say, Sultan?"

"I got one arm twisting the other to make me say no," Root said, crouching beside his shipment and playing a flashlight over it to see that everything he ordered was

FLOATING HUT—Deep in flowers and girls, Root barely heard the launch coming

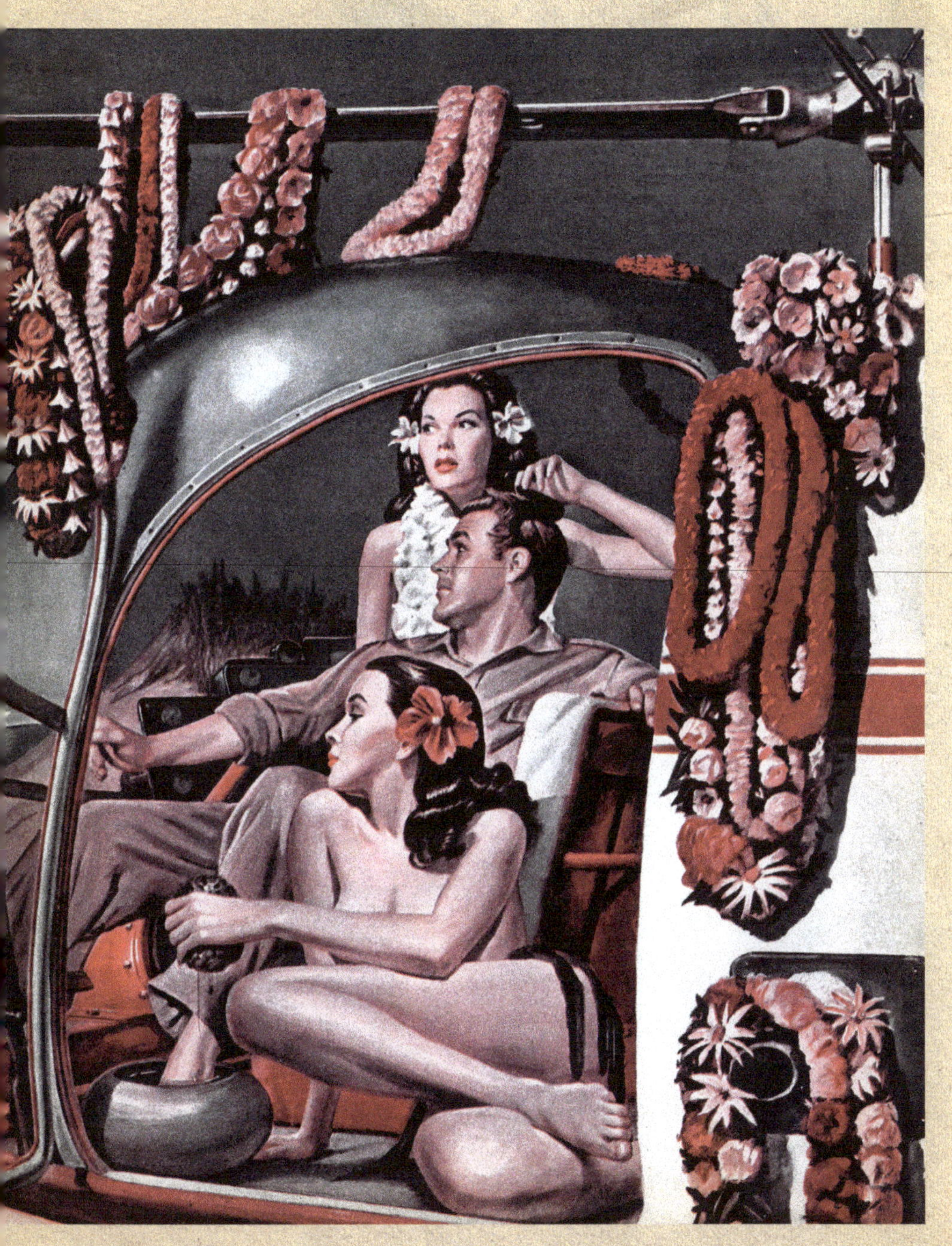

Illustrations by **Joe Little**

THE *Travis B. Chapman* docked at the Tubuai Atoll at 10:30 that night and Root drove the Jeep down to the beach half an hour later. His trade goods had already been put ashore and were standing in piles against the side of the shack Pennant had the girl in. Pennant was the captain of the *Chapman,* a big man with rimless glasses, a head like a cannonball and a body thick and squared off as a safe. He sat on a rickety chair, tilted back against the shack, while Dunlap, the *Chapman's* chief engineer, was inside with the girl.

"Hand over a five-spot and you're next, Sultan," Pennant said as the blond man got out of the Jeep.

"I'm asking about the kid," Root said. "What does she get out of it?"

"My fist in her ear if she asks as many questions as you do," Pennant said. "You worry too much. Well, what do you say, Sultan?"

"I got one arm twisting the other to make me say no," Root said, crouching beside his shipment and playing a flashlight over it to see that everything he ordered was there. "No time. I got to get this stuff on the 'copter and start making my rounds."

Through the wall of the shack, he could hear the girl asking the man with her when the ship would leave. She spoke in the soft, patient way of those from one of the more remote islands.

"I should have remembered you don't need the kind of pig I got in there," Pennant said. "Everyone knows you got a harem that spreads all over the Australs."

"Sure, I'm a regular stud," Root admitted. "Entire generations spring full-grown from my loins. Worried daddies tie their daughters to trees and guard them with cannons when I'm in the neighborhood. Here's your check and here's another list, Pennant. Everything seems to be here."

"Live and let live is what I always say," Pennant said, coming to stand beside the Jeep as Root began to put his things in it. "You got no call to get snotty when I'm making friendly conversation. It ain't on account of me conducting this little business here, is it? It ain't like I'm pointing a gun at her to make her do it."

"Pennant, there are maybe two billion souls in this world and you are looking at the only one who don't have a quarrel with anyone,"

Root said. "So climb off my back, because I'm not looking for things to be different. Four years with the Halls of Montezuma boys and a tin plate in my head from the fun fest on Okinawa made me into a devout noncombatant."

"Then don't make so many cracks," Pennant advised. "There's others don't feel that way."

He returned to his seat and Root continued to pile his packages into the Jeep. When he was finished he got in behind the wheel and as he drove off Pennant was kicking at the door of the shack and shouting for Dunlap to either come the hell out of there or hand out another five-spot.

From the beach, Root drove to the Times Square Bar, the only place to get a drink on Tubuai Atoll. Half a dozen sailors from the *Chapman* were there with girls from the island. Two couples were dancing to Sinatra's record of "I'll Never Smile Again." The slow tempo made it look as though they were up to their knees in tar. The rest were around two tables pushed together, the red-faced sailors bawling "I've Got Sixpence" at each other, and the black-haired island girls giggling as though their print dresses had feather ticklers built in where they'd achieve maximum results. Root sat down at the bar and said. "A beer, Charlie," and the bartender brought it and leaned toward him looking intense.

"You must give me your gun and show me how to use it," he whispered. "It's very important. I have to kill a man."

He was about 19, a tall boy whose hair stood on end as though it were wire. He came from one of the outlying islands and had been in Tubuai just a few months. His name was Bomira and he had brought a girl named Ouala with him. Dolph Redman, the famed "Baron of Tubuai," had rented them a tiny room, given Ouala a job in his general store, and Bomira one in his Times Square Bar.

"Who do you want to kill, Charlie?" Root grinned.

"Why is it something to laugh about?" the boy asked. "I would like to kill Captain Pennant. There, now you are not laughing any more. Should I tell you why I would like to kill him?"

"I think maybe I know, Charlie," Root said. "I wouldn't have been laughing if I realized it."

"He has her in a little dirty box on the beach and he is selling her to the other two," the boy said, leaning so close to Root they could have kissed each other. "Isn't that a good reason for me to kill him?"

"I couldn't say, Charlie." Root said. "But I don't have a gun, and anyway you'd be taking on a hell of an assignment if you never used one before. Pennant's strong as a gorilla and learned how to use his hands fighting in the ring. If he got close to you it would be all over, and I mean all over."

"Thank you for the advice, Mr. Root."

"Look, Charlie, I know how you feel about—"

"Thank you very much," the boy said stiffly. "Would you like another beer?"

"No, that's enough for me," Root sighed. "I got to get going."

He went outside and drove the Jeep for about four miles until he was at the isolated stretch of beach where he had landed the helicopter. He got his packages onto it, drove the Jeep a quarter of a mile inland and under some trees, then trotted back and was soon on his way to Rabaya. Fifty minutes later he saw the beach flares they always put out for him and settled the 'copter down at the center of the rectangle they formed. He threw several of the packages on the ground, then got down himself, picked them up and walked quickly toward the line of pole-straight *ludaya* trees that marked the end of the beach. He passed through them and into the exuberant growth of the island's lush foliage and went on for another half-mile, to come at last to a clearing. In it were two neat rows of thatched huts. All were dark. All were silent. He went directly toward one, got down on his knees and crawled inside.

"It would serve you right if I had gotten drunk and gone to sleep," the girl said. "Come quickly. I am cold waiting for you." She was number 64 on Root's list of 100-odd island ladies.

He took off his clothes and got under the blanket with her. She had curled up into a ball and her back was to him. He slipped one arm under her and put the other over to hold her tightly while he pressed his face into the fragrant warmth of the soft-piled hair at the back of her neck.

There is going to be trouble on Tubuai, isn't there?" she said. "Bomira is going to kill Captain Pennant."

"I doubt it," Root said. "He's talking about using a gun, but he doesn't even know how they work. Pennant will tear his head off if he gives him reason to."

"You are a nice man, but very stupid," she said, turning around in his arms and kissing him. "You think because I am waiting for you here and there are other girls waiting for you on all the other islands where you bring things from the ship that we are a people who have no pride and that things can be done to us just as you wish? 'Charlie' Bomira is from Marvuai and it was not too long ago that they were pirates there and used to raid the other islands and carry people off and do terrible things to them. Bomira would like to kill Captain Pennant the way the white man does. With a gun. But if he can't, he will do it the way his people used to. They have not forgotten."

"If I wanted a talky dame I could have stayed in Philadelphia," he said, putting his hand over her mouth and kissing her eyes. She touched her tongue to the palm of his hand and he took it off her mouth and kissed her. "Damn, I'm all mixed up again. Betty Grable, right?"

"No, Rita Hayworth," she said, and lifted her head quickly to bite his lip. "Betty Grable is tomorrow night on Tentatu. And the next night it is Lena Horne on Marvuai. And after that Linda Darnell ..."

"Got to do some switching around someplace," he said thoughtfully. "Saw a kid on a calendar a week ago that was just incredible. Something Monroe. Marian or Madeleine or something like that. Got to work her in some place. Not that she'll probably ever make it big, but you don't see a build like that every day, even around here."

He was on Marvuai two nights later and the next morning a boy shouted to him from outside the hut that a motor boat from Tubuai was nearing the island. He sat up and the girl next to him put her arm around his waist and pulled him down against her so she could kiss his back. He lay still enjoying it immensely and it wasn't until he heard the boat that he drew her arm from around him and stood up.

"I better put on a pair of pants," he said. "That's the one thing I remember about Philadelphia. People wear pants when they go outside."

He went down to the water and walked into it up to his knees. Dolph Redman cut the motor and the boat slid up to Root. He put out his hand to take Dolph's, then froze the motion as he saw "Charlie" Bomira lying in the bottom of the boat. Great lumps and bruises had blown his face up to twice its normal size, thickening his ears and sinking his dark eyes deep into pockets. His lips were torn, his nose a shapeless blob. His fingers fluttered over his body like crippled birds to touch his caved-in side and the ribs that poked through.

"I'll get someone to take charge of him," Redman said. "Then I'll tell you what it's all about."

Root went back through the people gathering at the water's edge. A distance from them along the beach, he sat down and a few minutes later Redman came walking toward him. A gray-haired, decisive-looking man past 50, Redman had lived in the Australs over 30 years and was more responsible than anyone else for the gradual development of Tubuai as a significant South Pacific trading port.

"Well, it was Pennant," he said sitting down next to Root. "The man must be crazy. He must have known there would be trouble over what he was doing. I guess he was actually looking for it. Why else would he bring the girl Ouala into the Times Square Bar and plunk her down at the bar right in front of the boy. She wouldn't take her eyes off the floor, but Pennant was having a fine time. He kept pushing at the boy, needling him, and finally he got what he was after—although maybe a little more than he bargained for at the beginning. The boy never said a word and Pennant had maybe a dozen or so of the men from his ship with him—Battleton and the engineer and some of the others—and they were having a good time, you know sort of nudging each other and waiting to see what would happen.

"And then all of a sudden the boy just reached across the bar and stuck a fork over his eye glasses and right down into his eye. Damnedest thing I've ever seen. If he'd pushed it in a little harder, it probably would have killed him. As it was, all it did was give him the excuse he'd been looking for.

"Well, I know you've seen people beaten up. Who hasn't? But Root, you never saw anything like this. I hope I never see anything like it again. The thing about it was that Pennant wasn't even angry. Even with blood running out of his eye where he'd been stuck, he wasn't angry. He just handed the glasses to one of the men and said, 'Now, there'll be some fun,' and then he pulled Bomira across the bar and started in.

"One punch and the boy went down. He started up and Pennant put his knee in his face and he went down again. He was a little slow getting up after that, so Pennant lifted him, bent him back over the bar and pounded him with the other hand. By then Ouala had started to scream and hide her face and Battleton and Dunlap were trying to pull Pennant off him. They wouldn't have had less of an effect on a bull elephant. Pennant just shoved them away and kept on with what he was doing.

"I don't know how often the boy went down or how often Pennant picked him up. Sometimes he wouldn't let him fall. He would catch him and push him up against a wall and hit him a few, then step back to catch him and do it again. The boy passed out three times. The first two times Pennant brought him out of it by pouring beer on him. The last one didn't work, so he picked him up and slammed him against the edge of the bar the way you'd try to break a broom stick. Of course that didn't work, either, but you saw what it did to his ribs. Looks to me as though one of them is poking back into his lung."

"There was no way anyone could stop him?" Root asked.

"Not that I know of," Redman said bitterly. "I don't carry a gun and nothing else would have done any good. Battleton kept tugging at him, but with that one arm he didn't have a chance. and the others were too frightened and probably a little too sick too to help him out. That brings up the question of what about you?"

"Me?"

THE CLASH—When Pennant tried to break the youngster against the bar, he found four steel prongs in his nose

"You knew there was going to be trouble," Redman said. "There's a general feeling you could be pretty rough if you ever opened up. Maybe you should have stayed around a while?"

"It's beginning to look as though I should have," Root said. "What about the girl?"

"Ouala? She went with Pennant. How can you explain something like that? After he finished with Bomira he went back to the ship and she ran along beside him begging him to take her with him. That was last night. I brought the boy back to my place and tried to patch him up a little so I could get him back out here before he died; he's going to. Early this morning I went down to see to my boat before starting out.

"Pennant was just in the process of throwing Ouala over the side of the *Chapman.* You could hear her screaming for him not to. Of course, she could swim like a fish and would have had no trouble reaching shore, but instead she swam around to the anchor chain and began to climb up it. When Pennant saw what she was doing, he stepped across the rail to wait for her and when she reached it he put his foot on her face and shoved her off. She fell and went under again and this time she just didn't come up. I guess she figured there was no point in it anymore."

"AFTER the war I swore I'd never let myself get in any kind of trouble again," Root said when Redman was finished. "Not for anything or anybody. But I guess you can't always stick to a thing like that. Where's Pennant now?"

"The *Chapman* left Tubuai a little before I did," Redman said. "Going east. They'll be coming into the coaling station at Bennett right around now and they'll probably stay there five or six hours. It ought to take about that long for them to coal up."

"All right," Root said. "I'll go get my things."

He returned to the hut of the girl he called Lena Horne. She was standing in it waiting for him, a slim, long-legged girl, full-breasted and with a face that smiled easily but now was mute as a cat's.

"What will you do?" she asked.

"I don't know," he said, sitting down and beginning to put on his shoes. "The French own these islands. I'll have to think about it on the way."

He flew directly to Bennett, and the men from the *Chapman* looked up, shading their eyes against the sun as he passed over them. They were sitting or lying on the beach a hundred yards from the coaling station docks. He landed on the other side of the island and walked back across it toward them, and they could see him all the way because Bennett is nothing but flat, sun-blasted rock and a mountain of coal. As he neared them, Pennant stood up, at the same time taking off his glasses.

"I'm taking you to Marvuai," Root said. "Ouala's dead and Bomira won't last more than a day."

"She could have swum ashore," Pennant said. "We were about to leave and I had no authority to take her with me. As for the kid, everyone saw him attack me. I got witnesses. Besides, what do you mean you're taking me anyplace? You ain't forgetting about all that suffering you did on Okinawa, are you? You ain't forgetting you're strictly a noncombatant. Here, hold my glasses, Bata. I don't like any son of a crumb telling me what he's going to do to me."

"Hold your own glasses," the one-armed mate said. "Didn't I tell you from now on I wouldn't give you the time of day if you needed it to stay alive?"

"Hold the goddam glasses and see that nothing happens to them," Pennant said, throwing them to him. "I'm getting tired of all this goddam whining. What did I do to them two that they weren't asking for?"

HE RAN forward and Root tried to hold his ground before him, but Pennant burst through his defending arms like a circus horse through a paper hoop, and then Root was down with the other astride him and already a hand was at his throat and his face was being pounded. Three, four times the other's heavy fist found him and then, almost sloth-like in his deliberateness, the blond man tugged away the hand from his throat and reached up to hook an arm around the sweat-gleaming head above him.

Hauling down on it, he tucked Pennant's head under his arm almost affectionately and at the same time drove his fist into his ribs. Body-bent and awkwardly positioned, Pennant reached back for Root's lower body, but another smash into his side interrupted it. Now he put both hands on the arm that encircled his head, intending to pull it away. But, still beneath him, Root brought his knee up between Pennant's legs and drew back on the arm about his head so that Pennant's body went forward and up, and for a second he seemed almost to be doing a headstand.

Then he came down heavily on his back and Root got an arm around his head again and, lying at right angles to him, was able to lift his hand high and bring it down into Pennant's body. Again and again he raised his hand and brought it down like a mace, slow-spacing it and hunching his shoulders against the hands that sought his face and throat.

"Kill him," Battleton said from the circle of men that had formed about them. "Break him apart. He did worse to that kid yesterday."

Root didn't answer. Pennant's first punch had broken his nose and blood was pouring down from it into his mouth. He hit Pennant again and knew that he had begun to break him up inside and he hit him still again, then stood up.

"Kill him," Battleton urged. "You got him, now. There ain't one of us who won't say you had to do it."

Root wiped the blood from his mouth, but there was no stopping the flow from his nose. Then Pennant had gotten to his hands and knees and Root took his head, almost like a man receiving a football punt, and tucked it between his legs so that he could bend over him and punch at his body some more with both hands.

Pennant was gasping, now, each hammer-like blow forcing the sound from him. He put his arms about the legs that imprisoned his head and pushed with his shoulders, but Root lowered himself on him and Pennant went face down in the sand, with Root's entire weight on his head and neck and the blond man's hands still thumping at his body. He was still conscious when Root rose, but his legs wouldn't support him and Root, moving more deliberately than ever, looped an arm carefully about Pennant's head, locked his hands together and poured all his strength into that tightening hold. When he stood up, Pennant

THE CASUALTY—Root dropped the trussed-up body to the natives, not knowing they would give it the *Djomindinari*

was unconscious.

"Get him on the 'copter," Root said to the one-armed man, wiping a hand across his face and bringing it away wet with blood. "You're in charge of the ship, Battleton. Get in touch with the owners as soon as you can and tell them everything that happened. There'll be a lot of hell handed out over it, but I guess it's gone along too far for anything to be done about that now. Tie him up, first. I don't want him getting loose and deciding he wants to try the dance floor again."

He brought Pennant back to Marvuai and Redman went white when he saw the trussed-up body.

"You should have brought him to the nearest French authorities," he said. "These people are too stirred up to handle a thing like this properly."

"I thought they ought to have first crack at him," Root said. "Hell, it's the twentieth century. You don't think they're going to do anything crazy, do you?"

"Yes, I do," Redman said. "Bomira died an hour ago."

The people took Pennant to an inlet into which, years earlier, their pirate ships had returned from raids. High rocks enclosed it on three sides. They untied him and threw him into the water and six two-man *tapangs* formed a loose circle about him as he bobbed in the water.

"The people of Marvuai stood or sat on the surrounding rocks and behaved exactly as though they were watching a cricket match," the *Sydney Dispatch* was to say in its report of the incident. "They cheered and applauded and some munched on fruit while it was going on. The girls of the island are known for their beauty and they made a lovely sight sitting one next to the other with their arms about their knees and flowers in their hair."

"It's an old game they used to play with their captives," Redman explained to Root just before it began. "Very simple. It's called a *djomindinari*. The only way you can translate that is boat-dance, which isn't exactly accurate. There he goes."

For some minutes, Pennant had been treading water inside the circle of boats. Now, apparently getting tired, he maneuvered toward one of them and lifted a hand out of the water as though to rest against its side.

"The man at the stern immediately brought his knife down on it," reads the report of the Government investigating board in charge of the case. It was from this report, incidentally, that the *Sydney Dispatch* obtained the information for its story. "He was very careful to sever just one finger. A moment later a man from another boat did the same thing to Pennant's other hand. By that time it had become apparent to Mr. Root and Mr. Redman that they intended to dismember him, yet keep him alive as long as possible while doing so. In the opinion of Mr. Root and Mr. Redman, Captain Pennant's ordeal lasted close to two hours. In that time they cut off his fingers one at a time and finally the hands themselves.

"When they had accomplished that, they began on his feet and treated them in much the same way. Captain Pennant made several attempts to drown himself, but these were all defeated. The men in the boats simply went into the water and held him above the surface while others continued to abuse him. After a while, the water itself was totally discolored by his blood and as they transferred their attack to his face and body, Mr. Redman recalls thinking that "He resembled nothing human at all, but an enormous sponge or porous ball or something of that sort." Some time before this point was reached, Mr. Root had turned his head away and did not look again until Captain Pennant was dead....

"Thank God it's all over," Redman said at last, and Root turned to see the men swimming back to their boats and lifting themselves out of the water, blood smeared over their entire bodies. Then he got up and started back along the beach to where he had left the 'copter. As he went, a voice called from behind him. He heard running feet and as he reached the plane, the girl he called Lena Horne threw her arms around him from behind.

"You don't usually go until much later," she said. "Aren't you going to come stay with me a while?"

"I've got to get back to Tubuai," he said. "People will be looking for me because of this thing and I may as well be where I can be found."

"But can't you stay with me just a little while first?" she asked.

"No, I guess not," he said, turning around, seeing no connection at all between what they had done to Pennant and the gentle, almost childlike innocence in her face, yet knowing it was there. "I guess maybe we've done as much of that as we're going to."

EDITOR'S NOTE: Following the hearings of the French investigating board, Root's helicopter service was discontinued and he served a year in prison for having brought Pennant to Marvuai. After being released to return to the States, Root entered the Army and took part in the Korean War. Since being discharged, he has married and is currently operating a small flying instruction school in one of the east coast cities. Those on Marvuai who sentenced Pennant to his fate and those who carried it out were arrested and jailed for 10- to 15-year terms. Some have already been released and all are expected to be out by 1964.

Redman still lives in the Australs. He is an old man, now, and has sold his various businesses on Tubuai and retired to the village on Rabaya where he has since taken a young wife. He is a genuine celebrity in the South Seas, a status that he recognizes and enjoys. He is easily accessible to interviewers, but since his story is so well-known, he soon falls back on the constant repetition of two or three key sentences.

"I can hear poor Pennant screaming like it was yesterday, and see those devils coming out of the water with their bodies red from his blood. I will never be able to erase those things from my mind as long as I live." ✳

"Penal Queen of Capt. 'Crazy's' Jungle Terror Colony"
Written as Roland Empey
Stag, November 1962
Illustration by Samson Pollen

with a rake. A man in a hurry,
Bosch. Wet and shiny of face,
head and glasses; thick shoulders hunched high enough to
hide his neck on both sides.

**Bosch had left Nigeria
with his infamous Butcher
Boys - assorted sizes, shapes
and colors, but all killers
for a price - when his scheme
to take over a native village
backfired. He had figured on
cleaning up by selling the
village girls in the Congo but
found himself dodging spears,
knives and related items of
cutlery instead.** The neighboring Cameroons provided the
next outlet for his enterprising nature, and taking over
Tapp's Bar, Tapp's General Store,
Tapp's All-Clothes Emporium, and
Tapp's Used Cars ("They're Tops
If They're Tapp's") in the town
of Dschang was the particular
goal he had in mind.

"Mr. Tapp was teaching me to
play the American tune 'Three

Men, October 1960
COVER ARTIST: NORMAN BAER

THE NYMPH WHO LEADS AN AFRICAN DEATH ARMY

"I AIN'T saying it wasn't a fair fight," Harry Tapp said not long after Max Bosch's Butcher Boys all but tore him apart. "There was 11 of them and one of me and that's no odds for any clean-living, red-blooded, high-minded type like H. Tapp to kick about. But Maxie shouldn't have gone and used that garden rake on me after the others threw me down. I mean that's the kind of thing you can call dirty pool."

He had been in his rooms above Tapp's Bar & Name-It at four in the morning teaching one of his Cameroon bar girls how to blow a trumpet when they busted in on him. There were eight of them

By WALTER KAYLIN
ART BY BOB SCHULZ

"KISS IT," "Aunt Edna" told the Bamileke chief, as Tapp passed out the guns. "Now you are my slave and you will die happy"

23

Illustration by **Bob Schulz**

I AIN'T saying it wasn't a fair fight," Harry Tapp said not long after Max Bosch's Butcher Boys all but tore him apart. "There was 11 of them and one of me, and that's no odds for any clean-living, red-blooded, high-minded type like H. Tapp to kick about. But Maxie shouldn't have gone and used that garden rake on me after the others throwed me down. I mean that's the kind of thing you can call dirty pool."

He had been in his rooms above Tapp's Bar & Name-It at four in the morning teaching one of his Cameroon bar girls how to blow a trumpet when they busted in on him. There were eight of them (not 11 as he claimed), but he was right about Bosch doing a plow job on him with a rake. A man in a hurry, Bosch. Wet and shiny of face, head and glasses; thick shoulders hunched high enough to hide his neck on both sides.

Bosch had left Nigeria with his infamous Butcher Boys—assorted sizes, shapes and colors, but all killers for a price—when his scheme to take over a native village backfired. He had figured on cleaning up by selling the village girls in the Congo but found himself dodging spears, knives and related items of cutlery instead. The neighboring Cameroons provided the next outlet for his enterprising nature, and taking over Tapp's Bar, Tapp's General Store, Tapp's All-Clothes Emporium and Tapp's Used Cars ("They're Tops if They're Tapp's") in the town of Dschang was the particular goal he had in mind.

"Mr. Tapp was teaching me to play the American tune 'Three Blind Mice' on his trumpet when Mr. Bosch and his friends entered," the girl, Umwame, said in her precise way at the hearings two months later, dealing with the "Hashish Hackings" that horrified the world. "I can recall no conversation. Mr. Bosch and Mr. Tapp simply flew upon each other in such a violent manner that I was terrified and drew the bedsheet over my head so I would not have to see."

The powerful American rose beside her like an overjoyed Roman candle and came down on the bald, squinting man who led the intruders. An excess of energy had always been Tapp's problem, and any outlet for its physical expression earned his roaring approval. In that first moment Bosch went down, with the big storekeeper powering over him into those still coming through the doorway. Of course, the odds guaranteed that he would not win, but the pounding assault of the knuckled bricks that were his hands was equal guarantee that teeth would be dislodged, noses mashed flat, and heads caved in before he was brought under control or run off.

This proved to be the case. Exuberance rather than anger was his dominant emotion, and he howled in triumph as his fists fell on those through whom he waded. A turbaned Algerian came at him low and encountered an uplifted knee that dropped him flat as a rug beneath his straining associates. A dead-panned Frenchman was lifted above Tapp's head and thrown up against a wall. A knife appeared in a down-driving hand, but fell harmlessly to the floor when the wrist above it was bent back and snapped like dry wood. He swung a man about himself by one ankle and threw him across the room, bowling over three others in the process. He fought in the mauling way of a gorilla surrounded by yapping dogs, but inevitably they had to bring him down and it was when that had been accomplished that Bosch ran the rake across his back. It exploded Tapp off the floor and free of those holding him and one head-down lunge took him across the room and out a window, an outstretched hand grabbing the trumpet as he went.

"I'll be back, Maxie, boy," he shouted up to the grinning man framed in the broken window. "Don't get yourself set up too comfortable. You ain't going to be staying around that long."

"Thanks for leaving your friend in the sack, here," the other called back. "It saves us the trouble of looking around."

The date of the incident was January 6, 1960. The place: Dschang in the Cameroons. A limp, listless, unimpressive African town, its nondescript business life controlled by the one-time soldier of fortune Harry Tapp. Sleepy-eyed Bamileke natives for the most part, a people dedicated to the principles of taking it slow and keeping out of the sun. A people firmly convinced that all white men were crazy. They ran around too much. So the take-over of Tapp's establishments by Max Bosch was of no particular interest to them. Yet, had they known what it would lead to, even these easygoing people would have protested. Because there is a direct line between the fight above Tapp's Bar & Name-It of January 6 and the horror of six weeks later, a horror described in this way by newsman Albert Ball in a dispatch distributed by the *Registered Press*:

DSCHANG, Cameroon, Feb. 23—*This city is a shambles. Seventy-four are known to be dead. A reliable count of the wounded has not yet been made, but it will undoubtedly come to at least twice that many.*

Why did it happen? Why? Stunned survivors ask it of one another, but none can supply the answer. All they know is that members of their own tribe—Bamilekes like themselves—swept down from the hills last night and fell upon the sleeping populace of Dschang with machete and bush knife to produce the pointless slaughter mentioned. Huts were broken into and set afire, women and children dying in them along with the men.

Marching in a ragged column to the accompaniment of a single trumpeter playing "Three Blind Mice," the tribesmen entered the town a little after midnight and ran riot for almost an hour before being dispersed and a handful captured by a detachment of French African troops.

As could have been predicted, all the prisoners—vacant-eyed young men for the most part—were found to be under the influence of hashish. Asked why they had done what they did, none had anything to say. There is no question of how or by whom. But why remains unanswered.

Immediately after his sudden departure from his Bar & Name-It, Tapp went into the hills above the town. He was pretty well battered up, his back bleeding badly, but he knew chances were excellent Bosch would send some of his Butcher Boys after him and decided to keep himself moving along.

The moon was out and patches of white light lay along the wooded trail he was traveling. Although blazing hot during the day, the Cameroon hill country gets cold at night.

He had been going perhaps two hours when he finally saw ahead of him the long, low, hut-like building he had been seeking. There were no lights in it, but as he approached, a figure detached itself from the darkness and the muzzle of a rifle barrel touched his chest.

"You're Mister Tapp," a voice informed him and he was able to make out a boy's thin, bored face beneath a turban of black cloth. "Why have you come here?"

"I've got to see Aunt Edna," Tapp said. "She knows me. It will be all right."

"She's sleeping," the boy said. "She'd cut my tongue out if I woke—"

"Let him in, let him in," a woman called irritably from inside and a blush of candlelight showed at one of the windows. "You already woke me with your jabbering."

The boy jerked his head toward the door and the big man pushed it open and went inside. She was sitting on a cot, legs crossed, elbow resting on her knee, chin in the palm of her hand. Her only garment was a tight-fitting, wrap-around print affair extending from her knees to her breasts. Below it her feet disappeared in shadow and above it her face was a dark, smooth, expressionless mask —small-featured save for the dark, wide eyes, the whole of it framed in a great, soft tumble of black hair. It was a knowing face, a cynical face, a face that would never show surprise or astonishment. Yet the girl herself was hardly more than 20.

"What happened to you?" she said. "You're white as a sheet and bleeding."

"Patch me up first and then we'll talk about it," he said. "I've got a proposition that might interest you."

"Money?" she asked.

"Money."

"That could interest me," she said standing up. "All right, lie down here. I don't have any whisky. You want to chew on some of the Happy Leaf to make it easier?"

"I'll be all right," he said, stretching out face down on her cot. "Save your stuff for the spooks that need it."

SHE had to cut his shirt and peel it off like strips of adhesive tape. His back was covered with blood, the rake marks running across like a set of parallel trenches. She had to improvise a swab and clean them out, and while she was at it he told her about Max Bosch running him out of Dschang.

"I'm beginning to get an idea of what your proposition is going to be," she said when she had finished cleaning him up but before she had applied any bandage to his back. "How does that feel?"

"It hurts," he said. "How about kissing it? Maybe that would help."

"You ought to have a dog lick it," she said. "There's something in their saliva that helps things heal."

"You'll do," he said.

She laughed and bent over him and began to run her tongue along the rake grooves. When she had finished, she cut strips off a clean white cloth and taped them to him.

"You want me to help you get your place back, don't you?" she said. "I remember you saying something about money. How much?"

"I've got half a dozen things going for me in Dschang," he said lying on his back now with the girl sitting next to him on the edge of the bed. "The bar, the stores, a couple of other things. We'll work out a reasonable percentage of the take and it will start coming to you the second I'm back behind the counter and Maxie is out. I'd attend to it myself only there are 14 of them or something and that's a little too much for even me to take on."

"It's too much for me, too," she said, frowning and shaking her head. "Except for Adrian outside and three others to get my merchandise for me, I don't have anybody. I know that crowd of Bosch's and we wouldn't have a chance against them. Of course, there's always one other possibility. Ugala and his hill people."

"You got most of them so softened up on your Happy Leaf they can hardly stand up," Tapp said. "Besides, what would there be in it for them? Why would they do it?"

"Leave that part of it to me," the girl said. "If I can get them to run Bosch out, I become a 33 percent partner in everything you've got in Dschang, right?"

"Twenty-five percent."

"Thirty-three."

"Thirty-three then, but you got to see I'm comfortable as long as I'm up here with you," he said and drew her face down to his chest. "Make out he got me with his rake right there. That's nice, sweetheart. That's very nice."

"Easy," she said as he drew her against him, turning sideways to receive the firm thrust of her breasts as his arms tightened about her. "Easy, Harry. Or quiet, anyway. It makes Adrian nervous to even think about someone doing this to me."

CHIEF Ugala and a dozen of his men arrived the next day. The chief was 400 pounds of butter-soft flesh covered here and there by a Hawaiian sport shirt made for a midget, a cowboy belt with a revolver in each holster, a pair of Bermuda shorts, a pair of thonged sandals and a black derby hat.

"I did not expect to see you here," he said to Tapp, the American sitting on a crate in front of the building and blowing softly into his trumpet, the girl standing next to him and the boy, Adrian, beyond. "I heard that you were no longer in Dschang, but I did not expect to see you here."

"I had to go someplace," Tapp said and bent forward with his trumpet aimed at the ground and blew a phrase of "Three Blind Mice." "This is as good as any."

"Oh, my, yes, yes, yes," the gigantic African beamed, his voice a fair approximation of the fog horn on a Hudson River ferry. "Our dear Aunt Edna is the one to help us forget all our troubles and misfortunes. You have our supplies, dear?"

"There's been a delay," the girl said. "It hasn't arrived yet."

"Oh, my, my, my, my, my," Ugala said in what was obviously genuine distress. Behind him his men shuffled their feet and looked glumly at one another. "What can have happened? Do you expect it shortly?"

"My men can only move at night," the girl shrugged. "Try tomorrow."

"We ask little of men or their gods," Ugala sighed, an exhalation not unlike that of a hippo heaving itself up out of water onto land. "Only enough to eat, an occasional woman, and the soothing comfort of the Happy Leaf. We will return in the morning and pray tonight that it awaits us."

"Those the clowns you're going to use to run Maxie Bosch out of Dschang?" Tapp inquired. "Hell, there ain't one of them that can walk across a room without falling on his ear. They been customers of yours too long, sweetheart. They're punchy."

"I told you to leave that to me," she said and turned to the boy. "Go check on the others. Tell them they're to stay out with the merchandise until I send for it. Tell them to keep themselves hidden. I don't want one of Ugala's sleepwalkers tumbling on them."

"You want to go with me?" the boy said to Tapp.

"That ain't considerate," the big man said. "It ain't right to leave a lady sitting around by herself."

"All right," Adrian said, shrugging it off, but his eyes closed to slits so nothing he felt would show through. "I'll be back in an hour."

They watched him disappear into the jungle, then went back into the long hut.

"I warned you once about him," the girl said. "There's no point in doing it again, is there?"

"Stop worrying," Tapp said and put his arms around her from behind, then bent over to kiss her neck and her ear, his hands working, pressing, coaxing at the front of her body. "My back's killing me. Everything's killing me. Take care of me, sweetheart. Be my ever-loving auntie with her own special bag of tricks."

The stall went on for eight more days. Each morning Ugala and his bearers arrived to inquire about their Happy Leaf, and each morning Aunt Edna shrugged and told them her shipment still hadn't arrived. Sadly unhappy about it at first, their attitude began to change as the days went by. They were feeling the deprivation and it showed. They grew irritable, impatient. They muttered among themselves and the beaming smile no longer appeared on Ugala's face, but was replaced by a brooding look of heavy-lidded distrust.

"Something is wrong here," he announced on the occasion of his eighth visit. "If your shipment had been hijacked I would have heard of it. Where is our supply, auntie dear? The sun has gone out of our lives and we are desolate and cold without it."

"I told you it hasn't arrived," the girl said. "When it does—"

"We do not believe you, auntie dear," the fat man said and moved with almost startling speed to pull one of his revolvers out and raise it an inch from her face. "You are deliberately—Aghhh!"

Tapp's trumpet had come down on his wrist at that point, coming down hard enough to jolt the gun out of his hand. Behind him some of his men had started forward, but stopped as Adrian swung his rifle in an easy arc to cover them all.

"That wasn't friendly," Tapp said and drove his fist into Ugala's face. "That wasn't—Christ, kid, you ain't what you look like."

The fat man was simply walking into him. Tapp backed up, threw an overhand right designed to tear an average man's head off his shoulders, but Ugala took it and kept rolling forward. Blood spilled out of his nose and mouth and he grunted as Tapp sunk both hands into his body, but still he came on until the American had been backed up against the hut and the other's great bulk had started bouncing into him. Once, twice, he withstood those elephantine lunges, then threw himself sideways to avoid the third. Ugala hit, staggered, bounced the wrong way and took a heavy punch to the back of the neck that finally dropped him. Once down, he showed no particular interest in getting up.

"The gun wasn't loaded," he sighed, big as a rubbery bear on all fours, blood spilling off his face to the ground. "I can't get bullets for it."

"Go back to your village," the girl said and motioned several of his men to come forward and help him up. "You will have your Happy Leaf when I can get it to you."

"You've got it," he said, sagging against the men who had lifted him. "Why are you doing this to me? Have I not always paid your price?"

"I didn't say I had it," the girl said, turning away. "I said I'll get it to you."

"You're pushing him pretty hard, sweetheart," Tapp said as the fat man returned to his litter. "He's pretty near ready to explode."

"No, he's not," the girl said. "None of them are. But they will be by the time I'm through with them."

"I'm beginning to get a little feeling that things are getting out of control, sweetheart," Tapp said.

"You're not getting worried, are you, Mister Tapp?" Adrian asked politely. "Aunt Edna knows what she's doing."

"I'm sure of it," Tapp said, looking at the calm-faced girl. "I'm just beginning to wish I did."

In the days that followed, Ugala continued to pay his hopeless visits. His hands shook now. His face twitched. He frequently pressed his hands to his lower body as though experiencing pain there. His people were in similarly bad shape.

"If there's a way of calling it off, I'd like to do it," Tapp said when the fat man—grey as putty and shaking so he could hardly speak—had been turned away for what was to be the last time. "I'll go back and take a crack at Bosch myself. This has just about stopped being my type of thing."

"May I try to blow your trumpet?" Adrian asked. "I very much enjoy that song you play."

"Take it with you," the girl said. "Go to the others and tell them to return with the merchandise tomorrow night. My partner is getting unhappy. After tomorrow he won't have any more reason to."

The boy sent his flat, no-comment look from one to the other, then turned abruptly and started into the jungle. They heard the trumpet sound and then the stuttering phrases that indicated he was trying to play "Three Blind Mice."

"Stop looking like that," the girl smiled going to Tapp and rising on her toes to kiss him. "This is not New York City or Hollywood. This is Africa. We do things differently here. How is your back? Perhaps I can do something for you."

"You're really something, sweetheart," Tapp said, shaking his head and grinning, then bending her bead back so he could kiss her throat. "The old back's killing me. Needs all kinds of attention. We ought to get right to it."

When Ugala returned the next night, perhaps 100 of his men were with him. At his word all fell on their faces while the fat man himself dropped to his knees before the cold-eyed girl. His face was ashen. His body shook as though with some terrible fever. He embraced her legs, pressing his face to them as though he were a terrified child.

"We can stand no more," he whispered. "What is it you wish of us? What must we do? We know you have that which we need."

The girl stepped back from him and took Adrian's rifle. The fat man sank back on his heels and groaned when she touched its muzzle to his quivering lips.

"Kiss it," she said. "Kiss it as a sign to your people that all of you must do as Aunt Edna commands. Regardless of what orders I give, all must accept and carry them out. Kiss it as a sign that you agree. Kiss it and you will have the Happy Leaf."

"We agree," he whispered and tears poured down his face as his tongue touched the gun. "We will do anything you say. We can do nothing else."

The leaves were brought in great baskets and thrown upon the ground like garbage for pigs. Yet, such was our condition that none resented this. Indeed as we dropped upon them—snuffing, grunting, pushing them into our mouths— what were we if not pigs?

This one did not contain Happy Leaves. No, my judges. This one contained 100 machetes and bush knives. Then the woman addressed us, tall and with her eyes flashing and her voice entering our hearts and bones and bellies.

"I want Dschang," she screamed. "You must take it for me. It has been agreed. There will be more Happy Leaf for all when it has been done. There will be no end—"

— from testimony given by the captured tribesman Akame Djor at the hearings following the massacre at Dschang.

TAPP came to his feet at her words, his mouth opening to roar a protest. But there was no point in even trying to. The tribesmen were howling, stamping, slicing the air with their knives. One among them didn't go for the idea.

"You must not do this, my people," the fat man cried raising his arms. "She is asking us to fall upon those of our own blood. Our brothers—"

They didn't have time for that kind of thing. A bush knife went into his side up to the handle. Others made contact as he began to sag. "No, my people," he said sadly through blood bubbling out of his mouth and fell like a collapsing tent to be cut apart by those surging over him.

And Tapp? Tapp was out of there by then.

Most of Dschang was asleep when he reached it. The huts and shacks of the natives were dark, the streets deserted. But light showed through the windows of the Bar & Name-It and he ran toward it and inside. Just Bosch and the girl, Umwame, were there. They were playing checkers, the pale, bald man behind the bar and the girl on a stool in front of it.

"Tapp," the number one Butcher Boy said and reached a hand under the bar. "I been expecting—"

"Not now, not now," Tapp said, but realized the other wouldn't hold up on whatever he was grabbing at. "All right, damn it, we'll try it this way."

Two steps carried him to a yard from the bar and the third sent him vaulting over it. Bosch tried to fall away from him, but Tapp came down spread wide and there was no getting out from under. The Butcher Boy went down with Tapp's foot on his wrist to keep his knife from coming into play, and Tapp's hand on his collar to lift his head and smash it against the floor, then lift it again and smash it again, and repeat still once more before hauling him to his feet and throwing him into the bottles and glasses behind the bar.

"Get hold of yourself, Maxie," Tapp said. "You know I could have finished you off just now. Only there's something else to take care of first. Aunt Edna and a million or so hopped-up tribesmen are on their way here and— Hear that? Hear that? That's that kid of hers with my

Dschang, Cameroon, Feb. 23— Led by a beautiful native woman called "Aunt Edna," a raging horde of hashish-drugged Bamileke natives descended upon this town last night to set its streets awash in blood.

Marching down from the hills to the tune of "Three Blind Mice," played on a trumpet, the machete-swinging tribesmen scattered throughout the city and cut down close to 100 men, women and children.

Native sources declare that one

slaughtered their own tribesmen, may have been the antagonism between two white men prominent in this area, Harry Trapp and Max Bosch, who had been contesting for control of various commercial enterprises here. The sources speculate that one or the other of the men encouraged last night's violence a means of getting the hand over his river tunately fo or not

"HAPPY LEAVES," Bamileke term for hashish drug, sent fierce tribe (above) into mad death ritual

horn. Maxie, we need your boys. And, Maxie, we need them in a hurry."

The trumpet was the first thing they heard, the tune disjointed and erratic but unmistakably an attempt at "Three Blind Mice." Then the voices. High-pitched, howling. Then the stamping feet.

"They're sleeping around," Bosch said, stooping to pull a long wooden box out from under the bar. "Umwame knows where and with who. She—"

"I will find them," the girl said, and ran across the room and out the door and right on out of town as well because by then the tribesmen were in the streets and invading the huts and the screams of those trapped had begun to be heard.

"Rifles," Bosch said, pulling a couple out of the box and giving one to Tapp. "There's nothing else we can do, is there?"

"Nothing," Tapp said. "Nothing at all."

They leaned on the bar from behind it and outside the sounds of violence grew steadily louder as the rampaging natives spilled through the streets. The sounds grew in intensity, reached a pitch to deafen strong ears, and then the doorway of the Bar & Name-It filled with the distorted faces and sweat-gleaming bodies of Aunt Edna's drug-maddened horde.

Behind the bar, the riflemen opened up and a shot exploded in the bell of Adrian's horn, shattering it and the boy's face behind it. It meant little to anyone. His associates poured over his body and Tapp and Bosch climbed onto the bar to dub their rifles down on a rolling carpet of upturned faces.

Bosch went first. Hands took knees, pulled him forward. He sent one agonizing look toward the ceiling, then was sucked into the mob as neatly and suddenly as a man falling down a manhole.

"You got me, you got me," Tapp roared, still towering over them and flailing his rifle. "But, gents, you're still going to have to work for it."

They made no attempt to defend themselves or avoid his blows, but tried only to get at him. Dozens were hit and fell, but others were there to replace them, and now the woman—wild eyed as any of them and carrying a machete—was moving toward him. He swung at her head, missed, dropped to his knees on the bar as her knife slashed his ankle, then grabbed her arm and fell back behind the bar dragging her down on top of him.

"Call them off, sweetheart," be panted in her ear. "Call them off or I'll break your back. Call them—"

But by then it was as much out of her hands as his. A tide of unseeing, unknowing men swept over the bar, tore Aunt Edna from his grip and moved in on Tapp. The bush knives fell indiscriminately, the arms that wielded them no longer able to stop, and Tapp went out without a murmur. Ten minutes later a detachment of French African troops were on the scene and ten minutes after that the pointless slaughter came to an end.

Incredibly, the boy Adrian had survived. His physical condition is hopeless, his face and body utterly destroyed by the rifle shot and his subsequent tramping beneath the feet of the rushing tribesmen. Yet, he is coherent in speech, lucid in thought, and it is his evidence that constitutes the most important information on the why of the incident at Dschang. According to him, Aunt Edna had thought for quite some time of attempting to take over the town and make herself its ruler. However, it was only when she thought about how to help Tapp in *his* effort that she realized it could serve her purpose as well.

Aunt Edna disappeared completely; there were rumors that she had escaped into the hills to begin her hashish campaign on another tribe, hoping to get another crack at Dschang and maybe the whole Cameroons. Probably no one will ever hear anything more of her until it is too late. ✱

"Bar Room Girl Who Touched Off a Tribal War"
Male, June 1960
Illustration by Charles Copeland

ed packaged goods and caused a full-scale epidemic."

Dr. Leroy Fothergill of the Fort Detrick staff has recently warned that saboteurs might introduce infection into plants turning out cosmetics, drugs and biological products such as vaccines, serums and anti-toxins. A woman would take in germs when she applied lipstick, and pass them on to the man she kissed. Or a team of spies disguised as municipal sanitation workers could steal a big water truck, fill the tank with bacterial solutions and cruise down the crowded city streets at 5 p.m. spraying a fine mist of odorless, colorless infection into the homeward-bound throngs.

There's one more thing you should know before you start feeling cocky.

Russia has her own huge arsenal of gas and germs.

In the chemical weapons

"THE ARMY'S TERRIFYING DEATH BUGS AND LOONY GAS"

— WRITING AS DAVID MARS —

Men, November 1960

COVER ARTIST: NORMAN BAER

RUSSIAN GAS ATTACK, simulated one, is put down by U.S. Army Decontamination

THE ARMY'S TERRIFYING DEATH BUGS AND LOONY GAS

Silent vapors that can force an enemy army to happily turn over its guns, tiny germs that will make a giant city writhe in diseased agony— This is CB Warfare—and the Pentagon prays it'll never have to use it

squad. Reds have ability to spread yellow fever here, Q-fever, even Bubonic plague

By DAVID MARS

WEIRD mask (above) will protect GIs against almost any Red chemical threat; strange weed below is newly discovered antidote to deadly nerve gas, which we have, Reds have, too

A STRANGE white powder floats down on the 10,000 Russian troops massed for attack along the West German border. A giddy, numb feeling sweeps through the ranks of foot soldiers. Men stagger, drop their rifles, fall. Ten seconds later 9000 of them are already dead . . .

A lone jet fighter sweeps down over the Soviet industrial plant at Magnitogorsk, laying a fine mist of odorless, colorless liquid. A few minutes later, 5,000 factory workers begin wandering aimlessly around in the plants. Many sit down on the floor and stare into space, smiling happily. Production creaks to a halt . . .

A muffled figure sits at the wheel of a sanitation truck, as the vehicle rumbles through the dark streets of Moscow, spraying the dirty gutters with "cleaning solution." A week later, three quarters of the population is dying of bubonic plague . . .

That's how World War Three may end. No guns, no atom bombs, no missiles. (*Continued on page* 70)

25

A STRANGE white powder floats down on the 10,000 Russian troops massed for attack along the West German border. A giddy, numb feeling sweeps through the ranks of foot soldiers. Men stagger, drop their rifles, fall. Ten seconds later 9,000 of them are already dead....

A lone jet fighter sweeps down over the Soviet industrial plant at Magnitogorsk, laying a fine mist of odorless, colorless liquid. A few minutes later, 5,000 factory workers begin wandering aimlessly around in the plants. Many sit down on the floor and stare into space, smiling happily. Production creaks to a halt....

A muffled figure sits at the wheel of a sanitation truck, as the vehicle rumbles through the dark streets of Moscow, spraying the dirty gutters with "cleaning solution." A week later, three quarters of the population is dying of bubonic plague....

That's how World War III may end. No guns, no atom bombs, no missiles. Just a few ounces of a concentrated substance mixed into a liquid or spray and spread over enemy cities, factories and troops.

And the age of gas and germ warfare has already begun. In heavily guarded laboratories, ringed by barbed wire and sharpshooting sentries, our Army scientists are working with a fantastic assortment of gases and bacteria that can affect man, his crops and his animals.

They can make men cry or drown them in their own body fluids. They can confuse people, frighten them or impair their mental balance. They can burn holes in flesh, paralyze or kill. They can poison food, water, clothes, cars, crops, cattle and household pets.

And they are only part of the astounding arsenal which might be used against us.

Major General Marshall Stubbs, Chief Chemical Officer of the US Army, a trim 54-year-old West Pointer with a Master's Degree from MIT, commands the 3,500 soldiers and 8,800 civilians of our Chemical Corps. His is one of the most crucial jobs in the free world today. Here's the story—based on an exclusive interview with General Stubbs and five of his senior scientists—of the fantastic gas and disease war which could face the United States.

At the Chemical Corps research and development center in heavily-guarded Fort Detrick, Maryland, the United States has substantial supplies of two types of gas ready for use. These are: (1) the burning Lewisite or mustard compound, (2) the so-called nerve gas or G-compound. The Army also has bacteria which can be delivered by spray or infected insects, spreading diseases among men, animals or crops. In Pine Bluff, Arkansas, a whole plant is busy producing these germs for the Corps.

This is what these weapons can do.

LET'S start with the least radical but still brutal mustard gas. Mustard gas is a powerful, blistering cloud that is both visible and smellable. It's most destructive to the eyes, skin and lungs, but will burn any part of the body it touches. A drop the size of a pinhead will make a blister the size of a quarter, and it does most damage in sweaty areas such as armpits, knees and crotch. While it may take a few hours before the burned skin turns red and even days before the painful blisters erupt, it hits and hurts much faster if it touches the eyes. If breathed, it produces a hoarse cough in the scorched windpipe. A man who inhales a lot faces possible pneumonia or death.

While mustard gas can be sprayed from low-flying aircraft, it can also be delivered in aerial bombs or in missiles fired from submarines off the coast. When a rocket loaded with mustard gas bursts, much of the contents will be scattered nearby and "settle out in droplets." These may form on the doorknob of a home, the steering wheel of a car or a bench in the park. A man will be burned if he touches a single droplet, but he's unlikely to die unless he inhales a quantity.

A much more lethal weapon than mustard is nerve gas, invented by Hitler's chemists just before the start of World War II. It was while researching for a better insecticide that the Germans hit on a group of compounds that had a lethal effect upon animals, too. Called the G-series, these nerve gases—Tabun, Sarin and Soman—are probably the most potent known to man. They've made most other gases obsolete.

Nerve gas can't be seen or smelled. Breathing only the vapors from three large drops of nerve gas can cause death in a few minutes. In 1945, US troops captured the German gas scientists and formulas. American experts tested the different nerve gases and decided that Sarin was the most effective. In recent years, US chemical warfare plants have manufactured millions of shells and bombs filled with Sarin. It isn't easy to handle, but there have been few mishaps because of extraordinary safety precautions.

How does a nerve gas work? As a vapor, it's breathed in through the nose or mouth. It hampers breathing, causes convulsions, paralysis and death. Even a tiny amount causes running nose, tightness of the chest, pinpointing of the pupils and breathing trouble. Then comes dizziness, twitching, excessive sweating, drooling, stomach cramps and involuntary urination and defecation. Finally breathing stops and the victim is dead. It may take less than 10 minutes.

It is surprising how little exposure to nerve gas is necessary to kill. Lieutenant Colonel Douglas Lindsey, Director of Medical Research at the Army Chemical Center, MD, says, "One deep breath may be sufficient…the exposed skin at the back of the hand or even a single ear lobe is a sufficient portal of entry for a tiny, but visible droplet which goes unnoticed."

That droplet can cripple or kill.

One missile could disperse enough Sarin to injure or kill one third of the population of an open area a full mile in diameter. Such a chunk of real estate in a big city would include tens of thousands of people, who'd probably have no masks and never know what hit them.

An even stranger chemical is now in the final stage of development by the Army. It's made from psycho-chemicals, solutions that can tranquilize, terrorize, confuse or derange a man without killing him. One solution simply puts a person to sleep for many hours. Another, a derivative of lysergic acid, can produce confusion and inability to carry out orders.

Some of the most frightening "mind-gases" have been extracted from well-known plants. Mescaline, derived from the peyote plant of the Southwest, and psilocybin, an extract from a Mexican mushroom, "produce hallucinations, depression, apathy and senseless elation for periods of 12 to 24 hours," said a reputable physician recently. What's worse, they muddle a man's sense of distance and his timing, so that a gassed pilot can't land a jet and a rifleman can't fire accurately.

Brigadier General Thomas R. Phillips tells about a carefully controlled experiment with a platoon of American GIs. "The gas, which is odorless and invisible, was allowed to drift to the platoon at drill. Within a short time, four of five of the men stopped drill and sat down. The sergeant struggled for a time to carry on the drill, but he too succumbed and sat down with the soldiers. Some of the men appeared to be disoriented, others were cheerful but just didn't care about anything. A lieutenant came over to try to restore order and discipline, but pretty soon he gave up—not caring about the drill any more than anyone else.

"The potentialities of such a weapon are obvious. No one is injured; they are completely normal when they recover. But while the effect lasts, enemy soldiers can come over, tie them up and take their guns. It is easy to imagine the Soviets making use of such a gas to quell a revolt or to win a minor war. The Soviets would never admit that a gas had been used. They would simply proclaim that the enemy soldiers had surrendered to join them."

But these psycho-chemicals—called "loony gas" by irreverent GIs—can be extremely important to the United States too. If there should be a World War III, erupting with a Soviet smash across Western Europe, these hallucinating gases might be very valuable in the US liberation of enemy-held areas. American planes and missiles could lay down a spray over the occupied cities, temporarily derange the Red garrisons without permanently hurting one anti-Soviet civilian, and free the capitals and industrial towns without the holocaust of nuclear attack.

Other chemicals in America's chemical arsenal attack a man's physical capacities. Some cause temporary blindness, temporary deafness, dizziness, nausea or mild paralysis. Lt. Colonel Lindsey reports that "the subject first loses ability to stand, and sinks quietly down on his haunches; then comes loss of function of the upper extremities. Depending on the dose, spontaneous recovery occurs in 1-24 hours."

All such war gases can be useful, but the emphasis has been on psycho-chemicals. One scientist-volunteer who took them has revealed his experience. Dr. Van Sim of the Fort Detrick labs told his fellow scientists that he found himself "perfectly content to enjoy my fantasies of color and vision…. I was notified on several occasions that I was not being very communicative—this is probably true. One of the most outstanding recollections was my reluctance to make simple decisions." Groggy as if half drunk, he was too limp to do anything.

In some ways, germs may be an even greater threat than gas. First, a much smaller quantity of germ-concentrate can do as big a job. According to General Stubbs, a mustard gas bomb the size of your fist has a thousand lethal doses. And you can get the same dosage from a test tube of nerve gas only as big as the top joint of your thumb. But the bacteria in a test tube of the same size could kill one billion people. That makes germs a million times more dangerous.

Second, gas only affects people in relatively small areas so it's best in big crowded cities. But bacteria can start epidemics that'll sweep across thousands of square miles. Ten large jet bombers, carrying 10,000 pounds each, could release enough germ vapor to reach 30 percent of the entire US population.

BW (bacteriological warfare) is a real and serious weapon. Many germs have been explored by US experts. Scientists know that plague, typhus, cholera or smallpox are best suited to kill a lot of people. To cause mass sickness that would cripple factories and armed forces, diseases such as rabbit fever and undulant fever might be used. There are selective bacteria to destroy chickens, cattle, horses, sheep. Chemical growth regulators now used to eliminate weeds can effectively wreck food plants.

General Stubbs' research teams have large greenhouses at Fort Detrick where they're studying the effects of BW products which can damage wheat, rice, cotton, barley, rye and oats. The Chemical Corps also has a plant in Pine Bluff, Arkansas to produce and store the BW weapons. Many of them have different life and strength. Some can survive being blown 20 or 30 miles by night winds. Most are not too likely to be released during the day, for sunlight kills most of them. Realistic planners don't expect the majority of bacteria sprayed out will do much damage, but such large numbers can be turned loose that vast damage will be done if only five percent are effective.

As for "insect warfare," it may be assumed that our scientists know something about the power of fleas infected with the plague, houseflies tainted with cholera, dysentery and anthrax; ticks with Colorado fever; tularemia and relapsing fever; and mosquitoes bearing malaria, dengue fever and yellow fever. These infecting insects could be used to menace and kill large population groups.

Today, both the free world and the Communist empire have many ways to spread diseases. Planes or missiles could release aerosol clouds—basically similar to the "bombs" used in your home to eliminate odors or kill insects, but loaded with bacteria. Or they might drop packages of dried but dangerous germs by parachutes from high altitude. Automatic timing devices would release the powdered infection a few thousand feet above the ground. A small "bomb" of bacteria might be put into the air-conditioning system of a key factory, telephone exchange, underground rocket base or the Pentagon itself. Such a direct delivery would also work for nerve or "loony" gas, but would require a larger amount and a bigger container of aerosol. The results would be a very high percentage of casualties, perhaps as much as three-quarters of the people in the building.

The same methods would be equally effective in an air-conditioned movie theater or office building. Since bacteria sprays are odorless and colorless, those who breathed in the infection would go home without any idea that the germs were incubating inside them. It might take as long as 14 days before they felt really sick. And even then they still might not realize they'd been hit with a BW attack.

Not long ago, the Chemical Corps experimented to find out how large an area could be covered by a harmless aerosol cloud released from a small ship off the Atlantic Coast. Hundreds of square miles were covered with the spray from simple, inexpensive, home-made equipment. An innocent looking "neutral" freighter with large tanks of bacteria and big efficient sprays could do ten times as much damage with only a small chance of detection. Or the germs might be smuggled ashore to be distributed silently in a hundred cities by enemy undercover saboteurs. General Stubbs confirms that BW material, in powder or liquid form, could easily be camouflaged as any one of dozens of items normally imported into the United States.

One of the most disturbing things about BW is that it is quite easy to produce the germs in big quantities. It takes hundreds of millions of dollars, huge factories and thousands of skilled men to manufacture A- or H-bombs. But a mere half-dozen scientists with $30,000 worth of equipment could make plenty of bacteria in any modest basement laboratory. One expert has even said that a single biologist could produce the germs without much more than the initial bacteria samples (cultures) and a bathtub. Thus, even a tiny nation with scanty resources can raise hell with giant neighbors by sneak BW attack. In the hands of irresponsible dictators in angry little nations, BW can be a real threat to world peace and health.

Any country launching a BW attack on another will almost certainly do it secretly. There'll be no declaration of war, and the country being infected won't even be sure who the enemy is. As a matter of fact, it might be some time before it's discovered that the increase in sickness is man-made. "If a saboteur had access to a food plant with wide distribution of its products, Congressman R. F. Sikes of Florida has pointed out, "he could easily poison enough food in one day's work to seriously incapacitate 500,000 people…. Imagine the havoc that would be created if saboteurs deliberately contaminated packaged goods and caused a full-scale epidemic."

Dr. Leroy Fothergill of the Fort Detrick staff has recently warned that saboteurs might introduce infection into plants turning out cosmetics, drugs and biological products such as vaccines, serums and anti-toxins. A woman would take in germs when she applied lipstick, and pass them on to the man she kissed. Or a team of spies disguised as municipal sanitation workers could steal a big water truck, fill the tank with bacterial solutions and cruise down the crowded city streets at 5 p.m., spraying a fine mist of odorless, colorless infection into the homeward-bound throngs.

There's one more thing you should know before you start feeling cocky.

Russia has her own huge arsenal of gas and germs.

In the chemical weapons field, the Red Army is known to have plenty of mustard (burning) gas and choking gas. And it's an ominous fact that one sixth of all ammunition issued to Russian divisions contain "chemical agents." The bulk of this is a German nerve gas called Tabun. In 1945, the Soviet Army grabbed the German gas factory itself, moved it back to Russia. "Presumably it is in operation," says Dr. William H. Summerson of the Pentagon's Research and Development Command.

The Russians' nerve gas will be a much greater threat than the burning mustards, because unlike mustard gas, most of the G-series compounds are both odorless and colorless. Not long ago, Dr. Cecil Coggins, former official of the Army Chemical Warfare Service, revealed that the Soviet stockpile of Tabun exceeds 50,000 tons.

The Soviets haven't been asleep in the psycho-chemical field either. Soviet Major General Drugov of the Military Medical Service has publicly announced that "special interest attaches itself to the so-called psychic poisons (mescaline, methedrine, lysergic acid derivatives), which are now used for the simulation of mental disease. Many of our scientists regard research on the actions of poisons and on the development of antidotes to be their patriotic duty." In plain language, this means that the Red Army has "loony gases" too. As for defenses, General Stubbs has learned that "They have a complete line of protective clothing which includes paper and oilskin overcoats, paper protective overalls and aprons, and a protective sheet which the soldier can lie on." And they've had plenty of practice with anti-gas clothing on maneuvers where live gas attacks are staged.

WHAT ABOUT Russian germ warfare weapons? You can get a pretty good idea from the *Soviet Medical Dictionary*, which coolly points out that "the following biological agents are believed to be suitable for use in bacteriological warfare: the plague, anthrax, undulant fever, tularemia, epidemic typhus, Rocky Mountain spotted fever, American encephalomyelitis of horses, yellow fever and botulism toxin. Some sources add to this list also cholera, rickettsia, Q-fever, smallpox. Recommended for infecting animals, in addition to anthrax and glanders, are foot-and-mouth disease, the Rift Valley fever, cattle plague and hog cholera. A number of methods of infecting agricultural plants have also been studied...the target of such weapons will be troops engaged in combat, large administrative and industrial centers, airports and air force and naval bases. They may also be used for infecting agricultural animals and large stock-farms, and for contaminating grain and industrial crops with a view to disrupting food supplies for the population... Special attention should be given the water supply system."

As if all these germs were not enough, the Soviets have begun treating their bacteria with radiation to produce mutations and new strains. These are not only harder to identify, but they're different enough so that the body's defenses against the original bug and the medicines used to treat patients can't help a bit. The Russians believe a bacterial attack can be extremely useful; before the dropping of an H-bomb, the germs weaken people's resistance so that many more would be destroyed by the thermo-nuclear weapon. If you're already sick, you're less likely to recover from radiation or the blast.

How can you protect yourself from Red gas or germs?

In a mustard gas attack, close all windows and turn off air conditioners as soon as a gas alarm is sounded. When the all clear is announced, open them to air the place out.

Sun and rain help to neutralize gases, but you can speed up the process by hosing down your car, exterior walls of the house and anything that has been contaminated. If any mustard gas touched you, wash the burning area gently with plenty of soap and water. Gasoline and other petroleum solvents will remove both mustard and nerve gases from objects with hard surfaces. Mustard soaks into many foods to some extent, penetrating up to about three-eighths of an inch, so throw them all out.

Civil Defense authorities are working on water purification now, so you aren't too likely to drink any mustard gas-tainted water from your kitchen faucet. But there's still the risk of eating meat from animals contaminated by one of the war gases. The Department of Health advises farmers to "slaughter these animals immediately to recover the edible portions of the carcass. Meat from animals exposed to mustard gas or one of the nerve gases should be boiled for one-half hour or more to insure that no traces of the gas remain in the meat."

Is there any protection against nerve gas? Yes, but you'll need two basic pieces of equipment to survive a nerve gas attack. The first is a gas mask, the second, chemically treated protective clothing. Those civilians who breathe in mild concentrations of nerve gas may survive after some weeks of misery, but those who inhale substantial amounts will die swiftly if they don't receive prompt and massive injections of atropine. Civil Defense units have been issued some of the excellent new M-52 masks that filter out both gas and bacteria, plus first-aid kits containing atropine and sterile hypodermics. *If* you don't get too much nerve gas and *if* somebody finds you in time and *if* that somebody has the atropine kit, you'll survive with no trouble at all.

The Army estimates that 25% of every troop unit nerve-gassed in the open is certain to die, and another quarter will have only a fair chance, even with the injection. And that's taking for granted that the troops will have masks on within 15 seconds after canisters of gas burst among them. If they take longer, many more than 25 percent will certainly perish.

If you do get splashed by drops of colorless nerve gas, you must immediately wash the skin with plenty of water. If droplets reach the eyes, they should be immediately washed out. If you eat or drink the nerve gas in food or water, you must wash out your stomach thoroughly. If clothing is contaminated, it should be thoroughly washed with a solution of alkali, or else buried or burned.

There isn't a great deal that anyone can do to defend himself against an attack if he doesn't have one of the new masks and doesn't take cover inside a shelter with germ filters over the air intake. The Chemical Corps is, however, trying to improve a system of detection devices. There's even a plan to impregnate the standard GI uniform with something that will react visibly to bacteria being sprayed. But civilians had better just close their windows tight and hope for plenty of sun. Federal Civil Defense brass advises that people should take all the usual precautions they would in an epidemic—but quadrupled. Where necessary, decontamination will be handled by special squads properly equipped, and local doctors and hospitals will be reinforced by teams of BW professionals who know about plagues and epidemics.

As for the psycho-chemicals or "loony gas," the best defense is the M-52 mask, which is still available only in extremely small quantities. The hallucinator shows up on military infra-red gas detectors such as the LOPAIR machine, but there's very little that a civilian can do about it. It doesn't linger too long, and there's no need for hosing down or decontaminating. General Stubbs hasn't released any specific figures on how long his "loony gases" remain effective in an area, but some outside scientists figure it can't be more than six to ten hours. As for the duration of the mental derangement, it may be anything from three hours to three days depending on the amount of psycho-chemical absorbed. Thus far, none of the US "loony gases" has left any of the human guinea pigs permanently disturbed.

Unfortunately for our chances of surviving a chemical or bacteriological attack, our defense preparations are riddled with apathy and stupidity, public and private. US Civil Defense is only a skeleton organization, with a tiny staff, a ridiculous budget and little equipment. The public hasn't taken the CW-BW menace seriously, and neither has Congress. As a result, millions of Americans who might be saved may die if an enemy hits with these new weapons within the next year or two. On March 9, 1960, Congressman Kenneth Hechler of West Virginia bluntly told the House of Representatives that "we are defenseless. Our people have never been told how to defend themselves against these awesome weapons, a full year after the chief of the Army Chemical Corps conceded that upwards of *30,000,000* citizens of the Soviet Union have been trained in defenses against chemical and biological warfare."

General Stubbs has repeatedly discussed the far-flung Russian civil defense outfit (called DOSAFF) which extends to every village, which has given millions of lectures, classes and demonstrations on CW and BW. He's told Congress that "Protective masks are sold by DOSAFF stores everywhere in the USSR, and protective equipment is maintained in office buildings, factories and key installations."

Do you have a mask?

Could you buy one if you wanted to?

Do you mind the reluctance and wrangling of US manufacturers whom the Army Chemical Corps has asked to please make them swiftly?

Stubbs is a serious, able soldier. He's not in the civil defense business, and he scrupulously avoids trouble with either the Office of Civil Defense Mobilization or Congress. He ran his entire research and development program for only $46,469,000 a year, and the total annual Chemical Corps budget was just $103,609,000. He knows that the Communists spend more money, train more people in CW and BW. He is also aware that one of the few deterrents to a Red gas and germ attack is the work his men are doing at Fort Detrick, at the Dugway Chemical Proving Grounds in Utah, at the Pine Bluffs bacteria plant and the Indiana factory that will soon start production of a new chemical agent.

General Stubbs also knows the dangers of panic sweeping through the civilian population, so he's always careful to point out that CW and BW aren't completely new and revolutionary weapons. He's right. While the latest gases are startling, choking fumes have been used as a military weapon for a long time. In 425 BC Spartans besieging Delium burned pitch, charcoal and sulphur to drive the defenders from the walls, and in 1456, Belgrade militia reversed this with a chemical smoke attack that scattered gasping Turkish divisions ringing the city. Union forces burned sulphur-saturated wood to choke the Confederate garrison in Charleston. The Federal brass had rejected a workable scheme to fire shells filled with chlorine on the Confederates. The French used tear gas against the Germans in August 1914, and on April 22, 1915, the Kaiser's forces at Ypres massacred entrenched British and

French battalions with the chlorine Lincoln's generals had spurned. The Allies were so impressed by the 5,000 casualties that the English hit back with their own chlorine six months later.

The gas war was on. Both sides produced masks to filter the choking fumes. Then the Germans introduced mustard gas on July 12, 1917, and it produced body blisters on British troops. Masks kept it from choking them, but it easily seeped through uniforms to burn flesh so badly that 14,276 Tommies had to go to aid stations. Not too many died, but the shocked, scorched survivors required weeks of care that tied up hospitals, ambulances, doctors, nurses and other skilled personnel. Then American doughboys were introduced to German gas on February 26, 1918, when the US 1st Division was plastered with a choking phosgene barrage near Ansauville, France. In June, the Yanks 1st Gas Regiment shelled the Kaiser's infantry with phosgene near Bois de Mort Mare in the first effective US chemical attack in American military history.

At the end of World War I, military statisticians noted that nearly one-third of the 272,138 American Expeditionary Force casualties were caused by gas. But only 2 percent were fatalities, in contrast to the 25 percent death rate among those struck by bullets and shells. US experts concluded that gas was more humane than "conventional weapons" which killed and maimed permanently. The burning mustard gas was found to be twice as effective as the various choking fumes, and five times as effective as either shrapnel or high explosive artillery shells.

But, both American and Russian chemists still had a lot to learn about gas. Of the 38 gases (15 choking, 4 blistering, 4 "vomiting agents," 3 "blood poisoning," and 12 crying) developed during World War I, only one was Russian and three American.

After the Kaiser surrendered, nobody used gas warfare for 17 years.

In 1936, Fascist Italy burned barefoot and half-naked Ethiopians with mustard gas. All major powers had large supplies of assorted gases in World War II, but none dared use them for fear of massive retaliation.

The deliberate military use of disease also has a long history, but one much more modest and less successful than gas warfare.

As far back as the 14th century the Tartars besieging the Italians in the Kaffa fortress tossed over the walls the bodies of soldiers who had died from the plague. This resulted in an outbreak of the disease among the Italians, who had to surrender the fortress. The Germans used anthrax and glanders against Allied military horses in both the US and France during World War I, and the Soviets report that similar attacks were attempted against Russian forces in 1917 and 1918. Moscow also charges that four secret Japanese BW detachments code-named "Nami 8604," "Detachment A 16644," "Detachment 731" and "Detachment 100," spread plague epidemics and infected reservoirs in China during World War II.

Today, the US is faced with a thoroughly modernized Red Army fully equipped to launch a blitz CW or BW attack. Soviet Defense Minister Zhukov has told the citizens of the USSR that "The next war will be characterized by…atomic, thermonuclear, chemical and bacteriological weapons."

Gen. Stubbs is gravely concerned about the great casualties America may suffer if the Russians catch us unawares. "It is my personal opinion that this is the sort of thing the Soviets can use and will use," he warned recently. All the experts agree with him. They know that CW and BW are no pipe dream, no science fiction fantasy. They wonder why neither the Congress nor the taxpayers seem at all worried.

Mustard gas.

Nerve gas.

Brain gas.

Bacteria.

Infected insects.

No masks.

No shelters.

It doesn't make sense. Even if you don't panic, you could let your congressman know how you feel about this fantastic situation. It can't hurt. He might vote more funds for the Chemical Corps and the Civil Defense masks, and the other defenses against BW and CW.

It might save your life. ✻

Pine glanced up at her in astonishment wondering if she were crazy or was just kidding. The hard pressure of the gun against his throat stopped him from asking. She was a startlingly beautiful girl, he realized, with eyes like pockets of black ink and teeth as even and white as rows of tiny sugar cubes. **Her bosom filled the jacket like a pair of boxing gloves stuck inside it.**

"There's nothing wrong with the way he's looking at you, Elena," the old man said irritably. "The poor devil's in no condition to care about women. Let him up."

The girl took the gun away from Pine's neck and he stood up. He was a long, lean man with the emaciated look that bore out his claim to having been a Nazi prisoner. The left side of his face was a mass of discolored flesh with white bone gleaming nakedly through the

Male, April 1962
COVER ARTIST: HARRY SCHAARE

THE YANK WHO
MILE DEATH TREK

By **WALTER KAYLIN**

Art by WALTER POPP

▶ The people of the village of Tovenau in Czechoslovakia's Capathian mountains, knew that the Germans were coming. It was the winter of 1943 and news of the crushing Nazi defeat at Stalingrad had filtered through even to this tiny hill town, which lay directly in the path of the Wehrmacht's retreat from Russia. Already the villagers were gathering up their sparse food supplies, preparing to hide in the hills until the Nazis had passed. An atmosphere of fear, verging on panic, ran through the narrow dirt streets as the desperate men and women went about the task of aban-

ENRAGED, Sgt. Pine leaped for the throat of the Nazi commander as he took hold of the Partisan girl

SURVIVED THE 3000 FROM STALINGRAD

In the winter of 1943, a huge German Army turned tail and fled out of Russia, while Soviet troops harried them at every step with fire, bombs and the worst weapon of all—starvation. In one of WWII's strangest accidents, a U.S. Tech Sergeant endured every horror of this retreat—until, in a weird twist of the wheel, he broke free, to engineer the downfall of 60,000 Nazi troops

Illustration by Walter Popp

THE people of the village of Tovenau in Czechoslovakia's Carpathian Mountains knew that the Germans were coming. It was the winter of 1943 and news of the crushing Nazi defeat at Stalingrad had filtered through even to this tiny hill town, which lay directly in the path of the *Wehrmacht's* retreat from Russia. Already the villagers were gathering up their sparse food supplies, preparing to hide in the hills until the Nazis had passed. An atmosphere of fear, verging on panic, ran through the narrow dirt streets as the desperate men and women went about the task of abandoning their homes. Guerrillas had reported that the vanguard of the German forces was only a few miles to the north.

But no one was prepared for the apparition that suddenly appeared on the outskirts of the village. It was a man and a horse, both so gaunt they resembled a single, huge skeleton covered by strips of cloth and dry hide. The rider stared straight ahead, his eyes burning in their dark sockets like bits of smoldering charcoal.

"It is Death himself," an aged woman whispered and crossed herself.

The horse, its bony head lowered, plodded forward until it tripped on a hidden wire stretched between a pair of stunted trees. The animal uttered a frightened whinny and collapsed in a pile of bones and mottled gray hide. The rider went down on top of him and slid off to land on his hands and knees in the snow. He started to get up, then froze in place as a rifle was touched to his neck. A second gun fired a single shot and the horse stopped screaming.

"United States Army," the man on the ground said. "Tech Sergeant. Vincent Pine. Escaped prisoner of the Nazi Fourth Army retreating from Stalingrad."

THE GUN went beneath his chin and poked his head up. The weapon was held by a tall girl in faded khaki trousers, ragged black boots and a ripped Czech Army jacket. She had a gypsy's wild face and her black hair was cut short as a wool cap. Next to her, also holding a rifle, was a burly old man with a thick, white, tobacco-stained beard which fell halfway down to his belt. He was the village's mayor.

"I don't like the way he's looking at me," the girl said, jabbing Pine's throat with the gun. "It offends me to be looked at that way. Warn him

not to, Preslov. I know how to deal with men who look at me as though
I'm a slut."

Pine glanced up at her in astonishment, wondering if she were
crazy or was just kidding. The hard pressure of the gun against his
throat stopped him from asking. She was a startlingly beautiful girl, he
realized, with eyes like pockets of black ink and teeth as even and white
as rows of tiny sugar cubes. Her bosom filled the jacket like a pair of
boxing gloves stuck inside it.

"There's nothing wrong with the way he's looking at you, Elena,"
the old man said irritably. "The poor devil's in no condition to care
about women. Let him up."

The girl took the gun away from Pine's neck and he stood up. He
was a long, lean man with the emaciated look that bore out his claim
to having been a Nazi prisoner. The left side of his face was a mass of
discolored flesh with white bone gleaming nakedly through the skin
near the jawline. Some of the villagers who had gathered looked away.

"You say you escaped from a Nazi army retreating from Stalingrad,"
the old man said. "How far away is this army?"

"Three miles and heading your way," Pine said. His voice and
manner were tough and urgent despite his beat-up physical condition.
"They're counting on using the Dukla Pass to cross the Carpathians.
What are you going to do about it?"

"We'll burn the village and hide in the forest," the old man shrugged
in response to Pine's question. "At least they won't get the little food we
have. What else can we do against an army of two hundred thousand
men? There are only 84 of us here and except for Elena, we are old
people and children. All the others are off fighting with the Partisans.
Even Elena is only home on leave."

"I've cracked a few heads since I joined the Partisans," the girl said,
glowering at the silent crowd around her. "But I've kept my morals.
I've never slept with any man except my husband and you all know he's
off at the front...." On and on she rambled, in the same vein. By now
Pine was sure she was insane or shell-shocked. There could be no other
explanation for this weirdly inappropriate obsession with her reputation.

"The Nazi Fourth has retreated across half of Russia. The men
are eating their own boots and knifing each other for dead rats," Pine
said, chopping the air with his hands to emphasize his points. "Typhus
is killing them off by the hundreds and dysentery has half of them too
weak to walk. They're in godawful shape but once they're on the other
side of the Carpathians, once they're through the Dukla Pass and back
in German-held territory, they'll rest, fatten up and be ready for action
again in a few weeks. One way or another we've got to stop them from

going through the pass. If we can do that, the whole cruddy bunch will surrender to your Partisans just to get fed. That'll put them out of the war for the duration. They—"

"There are only 84 people here," the old man repeated patiently. "How can 84…"

"What if this so-called American is a spy for the Germans?" another man cut in fearfully.

Preslov shook his head. "If that were true, he would not be urging us to fight." He studied the American thoughtfully, wondering how a man could be so close to collapse and still be filled with this burning desire to strike back at the enemy.

"Could we possibly contact the Partisans?" Pine asked. "Have them move in a detachment?"

"Not before the Germans arrived," Preslov muttered. "There is a Resistance artillery detachment 14 miles from here at Zoldau but we have no radio contact with them."

The old man hurriedly outlined the current conditions of the Partisan forces. In the confused backwash of the Nazi retreat, the movement was at its strongest point since the German conquest of Czechoslovakia. Thousands of men had joined in the past few weeks and increased Allied air drops had provided them with small artillery field pieces as well as rifles and machine guns. The movement even had its own "air force"—half a dozen patched-up civilian planes used mainly to spot *Wehrmacht* patrols.

"This artillery group at Zoldau," Pine said excitedly. "How long would it take to get a messenger through to them?"

"Three or four hours." The old man shrugged. "The woods are thick and the snow is deep. Maybe…."

"What kind of weapons do you have in the village?"

"One machine gun and several rifles. A little ammunition."

"It'll have to do," Pine grunted.

"What are you planning?" the old man asked.

"I just came through that pass," Pine said. "I saw a dozen places where the snow in the mountains is so heavy a sneeze could start an avalanche. A couple of well-placed howitzer shells could bring a million tons of the stuff crashing down. By the time the Germans dug their way out or found a new route, half of them will have starved to death. It'd take a whole Nazi army out of the war, maybe for months."

"But the artillery is 14 miles away," Preslov protested.

"Then we'll have to hold the Germans back until they can get here."

"Impossible," Preslov snorted.

"Not if we mount the machine gun above a narrow turn in the pass, where no more than a few men can get through at a time. We only have to hold out an hour or two before we get help."

"With a few old men and a girl?" Preslov said. "Most of the people here have never fired a gun in their lives."

"We have to try," Pine said grimly. "Think of it this way—you'll be accomplishing more in one day than the entire Czech resistance has since the start of the war."

They were silent for some moments when he had finished. Then a fat woman put her hands over her face and began to cry, the tears leaking through her fingers. "They will do terrible things to us," she sobbed. "They will beat us and burn us and rape us."

"Show me a man that won't," Elena said furiously. "They're all the same. Even our beloved Partisans. They've only got one thing on their minds. I spent more time shaking them out of my blankets than I did killing…"

CZECH PARTISANS (above) from region around Tovenau, where Pine escaped, were ready to cooperate when the American announced his daring "Snow Gun" plan . . .

"I will have to discuss it with my people," Preslov said. "You will wait here."

While Pine stood by impatiently, Preslov called an impromptu town meeting. The result of the meeting was later described by British war correspondent Hugh Bullitt as "an incredibly brave decision, especially in view of the fact that the Tovenau townspeople were largely untutored peasants, with no real understanding of the conflict swirling about them..."

"We will help you stop the Germans as best we can," Preslov said when he returned to Pine. "My grandson will go for the artillery group. He is only 12, but he runs like a deer. Now you must eat and rest. I will find the right place to set up the machine gun."

The American didn't protest when a woman led him to Preslov's hut. He lay down on the crude cot and tried to sleep. Through the doorway he could see a sullen, lead-colored sky above the snow-capped Carpathian peaks. Outside he could hear voices as Preslov's grandson was summoned and told what he must do. After a few minutes Elena came in carrying a bowl of soup and a tin of biscuits.

"Keep your hands to yourself," she shouted as soon as she was inside the door. "Pig! You're like all the others. I should have known."

SHE PUT the food on the floor and went toward Pine unbuttoning her jacket and screaming abuse at him. Now he realized her weird behavior was for the benefit of the other villagers, an act to convince them she was being true to her husband.

"Show some respect for a married woman," she screeched, sitting on the edge of Pine's bed. She peeled off her jacket and the shirt under it, revealing her firm, straining bosom.

"I don't want to be a killjoy, but I'd rather have the soup," Pine said meanly. "It's been two months since I had anything resembling a decent meal and..."

"Beast, beast," the girl howled, feverishly kissing his face and neck. "I'll teach you to behave that way with a good girl. I'll—"

"How much of this are you putting on?" Pine asked grabbing her wrists so she wouldn't slap him again. "I can't believe anyone's as big a nut as you're acting."

"And I can't believe anyone's as dead as you're acting," the girl said quietly. "I made a mistake. I'll go and let you have your soup."

"No, you don't," Pine said pulling her to him. His hands moved around to press on her back. "I'm not dead and you didn't make any mistake. Stick around for the sleigh ride."

"Filthy brute," the girl screamed happily, hooking an arm about his neck to yank him hard against her. "I refuse, I refuse. I'll be true to my husband."

After their lovemaking ended and the girl had departed, Pine slept, the first untroubled rest he had had since his capture by the Germans. The thought that in a few hours he would be able to strike back at his tormentors gave him a momentary feeling of peace....

TECH Sergeant Vincent Pine's strange journey across half of Europe had begun two months earlier. An ordnance expert, Pine had been at Stalingrad as a member of an American cadre instructing the Russians in the use of lend-lease equipment. In the final days of the frantic battle for the city, Captain Willi Jekel's First Scorpion Company, shock troops of the Nazi Fourth Army, spearheaded an abortive counterattack. They fought in the streets of the city for three days, then retreated with nothing to show for their efforts but a single Allied prisoner— Vincent Pine.

Like other POWs taken along on the Nazi's long trek out of Russia, Pine knew he was still alive only because he might be useful to the Germans as a hostage. The retreating *Wehrmacht* liked to drive groups of prisoners ahead of them, hoping that the sight of captive Russian soldiers would deter guerrilla bands from swooping down on their columns. Nine out of 10 times, this strategy failed.

A week after the retreat began, Pine was brought before Captain Jekel, an almost legendary figure on the Eastern Front. He had the thick, squared-off build of a concrete block and a head as bulky and bald as a gleaming helmet.

"So you're the American prize we picked up," The Nazi roared as Pine approached. "We will talk. You will tell me about your country and I will tell you about mine. But first I have an assignment for you. This burning of the villages is becoming an annoyance. We need the food these selfish Communists have been hoarding."

Jekel was standing in the burned out ruins of a Russian village with three of his junior officers. It was the third totally devastated small settlement they had come upon in as many days.

"What do you want me to do?" Pine asked. "Whip up a batch of cookies?"

At this point Pine was still a lounging, easygoing man. Born in Piedmont, Missouri, he had been a career soldier for ten years, the type who enjoyed the lazy pointlessness of peacetime army life. Even two years of war hadn't blunted his good nature. It was the brutalities of the German retreat which would produce the embittered hardcase who rode into Tovenau two months later.

"You are very amusing," Jekel complimented him, a beaming smile of approval on his broad, beefy face. "Very funny. But, no, we do not want your cookies. We will be at another village in an hour. When they realize who we are, the people will burn it as the others have done. But suppose they saw an American—a Russian ally—approaching—accompanied by two of our people, of course? They would permit him to enter, wouldn't they? He could talk to them. He could explain that we Germans intend them no harm, that we wish to be friendly with them. He could convince them not to burn their village. Then, when we arrived, the food would be there for us."

"Don't hold your breath that long, buddy," Pine said. "Cookies are the best I can do."

"Perhaps I can persuade you," Jekel said. Though his voice was still pleasant, his huge hands had become knotted fists.

As the big Nazi started toward him, Pine crouched a little with his hands going high and wide. When the two men were a foot apart, Jekel lifted a fist ear-high and chopped it down and in. As he did, Pine lunged forward, both hands open and grabbing. The movement brought him inside the German's chopping arc. As his hands closed on Jekel's collar, Pine tucked his chin against his chest, then turtled it straight out ahead of him. The top of his head slammed full into Jekel's broad face. The Nazi fell back with blood streaming from his broken nose.

"That was a very unwise thing to do," Jekel said, nodding as though he weren't at all angry and wiping blood from his face with the back of his wrist. "Very unwise. All right, hold him."

The three other Germans moved in on Pine. The lanky but agile American split one man's lip and popped a tooth out of another's mouth before they had him under control, his arms twisted back and pulled up, so that he was bent at the waist and hanging forward helplessly. At that point he was nothing but a target. Willi Jekel came toward him again, winding a length of iron chain around his fist.

When the chained fist smashed into the side of Pine's face, he and the men holding him lost their balance and stumbled back like drunks on ice. The Germans kept their grip on him however, pulling him around for another punch from Jekel. The second blow broke Pine's cheekbone. The third and last stretched him limp and unconscious in the snow.

"Put him in one of the ambulance trucks and see that he is cared for," Jekel ordered. "He will still do what we want. He must. We will starve if these cursed peasants continue to destroy their food."

Most of the Nazis still had several ounces of dried bread in their sacks when they began to retreat, but this meager food supply was quickly exhausted. Afterward, it became a pure and simple problem of living off the land. But since the peasants were burning their villages, this rapidly proved to be no solution to the German predicament.

Still, when a village was burned and deserted, the cats remained. Everything else living departed but the cats stayed behind—great, bloated, heavy-footed creatures padding about like old dogs. The Nazis killed and ate them; many were reduced to violent retching as a result, but when it was either cat meat or nothing, the men ate and retched and ate some more.

THEY ATE the mice that crawled into their blankets for warmth. They boiled and ate the lice that nested on their bodies. Horse was a delicacy and the roads leading back from Stalingrad were dotted with the skeletons of the beasts that had carried the Nazis forward to "certain victory" just months earlier. Most of the horses died of hunger or exhaustion after days of floundering through snow up to their bellies, but some were simply pulled down and killed by the ravenous German soldiers.

For several days after his vicious beating at Jekel's hands, Sergeant Pine rode in one of the lumbering ambulance trucks accompanying the column. He shared the rear of the vehicle with a German tank driver who bitterly resented Pine's presence. "Why don't we just drop this Yankee swine off in the snow?" the gunner would shout to Sherdel, the Nazi medical corpsman who was treating them. "Good German soldiers have to walk while he rides like a king and eats the food we should keep to ourselves."

The tank driver, his knee shattered by a shell splinter, had been brought into the truck screaming like a banshee. A glue-like fluid oozed out of the wound and a thigh bone protruded, jagged and raw. Sherdel, the medic, had bandaged splints about it but there were times when the man could not bear the pain, when he screamed and begged to die. Sherdel himself, a thin man with a face so devoid of expression it might have been formed in a wax mold, was suffering from scurvy which had rotted his gums to the point where an unbearable odor issued from his mouth.

"Captain Jekel knows what he's doing," Sherdel said in answer to the tank driver's question. "If things get worse, we might be able to barter prisoners for food. You never know."

As they continued to roll westward, the Russian guerrillas' harassment of the column continued. On one occasion a bomb exploded at the rear of the truck and a shrapnel splinter sliced off the head of a Nazi infantryman slogging behind their vehicle. Other soldiers plodded

past the decapitated body, too weary even to haul it to the side of
the road.

"Another mouth less to feed," Pine said sarcastically. It was one of
the first remarks the American had made since he'd been placed in the
truck. The condition of his face and mouth had made speech impossible.

In the Ukraine they hit black earth, which rain had turned into an
impassable mire. A hundred-mile-long column of tanks and other Nazi
Fourth Army vehicles sat helpless while guerrillas hit them with quick,
deadly night raids. Rumor had it that more than 5,000 men had fallen at
the guerrillas' hands in one night. Red army artillery boomed ominously
out of the north. In the ambulance truck, Sherdel and the tank driver
scratched lice from their bodies, cracked them between their nails and
cursed the leaders who had gotten them into such a mess. Pine listened
impassively.

"Tracks would roll right over this muck," the tank driver whined,
reduced to snivels and tears by his pain and the fear that a guerrilla
bullet would find him. "It's the wheels that are stopping us."

*(This same point was later made by a number of German generals
trying to explain their defeat in Russia. The trackless German vehicles, they
claimed, were simply no match in mobility in snow and mud for the Russian
vehicles—*Ed.*)*

The Fourth Army was bogged down in mud for three days before
the ground hardened sufficiently for their vehicles to start moving
again. By now Pine was out of the ambulance and plodding through the
slush with the Germans. He could see for miles along the black road,
a road clogged by the enormous, sluggish snake that was the German
army in sullen retreat.

"What a mess," he said to the soldiers who were guarding him.
"Half this crowd won't ever see Mama's *strudel* again." But the Germans
were too dispirited to even answer his taunts.

A SHORT time after leaving the ambulance, Pine was again brought
before Captain Willi Jekel. As before, he found the Nazi in a burned
out Russian village with several of his officers standing around him.
But something new had been added. A redheaded boy in a British
Army uniform sat in a chair with his arms and legs tied. He managed a
strained grin as Pine came up.

"Ah, the American Sergeant Pine again," Jekel greeted him in his
customarily exuberant way. "And this is the British Private Hawkins.
Private Roger Hawkins. Private Hawkins was taken at Stalingrad by
one of our other companies. He was doing the same kind of work there
you were."

Despite his bouncy manner, Jekel was showing the ravages of the disease that was sweeping through the entire German army. The flesh hung loose on his emaciated face, his eyes were holes black-ringed as though with India ink and his mouth was a cavernous wreck, the teeth rotting in the gums.

"What's on your mind, Jekel?" Pine asked.

"There was no food when we entered the village," the Nazi said with a wide movement of his huge arms. "The peasants even killed and burned their cats this time. I spoke to you about this matter before, American. Now I do it again. There is another village a short ride from here. These ignorant Russians are fond of Americans. If you explain to them—"

"No dice, Jekel," Pine said. "Now if you need help, bring in your friends again and let's get it—"

He stopped as Jekel reached into his pocket, took out the chain and begin winding it around his fist. He was being very orderly and methodical. When he had the chain wound to his satisfaction, he turned, slowly and deliberately, and drove his fist into Private Hawkins' chest, knocking the English youth over on his back, still tied to the chair. The boy's gasp was as sharp and clear as ripping cloth and his face distorted with pain as two of Jekel's men put the chair back on its legs. Once more the Nazi drew his chained fist back and the boy opened his mouth in an effort to speak, but no words came out.

"Wait a minute, Jekel," Pine cried.

"Yes?"

"Lay off him. I'll go."

"Don't do it, Yank," the boy wheezed. "The old lady hit me harder than that for pinching the girl downstairs."

"If they burn the village, I'll beat Private Hawkins till you won't recognize him," Jekel said. "And if you don't come back, I'll kill him."

"Stay away, Yank," the boy insisted. "It's all right with…."

"Bring the horse," Jekel commanded.

A decrepit grey nag was led over to them. Pine mounted and rode in the direction pointed out to him by Captain Jekel.

"The name of the village is Uvabelsk," Jekel called after him.

Uvabelsk was a guerrilla village. The men and women who lived there spent days at a time away from home in hit and run attacks on the Nazi hordes plodding across Russia. To those grim fighters—hardened to violence, hardened to atrocities—the fate of the English boy in Jekel's hands was of no great significance.

"Millions are dying here," their grizzled leader shrugged after Pine rode in. "One more makes no difference. We can not permit the Nazis to have our food. That is all there is to it. We will burn the village."

Pine tried to argue them out of it but he didn't have a chance. They were determined. The English private would have to be sacrificed to the Russians' efforts to grind down the retreating Nazis. If scurvy and typhus and lice and hunger were to be weapons in that vicious battle, let them be used with maximum effectiveness, the village leader declared.

"You will not find any villages here that will do what Jekel wants," the guerrilla went on. "It will be the same with all of them. Now, we must burn the village and flee. You are welcome to come with us."

"No, I'll go back," Pine said. "They'll kill him if I don't."

"At least have some food before you go," the guerrilla leader urged, pressing several thick chunks of bread into his hands. "Take some for your friend. Maybe you will be able to get it to him without the German noticing."

"It's worth a try," Pine said glumly.

He left shortly afterward. Minutes later, a ribbon of black smoke wound into the dear sky and the village of Uvabelsk went up in flames. Pine rode back in the direction he had come until he saw the black scorpion flags of Jekel's company flutter before him. The redheaded English boy still sat tied to his chair. His upper teeth were damped down hard over his lower lip and his face was white with expectation. He was frightened, but determined not to show it.

"Well?" Captain Jekel said.

"You saw the smoke," Pine said. "I couldn't do anything with them."

He turned away quickly, but not fast enough to prevent himself from seeing Jekel's chained fist make contact with the side of the boy's head. The chair went all the way over, so that Hawkins lay with his head in a pool of blood.

"Hand over the food the villagers gave you for Hawkins," Jekel sneered, guessing Pine's secret. "The boy will be your patient from now on. You will have other chances to spare him. Perhaps you'll be more successful next time."

But as the Nazis trudged westward, the experience of Uvabelsk was repeated in one village after another. The peasants sympathized with Pine's predicament but their primary goal was still to deprive the Nazis of food.

"We'd shoot our own mothers first," they said at Mov, tossing torches into their homes.

"Our souls would shrivel in Hell if we let them have so much as a crust of our bread," they said at Lubiovna, and did the same thing.

Tulitsky was a vast complex of tiny villages, perhaps two hundred of them. Their farm animals numbered in the hundreds. Fruits and vegetables flourished in their fields. Bread was made in every hut.

"We must have that food," Jekel roared at Pine and shook the battered Hawkins until it seemed his neck would snap. "I'll pound this whelp to pulp if we don't!"

"Don't do it, Yank," the boy rasped. "Just go and keep riding. Why the hell do you keep coming back?"

There were times Pine wondered why himself. The boy had been beaten and stomped until he looked as though he'd been run over by a tank. His face was a swollen mass of purplish bruises, the nose broken, his front teeth knocked out. Several ribs had been broken and it was agony for him to breathe. It was unlikely that even with the best of medical care, he could survive Jekel's tortures. Yet Pine kept coming back from his futile missions. Maybe it was Hawkins' boyishness that did it. Maybe that was what made the tough, hard-faced American determined to save him.

"I'll do all I can," he said now and mounted the grey horse. He was in Tulitsky an hour later. But here too the response was the same as he'd gotten everywhere else.

"We'd drown our children before we'd give the Nazis food," the head man said. Then the torches were applied. Thousands of villagers fled the blaze, carrying their possessions on their backs. Behind them Tulitsky burned to cinders and only the fat, padding cats remained to prowl its blackened ruins.

Jekel went berserk when he saw the black smoke rising. The savagery of his assault on Hawkins exceeded anything he had done before. He beat the boy to the ground with his chained fist, hitting him again and again. When the beating was over, the boy bled from a dozen places and could barely see. His voice was no more than a whisper, he sprawled on the ground—his body as disjointed and awkward as a corpse thrown off a truck. Pine knelt beside him.

"We'll be in the Carpathians in a day, Yank," Hawkins whispered as Pine tried to make him comfortable. "I heard them talking. They're going to go through the Dukla Pass. They've—" Pain sent a series of tremors through the boy's body. He bit down on his lip to keep from crying out. When the seizure passed, he spoke again: "The Krauts are too sick and hungry to go on much longer, but once they're through the Carpathians they'll be fed and taken care of. They'll re-group up and...."

Agony seized him again and he was unable to go on. A few minutes later they were ordered to get moving. Pine hoisted the semi-conscious boy onto the grey horse and the First Scorpion Company resumed its stumbling retreat.

It was a ghastly Captain Jekel who ordered Pine to ride ahead to Tovenau. The once powerful Nazi had lost a third of his weight and illness had lined and yellowed his flesh.

"Hawkins won't die, American," he swore, his eyes deep sockets of hate. "I promise you that. If we don't get food at Tovenau I'll do things to him you've never even seen in nightmares and still he won't die. That's my promise. Now go and remember what you'll see when you return if they burn that village."

Private Hawkins had already been taken off the grey horse when Pine approached him. The boy's eyes had a peculiar brightness the American hadn't seen there before. "Old Jekel's outsmarted himself," the boy chuckled weakly. "I'm bleeding real bad inside. He's killed me, that's what he's done. You can tell it, too, can't you, Yank?" Pine looked away to hide his pity. He knew Hawkins had spoken the truth—he would be dead before Pine even reached Tovenau. The American was horrified to discover that the fact almost gave him a feeling of relief. Now he was free to act.

Jekel could no longer use the English boy's life as a weapon against him.

"Tovenau is right on the other side of the Dukla Pass," the boy said. "Good luck, Yank."

"So long, buddy," Pine mumbled and mounted the grey horse.

For what seemed like an eternity he rode through the winding pass, lined on both sides by steep rock walls. With dull eyes, he studied the shelves of snow piled on the cliff tops, wondering what it would take to bring them crashing down.

Then he was in Tovenau, where his horse tripped over the hidden wire planted by Old Preslov and the other Partisans in the village…

About an hour after he fell asleep in Preslov's hut, Pine was awakened by the touch of Elena's hand on his shoulder. "The Germans are almost here," she said simply. "We have much to do."

Pine nodded and lurched to his feet. "By the way," he asked her teasingly, remembering their moments of lovemaking. "Didn't you say something about a husband?"

The black-haired girl shrugged. "You don't think he's so clean and chaste, do you? I'm as much entitled to a good time as he is. Especially when it might be my last. This plan of yours is crazy, American. The Germans will overrun us long before the Partisan artillery can get here."

When they went outside, the village looked deserted. Elena explained that the children and old women had been sent into the hills to hide. Preslov and the men of the town had already moved and taken their positions in the Dukla Pass, where Elena and the American were to join them. Preslov had tried to give Pine as much time to rest as possible.

A ten-minute walk through the snow brought them to the spot where the Partisans had dug in. Following Pine's instructions, they had mounted the machine gun on a ledge opposite a narrow point—less than 10 feet wide—in the pass. Sheer rock walls jutted up on both sides of the defile ahead. Some of the village men crouching behind trees and rocks carried rifles but most were armed with such makeshift weapons as pitchforks and clubs.

Old Preslov approached Pine and Elena. "All is ready," he said.

"Do you think your grandson made it?" The girl asked.

"He's strong and a fast runner," the old man said hopefully.

"We'd better keep talking to a minimum from now on," Pine murmured. "Voices carry a hell of a long way in cold air."

PINE APPOINTED himself to man the machine gun and Elena volunteered to feed him ammunition. The Partisans had already felled a large tree to provide cover for the gun. Now there was nothing to do but wait. The sun slowly went down, throwing ever-lengthening grey shadows over the expanses of snow.

Then the first, dark-uniformed figure crept through the defile. Half a minute later, another could be seen. Then another, until finally a line of a dozen men was visible, their breaths misting in the freezing air. "It's an advance patrol," Pine whispered. "Pass the word back to let them through."

Preslov started to protest but Pine silenced him: "We need time, remember? The sound of shots will speed up the movement of the main force."

Regretfully, Preslov gave the order. Soon the German scouts rounded another turn in the pass and were out of sight again.

"Have some of your men keep an eye on our rear," Pine said. "Those guys will be hustling back this way as soon as the shooting starts."

Overhead, the roar of a light aircraft engine could be heard. A small plane swooped down at treetop level over the pass, then banked to the right and disappeared in the grey sky. "That's one of ours," Preslov whispered in surprise.

"They could be checking on your grandson's story," Pine said hopefully.

"Which also means they probably haven't started moving the artillery yet," Elena added bitterly.

MARCHING THROUGH POLAND, these Nazi 4th Army men were pictured after battle with Sgt. Pine's partisan force

As evening came on, Pine prayed for bright moonlight. Even though the glare off the snow gave them better than normal night vision, the defile ahead was shrouded in shadows. In total darkness, enough Germans could slip through to quickly overrun the Partisans' precarious position.

Elena, crouched beside him, hissed a warning.

The plodding men of Captain Willi Jekel's First Scorpion Company looked more like a derelict rabble than crack German shock troops as they plodded through the pass in a ragged, four-abreast file. Pine looked for Jekel himself, hoping that he would be at the head of his company, but he couldn't spot the Nazi's block-like form.

"Let them reach that rock," Pine whispered to Preslov, indicating a black lump about 25 yards from the felled tree. "Tell your men to fire low. Aim for their middles."

They waited. The Nazis came on, more than 50 men visible now.

"All right," Pine said and opened up with the machine gun. Behind him and on both sides, he heard the sharp *whap-whap* of small caliber rifles. A dozen Scorpion men went down in the first burst. Others dropped on their faces, scrabbling in the snow for some kind of cover, or ran back toward the turn in the pass. A few, reduced to shambling, almost mindless robots by the long march, just stood there dazed. One by one they toppled, like stationary wooden targets. Then Pine lowered the gun's muzzle, sprayed the men who had thrown themselves to the ground until all of them were motionless mounds in the snow.

The skirmish took less than 20 seconds. When it was over, the defile was again empty and silent. "The rest are backed up around the bend," Pine told Elena. "We really took them by surprise."

"What will they do now?" she asked.

"Wait a few minutes then move in again," he guessed. "Chances are they'll figure it was a hit and run attack."

PINE WAS right. Five minutes later, a new group of Nazi soldiers ducked out of the defile. Only this time, they kept low and ran at a cautious crouch. Once more Pine felt the breech of the machine gun buck in his hands, saw Germans crumble in the snow.

At their rear the distinctive crack of German rifles could be heard. "The patrol is coming back," Pine shouted at Preslov. Unable to leave the machine gun, Pine darted anxious glances over his shoulder, saw the old men of Tovenau locked in hand to hand combat with the Nazi scouts.

Eight elderly villagers were killed in the fight, Pine learned a few minutes later. One of them—a man of 83—had perished of a heart attack while charging a burly Nazi non-com twice his size.

Once more the pass grew quiet. But Pine knew the Germans' next move would be a full-scale onslaught, against which the band of villagers would be helpless. With the inexorable force of an entire army backed up behind them, Jekel's troops would have to move soon. There was no time for subtle strategies under the circumstances.

"Oh, Jesus," Pine croaked as an armored halftrack swung around the bend, spitting fire from its gunslits. The American aimed at the small opening in front of the driver's eyes, but he knew it would be a miracle if he hit anything.

Like a huge armadillo, the car lunged up the slope toward their position. In its wake came a horde of Germans, a brown inundation engulfing the Partisans. A few Germans went down but the rest stormed through the villagers' panicky fire. "Fall back to the village!" Preslov bellowed, just before a shot burst his face apart. Pine swept the machine gun up in his arms and started running, the heat of the barrel penetrating the sleeves of his coat and searing his forearms. Elena, unencumbered, pounded past him.

Then Pine slipped on the wet ground, stumbled to his knees. The machine gun slithered from his hands and buried itself breech-first in the mud. The American regained his footing, sobbed in frustration as he yanked the weapon free. In back of him he heard a howl of animal rage. Whirling, he saw Willi Jekel's bull-like form running toward him. Hatred overcoming his fear, Pine raised the machine gun, cradling the barrel on his left forearm. He pressed the trigger but nothing happened. Realizing that mud had clogged the firing mechanism, he used the gun as a club, swinging it by the barrel. The heavy breech chopped into the side of Jekel's neck with a quivering thud. The blow would have killed a normal man, but it barely slowed Jekel down. The two men's bodies came together, hands ripping at each other's limbs, fingers clawing for eyes.

They were still struggling in the deep mud, like primeval lizards in a riverbed, when the first fusillade of shells whistled overhead. An explosion shook the ground beneath them.

Another. Then another. Light cracked open the dark sky over the Dukla Pass. The sound of the long-awaited Partisan artillery seemed to give Pine new, almost exultant strength. His hands had found a death grip on Jekel's throat. As they closed, he heard an awesome, ear-stunning roar—the unmistakable sound of an avalanche. He flung Jekel's limp body away from him, like a man tossing a dead rat in a garbage can, turned to see a white-and-brown cascade plunge into the pass. On and on it fell, filling the narrow defile with thousands of tons of snow and earth....

In his prize-winning article on the Tovenau action, correspondent Hugh Bullitt included a long interview with Vincent Pine, who remained in the army after the war. He is now the first sergeant of an armored company stationed in West Germany.

"After I killed Jekel, I cut out toward Zoldau, where I knew there was a heavy concentration of Partisans," Pine told the reporter. "Couldn't see any sense in going to Tovenau, since I knew Jekel's men were bound to take the place before I even reached it. I heard later the cruds wiped out all of the villagers they could get their hands on. I don't know what happened to Elena, but I figure she probably got clear. She was too tough and smart to hang around when it wouldn't do anybody any good."

The closing of the Dukla Pass stranded the bulk of the German Fourth Army.

"In the following weeks, bands of sick and starving Nazis actually sought out Partisans and begged to surrender," Bullitt wrote. "According to conservative estimates, the gallant sacrifice of the Tovenau villagers led to the death of at least 30,000 *Wehrmacht* soldiers. Perhaps a third of the Fourth Army eventually returned to its home territory, but it was never to be a significant element in the war again.

"Of Tovenau itself, nothing remains." ✳

"The Girl Trader"
Written as Roland Empey
Male, February 1971
Illustration by Samson Pollen

with 19 men aboard and Ensign
Ross Rogers in charge. Elsewhere, strung out over miles of
black ocean, were the rest of
the Indianapolis personnel, some
grouped together in twos and
threes, others alone.

The sun rose and blazed
down on them out of a cloudless sky. It burned them raw.
It played hell with their eyes.
Even closing them didn't help;
the blazing red ball burned
right through their lids. The
waves buffeted them, tossed them
about, exhausted them. Many
were still caught in the long,
sticky carpet of fuel oil, their
black heads poking up through
it like charred tree stumps. The
oil on their sun-scorched bodies
was an additional agony, a sandpaper scraping of bleeding skin.

The writhing, retching
torment of those who had swallowed the oil continued and some
pulled off their jackets and let
themselves sink rather than en-

Stag, May 1963
COVER ARTIST: MORT KÜNSTLER

While the men on the I-58 celebrated with sake, the survivors of the torpedoed Indianapolis floundered in the Pacific—and for three and a half days no one knew they were there. It was a wartime disaster that led to the only court-martial in history of a US Navy CO for losing his ship in action.

by WALTER KAYLIN

AT 11:30 on the night of July 29, 1945, Lieutenant Commander Mochitsura Hashimoto retired to the Shinto shrine aboard his submarine I-58 and said a brief prayer:

"Give us good hunting, all-knowing one," he pleaded. "Send us a great American ship to attack and sink."

Hashimoto had been praying for action for three and a half years, but his god had never answered him. He had been a torpedo officer in the attack on Pearl Harbor, but his ship had taken no active part in the assault. Later, he had been transferred to a submarine of the coastal defense class, but he hadn't seen an enemy ship during his entire tour. Still later, he had been given command of the powerful I-58, but he had encountered only one insignificant tanker and wasn't even sure he had hit *it*.

The failure of the I-58 to sight an American warship was particularly irritating to Hashimoto. One of the famed I-Class boats, the I-58 was one of the biggest, fastest and best-armed submarines in the world: 355 feet long, 30-foot beam, 2140 tons displacement. Two diesel engines produced 4700 horsepower and gave her a cruising speed of 14 knots on the surface and seven knots submerged. She had a range of 16,000 miles and could stay out of port for three months. She carried 19 wake-less, oxygen-fueled torpedoes that traveled at a fantastic 48 knots with a range of 17,000 feet.

In addition to its nineteen powerful Type-95 torpedoes, the I-58 carried six kaitens: human suicide torpedoes. The word kaiten means "revolving the heavens" or, more popularly, "turning the tide." Developed fairly late in the war,

... 108-Hour Mid-Ocean

Men clung to debris and each other. *Indianapolis* sank so fast—12 minutes—many of crew had no chance to grab life jackets.

the kaitens were the Japanese last hope of "turning the tide"—that is, throwing back the avalanching sweep of American conquest. The kaiten pilot came from the same mold as the kamikaze pilot. His only goal was to give his life for his Emperor, and his suicide craft had been armed with an explosive warhead to make that a certainty. Once he was shot out of the mother ship, there was no possibility of recovery.

Having sent off his prayer, of July 29, Hashimoto made his way to the conning tower, took a look about through the periscope and ordered the I-58 to surface. As usual there was nothing to be seen . . . nothing. The gods had ignored him again. Or had they?

"Bearing red, nine zero degrees, possible enemy ship!"

The roar had come from his chief torpedo officer, Toshio Tanaka. A black lump stood out against the horizon something less than six miles off, with the moon behind it. Hashimoto gave the order to dive, then picked up the object in his periscope again. An eerie, tingling sensation traveled down his spine. It was coming straight toward him and it was enormous—a black, looming monster of a ship.

"Torpedoes ready," he said hoarsely. "Kaitens prepare."

Still the huge ship plowed on toward him. (*Continued on page* 79)

Capt. Charles McVay, commanding *Indianapolis*, survived sinking to face Navy court.

Ordeal . . . 500 Dead . . .

300 Still Afloat . . .

A pilot spotted the survivors by accident and ships raced to scene. Last of 316 men rescued had been in water over four days.

AT 11:30 on the night of July 29, 1945, Lieutenant Commander Mochitsura Hashimoto retired to the Shinto shrine aboard his submarine I-58 and said a brief prayer:

"Give us good hunting, all-knowing one," he pleaded. "Send us a great American ship to attack and sink."

Hashimoto had been praying for action for three-and-a-half years, but his god had never answered him. He had been a torpedo officer in the attack on Pearl Harbor, but his ship had taken no active part in the assault. Later, he had been transferred to a submarine of the coastal defense class, but he hadn't seen an enemy ship during his entire tour. Still later, he had been given command of the powerful I-58, but he had encountered only one insignificant tanker and wasn't even sure he had hit *it*.

The failure of the I-58 to sight an American warship was particularly irritating to Hashimoto. One of the famed I-Class boats, the I-58 was one of the biggest, fastest and best-armed submarines in the world: 355 feet long, 30-foot beam, 2,140 tons displacement. Two diesel engines produced 4,700 horsepower and gave her a cruising speed of 14 knots on the surface and seven knots submerged. She had a range of 16,000 miles and could stay out of port for three months. She carried 19 wakeless, oxygen-fueled torpedoes that traveled at a fantastic 48 knots with a range of 17,000 feet.

In addition to its nineteen powerful Type-95 torpedoes, the I-58 carried six *kaitens*: human suicide torpedoes. The word *kaiten* means "revolving the heavens" or, more popularly, "turning the tide." Developed fairly late in the war, the kaitens were the Japanese last hope of "turning the tide"—that is, throwing back the avalanching sweep of American conquest. The kaiten pilot came from the same mold as the kamikaze pilot. His only goal was to give his life for his Emperor, and his suicide craft had been armed with an explosive warhead to make that a certainty. Once he was shot out of the mother ship, there was no possibility of recovery.

Having sent off his prayer of July 29, Hashimoto made his way to the conning tower, took a look about through the periscope and ordered the I-58 to surface. As usual there was nothing to be seen … nothing.

The gods had ignored him again. Or had they?

"Bearing red, nine zero degrees, possible enemy ship!"

The roar had come from his chief torpedo officer, Toshio Tanaka. A black lump stood out against the horizon something less than six miles off, with the moon behind it. Hashimoto gave the order to dive, then picked up the object in his periscope again. An eerie, tingling sensation traveled down his spine. It was coming straight toward him and it was enormous—a black, looming monster of a ship.

"Torpedoes ready," he said hoarsely. "Kaitens prepare."

Still the huge ship plowed on toward him.

Its straight-line approach awed Hashimoto, its towering bulk reached up into the sky like an enormous, rolling office building. Tension gripped the submarine commander and was quickly communicated to every man aboard the I-58. They stood still as statues. The only sound was the whispered plea of the kaitens to "Send us, send us, permit us a noble death."

The great ship didn't swerve, didn't zigzag. It came on as though it owned the seas. Hashimoto's face was damp with perspiration. He sucked in his breath, then let it out in a harsh, dry rasp:

"Fire torpedoes!"

The release-switch gunned the torpedoes out, one every three seconds. In a quarter of a minute, six were on their way, fanning out within a spread of three degrees. As they sped toward their oncoming target, Hashimoto hung onto the periscope as though frozen to it. Behind him his men were still, silent stone figures. Then …

"She's hit! She's hit!"

The submariners screamed for joy, hugged each other, begged for a chance to see. The great ship was reeling, rocking. A burst of orange flame shot up above her forward turret. Internal explosions spread long, jagged fissures across her massive hull. Sheets of blazing light rolled skyward, the disintegrating superstructure clearly visible against them.

Tears of joy filled Hashimoto's eyes, but he didn't forget his job. The big ship was still afloat. He would have to prepare to hit her again. Quickly he ordered the I-58 submerged and the torpedo tubes reloaded. As this was being done, the kaitens crowded around him—black-garbed, fanatical men—demanding that he explode them at the crippled ship. "Send us. Let us die in glory."

"We will see," Hashimoto promised them. "When we surface again, we will see what the situation is."

But when his periscope poked above the water again, Hashimoto met a sight he hadn't thought possible. All around him the seas were clear. The big warship, last seen belching her insides into the sky, had vanished. There was only one possible answer: she had sunk. The crew went wild again. Sake was brought and toasts were drunk. Even the disappointed kaitens managed to get into the spirit of the celebration.

EVERYONE in that exultant crew knew they had scored a tremendous victory. Yet not even Hashimoto himself had any idea of the actual scope of his accomplishment. In the 15 seconds it took for his three torpedoes to hit (three others missed), he had brought about the greatest sea disaster in the history of the United States Navy. At the very moment he and his men were going wild on sake, some 800 men were floundering in the black waters of the Pacific, *and for the next three and a half days, not a soul on earth knew they were there.* Close to 500 perished and it was just luck—sheer blind luck—that any at all were found and saved.

There had never before been such a snafu, such a combination of stupidity, incompetence and confusion. There was a court-martial as a result, the only court-martial in this nation's history of a commanding officer for losing his ship in action. Another result was a controversy that has raged within the Navy since 1945 and will undoubtedly continue for years to come. The controversy boils down to four words: Who was to blame…?

The cruiser *Indianapolis* came through the first three years of the war in better shape than many people thought she would. She had been commissioned ten years before the war began and well before radar had come into use. Accordingly, all the special equipment that was built right into the newer ships had to be piled aboard the *Indianapolis* before she could be sent out on her wartime assignments.

The result was to significantly decrease her stability. According to Admiral Raymond Spruance, Commander of the Fifth Fleet (who sometimes used the *Indianapolis* as his flagship), the big ship would sink quickly if she ever took a well-placed torpedo hit; her metacentric height (capacity for taking water inside the hull without capsizing) was inadequate.

Despite its vulnerability, the *Indianapolis* made significant contributions to the American effort at Iwo Jima and Okinawa, shooting down eight planes in that second campaign and raking the island with her heavy guns for a solid week before being hit by a kamikaze and having to withdraw. The suicide plane didn't hit the big cruiser directly, but its bomb plunged down through several decks, exploding in an oil bunker and damaging No. 4 shaft. Nine men were killed and 20 wounded.

Admiral Spruance moved over to the *New Mexico* and the

Indianapolis limped off to Keramo Retto to have her shaft repaired. Unfortunately, the job was botched and the big cruiser was next sent to Mare Island for major repairs.

When she was back in running order, she was sent to San Francisco to take on a top-secret cargo—a large crate and a small cylinder—and deliver it to Tinian. In the crate and cylinder were key elements of the first atom bomb scheduled for assembling in Tinian before being dropped on Japan. The *Indianapolis* left San Francisco on July 16. That same day Hashimoto's I-58 left the harbor of Kure on Honshu with orders to "harass enemy communications off the east coast of the Philippines."

The *Indianapolis* reached Tinian in ten days and unloaded her precious cargo. No one on board—including Captain Charles Butler McVay—knew what the cargo was, but the necessity for safe and fast delivery had been impressed on them and all hands felt pleased with their performance. The 2,090-mile leg from the Farallon Islands to Diamond Head on Oahu had been done in 74-and-a-half hours, a record that still stands.

The *Indianapolis'* next stop was Guam where she was to take on fuel, stores and ammunition, then proceed to Leyte for a 17-day retraining course before reporting to Vice Admiral Oldendorf, Commander of Task Force 95. Now that she was in tiptop shape again, Admiral Spruance was going to put his flag back aboard. How long that would be for was anybody's guess, but it was not expected to be too long. The Japanese were reeling under the blows of the B-29s; their surrender was expected any time now.

In this atmosphere of success and imminent victory, the *Indianapolis* sailed for Guam, took aboard the supplies being held there for her, then set out for Leyte.

THAT WAS July 27. The great old ship with her complement of almost 1,200 had just two days left to live....

The *Indianapolis* set out from Guam for Leyte at a time when certain safety precautions, routinely taken earlier in the war, were no longer considered essential. For one thing, a straight-line course between the two islands was taken rather than one of the more evasive routes that had been used earlier. For another, no escort was provided—the *Indianapolis* was on her own all the way. Finally, Captain McVay was told to "zigzag at your discretion" instead of being ordered to do so, as was done when the Japanese were still a threat.

For the next two days, things aboard the *Indianapolis* couldn't have been more relaxed. The men did their work, wrote letters, took their cholera shots. A movie was run off. The weather was hot at first, but then it began to fall off and by early evening of the 29th, the sea was fairly rough.

Texas-born Lieutenant (jg) Charles McKissick had the watch that evening, and Captain McVay came to the bridge several times to see that everything was all right. A fine-looking man of 46, Charles McVay was well liked by his officers and the enlisted men as well. He had been in the Navy 26 years and was accepted as a top-notch ship handler. Admiral Spruance himself had complimented him on his skill with the *Indianapolis*.

Now, on one of his visits to the bridge that fateful night of July 29, McVay said to McKissick "You may secure from zigzagging after twilight," which meant that if it were a dark night it would not be necessary to zigzag. Since it was indeed a dark night, McKissick gave the order to leave off zigzagging. From then on until the end, the *Indianapolis* traveled in a straight line.

As midnight neared, the *Indianapolis* was still surging steadily ahead at just under 16 knots. It was a hot night and many of the men had taken blankets out on deck, finding it too hot to sleep below. McKissick had completed his watch and been replaced by the gunnery officer, Commander Lipski. With Lipski on the bridge were Lieutenant Redmayne and Lieutenant (jg) McFarland. Third Class Vincent Allard was quartermaster of the watch. The sky was overcast, a few stars faintly visible. Captain McVay was asleep, but there was a voice tube beside him and he had given orders to be called in the event of anything unusual happening.

Two minutes after midnight....

A blast of incredible power rocked the great ship and a sheet of orange flame shot up high above it. A second blast close to the bridge followed the first and a pillar of water geysered up a hundred feet above the bow.

The blasts threw Captain McVay out of bed. His first thought was that the *Indianapolis* had been hit by another kamikaze. Naked (he slept that way), he made his way to the bridge to find the men of the watch unhurt and functioning, although all had been knocked down by the twin blasts. McVay realized now that it was no kamikaze that had hit the ship, but probably several torpedoes. Damage had been done—that was obvious. But it didn't seem to be too much to handle.

"Our list isn't too bad," he told Casey Moore, the damage control officer. "Go below and see how we're doing down there."

As Moore disappeared below, Captain McVay started back to his cabin to get his clothes. But his confidence of just a few moments earlier was already beginning to fade. The ship was behaving peculiarly: her bow was slipping into the sea rather than rising above it. The list was still only a few degrees to starboard, but the ship was slowing down, losing power. The lights weren't working. To a man of McVay's experience the meaning was clear: The *Indianapolis* had been gravely damaged below.

Quickly he instructed a radioman to send a distress signal, then put on his clothes and returned to the bridge. A moment later, Commander Joe Flynn climbed the ladder and joined him.

"We're taking water fast," Flynn said. "It looks to me as though we're through. I recommend we abandon her."

The second torpedo had been the crusher. It had blasted a tremendous hole amidships, blowing open the forward fire room (which immediately filled with water) and wrecking all power and communications systems in the forward half of the ship. All mains and oil tanks were ruptured, all cables set afire. A number of officers and men berthed forward were killed outright. The rest were trying to grope their way topside, stumbling through the black, spuming smoke, the maimed and burned screaming in pain, the unhurt trying to help their injured shipmates along.

Most of the foredeck was obscured from McVay's view by thick, furling smoke, but its radical downward tilt told him water was flooding in forward and pulling the bow down into the sea. Men were bunching up on the fantail and sliding down across the slanting oil-slicked deck toward the starboard rails. The stern was lifting, the bow dipping deeper. His ship's condition was now perfectly clear to McVay and he gave the only order left to give:

"Abandon ship! Abandon ship!"

They were over 300 miles from land and in waters teeming with sharks and barracuda. It was desperately urgent that rescuers come for them immediately, but none of McVay's messengers had returned from the radio shack. He decided to go see for himself. As he started down the ladder from the bridge, the *Indianapolis* heeled way over on her side. Already men were spilling into the water and McVay realized he'd never reach the radio room.

"Use the floater nets!" he shouted. "Get them against the stack."

But now the *Indianapolis* was tipping over still further, actually lying on her side with decks going straight up and down perpendicular to the water. She was settling quickly with the grey Pacific washing clear over her. Hundreds of men were in the water and scrambling about trying to find rafts or lifeboats to climb into—or debris to cling to. Many of the crew were naked, many badly hurt. The water was rising still higher over the big ship and now, a long, settling rush of it lifted McVay and carried him off. From the time of the first blast until the time the captain slid into the water, only 12 minutes had elapsed.

The *Indianapolis* went down in water two miles deep. Suction didn't prove to be the menace it has been in so many other sinkings. The big cruiser sank easily and almost without a ripple, disappearing beneath the surface and leaving some 800 men floundering about in the black night; the rest had been wiped out in the two torpedo explosions.

Some of the men died within minutes of entering the water. They were already in shock when they dropped in and they simply lacked the will and strength and awareness to carry on. But the rest swam quickly about—looking for something to help keep them afloat, looking for others to team up with. In those early minutes everyone's greatest fear was that he would find himself alone.

Most of the men had life jackets, but some didn't and the cries of these rose shrill and panicky: "Life jacket—for God's sake—somebody gimme a jacket…" Another thing spurring them all to desperate movement was the quick-spreading release of fuel oil from the ship. The black, vile substance seemed to be everywhere. Men were blinded as it washed again and again across their eyes. Others swallowed it and felt their insides turn to fire, and heaved and retched and vomited in an agony that was to last for days.

Captain McVay found himself at the head of a nine-man group clinging to three tied-together rafts. Separated from the others, they imagined themselves the only survivors, but at that time roughly two-thirds of the entire ship's complement was still flailing about in the water.

The central figures of one struggling group were Commander Lipski and Lieutenant Commander Lewis Haynes—Lipski badly burned over large areas of his body and dying, and Dr. Haynes in great pain from burnt hands. Around them were some 300 men of whom a number were already in bad shape from exposure, blast wounds and swallowing fuel oil.

It was Haynes' grim job to determine when a man was dead and his life jacket could be removed and given to someone else. Time and time again he swam up to limp, floating figures, checked a pulse, pulled an eyelid down, then gave the terse order: "Get his jacket. He's dead." The jacket would be removed and the dead shipmate would sink out of sight.

Lieutenant Commander Richard Redmayne commanded another group, one of a hundred or so men clinging to several rafts and some floating debris. Another group consisted of four rafts with 19 men aboard and Ensign Ross Rogers in charge. Elsewhere, strung out over miles of black ocean, were the rest of the *Indianapolis* personnel, some grouped together in twos and threes, others alone.

The sun rose and blazed down on them out of a cloudless sky. It burned them raw. It played hell with their eyes. Even closing them didn't help; the blazing red ball burned right through their lids. The waves buffeted them, tossed them about, exhausted them. Many were still caught in the long, sticky carpet of fuel oil, their black heads poking up through it like charred tree stumps. The oil on their sun-scorched bodies was an additional agony, a sandpaper scraping of bleeding skin.

The writhing, retching torment of those who had swallowed the oil continued and some pulled off their jackets and let themselves sink rather than endure it any longer. The jackets themselves were even becoming a problem, rubbing endlessly against necks and chins until they produced ugly, ulcerating sores. These were irritated still further by stinging salt water.

Several planes flew over that first day, land-based bombers flying out of Leyte and Guam, and the men howled their throats raw and waved their arms, but they weren't seen. Flares were fired from Captain McVay's rafts, but the big planes flew serenely on. Nothing about them even suggested that they were conducting a search. Was it possible that the *Indianapolis* hadn't even been missed yet? Was no one expecting her, looking for her, concerned about her?

Now a grim sullenness came over the men. The sun was pitiless. It dried their lips, turned their tongues to sticks of dry wood. Their mouths puffed up. They couldn't work their throats, couldn't swallow. Thirst was a problem now and the stronger among them swam close to the weaker ones to beg them, implore them, "Don't do it…don't do it, buddy…*for Christ sake, don't do it.*"

But thirst is a madness, and more and more of them found it twisting into their brains. "Don't do it, buddy. That's salt water. For God's sake, buddy—" But there was no longer any hope of holding some. The madness was in their eyes, their howls, their filth-laden curses.

They took huge mouthfuls of water and each one made them need more, more, and still more. The madness was an eruption of violence now—men roaring in rage and pain, striking out blindly. Then came the animal-like thrashings and writhings, then the gasps of torture beyond belief, then the moans of the dying and, finally, a blessed release in death. Only then was it safe to approach them again. The life jackets were removed, the bodies allowed to sink.

Late that first day, too, the sharks appeared. Terrified, some of the men shouted and flailed their arms about to drive them away, but the long, gliding monsters slipped in among them. Soon one howling man had been dragged down beneath the surface, then another. Some men forced themselves to float perfectly still in the water and these the sharks bypassed, but the active ones drew them like magnets. For all the rest of those long, horror-building hours, the sharks would stay with them.

Night came on—their second night in the water—bringing shivering cold and the fear of losing contact with one's friends. They had been in the water almost 24 hours and there was still no evidence of a search going on. Men felt the icy cold creeping up their bodies, numbing toes and legs, invading their stomachs. Some kicked and thrashed about in an effort to stay alive, but others were past caring. They lay stiff as boards in the water.

Tuesday was a blazer again. Men died of exposure and from drinking salt water and evidences of madness were everywhere. They imagined islands close by. They imagined the *Indianapolis* rising to the surface again and all of them climbing aboard. They imagined the Japanese submarine plowing into them and cutting them down with its machine guns. McVay continued to exercise an iron control over his group, as did Redmayne over his and young Rogers over his. Commander Haynes swam about his group—his burned hands useless—coaxing them, cajoling them, persuading them to keep calm and not give up hope.

For many of the men—the twos and threes and the isolated singles—the struggle was no longer worth it. Fifty hours in the sea had become too much for them. Many bled from shark bites. All were burned raw by the blazing sun. All had ulcerating neck sores from their life jackets. Many had been blinded by fuel oil. Others had been heaving arid gasping and vomiting it ever since they hit the water. All of them felt a violent, murderous hate against those who should have known they were out there, but who didn't.

One hour melted into another. 55…58…60….

Men tied their jackets together and tried to sleep. Some who succeeded never woke up again. Some chose to end it all by untying their jackets and slipping out of them. Those who continued the struggle had been reduced to limp bundles of laundry floating in the water.

Sixty-two hours…65… 70… The men were dying like flies. The dead floated in their life jackets among the living. The sharks nosed in among them taking what they wanted. That night a sun-crazed sailor screamed: "There's a Jap behind me!" and slashed the man beside him with a knife.

Seventy-two hours…74…78…their swollen tongues filled their mouths and most of them were incoherent, beyond speech. Their eyes were burning rivets. Their bodies twitched with the agony of their salt-encrusted sores. Their stomachs heaved and twisted and contorted. More and more life jackets were getting saturated and men died because they couldn't get out of them and so sank. The men in the water were past hope, past despair, past everything.

Eighty hours…82…84…

"A plane, a plane, it's a goddamn plane." A raw rasping voice, a strangled spitting of words. Then silence. Then: "He's hanging around. Maybe…maybe—"

The plane was a land-based Ventura piloted by Lieutenant (jg) Wilbur Gwinn USNR. Gwinn was having trouble with his radio antenna. It wasn't hanging properly. Moving aft to fix it, Gwinn glanced casually down and noticed a large oil slick on the water. Intrigued, he circled down further and suddenly sucked in his breath hard and widened his eyes in astonishment. The slick was dotted with men's heads. Lower still he could even make out arms waving. But who were they? Nothing had been heard of a ship being sunk. Quickly, he dropped all his life rafts. In the water men sobbed in relief.

"He sees us. He sees us. The son of a bitch sees us."

Quickly, Gwinn had his radio man send off a message to his commander at Peleliu and to the Command HQ in the Marianas: "Sighted 30 men in water, position 11 degrees 30' N, 133 degrees 30' E." Even as the message was being completed, Gwinn realized there were more than thirty men beneath him. His rough count came to about 150.

Once Gwinn's message was received, things happened fast. A PBY commanded by Lieutenant Adrian Marks flew out from Peleliu, arrived over the oil slick and began dropping all sorts of life-saving equipment—rafts, dye markers, ration cartons. In the water the dazed survivors steeled themselves to hang on a little longer…just a little longer.

"Oh, Lord, they know we're here," a man moaned. "Just let me hold on till they can get me out."

But even now, how long would that be? For some of the battered wrecks in the water, every minute counted. And out on the edge of the survivor area, men wondered if they had been seen at all. Some were miles from their nearest shipmate. And a 12- foot swell was running now, too strong for a PBY to land in. At least it was *supposed* to be too strong for a PBY to land in. But Marks had seen the men in the water and he wasn't about to go back without some of them.

"Will attempt open sea landing," he radioed his base, then started down.

It took several big bounces and half a dozen popped rivets, but finally the big plane was down on the water and taxiing slowly toward the shrieking, waving, pleading survivors. Marks concentrated on the men who were alone—he assumed the others were in better shape to hang on a little longer and he knew he could pick up just so many of them.

Ensign Morgan Hensley, a powerful man, strong as a bull in the chest and shoulders, was picked to pull in the survivors. Reaching down out of the port blister, he pulled the first man aboard.

"What ship?" the gasping, exhausted, oil-blackened survivor was asked.

"*Indianapolis.*"

The *Indianapolis?* The men on the PBY were dumbfounded. *It was the first anyone anywhere in the world knew that the great ship had been sunk—three-and-a-half days after it happened!*

A hero among heroes that dramatic night, Marks picked up 56 survivors before deciding that any more would endanger the plane and all those he had already taken aboard. But by then others were coming in to help out. Most significantly, ships were arriving: destroyer escorts *Cecil J. Doyle, Dufilho, Register* and *Ringness,* destroyer transport *Bassett,* destroyers *Madison* and *Ralph Talbot,* and still others.

By midnight the ships were on the scene. This was exactly four days--96 hours—from the time the *Indianapolis* went down. At noon the next day, 108 hours after the sinking, the last of the survivors was taken from the sea. *Ringness* had that honor and the further one of having Captain McVay in the group. Honors for rescuing the greatest number of survivors went to *Bassett* with 151.

It was estimated that approximately 800 men abandoned the *Indianapolis* when she sank. Of these, 316 survived. The rest—just under 500 men—died in the water. The first survivor was picked up August 2 and rescue operations were completed a day later. Yet it wasn't until August 15 that the Navy announced the *Indianapolis* had been sunk. This long delay, plus the fact that the announcement was made the same day the newspapers screamed the news that Japan had agreed to surrender, gave the general public the feeling that the Navy was trying to bury the story. An uproar arose, principally from the press and the relatives of those who had perished. Plainly, the *Indianapolis* catastrophe was not to be buried. Someone would have to bear the guilt. Someone would have to pay. But who?

Was it to be the routing officers at Guam who decided the *Indianapolis* didn't need an escort?

Was it to be the officers who assigned it Course Peddie—the straight-line route between Guam and Leyte—instead of a more evasive one?

Was it to be those who had given Captain McVay instructions to zigzag at his own discretion instead of ordering him to do so?

Was it to be Commodore Norman "Shorty" Gillette, acting commander of the Philippines Sea Frontier? Gillette had been sent a message from the Port Director at Guam informing him that the *Indianapolis* would enter his jurisdiction on July 31. Was Gillette at fault for not having reported the *Indianapolis'* non-arrival on the date she was expected?

Was it to be Rear Admiral Lynde McCormick who commanded the training unit in Leyte Gulf to which the *Indianapolis* had been assigned? McCormick had been sent the same message as Gillette. Should he have responded more quickly to the cruiser's non-arrival?

Was it to be McCormick's communications personnel? They had received the message concerning the *Indianapolis'* expected arrival in garbled form and been unable to decipher it. Yet, they hadn't asked that it be re-sent.

Was it to be Captain McVay?

At Admiral Chester Nimitz's order and well before the sinking of the *Indianapolis* had been made public, a court of inquiry presided over by Vice Admiral Charles Lockwood began looking into the matter. On August 20th the court announced its findings. These included a reprimand to Captain McVay for failing to zigzag on the night of the torpedo attack and for his inability to get off a distress message while the *Indianapolis'* communications systems were still functioning.

The court also recommended that McVay be court-martialed for (1) inefficiency and (2) for endangering the lives of others through negligence. The Navy's top brass was dead set against the court-martial, but Secretary of the Navy James Forrestal insisted it be held to satisfy the demands of the public.

The court-martial was held in Washington in 1945. Feelings ran high. A number of congressmen and members of the press let it be known that they thought Captain McVay was being made a scapegoat. Their fury was heightened when it was announced that Commander Hashimoto, destroyer of the *Indianapolis*, was being brought to Washington to testify. This was seen as an insult to McVay. There was speculation as to just how reliable a witness Hashimoto would be. This doubt can be seen in the first questions put to him.

Question: What is your religion?

Answer: I am a Shintoist.

Question: Do you know the difference between truth and falsehood?

Answer: I do.

A stocky, impassive man, Hashimoto testified that McVay's failure to zigzag had nothing to do with the sinking of the *Indianapolis*. He claimed he would have been able to sink her anyway, if not with conventional torpedoes, certainly with his kaitens.

But despite Hashimoto's testimony, McVay was found guilty of "hazarding his ship's safety through failure to zigzag" and sentenced to lose 100 numbers in grade. Of a second charge, "delay in issuing orders to abandon ship," he was acquitted. The court then recommended that McVay's sentence be remitted and he was returned to active duty. He retired from the Navy in 1949 with the rank of Rear Admiral.

Somewhere between Guam and Leyte, in water two miles deep, lies the broken, shattered hulk that was once the proud cruiser *Indianapolis*. More than 800 men share her grave. For them, the court-martial and all the excitement that went with it were meaningless. Yet, in an ironic way, their deaths will have meaning for others still to sail this nation's ships.

The sinking of the *Indianapolis* can be laid on no one man's doorstep. McVay didn't lose her, nor did Gillette or McCormick or any other single member of the personnel involved in her passage. All handled their responsibilities for the *Indianapolis* in ways that had become routine. Unfortunately, they had also become sloppy—loose, careless, casual. Too many things were taken for granted. When the *Indianapolis* didn't show up on time, it was simply taken for granted that she had encountered some routine delay. Delayed ships were no longer being checked on at that stage of the war.

Lay the death of a great ship and 800 men on the Navy's doorstep, but be assured there will never again be anything like it. Everything's been tightened, tautened, procedures sharpened. Today *nothing's* taken for granted, *nothing* considered routine.

From that viewpoint, the great ship and the 800 men who lie with her did not die in vain. *

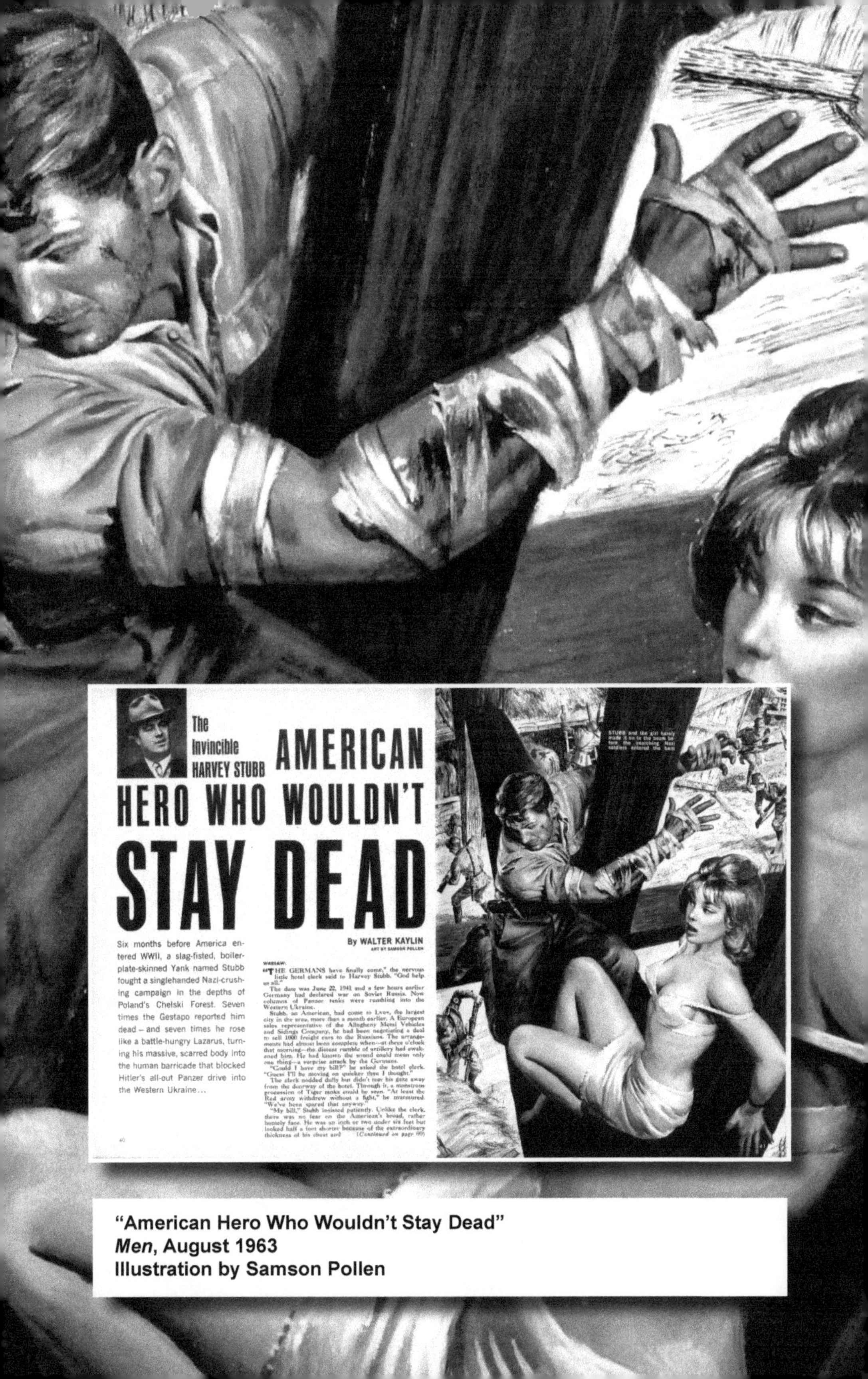

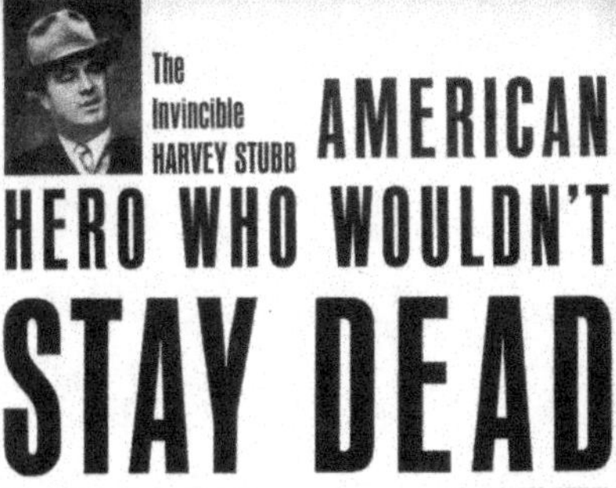

The Invincible HARVEY STUBB

AMERICAN HERO WHO WOULDN'T STAY DEAD

By WALTER KAYLIN
ART BY SAMSON POLLEN

Six months before America entered WWII, a slag-fisted, boiler-plate-skinned Yank named Stubb fought a singlehanded Nazi-crushing campaign in the depths of Poland's Chelski Forest. Seven times the Gestapo reported him dead — and seven times he rose like a battle-hungry Lazarus, turning his massive, scarred body into the human barricade that blocked Hitler's all-out Panzer drive into the Western Ukraine...

WARSAW:

"THE GERMANS have finally come," the nervous little hotel clerk said to Harvey Stubb. "God help us all."

The date was June 22, 1941 and a few hours earlier Germany had declared war on Soviet Russia. Now columns of Panzer tanks were rumbling into the Western Ukraine.

Stubb, an American, had come to Lvov, the largest city in the area, more than a month earlier. A European sales representative of the Allegheny Metal Vehicles and Sidings Company, he had been negotiating a deal to sell 1000 freight cars to the Russians. The arrangements had almost been complete when—at three o'clock that morning—the distant rumble of artillery had awakened him. He had known the sound could mean only one thing—a surprise attack by the Germans.

"Could I have my bill?" he asked the hotel clerk. "Guess I'll be moving on quicker than I thought."

The clerk nodded dully but didn't tear his gaze away from the doorway of the hotel. Through it, a monstrous procession of Tiger tanks could be seen. "At least the Red army withdrew without a fight," he murmured. "We've been spared that anyway."

"My bill," Stubb insisted patiently. Unlike the clerk, there was no fear on the American's broad, rather homely face. He was an inch or two under six feet but looked half a foot shorter because of the extraordinary thickness of his chest and *(Continued on page 60)*

40

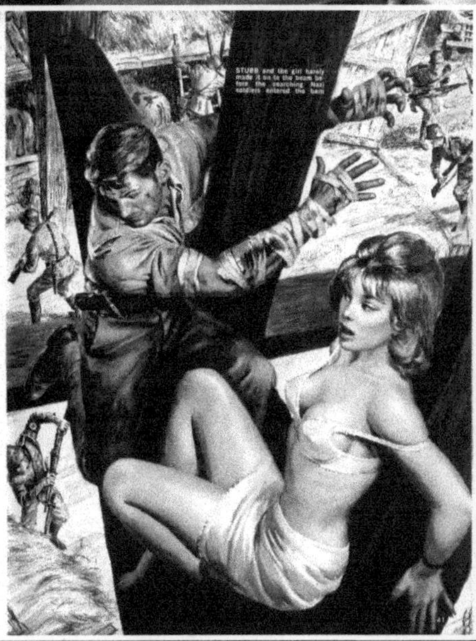

"American Hero Who Wouldn't Stay Dead"
Men, August 1963
Illustration by Samson Pollen

ters felt as though he were
being physically pounded -
"heavy leather mallets smashing my ears, an elephant's foot
stamping on my belly." Smoke
jetted above the enclosure,
squashing out into thick
clouds and the rumbling shed
its wraps to become a roar
of such cataclysmic violence
that Waters felt it grinding his heart and brain to
dust, shriveling his soul
under assaults that mocked its
existence. Then up from within
the bowels of that doomsday
clamor came the German rocket,
a finned and gleaming monster,
awesomely majestic in its slow,
probing rise. Ghostlike, it
slipped upward through the
billowing smoke and Agricola
spoke with lips gone grey in
fear and knowledge, but Waters
couldn't make out what he said.
Unhurriedly, the giant rocket
continued its vertical climb
until it was half a mile above

"MEET OUR TERMS OR WE DESTROY 500 MILLION PEOPLE"

— WRITING AS ROLAND EMPEY —

Men, October 1964

COVER ARTIST: GIL COHEN

"**P**REUFSTAND nine," Agricola whispered hoarsely, pointing into the stretch of fog-blurred tundra ahead of them—dwarf pines and spike-like bushes standing in hazy clumps about an expanse of grey-white ground frozen hard as stone. "Test area nine. **Rauchen Verboten, Rauchen Verboten,** see the signs? No Smoking. They intend to incinerate the world but they forbid smoking!"

The four men trudged on, the vague forms of others materializing out of the fog (Continued on page 90)

(Continued on page 90)

THE ALLIED raiding party swarmed into the bunker just as the nuclear murderers were launching the missiles

Illustrations by Earl Norem

PREUFSTAND nine," Agricola whispered hoarsely, pointing into the stretch of fog-blurred tundra ahead of them—dwarf pines and spike-like bushes standing in hazy clumps about an expanse of grey-white ground frozen hard as stone. "Test area nine. RAUCHEN VERBOTEN, RAUCHEN VERBOTEN, see the signs? NO SMOKING. They intend to incinerate the world, but they forbid smoking!"

The four men trudged on, the vague forms of others materializing out of the fog ahead of them, all moving across the frozen tundra toward a row of bulky buildings rising round-roofed and black against a slate-grey sky. All four wore the everyday clothes of the Arctic Outerlander—pants and a short coat of reindeer hide dyed a bright blue, heavy boots and gloves and a snug cap with a reindeer horn poking up above it. Two of the four were obviously Outerlanders, stocky men with broad, flat faces and Mongolian eyes. The other two were Paavo Agricola—balding, gnome-like, 66-year old Finnish nuclear scientist and founder of the short-lived "Bold Island Pantheist Union"—and Captain Harry Waters of the United States Air Force, a big man with a prairie squint and a nose banged flat in college football.

THE MIST-shrouded buildings loomed massively before the approaching men and finally they could see that each was a mighty lump of solid concrete girdled by a steel superstructure. "They've got forests of molybdenum steel piping in the foundations to act as flame deflectors," Agricola said in a low voice. "Also their recorder rooms, their catch tanks and their compressed nitrogen storage cylinders. Come, we're supposed to be at number four and remember you're supposed to be an Outerlander workman. There'll be nothing to do until after the firing. Then stay close to me and do what I do. You seem like a bright young man. You shouldn't have any trouble."

The four men joined a crowd of others behind an earthen wall enclosing the fourth of *preufstand* nine's launching pads. They were able to see the control center from where they stood—a concrete hut containing a periscope room, a recorder room, a workshop and several offices; a little beyond it were the powerhouse, the transformer station, an area for storing propellants, and concrete huts for the cable terminals and the firing and control equipment. Standing with Agricola among the silent Outerlanders, Waters could hear the hum and throb of motors and vehicles at the pad and several voices shouting orders in German.

"They're completing their check-offs," Agricola said cupping a hand to his ear to catch the German phrases. "The firing will take place in a few minutes. May I suggest that you refrain from shouting 'Wow' or 'Zowie' or anything of that sort? Remember you're supposed to be an Outerlander and the Outerlander vocabulary contains no such enthusiasm.

Waters was about to reply, but stopped as the scientist gripped his arm. Men were leaving the launching pad, first some drifting casually away, then others moving more quickly, and finally one in shirt sleeves despite the bitter cold running awkwardly and waving a hand for all clear. Agricola's hand gripped hard as a claw on Waters' arm and the old man's face was wreathed in perspiration. Some among the Outerlanders shuffled their feet like vaguely alarmed cattle, but most stood still as posts. A siren wailed. The old man breathed harsh as ripping cloth and said, "These things upset me so. Ahhhhhh."

An arrow of orange flame had burst up from the pad to achieve an eerie, quivering suspension against the grey sky. Its electrifying appearance was accompanied by a rolling, rumbling sound Waters was later to compare to "a million horses stampeding across a bass drum big as Lake Superior." Now the flame turned blinding yellow and an elongated diamond took shape within it. Sheets of steaming vapor rose high above the concrete enclosure and fell back hissing across its sloping surface. The rumbling grew in volume and took on a pulsating quality of such power that Waters felt as though he were being physically pounded—"heavy leather mallets smashing my ears, an elephant's foot stamping on my belly." Smoke jetted above the enclosure, squashing out into thick clouds and the rumbling shed its wraps to become a roar of such cataclysmic violence that Waters felt it grinding his heart and brain to dust, shriveling his soul under assaults that mocked its existence. Then up from within the bowels of that doomsday clamor came the German rocket, a finned and gleaming monster, awesomely majestic in its slow, probing rise. Ghost-like, it slipped upward through the billowing smoke and Agricola spoke with lips gone grey in fear and knowledge, but Waters couldn't make out what he said. Unhurriedly, the giant rocket continued its vertical climb until it was half a mile above its launching pad and tilting into trajectory, with its jet flung out behind in the shape of a yellow lance. Men were rising all over the area now to follow its course through binoculars, but soon these were put away as the rocket sped out of range on its way into that vast, bleak, uncharted stretch of Polar Ocean. Before long it would arc down and a bright yellow dye would mark where it hit the water. Then search planes would find the dye and map it to check the flight for accuracy.

"Compared to that monster, everything in your country's arsenal and Russia's are hardly more than toys," Agricola said, his face ashen, his hand still gripping Waters' arm. "If they've mastered the techniques required to put it on target, the days left us on this planet are few indeed."

"How long before they'll know?" Waters asked.

"Whether or not it reached its target? Oh, an hour or so I suppose. But, come, we're supposed to be helping clean up now. Stay close to me and keep your eyes on the ground."

THEIR clean-up job finally completed, the launching area already being prepared for another test, the Outerlanders left. German scientists stood in little groups discussing the flight, checking charts, examining pictures while technicians disconnected a weird assortment of complex instruments and drained the propellant tanks. Their age astonished Waters. None looked less than sixty and several could have been in their eighties and nineties.

"They're not exactly kids, are they?" he said.

"They are all of Hitler's time, and their Fuhrer's been dead 24 years—1945, wasn't it?" Agricola said. "Of course for them he's still alive. They are all old and mad but there are a number of authentic geniuses among them. My mind refuses to acknowledge what they're accomplishing here, but my eyes and ears tell me it's all true. Careful, now, careful."

Side by side and bent to a crouch, the two men moved about the testing area picking up debris left in the wake of the firing—bits of charred wood, chunks of mangled pipe, lengths of corroded wire. Gaseous odors still hung in the air and Agricola sniffed at them whispering sadly, "It would help if I could tell you the propellant they used, but everything is so new here, so unfamiliar. They are years beyond anything we've done elsewhere." They moved at their clean-up job within a group of silent Outerlanders while others—all young men, many less than 20, all carrying short clubs and with revolvers strapped about their waists, all with black swastikas sewn into their furs—pushed and shoved and hurried them along. These were the "Werewolves" of whom Agricola had already spoken to Waters, men born to Outerlander women of German fathers, "The women taken by force in every instance," according to Agricola, their offspring bitter, vicious men for the most part. Waters had seen the combined strains in their faces and the violence that flamed in their yellow eyes.

TOGETHER with a number of Outerlanders, they went through the earthen wall and were soon at the launching pad itself. They moved across the tundra in a silent, straggling group, the Werewolves jabbing them with their clubs to speed them along. The Outerlanders offered no resistance to this mistreatment and spoke no word of complaint. There was a time they had resisted the Germans bitterly, Agricola had said, but for many years now they'd kept under control through a program of drugs—"drugs that paralyze the will, but leave the body free to do its work." Drifting across the tundra like so many lost souls, they would return to their families now, and when the Germans needed them again, the Werewolves would come and rout them out. There was pity in Waters' eyes as he watched them, but something like impatience in his voice when he spoke to Agricola: "We won't be able to get much help from this crowd, will we? They're beat. They're just about out of the picture."

"You've met four or five who have somehow retained their strength and dignity," Agricola sighed. "All the rest have been rendered docile as sheep and from them you can expect no help at all."

"But I've got to get back to the carrier and four or five of them aren't enough to get me there," Waters said and there was a sudden tension in his voice, a sense of extreme agitation. "Hell, you're the expert. You're the authority. Isn't that how you see it? I've got to get back to the carrier before it's too late."

"Yes, you've got to get back to your carrier before it's too late," Agricola agreed, but this was an old man's voice, worn out and weary. "If it isn't too late already."

Some 24 years before the test launching described above, SS Hitler's Germany went up in smoke and the victorious Allies took over all elements of its weapons establishment left standing. A particularly significant "find" was made at Nordhausen where a V-2 rocket plant lay housed in a series of labyrinthine caves. In addition to the V-2, examination of the voluminous notes found there revealed plans for the more advanced but still practical A-9 and A-10 rockets—also some scattered references to still other rocket equipment of the sort quickly dismissed as "science fiction": rockets powered by atomic energy, rockets powered by solar batteries, rockets powered by molecular splinters whose total "lives" are measured in billionths of a second, rockets powered by rubidium and cesium ions, and so forth. Also found was a listing of the scientists by groups, each assigned a particular project. Searches were quickly made for the men listed, and most of them easily found. The one exception was the group, led by Reinhard Hauptmann, that had been assigned to the "science fiction" project.

In the years following the war, both the United States and Russia worked feverishly to acquire superiority in its rocket arsenal. The most important elements in this contest were the tools and machines developed by Germany during the war and the scientists who had worked on them. Intensive recruitment of German personnel brought Werner von Braun to the United States, heading up a contingent that included Hellmuth Schlitt, Krafft Ehricke, Herman Oberth and others of similar standing. Russia's Germans included Hans Hoch, Waldemar Wolf, Peter Lertes and Helmut Groettrup, who had worked with von Braun at the great Peenemunde plant.

Sparked by these men the two WWII victors were soon hip-deep in rocket plans and tests. Redstone, Jupiter, Explorer, Vanguard— these became familiar names to the rocket-conscious American public. In Russia it was the T-1, the T-2 and so forth. Of particular interest was the T-2 (also designated as M-103), which by the mid-sixties was acknowledged the most dependable and versatile rocket in the Russian arsenal. A two-stage rocket with an initial thrust of over 250,000 pounds and a second of over 75,000, a range of accuracy exceeding 1,500 miles, a velocity of over 5,000 miles an hour and an atomic warhead of about 700 pounds, T-2 was developed directly from the A-9 and A-10 plans found in the Nordhausen caves. The ironic significance here lies in the fact that Nordhausen was occupied by American troops originally, and handed over to the Russians with all its valuable plans and machinery untouched.

THE ROCKET race went on into 1968 with neither power achieving total dominance and amid growing signs that the world at large had grown sick of it and wanted it to end. Bundles of petitions to that effect arrived at the United Nations every day. Men and women prominent in the arts and sciences wrote impassioned books on the subject. Violent demonstrations were held in Washington and Moscow and London and Peking and Paris and a student uprising in Rome almost toppled the government. In Tokyo a crowd estimated at two million surged through the streets chanting "down, down, down the chute to shame and desolation," and in Finland a group of militant pacifists formed the Bold Island Pantheist Union, elected world-famed nuclear scientist Paavo Agricola their leader and prepared to "leave these centers of decay and worm-gnawed rot and found a better world on the clean, bold shores that dot the northern seas."

The Agricola group, some 300 men, women and children, steamed into the Barents Sea in August of that year with the fiery scientist at an amplified loud speaker leading them in their theme song, "Nature Clean, Nature Serene." Their ship was the eight-million-dollar yacht *Folly Girl* once owned by Panamanian shipping magnate Ricardo Lucerdo and renamed *God in Nature*. Glistening in fresh paint, *God in Nature* was escorted into the Barents Sea by a small fleet of tugs and private craft, all blowing horns and tooting whistles while Agricola howled at them through his loud speaker to "join us, join us, strike out for the clean, bold shores." After a few miles the escorting boats began to turn back, and when last seen, *God in Nature* was entering a bank of thick fog and proceeding on its own.

Through 1968 and into 1969 the rocket race went on, but with evidence mounting that a stalemate was being achieved. In all essentials the two great powers were apparently reaching a point of comparable development—in thrust, accuracy, velocity and size of warhead. The world spoke hopefully of a cut-off point, a point at which neither held any advantage over the other. Leading government figures seemed to share that hope. Conferences were held, technical discussions entered into. Progress was encouraging. A status quo would be agreed upon, arrived at, maintained. And then in March 1969 those hopes were shredded, shattered, trampled upon and the Damocletian sword of nuclear annihilation hung suspended over mankind's neck in clearer and more purposeful threat than it ever had before.

ON THE ninth day of that month a sealskin canoe was seen drifting in the Barents Sea three miles north of Kjelvik, Norway. The canoe was taken in tow by the trawler that had come upon it and soon it was seen that three men were in it, all unconscious, all in the last stages of physical deterioration. They were given emergency treatment and rushed to Kjelvik, but two died before they could be taken ashore and it was another 24 hours before hospital attendants realized the one survivor was Paavo Agricola. The scientist weighed less than seventy pounds and his entire body was covered with lacerated salt water sores. His pulse was erratic, his breathing irregular; his stomach a knotted lump unable to retain a cup of tea. Pain had etched itself deep into his face and he babbled wildly of "all the world's rivers filled bank to bank with corpses."

For several days it seemed unlikely that he would live, but eventually his body was restored to something like normal functioning and by the end of the week his survival was assured. During this period he spoke no rational word, but only continued his madman's babbling. It was felt that his mind had snapped under the strain of some terrible experience in the Polar Ocean and would never again work properly. Attempts to question him about the fate of the *God in Nature* party proved futile. He responded to all questions with a flood of uncontrollable tears or stared fixedly at the ceiling. He screamed of corpses in his sleep, seeing them once as forming a mountain high as Everest and then again as a carpet wide as the Sahara. He woke from these cruel visions with his bedclothes soaked in perspiration and had to be put in a strait jacket for several days following an attempt to throw himself out the window.

His state continued unchanged for several weeks. yet behind the madman's mask the powerful intellect that had won him the Nobel Prize and the respect of the international scientific community was slowly returning to work. There were occasional periods of calm and quiet and these lengthened and became more frequent. If he couldn't communicate, at least he no longer raved: The stunning moment finally arrived when he spoke quite clearly to a doctor asking him to "summon to my bedside the President of the United States, the Premier of the Soviet Union and all their chief military and scientific advisors." He was told this was impossible and immediately went into a two-day relapse during which he wept as before and screamed of "corpses piling up about the Empire State Building until it crashes beneath their weight…corpses filling Grand Canyon and rising high above its lip… corpses head to toe from Nome to Buenos Aires." When he returned once more to calm and clarity and repeated his demand, it was felt an attempt should be made to meet it. High Finnish officials converged on Washington and Moscow to state the case for their countryman. His contributions to science were stressed as were his well-known humanitarian instincts. Would it not be well to treat his demand with utmost seriousness? In view of the still unsolved mystery of the *God in Nature* party, would it not be well to hear what he had to say?

The Finns won their point and on April 19, some six weeks after he'd been fished out of the Barents Sea, Agricola sat in a wheelchair— pale, shrunken, all but swallowed up in a terrycloth robe—and spoke to a group of about a dozen Americans and Russians representing their countries' military-scientific establishments, each contingent including a government member of ambassadorial rank. When they emerged two hours later, all were grave, unsmiling and bluntly uncommunicative. "No comment" was all they would say to the clamoring press. But it was seen that they returned to their respective capitals and insisted on immediate consultations with their heads of state. These meetings were followed by a round of others involving all elements of the Government, the military and both nations' best scientific minds. The press and public demanded enlightenment, but a lid of secrecy sat tight over the matter and no official disclosures or unofficial "leaks" were made. Attempts to interview Agricola proved unavailing. Responding to a combined US-Russian request, the Finnish Government posted an armed guard at his door and permitted no one to enter his room save those on a top-secret list. The world waited and wondered and speculated as to what the scientist had revealed that would call for such an air of tension and urgency.

Today we know.

Steaming northward into the fog-shrouded Polar Ocean (Agricola told the group that met with him in the hospital), the *God in Nature* party had soon found itself in an endless expanse of silent sea and drifting icebergs. They were well supplied with food and sang cheerful songs, but as the days went by without their coming upon any islands suitable for settling, their original enthusiasm began to decline. The empty sea, the yellow haze, the silent, slipping bergs—these didn't make for an optimistic outlook. Where were the "bold, clean shores" they'd been promised? The only islands they saw were bleak rocks hardly larger than their yacht and usually covered by barking seals. They never came to a point of outright complaint, but it was obvious many would have preferred a return to the "centers of decay and worm-gnawed rot"

STUNNED, Agricola watched the missile hit the yacht . . .

to this endless drifting. In an effort to broaden their search, Agricola began to go off in the dinghy each day taking a few others with him and returning to the *God in Nature* just before nightfall.

RETURNING from one such search, the scientist saw at the very edge of the horizon a long, low blur of purple shadow. Excitedly, he pointed it out to his four companions. Each examined it through binoculars and came to the same conclusion—an island, a sizeable piece of land, the "bold, clean shore" they'd been seeking. Congratulating themselves on their discovery, they started back toward the yacht, seeing it tiny as a child's toy against a sweeping rim of pink-tinged sky. After some minutes they stopped to rest and gazed again at the yacht. In that moment a single flick of white light raced in an instantaneous arc across the horizon and deep beneath it the *God in Nature* disappeared. One moment it stood across the still seas from the men in the dinghy, sturdy and unmoving as though nailed in its place. The next it was gone. Gone with a finality so total it might never have been there at all.

The initial reaction of the men in the dinghy was that they'd witnessed an optical illusion. A cloud had settled over the yacht. Shadows created by the dying sun had somehow contrived to hide it. Something of that sort must have happened. So they continued rowing toward where they'd seen it last, expecting at every moment to see it again. Surely it would rise beyond that swell and their families and friends would be at the rail waving to them. But the minutes collected into hours and night turned the sky black and nowhere did they see the lights of the *God in Nature.* They rowed all that night and heard planes above them at one point, but these quickly left and they were alone again. Dawn found them exhausted by their effort and sick with worry and with memories of the white light they'd seen the night before looming large in their minds. At mid-day they crossed a patch of sea gleaming luminously yellow and Agricola groaned aloud in dawning realization.

They were rowing aimlessly now although in the general direction of the island they'd seen the night before and late that afternoon a chunk of charred wood drifted across their wake and seemed to have been torn from the deck of a ship. Before long other bits of related debris appeared and finally one with the words they'd been dreading: *God in*—. Strangely, none of them swore or screamed at this evidence of dark disaster. The entire episode still seemed unreal to them, uncanny. They rowed on, sluggishly now, listlessly, their faces frozen in dry-eyed grief and confusion.

Two nights later they reached the island, coming ashore on a strip of narrow beach dotted with small huts made from the skins of seals and reindeer. Here they encountered a people of such dull-eyed lethargy that it was immediately apparent they had been influenced by drugs. Racial cousins to the Lapps but long deprived of that energetic people's fierce pride and strength of purpose, the Outerlanders resembled nothing so much as a company of sleepwalkers. Most were so sunk in emotional inertia they didn't realize that newcomers had come among them. A half dozen exceptions included the brothers Warnak and Kart and the girl, Akam Luk—also several women so enfeebled by age that drugging them would have served no useful purpose. The young men and the fierce-eyed girl had come from another island only recently, leaving it because its herds of seals were dwindling and could no longer supply the current population with meat.

"If we had known how it would be here, we'd have stayed and starved," the girl said bitterly, and the two young men nodded in morose agreement. "There is horror here, and cruelty, and things far worse than that. Death lives here, death has made Apinak his home."

She spoke then of those who had established themselves on the other side of the island—"dirty men, dried up and old." She spoke of planes and trucks and machines and equipment and an impersonal use of the drug-weakened Outerlanders as though they were beasts for breeding and beasts of burden. She knew nothing of science and was unable to tell Agricola what the "invaders" were doing with their awesome machinery and their tall towers. "Could I see for myself?" the Finn asked. It could be arranged, the girl said. When next the Outerlanders were summoned to lift and carry and perform the other menial functions the "invaders" demanded of them, Agricola and those who had come with him could join them. Wearing Outerlander furs and employing the Outerlander sagging shuffle, they would have no trouble escaping detection.

So several days after they'd reached Apinak, Agricola and the others from the *God in Nature* joined a party of Outerlanders kicked and dragged out of their huts by Werewolf storm troopers, piled into trucks and rushed across the island. The girl and the brothers Warnak and Kart didn't join them, but hid in caves along the shore—the procedure they'd been following ever since arriving in Apinak. Half a mile in from the beach the island took on the character of the Siberian tundra—frozen ground, gnarled and stunted trees, thick mists. Mile after mile of it rolled by before the first concrete hut appeared, then quickly came another, then a square of ground with several airplanes clustered on it. And then, with violent suddenness, the whole bristling

sweep of construction and device that could only be a rocket center—
the component shop, the telemetering building, the assembly shop, the
maintenance workshop, the valve laboratory, the wind tunnel, the liquid
oxygen production plant, the fuel drums, the tank cars, the hangars,
the flame deflectors, the great launching pads and finally the rocket
itself, "the very epitome of destructive power," in Agricola's words, "a
product of genius run amok; smooth, sleek, enormous and indescribably
evil; an engine that made the very latest United States and Russian
weapons look like cap pistols; a monument to anti-man conceived in hate
and frenzy."

Stunned by what he had come upon in that desolate northland, it
took Agricola some minutes before he realized the men at the site were
all aged and all Germans. Then the full significance of what he had
stumbled upon hit home. Here, beyond all doubt, was the Reinhard
Hauptmann "science fiction" group of Nordhausen, missing since
1945 and generally assumed dead by their own hands. In this twilight
outpost they had continued with their experiments and carried through
a frightening number to successful conclusion. Here the Austrian
paperhanger still screamed and ranted and here men jumped to do his
bidding—"Burn! Kill! Ravage! Destroy! Consume the world in ashes!"
Listening to them speak, the distraught Agricola realized that was
exactly what they intended. They were in the final stages of their
testing programs. They had already designed and built a rocket that
could circle the globe and be brought down wherever they wished
it. Its performance was still erratic, however, but they were working
on that. When they could finally put it on target (a matter of a little
more time and testing) they would unleash an assault that would bring
Hitler's program to its logical climax. A belt of missiles extending
from one end of the island to the other would be readied, and at the
moment of *der tag* they would be loosed in one fateful hour on New
York, Moscow, London, Paris, Chicago, Rome, Leningrad, Los Angeles,
Tokyo, Peking, Stalingrad, Bucharest, Istanbul, Rio de Janeiro, Prague,
Warsaw, Jakarta, Sidney, Manila, Brussels, Belgrade and every other
of the world's great population centers. Half the world's inhabitants
would be reduced to ash and smoke and all the rest would crawl naked
and whimpering across a landscape gone dry as desert sand. The world
of rational men would come to an end in this, its sixtieth century, and
Adolf Anti-man would dance a jig on a column of corpses reaching to
the sun.

Overwhelmed by what I'd seen and heard, I went through my
Outerlander duties in a total daze," Agricola said to those who saw

him at the hospital. "The test missile was fired and I realized it would soon be able to do everything they hoped for. In some desperate way I managed to pull myself together and think of things to do. One fact became immediately obvious. I must come back. I must tell what I'd seen. I must sound the alarm.

He had completed his Outerlander duties and returned to the huts along the shore. He had spoken there to the two young men and the girl, explaining in simple terms the significance of what he'd seen and the importance of it being made known to the US and Russian military. "Even at this late hour they might somehow—somehow…." He wrung their hands, begged them to continue the hide-and-run tactics that had enabled them to avoid the German drugs, spoke feelingly of his hopes that they would meet again, and set out across the misty, storm-swept Polar Seas for Europe. In a pathetic attempt to improve low chances of navigating those treacherous waters and delivering his doomsday message, he had split his little *God in Nature* party in two and chosen two light sealskin Outerlander canoes to replace the bulky dinghy.

A description of the intrepid old Finn's miraculous return to Europe would be out of place in this narrative. It rates a staging all its own. It's enough to say he made it, his four companions dying in the effort (the two in the other canoe overturning and drowning in a storm; the two with him of exposure) and he himself suffering every agony the sea can inflict. He floated in off Norway with his skin cracked open in a hundred places and salt lining all its fissures, his heart, lungs, liver and kidneys all minutes away from conking out, his mind a hodge-podge assemblage of apocalyptic visions and nightmare fantasies and his mouth mumbling "corpses, corpses." It violated every principle of medical science that he should live or ever again communicate, but he did both. Six weeks after he'd been picked up outside Kjelvik, he spoke to a combined US-Russian scientific-military group in his hospital room.

Agricola's story induced expressions of horror in some quarters and skepticism or outright disbelief in others. There were those who said the "old boy" had lost his marbles. The *God in Nature* catastrophe (it was generally believed the yacht had gone down in a storm) had whirled him out of balance. His story was shot through with holes—

"They'd need ton upon ton upon ton of materiel for such projects. Where do they get it?"

"Isn't Hitler himself frequently 'seen' here and there by hysterics— in Spain and Argentina and Egypt?"

"A rocket able to reach and be brought down upon any point on the earth? Ridiculous! The science simply hasn't progressed that far. What do they use for a propellant?"

In response to this last, Professor William Frank of the President's Council of Science-Military Advisors recalled that the captured records and data of the Reinhard Hauptmann group showed them to have been exploring the theoretical possibilities of a photonic rocket—a rocket powered by the explosion resulting from a collision or anti-particles of "matter in reverse." The energy released in such an explosion would be thousands of times greater than that in the hydrogen-helium nuclear reaction and would presumably accomplish everything Agricola claimed to have seen. Could Hauptmann's group have gone off together 24 years before, kept themselves intact and undiscovered all this time and succeeded in developing their infernal machine—in Professor Frank's words, "the ultimate weapon?" The general view was that they hadn't, that nothing of the sort had happened, that Agricola's story was a complete fabrication, a fantasy conjured up in his fragmented mind. Yet if there were even a chance in a million ....

So it was decided that a joint US-Russian task force would be sent into the Polar Ocean to see for itself, but this quickly proved unworkable when agreement couldn't be reached as to whether an American or a Russian would command it. Two separate task forces were then decided upon, each to consist of an airplane carrier flying "searches" day and night and a flotilla of submarines to nose about the dark waters. Each carrier would also have two bombers aboard, each carrying the maximum bomb load its nation's weapons arsenal could provide.

Despite his weakened condition and his occasional lapses into despondency and hallucination, Agricola insisted on going along. This produced the expected squabble as to which force he'd go with, but a coin was flipped and he wound up on the American flattop *Concord.* He shared a room with a young flying officer named Harry Waters, a rangy southwesterner with demonstrated skills in all aspects of military service, a command of the Finnish language, and the easygoing manner necessary for getting along with the tempestuous scientist. Waters' instructions were direct and tersely stated—"Stay with him. Where he goes, you go. You're never more than a foot away from him. If we find this Martian nightmare he's running off about, you're in it down to the wire."

The US task force steamed out of Pearl Harbor on April 28, 1969, the Russian out of Murmansk a day later. Every conceivable precaution was taken to keep their sailing secret or rather camouflage them as routine military exercises. But tension was in the air and apprehension quickly ran its crackling course across the earth. Men ranted at being kept in the dark and in the same breath agreed it was "better not to know." All over the world, instinctive as animals crawling into their holes, men drew their curtains, shaded their lights and addressed each other in muted tones of fatalistic resignation. There were a few exceptions—in London where a screaming rush of naked women overflowed Piccadilly Circus and trampled scores to death under foot; in Johannesburg where a sudden outbreak of hacksaw murder clogged the streets with the heads and decapitated bodies of 23,000 Boers and tribesmen. For the most part, though, people tiptoed about and spoke in whispers. "Whose funeral are you going to?" ran the line under a cartoon in a New York newspaper. And the answer: "Mine, you fool. Mine."

AND IN the Polar Ocean too, the atmosphere was subdued and heavy. The submarines plowed their silent way ever further northward and rose to inspect each lump and blob of land that rose before them. The search planes whined off into the fog, disappearing from carrier view 10 feet past the flight deck and returned with their pilots shaking their heads and saying, "Not a thing, not a goddamn thing." Aboard the *Concord* Agricola took men by the sleeve and said, "Believe me, please believe me, it's there all right, I can assure you. It's long and flat and there isn't a tree on it any higher than a man's head. When we first saw it, it was just a purple shadow."

The days and nights went by and all reports continued negative. Agricola begged to go along on searches and he was finally permitted to, the lanky, patient Waters sitting beside him. There were times they flew 6 feet above the water and the frantic scientist "saw" Apinak a hundred times, but it was always a spit of sand or a clump of isolated sea rock when they reached it. After each flight, senior officers aboard the *Concord* would ask if he weren't satisfied now: "No offense, sir, but isn't it really possible you imagined the whole thing? You've seen for yourself there's no rocket installation out there, and each day we're costing the American taxpayer…." And almost weeping with frustration the old Finn would rage at them. "But it is out here someplace. You've got to keep looking. You've got to." For the Russians the expedition was no more fruitful. They too dug themselves through the fog and came back shaking their heads and muttering "Crazy old man, crazy old man, when will he stop wasting our time?"

And then in rapid-fire order came the two stunning events that shucked aside all lethargy and gave the operation the sense of violent urgency that marked it through all the fateful days that lay ahead. On its 22nd day of searching, the Russian carrier picked up a faint radio signal in an unfamiliar code. A team of cryptographers went to work immediately and four hours later succeeded in breaking it down. The message, unaddressed and lacking a closing signature, read— AMERICAN AND SOVIET CARRIER GROUPS PROCEEDING TOWARD YOU. EXACT LOCATION UNCERTAIN. ESSENTIAL THAT YOU COMPLETE YOUR FINAL PREPARATIONS IMMEDIATELY. The message was radioed to the *Concord* and its contents made known to all members of the Force. Scientists and military men aboard rushed to Agricola's cabin to apologize for having doubted him, but the little Finn brushed all that aside. "Don't waste time with such ridiculousness," he shouted, his frail body trembling in agitation. "Just find the station! Find the launching sites! Find them and do what you must."

The searches were intensified, the planes darting into every blur of shadow; threading their way back and forth through every cloud and bank of hanging fog. They returned to the carriers only to fuel up and then were off again, their pilots red-eyed and haggard and gobbling pills like candy to keep awake. The men of the submarine patrols drove themselves through a program every bit as demanding, rolling northward on their bleak, grey sweeps through waters uncharted and unknown, menaced time and again by mountainous masses of ice looming up before them—terrifying in their silent, glistening whiteness.

Well out on the western flank of the underseas patrol was the submarine *Bottlenose* (Commander Lester Hall). For over three weeks the *Bottlenose* conducted its searches without any positive results—an occasional rock or ice-strewn beach was the best it could report. But two days after receipt of the intercepted message, a wisp of movement far out ahead of the sub slowly resolved itself into the outlines of a freighter flying the Swedish flag. Commander Hall ordered full speed ahead and presently surfaced ordering the freighter to prepare for a boarding party. Lieutenant (jg) Albert Swift went aboard with a party of eight, intending to examine the freighter's cargo and papers. Watching from the *Bottlenose*, Commander Hall could see that Swift had been properly received and taken below. For 15 minutes activities aboard the freighter looked routine and normal enough for such an occasion. Then with several men still lounging along the rail and others going on about their everyday duties, an eruptive explosion buckled the freighter upward within a belching tower of black smoke. To the horrified watchers aboard the *Bottlenose*, it looked as though the freighter had broken in two with sufficient force to lift both flaming pieces clear of the water. Up they went and came down beneath a hissing mountain of sparks and steaming geysers to sink almost immediately, a great, black, funneling column of smoke rolling slowly over them.

COMMANDER Hall radioed the *Concord* describing what had happened and asking for instructions. He was told to stay at the site of the explosion and see if he could recover any debris. For perhaps six hours *Bottlenose* frogmen conducted a methodical search of the entire area amassing perhaps a hundred pounds of scorched wood fragments and bits of torn and twisted metal—some German lettering on several of the objects, some technical notations on others. The debris was brought back to the carrier and analyzed there, confirming the fact of Agricola's experience still again. The freighter had obviously been carrying materials for constructing rocket engines. The Swedish flag it flew could be assumed as simple camouflage. Everything pointed to a German ship and German cargo. *They'd need ton upon ton upon ton of materiel for such projects,* someone had jeered at Agricola's story. *Where do they get it?* The question had been answered.

Now something close to panic came down upon many in both task forces. The threat was clear and imminent, and still the rocket station lay hidden in the mists. Men spoke of those they'd left at home, and many were sure they'd never see them again. The searches were flown, but fog rolled out before the planes thick as cotton and visibility was a uniform zero. A Russian plane smashed apart on a spur of rock. An American plane missed the *Concord's* flight deck and plunged into the sea with all three men aboard lost.

Messages flew back and forth from one carrier to the other and the tiniest scrap of information was made immediately available to everyone involved. Agricola and Waters were flying 20 hours a day now. They'd been permanently assigned to a light torpedo bomber piloted by a stocky Bostonian named Hamilton. A good deal of the time Hamilton napped and Waters took the controls, but the pilot himself was flying the plane the dismal dusk-time Agricola squawked shrilly, "Look there! Look! Look!" The two younger men snapped their heads around just in time to catch the glint of metallic light that had caught his eye. It went on and off like a luminous pinpoint and Agricola whispered, "Apinak! It must be Apinak! It's *got* to be Apinak! They flew on circling downward and seeing the dot of light once more and then Hamilton cursed loudly and they all heard the rush of sound that was a plane coming in on their tail.

"Not ours," the pilot said tensely. "Hang on, professor. Take the gun, Harry. Let's see what we can do."

The plane had been stripped of all its armament except a turret machine gun and now Waters slid into place behind it. Hamilton was climbing straight upward, reaching for 10, 12, 16,000 feet with the other plane a gliding wraith climbing along beside him. Better than three miles up Hamilton leveled out briefly and began his dive and now Waters' gun was clattering fiercely, the big Westerner squinting into the gathering dusk and trying to pick out the plane screaming down the next chute. The noise of the gun and motor drowned out everything outside the plane, but he had a sense of movement more erratic and violent than need be and realized they were being hit and losing control. He turned his head to notice Agricola's face was white as chalk and his teeth bared back to the gums. Then a flaming flag unfurled at the nose of the plane, and Hamilton fell forward with streamers of blood unwinding down his face from the temple.

Fire roared large in front of the dying plane now and Waters scrambled toward it to take the controls from the dead man and try pulling out of the dive—a problem made still more difficult by the fact that the plane was still whirling, fluttering and splintering under the savage guns of its hunter. The Polar Ocean came up at them in a mad, swinging tilt and Waters howled himself into one final surge of strength, pulling the flame-ravaged, smoke-spewing nose upward and then flinging himself back toward the old Finn.

THE PLANE hit, bounced like a flat rock skipped across a stream, and came down with water flooding its shattered innards. Waters looped an arm around Agricola and beat a way outside for them both, going down with the old man and then coming up with him, their Mae Wests ballooning beneath them. Stroking powerfully, the big Westerner pushed them both clear of the plane just before a black avalanche fell on it from above with machine guns raking its quivering remains. "Lie limp, it's easier," Waters said and drew them both off into the darkness beyond the daggers of light thrown by the sinking plane. In the distance he could see a wide, flat shadow shaped like an upside-down saucer. He said, "Don't talk. Just stay limp. That ought to be Apinak and we ought to be there before sun up."

Waters' estimate proved to be correct and it was still dark when they crawled out of the water and lay gasping on the rocky beach. From where they were they could see the outlines of the Outerlander huts and after some minutes they rose and went toward them. Agricola remembered which was Akam Luk's and which was the brothers' Warnak and Kart. All three roused quickly in response to his whisper, and presently they were all in the girl's hut drinking a hot seafood soup and discussing their situation. By then Agricola and Waters had exchanged their clothes for suits of Outerlander fur.

Speaking rapidly in a Finnish dialect Waters was able to follow—although with difficulty—the girl brought them up to date on what had happened since Agricola left. There had been many more rocket tests, a number from stationary pads and a number from mobile launchers. Several freighters had arrived and the Werewolves had beaten the Outerlanders unmercifully to speed up the unloading. The pace of the entire operation had increased noticeably and all signs pointed to its climax being just a short time off.

"And our plane is gone," Waters said stonily. "No way we can get back to the carrier or even get in touch with them. My God, we really *are* in the soup, aren't we?"

He looked moodily off into space and the others watched him silently. Agricola was still exhausted from his ordeal in the blazing plane and the long haul through the water. Yet, even if he weren't, Waters would still be the focus of attention. Without anything having been said, it was understood that the tall young American would be calling the shots the rest of the way. He gnawed on his lower lip now, scratched a thumbnail along his jaw and said, "Maybe if I could see the station, it would help me come up with an idea. Any way that can be arranged?"

The girl said an Outerlander party was being taken to the rocket launching site early that morning. Just as Agricola and his *God in Nature* survivors had gone along with them months earlier, so could Waters go along, too. It required only that he join the beaten, shuffling crowd and move along in their dispirited way. Waters said fine and Agricola said he'd go along too. "Without me to explain things to you, you won't have any idea what it's all about. Need I remind you that you will be seeing the most advanced and complex rocket equipment existing anywhere on this earth?" Waters agreed that the scientist should join him. He also said yes when the two brothers said they wanted to go too—but he made it an emphatic "no" when the girl dropped her name in the hat. He said, "If something went wrong, it wouldn't do for all five of us to be caught in the same bag."

"And if the four of you get caught, what can I do here by myself?" the girl demanded.

"I don't know," Waters said, "but that's the way it has to be."

She took it with bad grace, shrugging sullenly and looking away from him, but she was on hand later to wish them well before the Werewolves came for them. Then she disappeared into the seaside caves to await their return.

The Outerlanders were driven to the launching sites in trucks, but one of the vehicles broke down on the way and the men it bore went the rest of the way on foot. Waters, Agricola and the two brothers were in this group, the four of them clumping along together with the scientist whispering information on everything they passed. At one point they came upon a radio tower—at another a cluster of airplanes with several middle-aged Germans and a number of young Werewolves tinkering with the engines—at another several rows of cottages—and then finally *preufstand* nine with Agricola whispering, "They intend to incinerate us all with what they've concentrated here—obliterate us, annihilate us, reduce the earth's three billion of us to a mountain of ash and a cloud of blue smoke...."

THEY WERE herded into a group at the *preufstand's* fourth launching pad and here Agricola pointed out the paraphernalia of the rocket station—the machines, the buildings, the storage area. Standing outside the earthen enclosure, the scientist listened to the German orders and, obviously jittery, suggested Waters "refrain from shouting 'Wow' or 'Zowie' or anything of that sort...." Then the flaming orange arrow shot skyward, the rumbling as of "a million horses stampeding across a bass drum big as Lake Superior" began and moments later the "ultimate weapon" rose in all its gleaming horror and Waters saw writhing, wriggling, whimpering Man standing naked and afraid at Armageddon....

"SORRY," Waters yelled as he knifed the struggling young Nazi. "But don't you guys know WWII's been over 25 years?"

He returned to the huts within a group of Outerlander workmen and spoke impatiently to Agricola of their stupefied state, their inability to help. There had been something like panic in his own voice that moment when he realized that he had to get back to the *Concord* and knew no way to do it. Their plane had been shot down and sunk. It would take him days, weeks to reach the carrier in an Outerlander canoe—if he were able to at all.

"Hell, there's got to be an idea, there's just got to be," he said back in the girl's hut and pacing up and down while the others watched him. "We've got the stuff aboard the *Concord* to put this outfit out of business, but what's it worth if I can't get back there and show them where to dump it? There ....."

The sound of an airplane brought him rushing to the door. A plane shot low over the Outerlander huts flying inland from the sea. Agricola spoke at Waters' elbow: "That could be their search plane. It probably wasn't a very long shot—just a final test for..."

"We passed their field on the way to the test area and then again coming back, didn't we?" Waters' voice was harsh and urgent: "It didn't look like much."

"They don't need many planes here," Agricola said. "Just a few to note where the rockets land and a few more to deal with intruders such as ourselves last night."

"Well, in that case..." He swung around on the girl and the Outerlander brothers: "We need a vehicle, a truck. We need some guns. Quick, how do we get them? Quick! We've..."

"There's a Werewolf guardpost at the end of the beach," the girl said. "There's always a truck there."

"How many Werewolves?"

"Oh, five, six, sometimes more."

"That's got to be it then." He took Agricola by the arm and pulled the old Finn up against him: "Old timer, you're not going to be in on this one. We're going to be moving too fast for you. You wouldn't be able to keep up. You'd slow us down."

"I know, my boy." The old man's voice shook: "But there must be something...."

Waters threw his arm out in a gesture wide and helpless, completing an arc that covered all the Outerlander huts and the blank-faced, drug-ravaged islanders moving dream-like and mute beside them. "See if you can get them out of here. Such poor, sad slobs. See what you can do."

He left the hut then with the three young Outerlanders coming quickly behind him. They ran down across the beach to the edge of the water and looked from there to the Werewolf guard but a hundred yards away. He spoke briefly to them there with the brothers nodding silently and the girl whispering, "Yes, yes, I'll do it, I'm not afraid." He put an arm around her and kissed her and felt her face, wet with perspiration. She said, "But hurry, hurry," her voice going down till he could hardly hear her: "Don't leave me too long."

She started along the beach toward the guard hut and Waters and the two brothers pulled off their clothes and ran into the water, each with an Outerlander seal-skinning knife in his teeth. They began swimming parallel to the beach and Waters squinted through the mist to see the girl still striding along, her hood pulled back now, her long hair falling, gleaming black about her shoulders. They flailed their arms like windmills trying to keep up, but they were still in the water when she rounded the edge of the hut and disappeared from view. They swam on till they were at a small out-jutting strip of beach and came ashore there, blowing like porpoises and rising immediately to their feet.

THE GUARDHOUSE stood back across the beach from where they had come in, a low, square building with mist blurring its outlines and an army truck up against one side. The three men started toward it, running low with the seal-skinning knives in their hands. They reached the rear of the hut to find a man hanging there upside down, an Outerlander being punished for some obscure offense. Dull-eyed and uncomplaining, he hung with his arms reaching down toward the ground and his back bare to reveal the welts and slashes that disfigured it. "Oh, the bastards." Waters panted and darted along the side of the hut until he was at a window and could peer inside.

The girl faced him from atop a wooden table against the far wall, slim-bodied and smiling, her heavy furs open to reveal the firm, rising pride of her lively breasts. She was dancing, stepping lightly along its center plank, her Oriental eyes gleaming wickedly, her hands flying about her body to touch it here then there as though calling attention to its varied perfections. Her black hair fell in thick, tumbling waves about her shoulders and she laughed and plunged her hands into it, her head going back, her teeth glistening wet and white against her ivoried skin.

A half-dozen Werewolves crouched in a semi-circle facing her, their heavy backs to the men at the window. Bull-necked and stocky, they pressed up close about the table, their blond-wolf faces lifted. The girl moved more quickly now, her laugh coming hoarse-voiced and mocking as they jostled each other aside to be the closest. Then heavy hands reached out for her and fear froze her face to a mask, and she kicked out violently, screaming, "Now! Now!" as Waters slid in through the window with the Outerlanders behind him.

In the very moment of their arrival, the hut became a maelstrom of whirling arms and glinting knives and powerful bodies in violent collision. Waters' first lunging rush brought his seal-skinning knife across a Werewolf throat, opening it wide as his arm, with blood gushing out in a torrent. All in the same stroke he swept the vicious blade into a mad-eyed blond-blurring face, felt pain and a deafening explosion alongside his head and bulled his way on with the knife whipping back and forth before him. He had a muddied sense of Warnak and Kart hurling themselves about like rubber balls and heard the girl scream in triumph, but blood was in his eyes and a bomb-burst of pain inside his head and he fought within a thickening cloud of black confusion. Bulky bodies fell away before him and blood spilled in hot sheets across his arms and legs and he continued to slash and heave himself about, even with the girl's arm tightening about his neck and her voice screaming in his ear. 'Stop! It's enough. It's enough." The floor was a swamp now with huge, fuzzy dolls sprawling everywhere, and he realized these were the Werewolves and they'd killed them all. "Their clothes." he said thickly. "Their clothes and their guns."

The switches were made, the girl shedding her own clothes and joining the men in Werewolf furs and swastikas. They found car keys in a drawer of the table and ran outside to the truck. The Outerlander hanging there gazed at them stolidly. They cut the rope and lowered him to the ground. He stared blankly as they clambered into the truck, then got to his feet and lumbered off into the mists. Waters took the wheel and the truck roared off toward the tundra interior—the girl with an eye swollen shut and her nose mashed flat, Warnak and Kart with faces cut and slashed to pulpy tatters, Waters with his ear pouring blood, his mouth a shambles.

They sped across that bleak, frozen ground and the dwarf pines rose up here and there like grotesque iron sentinels. No animals raced there, no birds flew. The sky was a primeval grey and cold as the ground itself. It was an empty land, a God-forgotten land and it was with a sense of physical shock that the four in the truck saw the tip of the radio tower up ahead of them and then the buildings, the cottages and the stretch of cleared, flat ground with the planes spread out across it.

"The one with the up and down tail, number one-two-three in from this end," Waters said slowing the truck down as men working on the planes looked up and watched them approaching. "It's an old World War II job, a *Jungmeister*. Not much for speed, but it handles easy and I'll have a chance of putting it down where I want. Okay? Everyone set?"

THEY muttered assent and Waters drove the truck onto the field, driving slowly past men at the various planes and exchanging Nazi salutes with them. As they approached the Bu. 133 *Jungmeister*, a thin-featured, balding man stared at them from the cockpit, then stepped quickly out of it onto the wing and down to the ground.

"Yes, what is it?" he said sharply in the Outerlanders' Finnish dialect. "Who sent you? What do you want?"

"We were sent…" Waters began heavily, his foot on the brake to hold the truck still. Several Werewolves drifted into view from beyond the plane and watched him curiously.

"What is it?" the German shouted. "What do you want? Who sent you? Who sent you?"

"We were sent…" Waters began again and realized he had nothing to add to that, nothing at all. And almost shrugging in his helplessness: "We were sent…"

Then he bounced his foot off the brake and onto the gas pedal and sent the big vehicle hurtling forward. It hit full into the clustered Werewolves with Waters flinging himself out of the seat, losing his balance and falling, rolling over once and coming up in a crouching rush aimed at the white-faced flyer. Guns popped behind him, voices roared savage oaths and the girl's scream rose and cut off suddenly at its peak of intensity. Hitting into the German flier with lowered head and shoulder, Waters slammed on over him and onto the wing of the plane. But as he scrambled for the cockpit, hands grabbed at his ankle and he felt himself being pulled back. The German was there, frenzied and screaming. "Let go of me, you son of a bitch," Waters gritted, kicking frantically then clawing his Werewolf revolver out and shooting the other full in the face.

A moment later he was piling into the cockpit and turning on the key the German had left there. Behind him the ground was littered with the dead and dying, but fighting still raged above them. The girl lay crumpled up on her side with her face toward him and a bullet hole in her forehead. Warnak and Kart fought back to back, but the Werewolves were pressing in on all sides and suddenly Waters saw them go down and sink from view as though beneath a muddy, surging tide.

"Lovely people," he said out loud, the plane trembling, quivering, beginning to roll forward. "Lovely, lovely people. Such a slamming around they took. Let's hope it was worth it."

The compact little single-seater was picking up speed now and elsewhere on the field, men were scrambling into others of Germany's World War II planes—a Me 109 fighter, a Dornier 217 dive-bomber. Waters increased his speed, felt a heavy *thunk!* as he plowed through a knot of howling Werewolves, then lifted the *Jungmeister* into the air and sped it toward a mountain of fog rolling in from the sea. Behind him the Messerschmitt's machine guns cracked briefly, then fell silent as Waters reached the fog and slid in out of sight. He knew the Dornier was somewhere above him climbing to a diving altitude and poising itself to shoot down. A single clear funnel was all it would need—a single shaft of open sky. He flipped on the radio, found the frequency he'd been using in Hamilton's plane, tried to keep his voice steady and said, "This is Waters calling the *Concord*. Waters calling the *Concord*. Come in, for God's sake. Come in, come in."

He was answered immediately, the voice spluttering with excitement: "Waters! Good Lord, we thought…"

"I know, I know, never mind that now. Look, I've been on Apinak," he said, quickly giving the island's approximate map coordinates. "I'm trying to get back to you in a German *Jungmeister*. They're trying to find me with a Messerschmitt and a dive-bomber. You're going to have to get to me first and bring me in. They…"

"We'll throw up everything we've got. Hang…"

"Fast, fast, move 'em fast. Remember it's a *Jungmeister*, a little single-seater son of a bitch. If I run out of fog before you find me, I'm dead."

"We're…"

"And you too, buddy. You're dead, too. All of us. We're all dead.

Come get me! Come get me! Come get me!"

He swung the plane frantically to avoid a patch of open sky and the Dornier screamed down at him. As though by sheer physical force Waters flung the *Jungmeister* back into thick fog and the juggernaut howled on past, then climbed once more to hunt and hover and swoop. He had the little plane darting about like a terrified mouse now and frequently through streaming wisps of fog he'd catch a glimpse of the great gliding brutes that stalked him. He spoke at times to the *Concord* saying he was still alive but desperate and pleading that they "Hurry up, can't you? Hurry and get me. How long do you think I can keep this up?" and being told, "We're trying, Waters, for God's sake, were trying, but we can't *find* you, we can't *find* you"—and the minutes limping by with a pale sun burning away more and more of his thinning protection until it seemed the hunters *must* get to him, *must* line him up in front of their obliterating guns—and then the horizon coming alive in a crosshatching tangle of streaking jets and the carrier-based fighters of the US and Russian task forces hurtling toward him to converge in a swooping, pinwheeling circus about the two German planes.

The Dornier went first, its deadly dive collapsing into a fluttering tumble with black smoke winding a flame-edged shroud about it and the grey seas blotting it up—neat, clean, perfect—as though it had never existed. The Messerschmitt hung on half a minute longer, hurling itself about like a maddened horse in a burning stable, with the carrier-based fighters circling in closer and more and more of their machine gun shells finding the mark until the German was literally being shot apart, chunks of wing and fuselage being ripped away, its nose in flames, its tail section hanging crazily, its carcass shredding, disintegrating, becoming a million flaming fragments blown over a mile of sullen sea.

Secure now but with the urgency of the task ahead tearing at his brain, Waters flew the *Jungmeister* out of cover and was immediately taken in tow by a quartet of fighters. With still others in front and behind they sped out to sea and presently the *Concord* came into view, its flight deck clear for receiving planes.

"Try it, Waters," the voice in his receiver spoke. "That little fellow ought to make it okay. Come in slow and catch us well up front. If…"

"Stop chattering, will you?" Waters said irritably. "I'm coming in."

He flew in over the carrier with the fighters falling away to give him room. Out past it he circled wide, flattening out and then coming straight in and decreasing speed until he was pancaking down and touching his wheels to the *Concord* deck and rolling along it. Men ran to him from all sides and as he jumped down to the deck some were already rolling the *Jungmeister* away to the side. Others, scientists, top military men, crowded around him, shouting questions—

"—Agricola?"

"—the photon rocket?"

"—is it true? Is it true?"

"—was the old man?"

"—your face. What happened?

And Waters, shouting, pushing his way through them: "Yes, it's true, it's true, it's all true—and they know we know about it now!"

"Calm down, man," someone told him. "We sent four planeloads of paratroops to the island as soon as you gave us the position. They should be bailing out by now."

"There may not be time," Waters said. "Better to bomb them out now, even if it means killing our own men!"

It took valuable minutes of argument but finally the commander of the force agreed with him.

THEN UP on enormous elevators came two Navy "Executioners," 1969 improvements on the powerful A3J "Vigilantes" of a decade earlier— attack bombers specially designed to carry thermonuclear bombs at high altitudes at Mach 2.5 speeds. Their crews were already at their stations, but frantic hands helped push Waters along and into the *Perfect Patsy* (the other was *Rhoda's Reward*). The seat next to the grim-faced pilot (Captain Glenn Hartman) was quickly vacated for him and he dropped into it. Then the big plane bumped along the flight deck and lifted into the air, with *Rhoda's Reward* falling in on its left and two Russian bombers appearing almost immediately on its right. Fighter planes from both carriers shot ahead of them to form a fanned-out screen with still more coming up behind and *Perfect Patsy's* radio crackled with the crisp, clean tones of a *Concord* signalman filling the air with orders and atmospheric reports, then turning frantic and squawking: *"Something's happening in Buenos Aires—report coming in— some sort of explosion—big fires everywhere—heard it at a thousand miles."*

"It's started," Waters roared. "Oh, Lord, oh, Lord, let's get this pile of junk moving. That way, that way, straight into the sun. Lord…."

They raced on, climbing high above the fog and straining to see down through it. The grey of sea and sky closed them in like a muffling blanket. Waters tasted blood in his ruined mouth and wondered how long ago it was that he'd been hit—a week, a year, a century? They flew on through an enveloping greyness stretching to infinity and beyond and then the *Concord* signalman was with them again, his voice high-pitched as a woman in flames:

"Leningrad, the same thing's happening in Leningrad—explosion—

fires—dead people everywhere—nothing left of it—nothing—nothin.....

Numbed with horror they piled along and Waters felt his body giving away under the strain—his heart pumping erratically, a great fist beating at his brain, his stomach churning as though a tangle of snakes inside were devouring each other and themselves. And the signalman still again, sobbing brokenly now. *"Frisco, Frisco's gone—nothing but smoke and ash—fire going out onto the ocean—dead..."*

And then Waters screaming the words, his eyes a madman's— *"LOOK THERE! LOOK THERE! LOOK AT IT!"*

A pillar of billowing smoke stretched up into the sky before them and above its spreading peak hung a rocket of power past all conceiving. The very symbol of mindless authority, it dominated that endless sky like Deity's finger held high for all the world's groveling worship. Made by Man, it now owned him and seemed to sense this and indicate it—tilting itself casually into trajectory as though this were a thing rationally decided within its own furnace-heart. Then, sublime in the knowledge of its utter invincibility, it sped off on its destructive mission leaving its burning wake spread across the sky.

"The site." His hands to his head as though to keep it from exploding, Waters was shouting the words in Hartman's ear: "The site!"

Hartman nodded, shouted something into his intercom, wound *Perfect Patsy* out past the column of smoke and then brought it around heading straight for it. Behind it were *Rhoda's Reward* and the two Russians with all the fighters scurrying to get out of range. Through the roaring din of their own plane and the rumbling of the rocket-firing below came the remote screech of the *Concord* signalman: *"Manila— half Luzon—fires jumping to other islands—estimated ten million."*

Now they could see the site clearly, line after line of the giant rockets. Hartman was going in for the bomb run when, suddenly, the situation changed. Far below, dozens of tiny figures swarmed onto the site, men armed with submachine guns and rifles. "It's the paratroops," Hartman shouted. "They've reached the target. I can't drop the bomb now, damn it! I can't!"

In less than five minutes of bloody combat, the combined Russian and American force had conquered the Nazi base, butchering the old scientists and their Werewolf minions with relentless fury. As Waters and Hartman watched from the circling plane, an explosive charge shattered one of the launch towers and the missile it held crashed over on its side like a toppling chimney. Inside the blockhouses, other paratroops were smashing the missile control mechanisms.

The battle for Apinak was over—but the victors still didn't know that if they had reached the site only a quarter of an hour earlier,

30,000,000 lives would have been saved....

From Apinak, the *Concord* sailed to California to help in the vast disaster area that had been established there. San Francisco was no more and everything between Santa Rosa and Salinas was grey-ash wasteland. Buenos Aires, Leningrad, Rome and Manila had suffered similar fates. An estimated 30,000,000 people had died and perhaps twice that many more burned or otherwise maimed.

As the peoples of the world set to work to rebuild, many pondered the catastrophe and looked for meaning in it. Some saw God's hand in the matter, supporting this view with the Old Testament tale of Sodom and Gomorrah. For these the destruction of five of the world's great cities with all their inhabitants was still just a warning—"Repent ye for the Kingdom of Heaven is at hand." They filled the churches and gave their money to total strangers and many went off to live in caves.

Others saw it as a triumph of the machine and devoted their energies to getting their creature back under control. The secret factories in Germany's forests that had supplied the Apinak center were located and destroyed. The vessels that had carried the supplies were sunk. A United Nations relief exposition went up to the Polar Ocean to visit all Outerlander islands. At one point a wild rumor swept the world that Hauptmann and several of his best workers had escaped and were already back in business on still another island, but this was quickly dismissed as inconceivable.

As THE central figures in the adventure, Waters and Agricola were besieged with publishing offers. His nerves shattered by what he'd seen and endured, Waters was unable to respond for several months. During this period, the pilot Glenn Hartman and 17 others who had flown off the two carriers sold their recollections to various newspapers and magazines. Warned that if he waited much longer his own version would be "old hat," Waters finally got to work and wrote his *Apinak Adventure.* The book had a phenomenal sale, was translated into 83 languages and will undoubtedly continue paying royalties to Waters for the rest of his life. A movie of it is now being prepared and an intensive search is underway to find unknowns for the roles of Waters, Agricola and Akam Luk. The girl will not die in the picture, but return to the carrier with Waters in the *Jungmeister* and marry him later. It's felt that the general public won't take to the picture unless it ends on a note of happiness and hope for the future. ✱

'RED BARON' PILOTS WHO HEISTED A MID-WEST TOWN

AT a little after 11 o'clock on August 6, a small van drove into Duren, New Mexico, coming from the east, and parked in front of Atkins' Department Store. Signs on both sides of the van read, "Somers & Boyle, 'Everything For The Patio'." Two men were in the store. The driver got out and went into the store and the other man stayed in the van reading a comic book.

About five minutes later the driver came out and was heard to say, "Something's fouled up. They don't know anything about our making a delivery. You drive fifteen hundred miles to deliver a load of stuff and the place you deliver it to asks you what you're doing here. Well, I've got Atkins himself checking into it and he'll be out in a couple of minutes to tell us what's what."

The driver was a pock-marked, balding man, probably in his early thirties. He didn't get back in the van, but stood close to it on the sidewalk with a toothpick in his mouth and his hands jammed into his trouser pockets, facing the store. His partner, a bulky, thick-necked, older man, didn't look too bright, reading *Blondie* with his mouth hanging open and a greasy cap pulled down low on his forehead.

There was a similar kind of confusion going on across the street. A curly-haired man in a Southwestern Telephone Company uniform had driven up to the Exchange in a Company jeep and gone inside, calling out cheerfully, "All right, what's the trouble? Doesn't anyone around him know how to handle *(Continued on page 68)*

"'Red Baron' Pilots Who Heisted a Mid-West Town"
Written as Roland Empey
Men, April 1974
Illustration by Samson Pollen

as stones and never blinked. You
couldn't believe they saw anything, but the truth is they
never missed a thing. He wasn't
particularly big, but he was
hard as rock all over, with
hands like saws or iron mallets. He worked for Tono Phul,
the Malayan tin king. Tono Phul
used to entertain his guests
by having the Filipino break
two by fours in half with his
karate chops. I saw him break a
desk apart that way. Once, Tono
Phul put him in a cage with an
orangutan. The Filipino broke
the ape's neck and then kicked
it to death. He was the worst
thing that ever came down the
pike, and when Tono Phul had
him tie me to a pool table and
work me over, I was sure my time
had come."

He had been with Scotland
Yard and working on a heroin-smuggling case at the time,
William Clive goes on to explain. His investigation had

"DETECTIVE WILLIAM CLIVE:
IS HE THE REAL JAMES BOND?"

— WRITING AS ROLAND EMPEY —

Male, January 1966

COVER ARTIST: MORT KÜNSTLER

Tall, iceberg-eyed, cruelly handsome, he's prowled the dark back alleys of the world, taking on everything from Red spies to underworld killers in his constant striving for excitement, seasoning his violent life with generous helpings of young, luscious, willing women. Now MALE presents an exclusive report on the man who, insiders claim, was Ian Fleming's living model for the famous Agent 007 . . .
Detective William Clive:
IS HE THE REAL
JAMES BOND?
28

TRINIDAD:

"**W**HAT was the worst experience I ever had?" The tall, lean-faced man with the grey-blue eyes permits himself a patient smile. It touches his mouth and for a moment softens its hard, almost cruel line. "I suppose the worst experience I ever had was when the Filipino tied me to a pool table and gave me a going over using *karate* chops. He was a wonder, that chap. He kept me going for almost an hour before I fainted."

The conversation takes place in King Arthur's Celebrity Palace on Volcano Street in Port of Spain, Trinidad. The

"SEE HOW I break boards?" the Filipino said. "Now we will try the same thing on your legs . . ."

29

Illustration by Gil Cohen

"What was the worst experience I ever had?" The tall, lean-faced man with the grey-blue eyes permits himself a patient smile. It touches his mouth and for a moment softens its hard, almost cruel line. "I suppose the worst experience I ever had was when the Filipino tied me to a pool table and gave me a going-over using karate chops. He was a wonder, that chap. He kept me going for almost an hour before I fainted."

The conversation takes place in King Arthur's Celebrity Palace on Volcano Street in Port of Spain, Trinidad. The Celebrity Palace is a small, dimly lit cafe with King Arthur himself behind the bar—an enormous and jovial man who smokes cigars and wears Hawaiian sports shirts. King Arthur was once one of the island's leading calypso singers, but hard usage and a great deal of whiskey have reduced his voice to a croak and he no longer entertains. But every record on the juke box is one of his and the sound of his roaring, rollicking "Honey Man" choruses never lets up.

"De poppa sit in de maple tree—
De mama sit in de tree with he—
Dey sit all night and de aujourd hui
Dey drink de gin and it squirt on me…"

"If you don't like my singing, go drink somewhere else," he tells anyone asking for some other artist. "For me, King Arthur is the best." He grins ferociously when he says this and few of his customers ever press the point.

The tall man with the icy eyes sits at the end of the bar where it bends and reaches the ceiling-high mirrors. He drinks bourbon on the rocks in double shots and has been known to down as many as a dozen without it showing any effect. He exchanges a few words with King Arthur from time to time, but other than that he keeps to himself. However, the tourists who crowd the little cafe will frequently engage him in conversation—most often a giggling woman with a camera slung about her neck. Some want his autograph and some ask if he'll pose for a picture. The more intense ask: "Is it true what they say about you, Mister Clive?" or "What was the worst experience you ever had, Mister Clive?" In most cases he'll excuse himself and say he has an appointment. But to those wondering about the worst experience he ever had, he'll sometimes give the answer quoted above. If they press him for details he'll say—

"The Filipino was more of an animal than a man. All you had to do was look in his eyes to realize there was something all wrong there. His eyes were dull as stones and never blinked. You couldn't believe they saw anything, but the truth is they never missed a thing. He wasn't particularly big, but he was hard as rock all over, with hands like saws or iron mallets. He worked for Tono Phul, the Malayan tin king. Tono Phul used to entertain his guests by having the Filipino break two by fours in half with his karate chops. I saw him break a desk apart that way. Once, Tono Phul put him in a cage with an orangutan. The Filipino broke the ape's neck and then kicked it to death. He was the worst thing that ever came down the pike, and when Tono Phul had him tie me to a pool table and work me over, I was sure my time had come."

He had been with Scotland Yard and working on a heroin-smuggling case at the time, William Clive goes on to explain. His investigation had taken him to Kuala Lumpur in the guise of a business man surveying Malaya for export-import possibilities. There he had been contacted by millionaire tin-mine owner Tono Phul, the suspected kingpin of Malayan narcotics. Invited to the Malay's sumptuous home outside the city, Clive had been entertained royally for three days. Among the entertainments was a Eurasian girl of overwhelming loveliness—tall, sinuous, full-breasted, her long hair black and gleaming. The girl had been put at Clive's sole disposal and he had enjoyed her fully even when he realized she was trying to pump him for information.

On the evening of his third day with the Malay millionaire, he had been drugged at dinner and come to spread-eagled across a pool table with Tono Phul sitting on a high stool watching him. The girl stood nearby, also watching. "I think you have come to Malaya to learn certain things about me, Mister Clive," he said. "You are an extremely clever and capable man and I would like to know what you have learned so far." Clive insisted he was in Malaya on private business and finally Tono Phul shrugged and beckoned to the Filipino.

"He had been standing out of my range of vision, but now he came up to the table," Clive says to his female questioners. "He was stripped to the waist and I could see the muscles twitching and stretching under his skin like snakes. His face was dead as stone. He held his hand a foot over my throat with the edge straight down like a knife. I'd already seen him break furniture with that hand and pulverize the big ape. Tono Phul asked me again to tell him what I'd learned. I said he had me wrong, I'd come to Kuala Lumpur on business. He nodded at the Filipino and the Filipino brought the side of his hand down on my throat."

It hadn't been a particularly hard shot, Clive continues. But it sped burning jolts of twisting pain throughout his body. It was as though his nervous system had burst into flame at a hundred different points. A second blow redoubled his anguish. The Filipino's stone face blurred before him and he could see Tono Phul's behind it with his lips forming the words, "Tell me." He heard himself scream, "I don't know, I don't know" and was hit again and again and again, each of the deft raps triggering a bolt of explosive, spreading pain within him. He estimated that it kept up for almost an hour before he finally passed out.

"I came to in a truck," he concludes. "The Filipino was driving and Tono Phul was sitting beside him. The Eurasian girl was feeling my head and smiling sympathetically. They took me to a hospital in Kuala Lumpur and Tono Phul said a bullock had rolled on me and the hospital should send him the bill for my treatment. I was in the hospital for five weeks and came out to learn that the Malayan Constabulary, using certain material I'd been supplying Scotland Yard, had arrested Tono Phul and charged him with heading up an international heroin-smuggling ring stretching into five continents. The Filipino had been killed fighting the police when they came."

When he's finished, Clive excuses himself and sends his gasping questioner on her way. But, if she's young and pretty—as sometimes happens—he buys her a drink and then maybe another and then they'll get up and leave the Celebrity Palace together. As he pays, Clive probably tips King Arthur a wink. The wink says as clearly as spoken words: "What a cinch! Easy as shooting fish in a barrel."

THE FILIPINO incident will ring a bell with many who read it here. They'll recall it from the Ian Fleming book *Goldfinger* and from the picture of the same name. The only significant difference is that in *Goldfinger* the karate expert is a Korean, not a Filipino.

Readers will also recognize the grey-blue eyes and the hard, cruel mouth mentioned above. They are well-known features of Ian Fleming's internationally known secret agent, James Bond. The physical similarity between the fictional Bond and the real-life William Clive is not surprising. In the view of many who would conceivably know, it was the young Scotland Yard detective who inspired Fleming to create

DETECTIVE
WILLIAM CLIVE

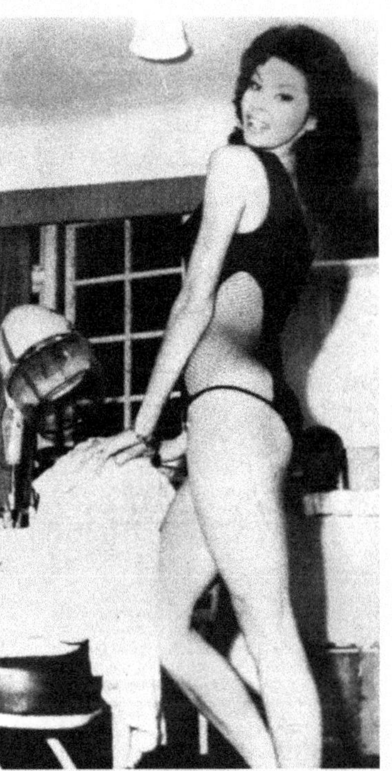

LIKE BOND (as portrayed above by Sean Connery), Clive
tangled with—and destroyed—world's most sinister criminals

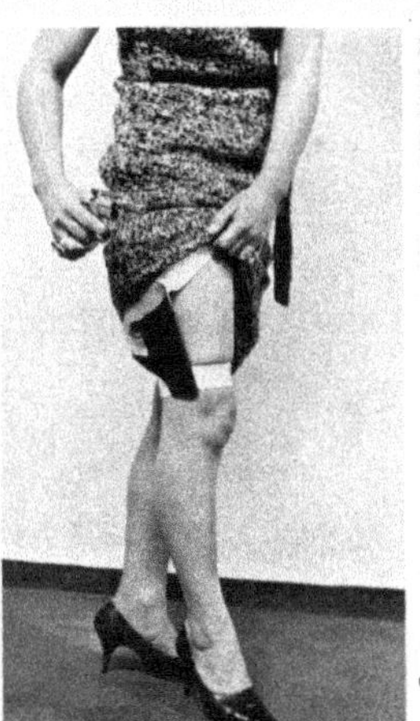

IN BEST BOND MANNER, Clive combined lovemaking with other interests, like gambling, skindiving (above left),
and strange weapons (ctr.), usually preferred his women to be young, exotic, beautiful and long-legged (rt.)

James Bond.

Consider these other similarities. Like Bond, William Clive is a motor car buff and like Bond he leans toward English Bentleys—the older Continental model with a heavy six-cylinder engine and a 13:40 back-axle ratio. It's the car William Clive still drives today, fitted with an Arnott super-charger that enables it to hit speeds well over 100 miles an hour. In *On Her Majesty's Secret Service,* Bond finds himself chasing a blazingly beautiful girl in a low, white Lancia Flamina Zagato Spyder. The chase went on for miles along the winding roads and through the villages of southern France and he finally lost her in the narrow, traffic-clogged streets of Montreuil. But before he'd given up the chase, Bond had reached a speed of 125 miles an hour. Clive was once asked about that by a redheaded American girl in black shorts and a crimson halter. She spoke to him in the Celebrity Palace: "I'm sure a hundred and twenty five miles an hour in a Bentley is an exaggeration. Did *you* ever do it?"

"NOT VERY often," Clive admitted, eyeing her slim, tanned legs and the firm, rounded swell of her breasts against the crimson halter. "But I was once chased along the Via Mercurio by three killers hired by Aunt Tina Lola. Auntie was involved in a scheme to steal ten million dollars worth of paintings out of the Vatican and since I'd learned how she intended to do it, she had her people shooting for permanence. I was out for a spin with two girls—starlets from the film colony in Rome— when this black limousine got on my tail. I pushed my vehicle up to 127 but I still couldn't shake them. Fortunately, they didn't know about the brace of 30 caliber machine guns I'd rigged up in my car trunk for just such emergencies. Things worked by remote control. All I had to do was push a button on the dashboard, the trunk door flipped up and I let go with a twenty second burst that blew the limousine's front wheels and killed the driver. Car went right off the road, skidded about 200 feet on its roof and burst into flames. The poor devils inside were all incinerated, I suppose. Didn't take time to look. The ladies and I were late for a luncheon engagement...."

The girl looked doubtful. Clive took her by the arm. "Come with me, my dear. I'll be happy to take you for a spin in my car." On the way out he tipped King Arthur a quick wink.

Like Bond, William Clive comes from Scotland, and like Bond, his past is shrouded in mystery. Little is known of his family or early life, but it's been established that he was in London in his early teens and already showing the hard-breathing interests that would distinguish his career—sex and gambling. At 17 he had the tough, cynical manner of a much older man and a cool eye that looked at women as though he were undressing them. Yet, it would be a mistake to say of Clive—or of Bond—that he chased women indiscriminately. The girl must be young. She must be beautiful. She must be exciting. She must be unusual. So it was that even as a very young man Clive was seen in the company of sultry-eyed Eurasians and sleek West Indians and dazzling French and Italian women while all his contemporaries settled for the mousy little shop girls that live in droves in London.

But for the most part they were girls with expensive tastes, too. And at this time Clive was working as an automobile mechanic for a fairly low salary. How then could he afford to carry on such a busy love life? Answer—by gambling. Like Bond, he was drawn to cards and, like the fabulous 007, he handled them with fantastic skill. *Chemin-de-fer* played in elegant gambling clubs was his favorite (Bond's too), but he was also wild for bridge and poker. An utterly honest player himself, he quickly developed an intense loathing for anyone who cheated. Even before he joined Scotland Yard, he had frequently worked as a gambling detective—a man hired by someone who suspects he's being cheated at cards, and whose assignment is to catch the cheater in the act. One of Clive's entrapments is still remembered and often discussed at the famous Black Prince Poker Club in London. (It's worth pointing out that James Bond is hired to catch Goldfinger cheating at gin rummy and later does the same thing to German nuclear genius, Hugo Drax in *Moonraker*.)

THAT WAS in 1938, when Clive was 19 or so. He had already struck up an acquaintance with Peter Riverton, the playboy Earl of Cheffland. Riverton told him he felt he was being cheated at poker by one of the players in his regular game—a red-faced Hungarian named Chosek. He'd pay Clive a thousand pounds if he could find out how it was being done. Clive accepted the offer and the next time the poker group met, he was one of the ten or so men who gathered to watch them play.

"The game was draw poker and six were playing," he will say, describing the incident. "It was a continuing game. That is to say it was held once a week with the same six men playing each time. They played at a round table and as generally happens in such games, they always took the same seats, Peter Riverton and the Hungarian, Chosek, sitting opposite each other. I noticed immediately that Riverton had his back to the bar and that being farsighted, he had to hold his cards well out in front of him to see them. The bartender was a tall, hungry looking chap named Griffin, very busy polishing his glasses every second he wasn't making a drink. All right, Griffin was obviously able to see Riverton's cards and he was somehow signaling Chosek. But how? That was the thing I couldn't make out. How was he doing it?"

The game went on for hours with the stakes getting steadily higher, Clive continues. When it reached fifty pounds ($250) ante and a hundred pounds to open, two of the players dropped out.

When those stakes were doubled, two more dropped out, leaving just Riverton and Chosek in a head-to-head contest. Until then, Riverton had been holding his own, but now luck started turning against him. He began losing hands on an average of four out of every five. When he had a hand good enough to stay in with, Chosek managed to have one just a bit better. When he had a powerhouse, Chosek always had nothing at all and dropped out before he could lose much. Riverton's losses mounted quickly and the red-faced Chosek grew increasingly sympathetic. "Too bad, old fellow," he said on several occasions, shaking his head. "Cards just not coming your way tonight."

Still apparently watching the game, Clive had his entire concentration on the bartender, Griffin. The lights above the bar were dim and the bartender himself could hardly be seen, but the glasses he kept polishing gleamed and sparkled. And now Clive noticed something about that neat line-up. Griffin's glasses were arranged in four rows, 13 to each row. "Each row could stand for a different suit," he realized. "The first one clubs, the second diamonds, and so forth." He watched still more closely. Riverton was dealt five cards. He held them well out to see them. Griffin's white hands appeared above the bar polishing glasses—the first and third glasses in row number one, the sixth in row number two, the ninth in row number three, the eleventh in row number four. Quickly, Clive looked at Riverton's hand. He held the Ace and Three of Clubs, the Six of Diamonds, the Nine of Hearts and the Jack of Spades. The glasses Griffin had polished conformed to the cards in Riverton's hand! How simple! From his vantage point behind the bar, Griffin had no difficulty seeing Riverton's cards. Since the glasses before him stood for the 52 cards in a deck, all he had to do was polish the appropriate glasses to show Chosek what Riverton held. Then, polishing again, he was able to show the Hungarian what Riverton kept and what he drew.

Clive's way of dealing with the situation was pure Bond. On the pretext of having to leave the room, he slipped behind the bar, dragged Griffin down to the floor holding a hand over his mouth, and knocked him cold with a right hand punch. Then he took his place and began polishing glasses to indicate Riverton's cards to Chosek. But he made a point of getting them wrong, showing Riverton as holding much weaker hands than he actually did. Four times in a row Chosek bet heavily being sure he had the hand won. Each time he lost and each time his face got redder and his temper got worse. The fifth time it happened, he jumped up from the table and strode to the bar saying he wanted a drink. Clive stepped forward to serve him.

"May I help you, sir?" The regular bartender's been taken sick. I'm taking his place."

IN THAT second, Chosek knew what had happened and knew he'd been caught. Without a word he returned to the table and wrote out a check covering all the money he'd taken from Riverton during their poker sessions. Then in utter silence, he left the Black Prince Poker Club, never to return. "A messy business," Clive says of the incident. "Fantastic that a man could be so greedy. I mean Chosek was a fine card player, and would have won a sizeable sum of money even without cheating. Poor Riverton could hardly tell his ace from his elbow."

It was the War that indirectly brought Clive into detective work. In those early years when Britain fought alone, it was essential that she get the most out of her limited manpower. So, every effort was made to place each man where he would be of greatest value. Clive had a flair for languages, a love of violence and the cold nerve of a safecracker. It was perfectly natural, then, that he be picked for Intelligence work. With only the briefest of preparation, he was parachuted into Occupied France on the first of the many sabotage missions that filled his army career.

To name just the highspots of those flaming years: He took part in the famous raid on the lighthouse outside Calais. It was Clive alone who signaled four incoming German ships incorrectly, thus causing them to smash up on the rocks.

He penetrated Gestapo headquarters in Paris wearing the uniform of an SS man, and succeeded in photographing the order that would send 10,000 Frenchmen to the Eastern Front as slave laborers. The orders gave the route of the train to be used and the Marquis were able to attack it, free the 10,000 men and kill over 600 Nazi SS guards in the process.

He frogmanned his way into the harbor at Marseilles and sank three heavy coal barges, thus blocking in eight Nazi submarines for five hours at a time they were desperately needed in the English Channel.

He took the identity of a German army doctor for four months and succeeded in attaching himself to the group attending to Marshal Rommel during one of the Desert Fox's several hospitalizations. While on this assignment, he was able to eavesdrop on conversations between Rommel and several of his senior officers and thus learned the general nature of his plans at El Alamein. This information was later to prove invaluable in helping the British formulate their own strategy for that all-important battle.

He led daring raids deep behind the Axis lines but also killed as a lone assassin. He infiltrated carefully guarded installations in the guise of a German, an Italian and a Vichy Frenchman. He romanced the mistress of Italian artillery general Vito Bona and learned from her when that flamboyant general would embark for the fighting in Sicily. He toughened perceptibly during those violent years, the mouth turning hard and cruel, the eyes taking on a steely glitter. He was wounded seriously four times and came to the conclusion that he was living on borrowed time and would certainly be dead by 45. (Students of James Bond will recall that 007 came to the same conclusion.) He learned to pretend to be in love when his current assignment required it and this helped develop the sardonic cynicism that characterized his post-war personality. He came out of the war as hard as shiny steel, seeing life ahead of him as a day-to-day thing, and ready to keep right on using all the tough skills he'd learned in Service.

"I WAS AS still steamed up for action when I stepped out of the uniform," he says now. "Wanted work somewhat along the same lines of the things I'd done in the Army. That meant Scotland Yard. Fortunately, I was well recommended and my application was favorably acted upon. Even with that, however, I would normally have had to look forward to years of routine, humdrum work at the bottom of the ladder. But those weren't normal times. The boys were back from service and thousands of them wanted something better than their old jobs. They wanted the big money and they wanted it fast and they didn't care how they got it. That was the time of the Knock-Over Mobs—a bad time in London."

The Knock-Over Mobs were groups of heavily armed former servicemen who roved the roads in radio-equipped cars, waylaying mail trucks, bank vans and any other sort of vehicle that promised some sort of haul. In an effort to combat them, Scotland Yard found it necessary to put a number of men in the field who hadn't received anything like adequate training. Clive was one of them. He was also one of the few who survived and stayed with the Yard. Most of the other new men— reduced to working in pairs and sometimes even as individuals—were unable to hold their own with the well-organized ex-servicemen. Some were killed and others too badly battered up to continue. Those who did last were not only the toughest physically and mentally, but also those who knew how to improvise new methods to meet the new situation.

So it was that Clive developed his heel knives—weapons that would later become a standard part of James Bond's armaments. Hidden inside detachable heels and small enough to be palmed, they could be gotten to under almost any circumstances and several times saved his life. So too did he make a thorough survey of every known make of revolver and decided on the Walther PPK as the best suited to his needs—the same gun James Bond used during one phase of his career, although switching to the Beretta at another. Forced on two occasions to swim for his life, he got into the habit of wearing loafers or slip-ons—shoes that could be kicked off in a second—another 007 specialty. He also developed a remarkable ability to improvise weapons from anything that came to hand—a belt buckle, a wrist watch, a camera, a fistful of coins, his tie used as a strangling rope. There also grew within him (it must be admitted) a streak of sadism. He trapped Jeff Hawley of the Liverpool Knock-Over Mob in an open manhole and could have taken him into custody with ease, but instead he kept that giant hoodlum thrashing about in the muck and filth of the sewer for over an hour before he let him out. James Bond addicts will recall 007 sneaking up behind the crouching figure of the German, Krebs, in *Moonraker* and kicking him a yard through the air so his head hit a wall and he was knocked unconscious. As with Clive and Jeff Hawley, the matter could have been handled less drastically.

"I was involved in the Knock-Over Mobs operations for four years," Clive will say today, sitting in the corner of King Arthur's Celebrity Palace. "It was tough work and it was dirty work. Few people realized then or realize today how beautifully organized the Mobs were. They had a central headquarters, a clear-cut chain of command, a wonderfully set up radio communications system. The only way to learn anything about them was to infiltrate them, join them, pretend to be one of them.

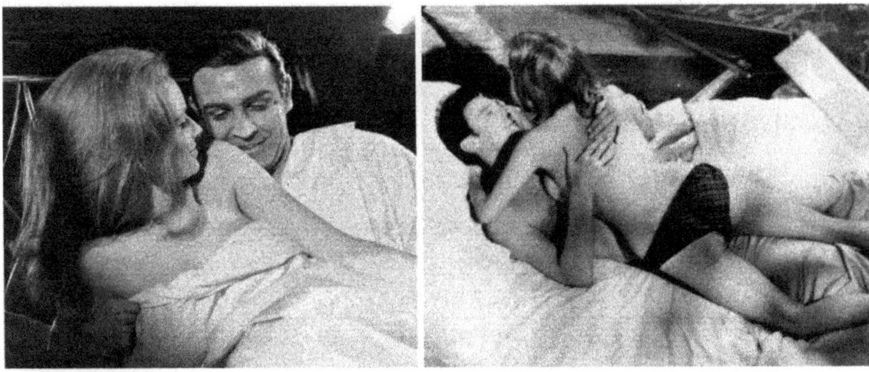

UNCANNY similarities between Bond character *(above)* and real-life agent Bill Clive included marriage to girl who was later murdered, ability to kill without mercy, preference for operating on his own . . .

Working on this principle, he at one time became right hand man to the 400-pound crime overlord Ira Swing. At another time he conducted a sizzling three-month affair with black-eyed mob queen Lottie Sykes. He functioned as a gunner in some mobs and a planner in others. He romanced his way into some women's confidence and fought with their men to establish his authenticity. In all cases he turned on them as soon as he had the evidence the Yard needed and then went on to something else with their curses ringing in his ears. His whole life sharpened, tautened. He drove faster, gambled for even higher stakes, was more and more reckless in his pursuit of beautiful women.

By 1951, the Knock-Over Mobs had been effectively broken up and Clive was being moved up to still more demanding assignments. There were three years operating out of the Yard's Singapore office on such matters as narcotics smuggling and international prostitution. It was during this period that he had his run-in with Malay millionaire Tono Phul and his Filipino karate specialist. There were two years on a counterfeiting assignment in Hong Kong and it was here that he had his affair with the bohemian artist, Loma Wax. Of Clive's many affairs, the one with Loma was unusual because he asked the lovely, cool-eyed girl to marry him and she said yes. But before they could set a date, Clive got himself involved in a gunfight on a dark street with a crew of Chinese killers. The girl was with him. He killed all three of his ambushers. But before he accomplished this, a shot ripped open the back of Loma's head. His eyes glittering, his mouth more than ever a cruel, hard line, Clive went on to still other cases, his fantastic skills and icicle nerves sending him up to a special status at the Yard. He took orders and carried them out, but to a great extent he had become a law unto himself making life and death decisions of a sort all other senior officers asked for instructions on.

Convinced that he wouldn't live past 45, he saw no point in planning for the future. Yet, his gambling winnings were such that he was able to put some money away despite himself and one day he bought himself a tiny cottage on Napoleon Lake in Trinidad. By that time Ian Fleming, a former consultant to the London *Times* turned suspense novelist, was spending time in the West Indies himself.

Did the two men meet and did Clive discuss his background and methods? There's no sure way of knowing. Fleming is dead and Clive is semi-retired and spending almost all his time playing bridge and *chemin-de-fer* at Port of Spain's swank Ace-Queen Club or drinking at King Arthur's Celebrity Palace. Of course, there are still women in his life—a great many of them—all long-legged, vibrant girls who know how to have a good time. And of course there are the tourists too, the camera-carrying travelers from America and Europe who corner him in King Arthur's and ask the inevitable questions:

"…the worst experience you ever had?"

"…true about the Bentley?"

"…prefer the Walther to the Beretta?"

"…James Bond?"

To this last he'll generally tip King Arthur a wink, direct a puzzled look at the ceiling and say, "James Bond? Don't know the name. Chap in a book, you say. Can't say I've ever come across him." Then he'll excuse himself and leave, with the mocking words on the jukebox rising above the tourists' disappointed voices:

> *"De poppa sit in de maple tree—*
> *De mama sit in de tree with he—*
> *Dey sit all night and de* aujourd hui
> *Dey drink de gin and it squirt on me."* *

his gleaming head. The crunch
had the splintering sound of
wood broken apart by a sledge,
and blood spurted from his ear
as though a faucet had been
turned on somewhere inside.
"THE LITTLE MAN DOTH STING -" He
came on batting with his huge
hands and Hall flailed back at
him with the iron bar, repeatedly cracking it down on his
head and neck and shoulders and
falling back again and again
as the blood-drenched giant
kept coming in at him, his voice
incredibly calm despite its
ear-shattering volume. "SUCH VI-
CIOUS BLOWS BEAR WITNESS TO A
HEART UNCLEAN. THE LITTLE MAN
DOTH SPEND HIMSELF IN HATE -"

The bar thudded down, and
again. One of the giant's eyes
rolled wildly, a lamp blown out,
and went dead. "THE LITTLE MAN
DOTH MAKE HIS BED IN HELL'S -"
Quick, flickering images passed
through Hall's mind; of Lustizo
and Oltami locked in mortal

Suspense Booklength

Golden-Legged Girl at Call-Doll Motel

$3.95 Thriller about Sin and Savagery in a Border Helltown "Violent and sexy"
ST. LOUIS POST-DISPATCH

Capt. Harry Moore
One-Man Army Who Turned Back the Cong at Viet Ridge

The Motorbike Girls and Their Wild Love Lives

"BUILDING VULTURES" They Make Millions Keeping You in Crummy Housing

The Corrupt Young Nymphs of Saigon, WORLD'S WILDEST CITY

"THE BLACK LACE BLONDE, THE YANK JUNGLE FIGHTER AND THE CHICOM PLOT TO GRAB THE MID-PACIFIC"

— WRITING AS ROLAND EMPEY —

Men, July 1966

COVER ARTIST: CHARLES COPELAND

"THE waters did part and the land did rise up black and steaming and the scattered peoples of Asia did press their foreheads to the ground and know him as the Golden Messiah."
The deep tones resounded through the jungle clearing and the natives lying prostrate in the mud groaned as though in physical pain or ecstasy. Stringy Bulyaros with their teeth filed down to points, stunted, pigmy-like Igarots, cave-dwelling Atamaris, tattooed Shamats from the tree-
"THIS'LL teach you not to bother me when I'm busy," Hall roared

THE BLACK LACE BLONDE,
THE
YANK JUNGLE FIGHTER,
AND THE
CHICOM PLOT TO GRAB THE MID-PACIFIC

By ROLAND EMPEY

ART BY GIL COHEN

The most deadly Red Chinese agent alive, he had set himself up as an emperor of half a million Philippine rain forest savages. Now he was leading his crazed followers on a blood-soaked march to Manila —and only a bare-knuckled U.S. jungle ace and a golden-haired, lush-curved girl stood between him and his relentless drive to crush America's staunchest Asian ally

Illustration by **Gil Cohen**

THE waters did part and the land did rise up black and steaming and the scattered peoples of Asia did press their foreheads to the ground and know him as the Golden Messiah."

The deep tones resounded through the jungle clearing and the natives lying prostrate in the mud groaned as though in physical pain or ecstasy. Stringy Bulyaros with their teeth filed down to points, stunted, pigmy-like Igarots, cave-dwelling Atamaris, tattooed Shamats from the tree-top huts of Shamat Ridge, all of them primitive peoples from the black swamp-jungles of northern Luzon. The figure on the three-top platform stood motionless before them, a towering mountain of a man close to seven feet tall, high cheekbones, slanted yellow-flecked eyes, his great skull shaved and gleaming in the light of a thousand torches, his massive body covered with a flowing, blood-red robe. A blonde young woman in green skirt, blouse and high-heeled shoes sat on a camp chair beside the platform, her legs crossed, a notebook open on her knee. Several frozen-faced Chinese stood in a clump behind her, silent, ramrod-straight, dressed in sandals and blue kimonos with saw-toothed, double-edged short swords strapped to their wrists.

"To him did gather all whose hearts cried out …."

JUST OUTSIDE the clearing, four men crouched in thick foliage and watched the weird scene unwinding before them. Three were Filipinos in the tan uniforms and wraparound leggings of the Philippine Constabulary. The fourth was Henry Hall, the Constabulary's American advisor and jungle specialist—a tall man with a hard, jutting face and a slope-shouldered build suggesting great power. It was Hall who spoke now, his voice a hoarse whisper, "He's got them scared to the point of total submission. He'll make his pitch for the collection now. And it better be a good one. Papa Mao didn't send him out here to bring him home an empty bag."

"Papa Mao?" The Filipino, Asayan, was speaking, a slender boy in his late teens. "You mean this is the work of the Reds?"

"Hell, yes." Hall was impatient. "He sells himself as the Golden Messiah, and then hands them over to Papa Mao to do with as he wants. That's what it's all about."

"And the girl?"

"Lily Hart," Hall said, shrugging. "Lily's a rough, tough little tomato, but she's all right. Trouble is she always winds up in bad company—crooks, smugglers, strongarm guys and now this big baboon. She's never learned to stay out of trouble."

"*...need no lands, no beasts, no paper money, no possessions of any sort. All these will become as one to be administered by the Golden Messia....*"

The giant Mongol urged his listeners to give freely of their worldly goods, then stepped down from his platform and disappeared into a conical tent. The girl, a ballpoint pen poised over her notebook, urged the natives forward. They began to shuffle past her in a long, winding line, each stopping briefly to mumble to her and wait while she made an entry in her book. "Telling her how much they're handing over to the Messiah," Hall said. "It's got to be all they've got. If one of them tried to get away with less—Hey! Watch this. You'll see what I mean."

THE GIRL had stopped one of the Bulyaros, a tall, boney man with mud matting his hair and the gaping, tooth-crammed mouth of a crocodile. She spoke sharply to him. He shrugged, muttered something, looked away from her. The girl motioned to the Chinese guard behind her. Half a dozen of them padded swiftly past her and grabbed the Bulyaro. He struggled frantically, his voice rising in a terrified screech. Others among the Chinese were lowering an iron cage down from a tree by a heavy rope. Screaming shrilly now, the native was thrown into the cage and its iron door banged shut. Then it was pulled up some 50 feet in the air with the Chinese yanking on its dangling rope to swing it.

At first it traveled an arc of only a few feet, but this enlarged rapidly until the cage was whirling wildly through heavy branches and smashing off tree trunks—great echoing *CLAAANNNNGGGs* and BOOOOOMMMMMs signaling each crashing contact with the Bulyaro imprisoned inside howling like a crazed dog. Below him the others stared up in uncomprehending fear or giggled hysterically, and the Chinese had to push in among them and herd them along like sheep to start them filing past the girl again.

"Well, that's it, gents," Hall said. "No choice but to go in there and take him."

"Take him?" The Filipino, Lustizo, made no effort to hide his disgust of a plan he considered insane. "We are going to take the Messiah? There are just four of us and you think we're going to take the Messiah?" Lustizo was a stocky, grizzled old timer with a cavalryman's bandy legs and awkward gait.

"We've got no choice," Hall shrugged. He hefted an iron bar a foot

CHICOM High Command in Peking (above) ordered fanatic Ara Moule to set up Red beachhead on islands. Many innocent natives (like man on left) lost their lives for listening to tyrant . . .

BOMBSHELL of a blonde (above) was determined to stop Red takeover, even though her certain death was the price if she failed

and a half long and rapped it against the palm of his hand. "You see the state he's got these poor birds in. They'll butcher their babies if he tells them to. Add them to the millions he's been lining up all over the Philippines the past two years and you get an idea of what's about ready to happen. A takeover. A march on Manila and then hand the whole country over to Mao. Sorry, gents, but we've got no choice. We take him now or by God he's going to wind up taking the whole country." He swung his heavy bar like a baseball bat and said, "What do you think is going to happen when I lay this across that skull of his?"

"With a head like that, you're going to wind up holding an iron pretzel," Lustizo grunted. "We can amuse ourselves trying to straighten it out while we're swinging in his little bird cage."

Ara Moule's rise to power in the Philippine jungles was unique. A man of incredible physical strength, Ara Moule was also an impressive intellectual, a gifted linguist, a translator of Shakespeare into four obscure Mongolian dialects, a mathematician and a champion chess player. A dedicated Communist, Moule arrived in northern Luzon in 1960 and immediately began the incredible effort that would one day cast his looming shadow across Manila itself.

"I am the Messiah to the Asians, God's Golden One sent to raise you from the mire"—was the heart of his gospel, and its impact was immediate. To primitive jungle peoples he was clearly a god-man from another time, if not another place, a creature for them to bow down before and

worship. In most cases a single attendance at one of his "Acceptance Meetings" was all that was needed to convert them. His jungle march was a series of spectacular triumphs—at one meeting, 6,000 tribesmen accepting him, 10,000 at another, a fantastic 40,000 bending before him like a field of wheat on the rocks above Muraya Falls. Lands, animals and possessions of all sorts were handed over to him, and his army of "True Believers" swelled to the hundreds of thousands with cells and offshoots on every inhabited island of the Philippines. For well over a year that wild expansion went on, while the government at Manila wondered what it meant and where it would end. Then, at last the sense of threat became too great to ignore. A meeting of all government security elements was held, and the American, Henry Hall, was asked to conduct a personal investigation of Ara Moule, or as he called himself, "the Golden Messiah," and make recommendations as to how he should be dealt with.

Hall was, naturally, picked for the job. A Texan distantly related to the old-time badman Wesley Hardin, Hall had arrived in Manila in 1958 as first mate of the Gulf & Peninsula Line merchant ship *Leslie Owen Kling* out of New Orleans. Hall was 27 then, but he'd already had 14 years of shifting for himself and had worked as a truck driver, lumberjack, circus wire walker, longshoreman, telephone lineman and airline mechanic—among others. He had also had 16 professional fights under the name of Kid Dallas and fought in the Korean War. Plainly he was a man with an urge to keep moving. At Manila he decided he'd had enough of merchant marining. "Pay me off, Cap. I'm going to stay and see what kind of a town this is."

He had taken a room in the *tondo*, Manila's Malay section, intending only to stay until his money ran out, then get another berth on a ship and move elsewhere. But in the steaming, seething *tondo* he had stumbled quite by accident into a group of malcontents planning to blow up Malacañan Palace, the Philippine White House. He had bought himself a rusty Colt revolver in a hock shop, burst into the basement where the bomb throwers were making their plans, cowed them into an acceptance of his authority and turned them over to the Constabulary. His manner had impressed the Government's Security Chiefs and it had been suggested that he take on specific assignments.

In the three years that followed, Hall had become an increasingly important cog in the Philippine Security machine. He had taken part in raids deep into Mindanao and other southern islands to round up sabotage gangs planning raids on Manila. He had led the small-arms attacks that netted three different smuggler gangs in the Sulu Sea and had personally brought in the terrorist Manuel Chazo after a two-month chase through 14 islands. The capture of Chazo was viewed as a classic of its kind: Two strong, skilled men using all their resources in a relentless duel that ended only when one had pushed himself to a point of total exhaustion. It was Chazo who had run and fought himself out of breath and strength and heart, and it was Henry Hall who tied him up like a trussed pig and hauled him back through 1,100 miles of jungle to Manila.

With the Chazo capture, Hall was clearly established as the most skilled of all the Constabulary's jungle hunters. When the decision came to find someone to investigate the terrifying Messiah sweeping on toward Manila supported by thousands upon thousands of primitive tribesmen who were turning their weapons, their possessions and their very souls over to him, it was inevitable that Hall would be picked. "Take as many men as you need," he was urged. "Make whatever preparations you require. But let us know the nature of this roaring fire burning through our jungles. Let us know what we must do to check it."

HE HAD decided that three men would be sufficient. Young Asayan, a tracker with the ears and eyes of a panther. The tough, experienced Lustizo, a grouchy man but dependable and incapable of panic, and the silent, moody sharpshooter, Luis Oltami. Oltami, a loner, was a death-obsessed man who would provide the single most bizarre note in all the bizarre proceedings to follow.

Hall's little party was flown up to Baguio in the Benguet Mountains from Manila in early May of 1962. The summer capital was well into its social season. The streets were crammed with tourists in Hawaiian shirts snapping pictures or going off on horseback parties to Bontoc or the Ifugao rice terraces at Banaue. Scores of wealthy Filipinos had come for the boating and dances, the slim-waisted, black-eyed young women in their shawl-like *ternos* with the great puffed sleeves, the men astonishingly cool-looking in sheer *barong Tagalog* shirts.

Hall's party had time for none of that, though. They stopped only long enough to check their weapons and equipment and to interview a native claiming to have been at one of the Messiah's meetings some weeks earlier. Hall quickly found the native had nothing of importance to tell and was probably only hoping for a *peso* for his "information." Hall laughed a "good try" and gave him the peso. Soon after that the four men were on their way northward in a Jeep, a Baguio constable driving. Well above the city they hit black jungle too thick for a vehicle to penetrate. The Jeep halted and the four men went ahead on foot.

Their trek northward went on for 38 days.

"At least we're getting closer to him," Hass said as they began encountering first, determined silence and then, transparent fear. "We're moving onto his home grounds."

It was the tracker, Asayan, who finally located him. They were hunting in pairs by then—Asayan and Lustizo together, Hall with the silent Oltami. Later, they would meet at a pre-arranged time. When they met this time it was immediately clear to Hall that something important had happened. The boy was eager with excitement, and even the phlegmatic Lustizo showed tension.

"He's on the other side of the Chafaya River," Asayan said, eyes glittering. "He has many Chinese with him and a white girl and there will be a meeting for the natives tomorrow night."

Hall questioned him sharply to find out exactly where the meeting would be held. The boy drew a crude but accurate map showing the trails he'd followed to the Chafaya and the point where he'd paddled across in a derelict *banca*—a crude canoe. Once Hall was sure he could get there, he told them his plan. "I'm going to go get a look at him myself. It's essential that we find out what's going on without him being aware of it. One man has a better chance of moving around undetected than four, so the three of you will wait here until I return. We'll figure our next step then." They had agreed upon a time for his return and what would be done if he didn't make it: Lustizo would assume command and one man would return to Baguio for further instructions. The other two would continue to track the Messiah.

Hall left them within an hour of the boy's return, a submachine gun in one hand, a machete for hacking through the underbrush in the other, and his heavy iron pipe strapped to his back. It was after nightfall when he reached the Chafaya, located Asayan's *banca* and paddled across. Less than an hour later he was at the Messiah's encampment and worming his way through thick brush, close enough to see and hear what was going on.

HALL KEPT his vigil all that night. His vantage point enabled him to hear the Messiah in his talks with the Chinese before the meeting and from the talk he began to get a glimmer of what his "mission" was all about. He saw the girl, Lily Hart, and grunted a curse, wishing she weren't mixed up in it. Then came the meeting itself, with the natives collapsing in groveling fear before the giant, red-robed Messiah and swearing to hand over all they owned. There were two who were evasive in listing what they had. Both were thrown into the iron cage and sent smashing into branches and tree trunks. When the meeting ended, both men were still in the blood-spattered cage, both smashed to pulp, both long since dead.

"Well, there's no secret about him anymore," Hall said when he rejoined the others in his party the next morning. "He's a Red or at least working for them. We'll stay close to him and I'll try and figure out our next move. It's a cinch we're going to have to do *something*. He's a dangerous man, and if he's not stopped soon it's going to be too late to stop him at all."

Now, three nights later, Hall and the three constables crouched under cover while Ara Moule, the Golden Messiah, thundered at an acre of assembled trembling natives that he was "one risen up in shining glory all clad in robes of quivering flame." Later in the meeting, a Bulyaro who had tried to hold out was thrown into the iron box and smashed to death. A little after that Hall took a few tentative swings with his iron pipe and said, "We're going to have to go in and take him."

The project was greeted with less than enthusiasm by the three constables, and Lustizo described it bluntly as "crazy." But Hall insisted they had no choice. "We take him now or he winds up taking us. Let's move out, gents. We're wasting time talking."

They moved forward on their bellies, circling toward the encampment—the Golden Messiah's conical tent rising high among a half dozen smaller ones. Most of the natives had filed past Lily Hart and were straggling off into the jungle. The dead Bulyaro lay huddled in a corner of the gently swinging cage, a grotesquely twisted arm sticking out through the bars. Several of the Chinese had gone into the Messiah's tent and others lounged about in front of it. The last of the natives mumbled the worth of his wealth to the girl and trotted into the underbrush. She folded her notebook to the last page used and took it into the Messiah's tent. Hall and the three Constables inched their way forward until they were close enough to hear the Chinese talking and see the open flap of the tent and those who were clustered inside.

"We're going to have to pull the damn thing down on them," Hall said. "It's one of those heavy felt and canvas jobs. If we work it right, we'll hook them like fish in a net."

He sent Lustizo and Asayan around to the back of the tent, each of them taking up positions under cover and about 10 yards apart. He waited in front with Oltami until they were in place. Then he said, "You can see three of the four ropes that are holding it in place, Luis. Slash them and it will all come down. Questions?"

Oltami shrugged, said "I see if I can do it" and adjusted his rifle to his shoulder. The others all held submachine guns. Hall said, "It's got to be fast, Luis. We can't have too many of them flying at us." Oltami nodded, and ripped off three shots, one on top of the other. The tent collapsed like a great bladder with the air suddenly whooshed out of it.

The Chinese standing guard outside ran about blindly, like ants blown out of a sand hill, their high-pitched, cackling voices drowned out in the hard, rapping sounds of submachine gunfire. Hall covering the front, Lustizo and Asayan the back. Hall signaled the firing to stop, shouting, "Stay still and no one else will be hurt."

Two MEN lay dead in front of the tent and another moaned softly.

For perhaps half a minute nothing happened. Then one of the lumpish mounds began moving toward the front flap and the girl came out patting her blond hair back into place and cursing Hall in longshoreman language. The big-shouldered Texan shook his head sympathetically and said, "I know, Lily. Life's full of these lousy little breaks" and shouted again, "All right, Moule, I want you now. Just you. Let's—" He stopped as the four Chinese in front of the tent bounced to their feet and rushed toward him, their short swords swinging. His burst of fire exploded full into them and sent them reeling along five yards of jungle, mud-like dolls spilled out of a child's runaway baby carriage; three were dead and one rolled into a quivering ball with his chin against his knees and blood bubbling up out of his mouth. Hall shouted, "It didn't work, Moule. Come on out. Now."

There was silence. Nothing moved. Hall scooped up a bundle of thin sticks and, lighting a match, made them into a torch. He shouted, "Come on out, Moule. Or else I'm sending you up in flames." And to the girl: "Warn him, Lily." She was standing perfectly still with both hands still at her hair. She said, "You wouldn't," and Hall started forward carrying his torch. She called out, "You'd better come out. I think the snake will do it."

Silence again, the collapsed tent perfectly still. Hall took a step forward and then the tent bulged hugely upward and Ara Moule, the Golden Messiah, came out of it, his face wearing the calm, serene smile of a gigantic Buddha, his enormous red-robed body catching glints of dazzling light so that it seemed he walked in flame, his naked skull gleaming like polished ivory. Hall heard Oltami gasp behind him, and turned quickly to see the Filipino raise a trembling hand to his mouth. "Get hold of yourself," the Texan said sharply and turned back to the Golden Messiah advancing toward them, a soft-pacing giant of a man, with footfalls light as a jungle cat's.

"You wanted me," he said still smiling, his voice a deep, resonant bass, but quiet and even gentle. "I am here. I am the Messiah sent to free the Asians—"

"Tell it to me on the way, kid," Hall said. "I'm taking you to Manila."

"Are you?" the Messiah said nodding and chuckling softly. "Well, we shall see. Yes, that will be very interesting to see."

THEY STARTED back through the jungle, leaving Lustizo and Asayan to guard the Chinese who were bogged down in the tent. Hall had told the two Filipinos the route he would take and it had been agreed they would try to hold up the Chinese for an hour, then hurry to catch up. Hall had tied the Messiah's hands behind him, taken the girl by the arm and said "I'll break your neck if you try anything, Lily." Then the little party had started out with Oltami leading the way and Hall himself bringing up the rear, his submachine gun in one hand, his iron bar across his back.

They went due south, moving much slower than Hall had intended, their pace kept down by Lily Hart's difficulties. The girl slipped and stumbled in her high heels, but refused when Hall suggested she take them off. "What do you think I am, a savage? I come from Buffalo, New York." Hall told her brusquely, "Suit yourself, just keep moving along," He jabbed her rump with the iron bar when she began to slow up still more. She screamed and tried to scratch him, but he kept jabbing her along, saying, "Now Lily, now Lily, let's keep moving." Ahead of her the Golden Messiah marched steadily along, sometimes humming to himself, sometimes addressing a remark or two to Oltami's back, "Such a fine-looking young man. Knowest thou the peace of acceptance, young man? Hast heard me speak, young man? Hast heard the Messiah address his flock?"

They moved through black jungle. A pale moon filtered through the leaves in some places and was unable to pierce their thickness in others. They moved to the buzzing-hacking-sawing sound of trillions of insects and heard the occasional cry of a *junlu* parrot and once the chattering of a troop of yellow-eyed *garo* monkeys racing above them and another time the deep, coughing roar of a Luzon tiger. The girl cursed bitterly at the beginning, but fell silent as the hours crawled by and where once Hall had been poking her with his iron bar, he began putting a hand on her arm to help her along. Up in front Oltami had begun darting about to pull branches out of the way for the Messiah walking calmly along behind him. The giant's hands were still tied behind his back, but he moved with an incredible grace and balance nevertheless and had no trouble keeping his footing. "Dost know of my work in these jungles, young man? Dost know of the light that glowest in the hearts of all who accept the Golden Messiah? Dost know the truth that—?" And Henry Hall talking to the girl: "How many poor slobs did he break apart in the little cage, Lily? A little con game or a little drunk-rolling's one thing, but this is something else. This is murder and treason and selling out a whole goddamn country —" And the girl, stumbling, slipping, her skirt and blouse ripped and spattered with mud, her hair hanging in matted ropes, her voice a weary whine: "Let me alone, can't you? Can't you?"

Morning was almost on them when they heard the shots behind them. Submachine gunfire, unmistakably. Hall shoved the Messiah and the girl into a thick clump of trees, ordered Oltami to keep them covered, and raced back along the way they had come. The firing stopped, then started up again, and he froze, suddenly aware of someone crashing toward him through the underbrush. He ducked behind a tree, waiting for whoever it was to draw abreast, then popped out, snaking an arm around a sweaty head and found himself holding Lustizo.

"They killed Asayan," the Filipino gasped as soon as he recognized Hall. "Cut him in half with their little swords."

"Keep going!" Hall snapped, turning him loose. "Make a racket. Move!"

THE FILIPINO lumbered off into the brush. Hall fell back behind his tree again. Moments later, six Chinese came into view, running low to the ground like dogs on the scent—faces blank as though carved in stone, short swords in their hands, kimonos bunched about their waists. 50 yards—30—10—and then Hall was out in front of them, his submachine gun clattering as its muzzle swept back and forth. They went down like tenpins and one skidded along the ground, his sword a darting snake's tongue, and Hall had to fire a burst into his head to keep from being slashed. Then, sure he'd accounted for all six, he ran back after Lustizo, met the Filipino coming toward him, and barked, "Come on, we're making too much noise."

He led the way to where he'd left the other three. By now morning was a thin, pale grey leaking out ahead of them. Hall rammed through brush and foliage, with Lustizo blundering along behind him breathing like ripping cloth. Hall roared a curse as he saw Oltami hacking away with a knife at the rope around the Messiah's wrists, his movements frantic, his eyes bulging in a madman's unreasoning fear. *"He is the Messiah! He is the Golden One sent to free Asia! We must exalt and worship him. We must—"* The words spiraled into a strangled screech as Lustizo came down on him, but in that moment the Messiah's freed hands flew upward, with the rope dropping away and his voice going off like a cannon, "HAVE FAITH. HAVE AT THEE!"

In that instant, Hall smashed him with the iron bar, smashing it into the side of his gleaming head. The *crunch* had the splintering sound of wood broken apart by a sledge, and blood spurted from his ear as though a faucet had been turned on somewhere inside. "THE LITTLE

MAN DOTH STING—" He came on batting with his huge hands and Hall flailed back at him with the iron bar, repeatedly cracking it down on his head and neck and shoulders and falling back again and again as the blood-drenched giant kept coming in at him, his voice incredibly calm despite its ear-shattering volume. "SUCH VICIOUS BLOWS BEAR WITNESS TO A HEART UNCLEAN. THE LITTLE MAN DOTH SPEND HIMSELF IN HATE—"

The bar thudded down, and again. One of the giant's eyes rolled wildly, a lamp blown out, and went dead. "THE LITTLE MAN DOTH MAKE HIS BED IN HELL'S—" Quick, flickering images passed through Hall's mind; of Lustizo and Oltami locked in mortal combat, of the girl on her knees, screaming hysterically, hands at her mouth. Then, a blur of wiping movement. "NOW, LITTLE MAN—" and the bar had been plucked from his hands, with the battered Messiah marching forward and twirling it like a baton. Scrambling, scuttling, Hall leaped out of range, yanked up his submachine gun and fired off a single shot—then another and another and a fourth and a fifth. All five thumped into that bear-like body, sending the Messiah stumbling, falling, and rising again and suddenly Hall was lying on his back, the great Mongol looming over him and then his sixth shot hit home and blew the Messiah over on his side, his neck twisted and his face in the mud.

Slowly, the Texan rose to his feet and stared down in disbelief and something like shock at the man he'd fought. Lustizo and the girl came to join him. Oltami was lying dead where Lustizo had split his head with a machete. "I can't believe this," Hall said hoarsely. "He wasn't human. Look at him." The giant's face was unrecognizable, every bone in it broken, every feature smashed and shapeless. Blood dribbled from a dozen places on his body. He lay like a beached whale with one staring eye open and Hall muttered, "Can't seem to think. The old head's not working. What do we do now? What—?"

The girl screamed. Lustizo crossed himself. The Messiah was stirring, moving. They fell back from him in a panic, watching as he sat up, then got to his knees. Fall came up behind him quickly to pull his arms behind his back and tie his wrists together. "We resume our journey, little man," the Mongol said, struggling painfully to his feet and swaying drunkenly when he finally stood erect. His voice was heavy, slow, pontifical. "We go on to the end, little man."

They reached the village complex of Ago Ago 18 miles above Baguio some 22 days later. They had draped the Messiah across a bullock most of the way and the girl had ridden a little *ascuilo* burro. Lustizo had bought both animals at an Igarot village, paying for them

with his submachine gun and machete. They'd gone under cover
on dozens of occasions while hordes of frenzied natives beat the
underbrush searching for the Messiah. They had floated down rivers
lying on lashed-together logs with brush piled above them looking
like something broken loose from a river bank. The girl went thin and
silent, her face a bleeding network of sores and scratches, her clothes
reduced to rags. Hall and Lustizo were bone-weary and emotionally
exhausted; the Filipino crossed himself frequently, muttered to himself
and refused to look at the Mongol. The Messiah himself seemed to have
withdrawn to some inner world. He went for six days without saying a
word, then looked at Hall and said, "You are new here. Come, tell me of
your former life. Didst know thou many women?" Lustizo had snarled,
"Kill him, kill him," and made an unsuccessful grab for Hall's gun. "He's
the devil incarnate." Hall had answered, "Take it easy, we'll be out of
it soon."

They had encountered natives of the sophisticated Parawyo tribes
three weeks after they'd started out and induced them to send runners
to Baguio with a message for Constabulary headquarters there. Two
days later they came into Ago Ago and were met by a force of heavily
armed police.

"There's a big crowd of natives moving this way, coming out of
the jungles," the lieutenant in command said to Hall, explaining their
grenades and automatic weapons. "We could be in for trouble."

The plan had been to move the Messiah to Baguio in a Jeep convoy
with the Constables as guard, then fly him down to Manila, but the
natives formed too fast for that. They came into Ago Ago in great,
settling waves, and there was a watchful calm about them more ominous
than any frenzy would have been. They filled every inch of space within
the sprawling village, standing, sitting, lying in the dusty alleys. And
they had only one question for the Constabulary lieutenant: "Why have
you taken our Messiah from us?"

"We'll never get him down to Baguio," the lieutenant said nervously
to Hall. "They want some kind of a hearing right here. If we don't give
it to them, they'll use force to free him so they can take him back into
the jungle."

"He's been acting nutty ever since our brawl," Hall said. "He's got
six bullets in him and he took a God-awful pasting back there and it's all
probably thrown him out of kilter. Maybe if we give him a hearing he'll
reveal himself. The poor bastards might want a messiah, but they don't
want their messiah to be a nut."

The hearing was held in the village meeting house, a long, rambling
building with benches around the back and down both sides. A desk

and several chairs were placed in front. The afternoon of the hearing, the Constable lieutenant and several others sat at the desk. The natives were everywhere else, on the benches and filling up all the space inside and outside the building, flowing back to the very edges of the village. When the Messiah was led in, a murmur of resentment went through them, picking up volume gradually until it had become a deep-throated roar of sullen rage. Many hadn't seen the giant Mongol since he'd been brought in, and his broken face and the unmistakable evidence of his great pain put them in a fury. Many would have charged the grim-faced Constables even then, but the Messiah was told he could speak and the tribesmen held off.

"I am the Golden One, the Messiah long promised to the lowly and common-born of Asia," the giant Mongol said, and his voice had all the calm authority of his jungle Acceptance Meetings. Standing at a window inside the building, Hall cursed softly and knew they'd been beaten. The Messiah was the Messiah of old. The natives would never let him go. "Tell those who bear witness to his pervasive goodness—" The deep voice rolled on and the words were a majestic waterfall, words most of his listeners didn't understand, yet words that swept them along on their rising, booming crest. "Come within the parting of the heavens and God's eye was a piercing—" We're beaten, Hall thought resignedly. That long, violent hunt, all for nothing. He's beaten us. "Steaming mists did part and the clear light—"

"Liar! Liar! Liar!"

The words went off like a clanging bell and in a moment the room was in a tumult. "He's a Red! He's working for the Chinese Reds! Everything he's done has been—" The girl, Lily Hart, was on her feet and pointing a quivering finger. A native tried to pull her down, but she struggled free of him and continued to scream, "Liar! Red! Chicom!"

THEN, THOUGH her mouth was still working, no one could hear her. The Messiah had risen to his feet and the Constables were grabbing for him. Their efforts were as ineffective as butterflies trying to pin a bull. With a huge heave of his arms and shoulders he flung them back and lunged into the howling natives. His bolting path led him straight at the girl and as he crashed over her, her head snapped over her neck, grotesquely broken.

Slugging his way through wild-eyed natives, Hall flung himself into the Mongol's path. He made one brief attempt to overcome the huge figure and hold it in its place. Then he seemed to hear a voice murmur "No, not this time, little man," and a hand like a flat iron came down on his head and sent him spinning up against a wall of the room. Dazed, he stumbled toward a window, saw the Messiah go through it ahead of him and saw the natives outside rise up like a tidal wave to receive him. For one shattering second he saw the calm, broken face rising high above that seething mass and the great booming voice rang out: "Now I go to fulfill my true destiny!" And then the bear-like figure disappeared as the wave of human bodies rolled over it.

They've turned on him, Hall realized numbly. They're trampling him to death...

It was some time before the Constables could break into the knot of struggling natives. When they did there were some who wished they hadn't. They'd gone in to find the Golden Messiah and bring him out. But all that was left was a few shredded fragments, barely enough to fill a small paper bag. That, and something to wash away with a bucket of soapy water.

It was, Hall reflected later, a fitting destiny for this Messiah of evil destruction. ✳

I EDITED that [Magazine Management] stuff, I read it all. I went from that to *The Saturday Evening Post*. The very first day at the *Post,* I edited a piece by John O'Hara and Hannah Arendt. She said, 'Come on, vat are you *doink?'*

"I said, 'You're okay Arendt, but you're no Walter Kaylin.'"

Mel Shestack
in conversation with Josh Alan Friedman

Let old Dick -"

"Get the hell away from me," she muttered. "I don't want company."

He dropped down beside her, slipping an arm around her shoulders and pawing at her breasts. "Tell old Dick your troubles. Tell old Dick who slugged you in the mouth, and old Dick will tear him in half clear up to the Adam's apple. Let old Dick be nice to you, beautiful."

But the girl laughed shakily and twisted away from him, still patting her mouth with the handkerchief. "Don't get such silly ideas, Dickie boy. I'm Duke's whore. Haven't I told you that often enough? I'm Duke's whore ...."

It was some two months earlier that Dick Billings, an agent of the Central Bureau of Investigative Intelligence, was called into his bureau's office in Washington, DC.

"SURF PACK ASSASSINS"

— WRITING AS ROLAND EMPEY —

Male, August 1967

COVER ARTIST: MORT KÜNSTLER

"HIT the suds!" Cy Boardman hollered as he caught a five-foot wave that sectioned ahead of him. "Hang ten, you no-good!" whooped lean, black-haired. hawk-faced Boardman. He rode the soup right onto the grey-white sands of Cavite Beach in Luzon in the Philippines.

Eight others of the WOOSS (World's Our Oyster Surfing Society) came swirling along behind him: Tex Neeley belly-boarding for laughs with his red beard looking like a sponge pasted onto his chin; Maggie Huntington, cool and precise in a white bikini and looking as though she might start buffing her nails on the way in; Phil Taber, Arnie Leach,

They were a wild group of young Americans on a surfing-and-sex binge that had taken them halfway across the world—and lurking among them was a Red killmaster out to trigger a three-continent orgy of subversion and murder. Then a Yank undercover man infiltrated their treacherous ranks, moving up a girl-by-girl, thrill-by-thrill ladder in search of his deadly quarry, aware that a single false move would throw him into the path of a tidal wave of violent revenge . . .

They Lived for Sin, Sun and Sudden Death

SURF PACK

Illustrations by **Earl Norem**

HIT the suds!" Cy Boardman hollered as he caught a five-foot wave that sectioned ahead of him. "Hang ten, you no-good!" whooped lean, black-haired, hawk-faced Boardman. He rode the soup right onto the grey-white sands of Cavite Beach in Luzon in the Philippines.

Eight others of the WOOSS (World's Our Oyster Surfing Society) came swirling along behind him: Tex Neeley, belly-boarding for laughs with his red beard looking like a sponge pasted onto his chin; Maggie Huntington, cool and precise in a white bikini and looking as though she might start buffing her nails on the way in; Phil Taber, Arnie Leach, red-haired Mavis Hunter, freckle-faced Kelly Stevenson riding big Ed Taylor's shoulders, pounding his head with her fists and screaming in wild laughter, "Keep me dry, you bastard. That's the deal. Keep me dry and I'll give you a night you'll remember when you're a hundred." And Dick Billings, stunting on the board with one leg out sideways and both arms flailing; jug-eared Dick Billings, the smallest of the men at 5'7" and 140 pounds and with a wide-eyed, rubbery face that lent itself to the kind of clowning he was always doing.

"Oh, that's bitching."

"Pour right into it."

"Get Arnie riding the nose."

"Hang ten, baby, hang ten."

THEY DROPPED off near the beach, jounced around in the water splashing each other, then paddled back out and sat there bobbing like ducks until a six-footer came rolling in. Then they were up on their boards and riding it in with Boardman and Maggie Huntington and Tex Neeley slipping into the curl and wheeling inside it smooth and easy as roller skating along a sidewalk, and the others clubbing ahead the best they could, some teetering, some floundering, Dick Billings tumbling off his board with both feet and hands grabbing.

"Save this poor lost soul!" Dick howled and the others laughed. And Cy Boardman shouted back, "Drown, you crud. You'll never find a better resting place."

They kept at it for three hours until late in the afternoon. Twenty-five years earlier Cavite Beach had run red with the blood of American and Japanese soldiers, but all evidence of that violent time had long since passed. Now, several toy-like outrigger fishing boats sat far out in the water, pasted up against a pink-ribbed sky. The beach was calm, serene, incredibly peaceful.

A solemn-faced, half-naked boy of eight or nine squatted on his heels in the sand; Tex Neeley handed him a peso; the boy grinned and stuffed it in his shorts in front. Tex peeked and roared, "The little cockroach has a hundred more in there." The sun came down like a red disc on a string, falling rapidly, flattening out against the horizon. The surfers took their final rides, then pulled on jeans and sweatshirts from a black hearse and a wooden station wagon standing side by side on the beach. They were cumbersome old vehicles, all right, but just right for loading in the long boards.

"Be nice if Steve and Duke and Molly get here soon." Dick Billings put a goat-like bray in his voice and made his teeth chatter. "That son of a bitch Duke, how could he have forgotten all that good booze?"

Duke Mann had been in charge of loading up their vehicles in Manila and somehow or other he had mislaid their entire stock of beer and whiskey. After they had reached Cavite, he and Steve Paris said they'd go back and see if they could track it down and Molly Diamond had said she'd go along. Long-legged Molly, with her great mass of blonde hair and her flat statement that "I'm Duke's whore. Don't any of you other dogs start panting around."

The surfers built a fire on the beach. They began nibbling on sandwiches and talking about some of the places they had surfed over the past few months—Malibu in Southern California, of course, but some beaches in Rhode Island and South Carolina, too, and Boardman and Taylor and Kelly Stevenson went into raves about the twenty-footers at Hawaii they'd taken on a year earlier. A full moon close enough to touch sent paths of white shimmering across the water, and Arnie, the "supplier," handed out marijuana cigarettes, but clown-faced Dick Billings spoke for all of them when he said, "Give me that old-time religion. I want it hot and rough and flowing. A hundred and twenty proof rotgut's about right, with a couple of monkey rumps floating around for taste."

They got tense and edgy waiting and some of them began talking about driving into Manila and getting hotel rooms and "The hell with the three of them." But a little after nine o'clock they heard the Jeep coughing and stuttering up toward them and pretty soon they could make it out, bucking along the sand. Then they heard Duke hollering, "We found the stuff, it was still sitting on the deck where I left it." And Molly Diamond shouted "Stop screeching, baby, we'll be there in a minute."

THE JEEP reached them and Duke and Steve and Molly got out, grinning in triumph. Then someone said, "What took you creeps so long?" And Molly said, "Oh, you know Duke, he had to go visiting every boat along the dock there. The sociable kid. Always looking for someone to chatter with." She was wearing shorts and one of Duke's jackets and one of his yachting caps, and she had her arm hooked through his. Then he untangled himself from her grip, and said, "Come on, let's get the stuff out of the Jeep, everyone's all worked up to a big thirst by now." He was a stocky, bull-necked man with a tough, almost arrogant style.

The liquor and beer were piled up at the fire and everyone got to them in a big rush. The booze flowed, the beer spilled over, and every now and then someone laughed out of the sheer greatness of the situation—the whiskey available in unlimited quantities, the surf hissing up against the beach, the moon throwing a broad white path across the glittering water. They sang crazy verses to *Humoresque,* shouting themselves hoarse.

Dick Billings led them, a scrawny figure prancing about in front of them and flailing his arms. They laughed at his gyrations and howled in glee when he poured a drink over his head.

They began drinking faster, and Kelly Stevenson and big Ed Taylor went into the thick shrubbery at the edge of the beach. Kelly laughed, "We're going to study nature. We're going to learn all about the birds and the bees."

BOARDMAN shouted at poker-faced Steve Paris, "Hundred bucks if I polish off the whole bottle. Hundred bucks, right? All right, here we go, here we go." He stood wide-legged with a pint of liquor tilted into his mouth and his throat gulping, working like a python swallowing a pig, and they gathered around him chanting, "One-two-three-four." His face turned purple and black, and suddenly his legs were out from under him as though they'd been pulled away by a rope, and he was down on all fours mumbling, "Sick—getting so goddam sick," and the others were screeching in laughter, pointing at him, and Steve Paris was saying, "Hundred bucks still sitting here for anyone else who wants to try. Make your play, gents, make your play."

They steamed up quickly, the men grabbing for the women; and Arnie Leach and red-haired Mavis Hunter got themselves into a tangle of arms and legs. Phil Taber crawled up beside them to kiss Mavis's neck and back, saying, "Go on with what you're doing. Don't pay any attention to me."

They howled at the moon, opened more bottles, and Tex Neeley lay soggy and sodden on his back. The sleek, dark-haired Maggie Huntington squatted on his chest. "Drink this, you stupid moron," she demanded, pulling his mouth open with her hand in his beard and pouring in a bottle of beer. He gasped, snorted, tried to twist his face away, but she had him too firmly. "Drink it, stupid." The others had gathered around, cheering her on. "Drown him, Maggie. Pour it in till it comes out his ears."

Neely gagged, upchucked beer all over his chest.

"Filthy pig," the girl said calmly. She took him by the ears and began banging his head on the ground. "Filthy, filthy, filthy."

Neeley bellowed like a demented bull. "Don't be mad, angel. I'll be a good boy. I'll be neat."

Dick Billings banged out chords on a guitar.

KELLY Stevenson and Ed Taylor rolled out of the bushes, the girl all but swallowed up in the man's huge embrace, his mouth pressing hard on hers. Someone flipped on a transistor radio. An accented voice rose quickly: *"Manila docks. Adavi Lomo, a guiding spirit of the Asian-African Conference held in Morocco half a year ago, was found dead of gunshot wounds in his cabin cruiser,* African Freedom, *early this evening as it lay tied up against a wharf of the Manila docks. A revolver lying close to his body suggested the strong probability that Mister Lomo had taken his own life. Mister Lomo, an Ethiopian, was a major force for law and order in the Dark Continent and his death will undoubtedly be a serious blow...."*

Someone switched the station to a jazz music program. Arnie Leach and red-haired Mavis Hunter began dancing slowly with Phil Taber bobbing around them, laughing and making an elaborate thing out of cutting in, the three of them somewhat younger than the others, none over 21. Dick Billings jigged across the beach, kicking up his heels, still strumming chords on his guitar. He reached the shrubbery at the far end of the beach. A scream directed his stare to a point under a *yacca* tree some 10 yards away. Molly Diamond lay there with Duke Mann standing over her and bent down toward her, his hand raised for a backhand chop. The girl's voice was a wail, "The *African Freedom.* That's the boat you went visiting on. You were talking to that man with the white robe and the red fez and now he's dead. I remember, you were talking to that man."

"You're imagining things," Duke Mann said, and his hand came down to smash her mouth. She screamed and he hit her again, and blood began trickling down from a corner of her mouth. "You're imagining things, baby. You couldn't have seen me on the *African Freedom.* You're imagining things. You must be imagining things."

HER HEAD jolted each time he hit her, and she screamed, begging him to stop. "My face. Don't mark up my face. Please, please."

He finally stopped and she whimpered, "I didn't see you go anywhere, Duke. You were with me all the time. Don't hit me again, honey. My face."

He spoke sympathetically, "You're all right, Molly. Anyone that learns as fast as you do probably heals up overnight."

HE PATTED her head and went back to the others. The girl sat up and began dabbing at her face with a handkerchief. Dick Billings pranced toward her, strumming the guitar and shouting, "What are you doing all alone, beautiful? Let old Dick—"

"Get the hell away from me," she muttered. "I don't want company."

He dropped down beside her, slipping an arm around her shoulders and pawing at her breasts. "Tell old Dick your troubles. Tell old Dick who slugged you in the mouth, and old Dick will tear him in half clear up to the Adam's apple. Let old Dick be nice to you, beautiful."

But the girl laughed shakily and twisted away from him, still patting her mouth with the handkerchief. "Don't get such silly ideas, Dickie boy. I'm Duke's whore. Haven't I told you that often enough? I'm Duke's whore...."

It was some two months earlier that Dick Billings, an agent of the Central Bureau of Investigative Intelligence, was called into his bureau's office in Washington, DC. Billings was a sandy-haired man of routine appearance, average in height or even a little smaller, the sort of man who would go unnoticed in almost any crowd. Billings' interviewer that day was the bespectacled, scholarly-looking Arthur Cole, the head of the Bureau since its founding in 1949. To Billings, Cole said, "Something has come up, Dick. Something in the line of murder."

He went on to explain, "An organization of Asian and African statesmen was recently formed to plan a resistance to the expansion of Communism and other left wingisms in Asia and Africa. They held their first and only meeting to date in Morocco about three months ago. When it was over they all went off in different directions to raise funds for their work—some 45 of them going off to about that many countries around the world. One delegation went to Paris, and the day after they arrived their principal member was run down by a car in the street and killed. A few days later a key member of the delegation that had gone to Rome fell six stories out of his hotel room. Killed, of course. London, West Berlin, Brussels. Same sort of thing happened.

Delegates from the conference met with accidents. Perfectly reasonable accidents. The sort of thing that happens around the world thousands of times a day. But these were particular people it was happening to, and so we decided to investigate. Well, we've been investigating for almost three months now, and we still don't have a damn thing to go on. Well, one little thing, actually, but it's so damn silly it almost embarrasses me to talk about it. Still, it's the thing I've called you in on."

In each instance of a killing, Cole said, a particular group of surf riders had been somewhere fairly close by. "Within a hundred miles, anyway." Of course, the odds were 9 out of 10 that it was just coincidence. They were a wild group that traveled around the world looking for great waves to ride, and they were capable of showing up anywhere. "Most of them are nuts, half-wits, anything-for-a-thrill kind of jerks," Cole went on. "It's insane to think any of them could have the kind of discipline necessary to take part in a murder plot, but we've decided we've got to take a good close look at them anyway and you're the guy we picked to do it. How does it sound?"

Billings laughed. "I knew I should never have let you know I went surfing in my free time. All right, maybe you better give me what you have on each of these people individually."

Cole took a bulky folder out of his desk and drew out some pictures and printed matter. Handing over the pictures to Billings one at a time, he read off a sentence or two applicable to each.

"Cyrus Boardman. Rich man's son. Has enough money of his own to keep the group afloat whenever things get a little tight. Surfs well enough to win big competitions.

"Ed Taylor. No occupation, no money, but he's got a way of latching onto people who take care of him. Right now, it's Kelly Stevenson.

"That's Kelly. Cute kid, isn't she? Well, Kelly pays the bills and it's Ed's job to keep Kelly happy. So far, I guess, he's doing okay.

"Tex Neeley. A real kook. Gets his kicks out of having women slap him around. He's got a good one doing it, too. Maggie Huntington. That's Maggie. Thinks no more about breaking a bottle over his head than she does about taking a drink.

"Phil Taber, Arnie Leach and Mavis Hunter. Wild kids, plain and simple. The two guys share the girl and they all seem to get along okay. Arnie's got a contact someplace that keeps him supplied with marijuana, but we're not interested in that."

"Duke Mann. Used to drive racing cars. Lost his taste for it after he almost got killed in an accident two years ago. Tough sort of bird. Likes to hit people.

"Steve Paris. Last one to join up. Don't know much about him. He and Duke Mann have gotten close.

"Molly Diamond. How do you like that for a doll? Ever see a prettier pair of legs? Molly used to sing with bands. Played piano, too, I think. Talented girl, but it looks as though Mann has started roughing her up."

"Looks like kind of a messy crowd," Billings said thoughtfully. "Well, where do I fit in? How do you want to work it?"

"They came back to the States a few days ago and they've been surfing at some of the Florida beaches," Cole said. "You'll join them and work your way into the group. We'll see you have some money, so they'll be glad to see you. The main thing is to play it as loose and nutty as they do. Whatever comes up, you're for it, anything at all. Once you're in, well, hell, you've been with us long enough, Dick. You'll know what to do. "

"I take it you don't want me to use this serious, everyday personality of mine," Billings laughed.

"No, we want you to be as much of a kook as any of them," Cole said. "Put yourself over as some sort of nutty, good-natured clown."

It wasn't too long before Billings made contact with the World's Our Oyster Surfing Society. It was on an isolated beach on the West Coast of Florida. The day was sunny, the waves small but well-formed. Two of the surfers were sitting on the beach when Billings drove up in the ancient and dilapidated school bus his CBII headquarters had managed to locate for him. As he got out fully dressed and carrying his board, the two surfers watched him intently and he recognized Cy Boardman and Duke Mann. The others were all out riding the waves. Billings waved at the two on the beach but they didn't wave back. He saw their vehicles parked behind them—a hearse, an old wooden station wagon and a Jeep. He went down to the edge of the water carrying his board and watched a few minutes, then put the board into the water and got on it to start paddling out. The two surfers got to their feet laughing, and Boardman, shouted after him, "Hey fella, didn't you forget something?"

Billings cupped a hand to his ear. Boardman shouted. "Your clothes, you're wearing your clothes."

Billings yanked off one shoe and threw it high in the air, then resumed his paddling. They were all watching him by then, the two standing on the beach and the others sitting on their boards in the water. Billings picked out the wave he wanted traveling shoreward and got to his feet to ride it in. He was only a so-so surfer, but he didn't mind taking chances and now he made himself into a ballet-type godling, balancing on one foot with both arms out sidewards and his head way out in front. It was a crazy pose and he was able to hold it for only 10 seconds, but the others cheered and applauded when he went off the board and they gathered around him when he straggled onto the beach.

"Lost your marbles, fella?"

"Son-of-a-bitch couldn't even wait to get out of his clothes."

"Give it a pretty good ride."

"Try it again, guy."

Billings surfed with them the rest of the day, doing the clown act he and Cole had decided on. He howled, waved his arms, took a few unnecessary tumbles but managed to put together a few good rides, too. The surfers didn't admit him into their circle, but they grinned and waved at him while he was riding the waves, and Taber and Leach talked to him a little, asking how long he'd been surfing and if he knew any spots where the waves were particularly good.

A little before sundown Billings told them goodbye and got into his bus as though to drive off. But the beat-up old vehicle wouldn't start. He'd seen to that earlier. He'd lifted the hood, peered inside, found a few rusty parts to grab loose and fling back over his shoulder. Then he'd grabbed up a hunting knife from his gear and walked around the bus slashing all the tires. When he had it sitting on four mangled flats, he put the board under his arm and started off. After a few moments someone came running up behind him and grabbed his arm—freckle-faced Kelly Stevenson.

"You better stay with us, nutty," she said, laughing, hooking her arm through his. "You're too dumb to go wandering around this earth by yourself."

"I agree, I agree," Billings wailed, going back toward the others with her. I need someone to look after me."

Once he'd made this original breakthrough, Billings had no trouble winning total acceptance from the surfers. He drank hard enough, surfed furiously enough, and carried on in a crazy enough way to justify it. But at no point did he see anything at all to indicate they might be connected with the "accidents" Cole had mentioned to him. He had never seen such a crowd of "bubble heads" and hadn't even thought they existed. They seemed incapable of sustaining a serious thought or holding a sensible conversation. The "great wave" dominated all their discussions, the "great wave" that would give them a better ride than they'd ever had before. And as they moved up the coast of Florida and into Georgia and from there into the Carolinas, surfing, surfing, surfing every beach they could find, he became increasingly convinced that nothing else ever entered their minds. It seemed incredible, but there it was; they wanted nothing in life but to search out the great waves and ride them shoreward, bending their bodies into the scooped out "curl" and whooping as they powered out ahead of it.

I'M ON a wild goose chase," Billings confided to Cole on the telephone. "If any of these goons are murderers, I'm the king of the Cannibal Islands."

"Maybe you're right," Cole said thoughtfully, "but stay with it a little longer anyway. We've got one of these Asian-African delegations in Washington and it's making us nervous. Rom Nikki of Nigeria is the head of it, and he's one of the toughest anti-Communists on the African continent. We've got half our personnel working on this thing and you'd better stay with it, too."

"Will do," Billings said.

The surfers moved up over the North Carolina border into Virginia, and any day the weather turned cold they put on gleaming wetsuits, but nothing stopped them from surfing. "Find the great wave!" was their battle cry and they sent out parties to search for remote beaches. One day Maggie Huntington even suggested she and Billings go off on such

"THIS is a fine old hearse," Molly said, grabbing Billings. "Now let's put a little life into it . . . "

a search. "Come on, nutsy, let's see what we can dig up."

Billings was surprised. He'd gotten too used to seeing Maggie slapping Tex Neeley around to think they were ever separated. He said, "What about old Tex? How's he going to like that?"

The girl laughed, "I'm punishing him. No sweet little kick in the face for him today."

They went off in the Jeep. Neeley glowered and the others opened a case of brandy to start the day. They took a basket of sandwiches and a bucket of chilled beer with them and headed back the way they'd come, re-crossing the North Carolina border and scouting out the beaches along a stretch of rugged coast there. Billings drove and the girl sat beside him wearing a white bathing suit and a parka with the hood back. Her dark hair tumbled soft and glossy over her shoulders and her eyes were fixed straight ahead. When Billings fell into character and began driving crazily and making rubbery faces, she spoke abruptly, "You can stop putting it on. You're not as big a goof as you're always letting on."

They drove a while longer, and Billings said, "How about you, Maggie? Are you all you're cracking yourself up to be? I'm talking about that wacky act you've worked out with Tex Neeley."

"He's a Texan, all right, but his name isn't Neeley," the girl said. "It's Archer and he's heir to one of the biggest oil fortunes in the state. I want a piece of it. If I've got to dance on his head to keep him happy, I'm all for dancing. Maybe there were a couple of times I almost threw up when I was through with him, but if he likes it, that's all that counts."

"Who's blaming you?" Billings shrugged.

They moved out along the beach, bumping along on sand and rocks. When they hit impassable stretches, they went back away from the water; then they reached some sort of makeshift road and continued along it until they could come back down and proceed alongside the water again. The beaches were generally rough and rocky and deserted, and the waves were obviously all wrong for surfing. After a while they decided to stop and have a bite to eat even though they still had not succeeded in their mission. They got out of the Jeep and sat in its shade on the ocean side, and the girl unpacked the sandwiches and beer and handed one of each over to Billings.

"Peaceful," he said. "Everything nice and calm and peaceful."

The sun was directly overhead by then. The girl had taken off her parka and flung it back in the Jeep. Her skin was dark against the white of her suit, her bristling black hair blown by wayward breezes. Billings said, "I've got to say this, Maggie. All that junk you do with Neeley or whatever his name is—it's a waste of good womanhood. You know, it really is. You could…"

He stopped suddenly, stunned by what he saw. The girl was biting down on her lower lip, gulping. Tears had started down her cheeks. "What the hell," he said. "I didn't want to get you upset, Maggie. I just couldn't help thinking."

SHE PUT her face in her hands. Her shoulders shook. He put an arm around her, "Maggie, come on, get hold of yourself." He smoothed her hair, patted her cheek. She turned into him like a frightened child and he felt her trembling, wet face lifting to his. He kissed her, and then she was sighing and burrowing up against his chest and he was pressing his hands hard against her back and rolling his body against hers to settle her deeper into the shade of the Jeep. A sudden fierceness possessed them both, the fierceness of needs repressed, and their hands were demanding each other's bodies, their mouths exploring. They rolled up against a Jeep wheel and now their bodies were straining to express their surging requirements. In a moment of violent exaltation, they'd achieved an explosive merging of their beings, the girl's breasts lifting in desperate demand against Billings' chest, their very pulse and tissue meshing and becoming one. Panting, they clung together in quivering intensity. Then they fell back sighing and smiling at each other with something like gratitude.

"I don't even remember if I finished my beer," Billings said. "That shows how great I feel."

"You didn't," the girl laughed. "Most of it is still in the bottle."

They got back in the Jeep soon after that and continued looking for the "great wave" or even an "okay wave," but the surf was all wrong and they found nothing. Later in the afternoon the girl said, "We gave it a good try," and they started back toward where they had left the others, Billings driving and Maggie resting her head against his shoulder. They arrived to find the hearse. A number of the surfers were gone. Only Mavis Hunter, Phil Taber and Arnie Leach were there, sitting around a small fire cooking hot dogs. Cy Boardman was in the water fifty yards up the beach riding a small wave.

"The others went off scouting out locations along the Virginia coast," Mavis said. "They ought to be back soon."

It was at that point that the hand of dread grabbed at Billings' heart. Someone turned on the radio. A newscaster was already announcing the kind of news Billings had steeled himself to expect:

"Freak accident killed Rom Nikki and his wife this afternoon. The noted Nigerian diplomat was head of the Asian-African delegation that has been in the city for this past week. An explosion of as yet undetermined origin blew up the trailer where Mister Nikki and his wife were staying while he worked on an address he hoped would be entered in the Congressional Record. Mister Nikki was a forthright and determined leader in the fight for Asian and African independence and his presence will be sorely missed. Tributes have been pouring into his delegation's headquarters from all over the world."

"Oh, turn that junk off and get some music," Mavis said, and Taber twisted the dial until he picked up a tune by The Mamas and the Papas, "My Heart Stood Still." Their voices came in, one upon the other, like great bells. Boardman came back along the beach and they all sat in a circle around the fire with Mavis singing along with the radio group, her fingers snapping, her red hair falling thick and luxurious below her shoulders. Maggie lay down beside Billings with her head in his lap. She reached a hand up to touch his cheek, "You all right, Dickie boy? You look like your mind's a million miles away."

"What mind?" Billings said pushing himself back into his familiar role of the nut, the clown. "That's the first time anyone ever said I had one."

But his mind was actually racing, seething, trying to analyze the news he'd just heard. Still another key delegate from the Asian-African conference had been killed, this one right in Washington. And the surfers had been exploring up in that direction that afternoon. Had they gone into the capitol, or was this still another coincidence—a politically explosive death that just happened to have occurred while they were close by?

THE SURFERS themselves arrived soon after sundown and, as though to answer Billings' unspoken question, the first thing Duke Mann said was, "Well, we went all the way into Washington, but we didn't find a single decent surf to ride. Guess we'll have to quit this part of the country. Maybe quit the country entirely. I hear they've got waves in the Philippines that are as good as anywhere else in the world."

"Better than Hawaii?" Boardman asked incredulously. "Better than Madagascar?"

"The best," Mann insisted. "The very best. In fact the more I think about it, the surer I am that's where we ought to be heading."

Billings tried to concentrate on what they were saying, but something else kept pushing through. He had to talk to Cole. That was essential. But how to go about it? The surfers had started partying. Duke Mann beat out rhythms on two empty five-gallon cans. Kelly Stevenson and Ed Taylor danced. Everyone else picked up the beat and banged their hands together. The fire fingered their faces in the darkness. Maggie Huntington remained cold-eyed and indifferent as Tex Neeley pushed his face hopefully against her shoulder. Mavis Hunter laughed and said, "Now boys, now boys," as Phil Taber and Arnie Leach traded insults across her. Molly Diamond stood behind Duke, twisting her finger in his hair as he crouched over his oil can drums.

"Dull party!" Billings shouted suddenly, jumping to his feet and flourishing a bottle of bourbon. "Where's the action!" He turned the bottle up over his mouth, gulped some down, then jumped into the center of their circle pushing Kelly Stevenson and the grinning Ed Taylor aside, roaring, "What's the matter, don't you know any steps? Here, let me show you some real dancing."

Then he went into a prancing, leaping, crazy-legged dance, keeping it up even as he gulped down another and still-another mouthful of bourbon. The surfers howled their enjoyment, and Duke Mann began speeding up his beat so that Billings had to dance still faster to keep up with him. He fell once but bounced right up and kept on dancing. He drank, staggered, fell to all fours and looked vacantly about at the laughing faces pressed all about him.

"He's had it."

"Drunk as a skunk."

"Eyes like poached eggs."

"Look out, he's going to try it again."

Billings clambered to his feet once more, took another swig of the bottle but most of it ran down his chin. He tried a couple of clumsy steps, but stumbled and almost fell again, and pushed himself out of the circle, mumbling, "Fresh air, gotta get some fresh air." He staggered across the sand, fell into the seat of the Jeep. That made them laugh all the harder.

"Going off for a ride to get some fresh air."

"Run himself right into the ocean."

"Crazy nut."

"Look at that for steering."

Billings had gotten the Jeep started and now it was weaving back and forth across the sand. The vehicle jerked, stalled. He got it started again, pushed it into its weaving course. The laughing surfers fell away behind him. He got the Jeep out to a dirt road running parallel to the beach and sufficiently far away so that he knew they couldn't hear it anymore. Then he straightened up, came down hard on the accelerator, and was soon tearing along, handling the wheel with his customary skill. Presently he pulled to a stop at a roadside telephone booth. Moments later he was speaking to Cole and the CBII chief was saying, "Well, what have you got for us, Dick? Lord, that was a mess today. There wasn't enough left of Rom Nikki and his wife to put in a paper bag. Not a paper bag."

"No chance it was a legitimate accident?' Billings asked.

"No chance at all," Cole said firmly. "Now, tell me what you know."

As quickly as possible Billings went through the events of the day. When he was finished, Cole said, "Bad, bad, I guess we botched it. Rom

Nikki was one of these tough birds who's sure he can do everything himself. Wouldn't let us give him any kind of protection. He had his trailer in a patch of woods a little outside the city and blowing it up wasn't much of a problem. We'll see that it gets into the papers as an accident, but one of Rom Nikki's Nigerian guards is sure he saw a man wearing just a pair of shorts running through the trees there a few moments before the explosion. Could have been one of your surfers, couldn't it?'

"Mann, Paris, Taylor, Neeley, they were all wearing shorts and a sweatshirt when they went off today," Billings said. "Could have been any one of them. Incidentally, Maggie said Neeley's real name is Archer and he's got a lot of money coming to him in Texas oil. You want to check that?"

Cole said, "She's right. We've got that already. We also know that he tried to get into China from Hong Kong about a year ago. But he got into some trouble on the border there—something about a rape—and the Chinese wouldn't let him in. Look, there's something else, Dick." His voice took on a note of urgency. "There's another Asian-African Conference scheduled for next month. If anyone wants to disrupt the whole movement, that would be the place to do it."

"Where is it going to be?" Billings demanded.

Cole spoke carefully. "I'm the only one in the Bureau who's been told, Dick. Our thinking is that the fewer people knowing about it, the better chance it has of coming off all right. Sorry."

What was it Duke Mann had said when the surfers got back from Washington? *Guess we'll have to quit this part of the country. Maybe quit the country entirely. I hear they've got waves in the Philippines that are as good as anywhere else in the world.*

Billings said, "Is that meeting in the Philippines?"

Cole drew in his breath with the sound of ripping cloth. "Where did you hear that?"

Billings said, "I've got to get up to see you, Arthur." Cole started to say something, but Billings cut in on him, "Figure on me first thing in the morning. I'll work out a way." He muttered to himself, thinking hard. *"Damn, damn"*—then snapped his fingers. "All right, I've got it. Use the New Jersey Avenue medical thing, the Doctor Zeno office. Have Adam with you, Adam Ross." He thought a moment, then said, "Maybe you'd better have Mary, too. She might come in handy. Let her be the receptionist."

Cole didn't try to hide his worry. "I wish I had a better feel of this thing, Dick. It's as though it's all getting away from us. I don't know, I don't know."

Billings said, "I've got something in mind, Arthur. At least let me talk to you about it."

"All right," Cole said gloomily. "I don't have anything better to offer, myself. We'll do the Doctor Zeno thing in the morning."

Billings hung up and got back in the car. He sat quietly for a few minutes thinking over what he was going to do. Then he started driving back toward where he had left the surfers. About half a mile from their site, he left the road and approached the beach. Clumps of rock edged its border farthest back from the water, some of them rising up three or four feet from the ground. Billings drove carefully along beside them, then faced the Jeep into them, and stopped. Then he got out of the Jeep.

He raised the hood, reached his hands in to get them greasy, then spread the grease all over his face and clothes. Then he got back into the Jeep, started it going and jumped out the open door seconds before it smashed into the rocks. He gazed approvingly at the hanging door, the shattered headlights, the mangled fender, the beaten-in grille. He looked around on the ground, picked up a piece of sea glass and gouged his forearm spilling blood down across his wrist and hand. He used the same glass to scratch up his face and chest and legs. He took hold of a side of the car with one hand, gripping it firmly, then began turning away so that the strain of the movement went into his shoulder. Sweat beaded his face and forehead. He had a trick shoulder. He knew how to throw it out of its socket. He'd done it before, but it hurt like hell just the same. He grunted, bit at a quivering lower lip, then gasped at the tearing result he had achieved. The arm hung loose. He sank to the sand and leaned against a wheel of the damaged Jeep, panting.

The minutes slipped by becoming hours. If they came and found him, okay. If not, okay, too. He dozed a little, but only fitfully. At about three in the morning he got up and started along the beach toward where he had left the surfers. He walked slowly, staggering a little, holding his hand up to his damaged shoulder. He heard the surfers before he saw them, they were whooping, hollering. Then he caught the flicker of their fire, and a few moments later he stood where he could see them, the fire and a full moon showing them all to him perfectly.

ARNIE Leach, Phil Taber and Mavis Hunter were together as usual. They looked surprisingly young and they weren't saying anything. Boardman was asleep. Kelly Stevenson and Ed Taylor lay side by side on their stomachs, watching what was going on in the center of their circle, both of them grinning. Molly Diamond stood alone, long-legged and pretty but her face was unhappy. Tex Neeley and Maggie Huntington were playing "bullfight," the girl flapping a sweat shirt and Tex bellowing and lunging at it. He held his fingers up beside his head for horns. Duke Mann and Steve Paris stood close by, holding long sticks. When Tex missed his sixth lunge and dropped to all fours, panting, Maggie called out briskly, "Bandilleros." Mann and Paris handed her the sticks and she began jabbing Neeley in the side, shouting, "Huh! Toro, toro, toro!"

Kelly Stevenson and Ed Taylor laughed, enjoying the spectacle, but Leach and Taber and red-haired Mavis Hunter looked uncomfortable and Molly Diamond called out, "Isn't that enough, Maggie? Maybe we should try to find Dick." But the bullfight participants paid no attention to her. Slim-bodied in a bikini, her bush jacket flapping open, Maggie Huntington continued to poke Neeley with the sticks until he came suddenly to his knees, flinging his arms around her waist and pressing his face to her belly. She laughed and let him kiss her there, and he rose to his feet lifting her up above him and roaring, "Queen of the universe, goddess of all creation, empress."

"My God, look there!" Mavis Hunter said, pointing. Dick Billings staggered toward them, blood-smeared and filthy, one arm hanging limp and useless. Neeley lowered Maggie to the ground, and the others stood staring as Billings approached them. "Accident," he muttered. "Ran the damn Jeep into some rocks. Beat it up pretty bad."

MAVIS and Molly Diamond ran up to lower him onto a log. He winced as they touched his arm. "Shoulder…hurts like hell." Leach brought him a drink. Duke Mann said coldly, "God damn, God damn, where did you leave the Jeep?" Billings told him. Mann and Paris went off to look for it.

Kelly Stevenson said, "We don't have anything in the line of medical supplies except band-aids and aspirin."

"And booze," Ed Taylor laughed. "Plenty of booze."

"I'll have to get to a doctor," Billings said. "The arm's hurting like hell. There'd be someone up in Washington."

"I'll drive you up in the station wagon," Molly Diamond said.

"Duke will break your neck if you try to," Maggie Huntington said. "Isn't he sore enough because of the Jeep?"

"Then I'll drive him," Arnie Leach said. "Duke won't break my neck."

"Won't he?" Maggie laughed. "Are you sure you want to find out?"

Arnie's face went red and he turned away. "Hold his hand, baby," Maggie said to Mavis Hunter. "He's all upset."

"Maybe someone could flag a truck down for me," Billings said wearily. "Nobody has to go out of their way. Just get me a ride."

In the end that was what they decided to do. As soon as the sun came up Leach and Taber went out to the road with him and flagged down a janitorial supplies truck. The driver said sure, he was going to Washington, and Billings got in beside him. "If I don't make it back before you leave, hang onto my board," he said. "I'll see you someplace this century or the next one."

The truck driver wasn't interested in conversation, so he was able to think about the surfers. There was some sort of split among them, he realized. Mann and Maggie Huntington and Tex Neeley and Steve Paris were the "in" group. Molly Diamond wasn't exactly one of them, but she was too involved with Duke Mann to be separated from them. Kelly Stevenson and Ed Taylor had some private thing all their own although they sort of hovered on the outside of the Mann-Maggie Huntington group. Arnie Leach, Phil Taber and Mavis Hunter were a group all their own; they had a crazy thing going among the three of them, but every now and then they looked as if they thought the Mann-Huntington stuff was too rough for them and they wanted to pull out. Boardman was a loner—the best surfer among them, a detached, good-looking man who couldn't take a drink without taking another and another until he fell unconscious.

Billings was still working out relationships among the surfers when the driver let him off in Washington a few blocks from the New Jersey

Avenue address he wanted. A few minutes later Billings entered a small office building, taking a self-service elevator to the third floor and going into an office with DOCTOR EDWARD ZENO, GENERAL PRACTITIONER on the door. A slim, blond, bright-faced girl in a polka dot dress sitting at the receptionist's desk said, "Hi, Dick" and shook her head pityingly at his battered up condition. "You really did a convincing job. You'll do that thing to your arm once too often and you'll never get it back in again."

This was Mary Hazlitt, Cole's private secretary. "My good right arm," according to Cole himself. Billings kissed her, said, "Mmmm, you smell good."

The girl laughed. "Will you have time to take me out for a drink tonight? It's been so long."

Billings sighed, "Not tonight, angel. I've got to get back as soon as I finish up here. Okay for me to go in?"

She nodded, pressed an intercom button, pointed at a door to an inner office. Billings opened it and went in. Cole was there, also a tall powerfully built Negro wearing a sports jacket and an open throated shirt. This was Adam Ross, a CBII agent who had worked on a number of assignments with Billings through the years. The men shook hands, and Billings said to Cole, "Throw this thing in for me, Arthur," motioning at his shoulder. To Ross he said, "You hold me, Adam. If I faint don't bother throwing any whiskey down my throat. I've had enough in the last few weeks to last me a lifetime."

Ross laughed, slipped an arm like a steel bar around Billings' back, and held him so he couldn't move while Cole raised his hanging arm and gave it a sudden, powerful twist. The arm popped back into place and Billings swore softly as pain bolted through his body. Then he said, "The trouble with me is I've got to get too realistic about things."

He flexed his arm, rubbed the shoulder, then spoke to Cole, "I'm beginning to feel sure there's a terrorist group among the surfers, but that they're not all in it. These kids Leach, Taber and Mavis Hunter—I can't imagine they know anything about what's going on. Cy Boardman—too much of a lush for anyone to take a chance on. Taylor and Kelly Stevenson—maybe, maybe not. Same for Molly Diamond, although I really can't figure her. Another thing I can't figure out is who's in charge. Mann puts himself across as a tough bird, but I've got a feeling he's just a strong-arm guy and someone else calls his shots— just a hunch. And that Maggie Huntington-Tex Neeley combination— well, sometimes that pervert act of theirs looks real, but other times it's as phony as an eight-dollar bill."

Cole spoke impatiently, "You didn't throw your arm out of joint so you'd be able to come up and tell me that kind of chitchat. What do you have in mind?"

"I think we've got to get a double game going with them," Billings said. "We've got to give them something specific to go after and we've got to be there to grab them when they do. We can't set up any of the legitimate Asian-African delegates as clay pigeons, but there's no reason we can't *invent* one."

Adam Ross shook his head and laughed, "I'm beginning to see what I'm doing here."

"Wilmeth Siki, brilliant British-educated Senegalese who has been electrifying the people of Senegal with his pro-Democracy, anti-Communist speeches," Billings said. "That's you, Adam."

Now Billings turned to Cole, "You'd have to get the cooperation of the head of the Senegalese delegation, and if he won't give it to you, we'll have to get another one. The point is to let the word leak out that this great, magnetic, overwhelming personality is going to the Philippines where he will undoubtedly electrify the Conference just as he has been doing in Senegal. That will make him a natural for an assassination attempt; in fact, it will make it inevitable that they go for him. Naturally, we've got a hundred plainclothes men guarding Adam every second he's there, and as soon as they make their move, we grab them."

The other two were silent. Billings said, "Look, we're not really sure the surfers have had anything at all to do with these Asian-African killings. We know a group of them were in Washington yesterday. If they *are* involved in these things there isn't a thing we can do about it yet, because we simply don't have anything on them—not a thing. All we know is that they're going to the Philippines and that's where the next Conference is going to be held—and that might just be coincidence. And if they are involved, we don't know if they're in it alone or if there are others working with them. In short, we're no place unless we can draw them out, make them commit themselves, give them the chance to do it anyway. Now, how can there be a better way to do it than the way I just described?"

Adam Ross shrugged, "Why not? I'd get a bang out of it anyway. Wilmeth Siki, brilliant, British-educated."

"All right, quit the clowning," Cole snapped. "Let me think a minute." He walked up and down, scratching his jaw with a thumbnail. "I want to study it another day or so, but I think we'll probably do it. Leaking the damn thing properly will be a problem in itself. I mean the Conference itself is secret. Oh, well, I'll figure a way, I'll figure a way. Well, you'd better take off, Dick. We don't want your surfers going off someplace without you."

Billings said, "Give me five minutes with Mary. I haven't seen her in months." He shook hands with both men and went out to the receptionist's desk. Mary Hazlitt made a face at him. "Are you really going back so soon? That doesn't seem fair, Dick. We ought to at least have time for a drink."

Billings spread his hands helplessly. "Kind of a big nasty thing we're working on, Mary. It'll keep me tied up for quite a while, yet." He sat on the edge of the desk and she came around to rub his leg. He grinned and put his arms around her waist, clasping his hands behind her. She kissed him, a clean, fresh kiss, her mouth as sweet as a minty flower. He said, "Yum yum, don't do that again or I'll change my mind about going."

SHE SAID, "It's not fair. You've been away long enough. Why can't they send Adam instead?"

"Adam's got a girl, too, angel," Billings said, kissing her. "Besides, he's going to be away himself. He's in this thing, too."

Mary said, "I didn't know Adam was a surfer."

Billings said, "He isn't." He laughed, "Adam is more the dynamic, brilliant, diplomatic type." He pushed himself off the desk and kissed her again. "Stop fussing, angel. It's the job. If you don't like the hours you should have taken up with a baseball player."

"I thought they played night games, too," the girl said. "I wouldn't like that."

"Aren't you the sexy one?" Billings laughed. Then he kissed her still again and left. Outside the building he walked a few blocks, then began flapping his thumb to catch a ride. It took a while before a van picked him up, and it was late in the afternoon when he returned to the surfers.

All of them were out riding the waves when he arrived except Maggie Huntington and Tex Neeley. Maggie was sitting on a log reading a magazine and Tex was standing behind her, brushing her hair. Billings strode up to them, grinning and waving his arm so they could see it was okay. "Got a doc to throw it back into place for me. Good as new. Think I'll get my board and get in a little ride before it gets too dark."

It was a week later that the surfers left for the Philippines on a freighter of the Michaelson Line. It developed that Boardman's father was a majority stockholder in the company and since the freighter was traveling light, there was no problem getting them all aboard. Their vehicles went, too. By the time of their departure, Billings had spoken once more with Cole by telephone.

"The Conference is going to be held at Batagapan," Cole had said tersely. "It's an obscure little town a little above Manila. It was picked because it's off the beaten track. But it doesn't take too long to get to, either."

"What about Adam?" Billings had asked.

"He's in Africa already," Cole had said. "He's coming up as Wilmeth Siki, a key member of the Senegalese delegation. We've done a good job keeping the Conference officially secret, yet we've let the word leak out that something big will be going on at Batagapan with this Siki character there dominating the festivities. Any indication your surfers have picked it up?"

"None, but I wouldn't know about it if they had," Billings had said. "There's an in crowd and an out crowd here, and I'm definitely not one of the ins."

"You don't think they've twisted to you, do you?" Cole asked sharply. "There's been 11 of these Asian-African delegates killed over the past five months," Cole had said. "Everyone looked like an accident and every one was a murder. That means whoever did it is awful damn tough and awful damn capable. It's too late to get you out of there. That would tip our hand. Just watch yourself, Dick. Sit with your back to the wall."

They talked a few minutes longer, and Cole gave Billings some idea of the physical circumstances under which the Conference would be held. A number of open-sided tents would be put up for the various committees of the conference to meet in—the Financial Committee, the Policy Committee, and so forth. When all the delegates of the Conference met to hear the principal speeches, they would gather on a long grassy expanse with the platform at one end. The Asians and Africans would provide their own security, but a group of CBII men would also be there under the leadership of Cole himself. "I'm jumpy as a cat about this thing, Dick," Cole admitted. "That's why I want to be there. We know so damn little about what we're up against."

The trip across the ocean was uneventful and if they suspected Billings, none of the surfers gave any evidence of it. They drank a lot and talked about different waves they had ridden and brawls they had thrown, and gathered at the rail to watch porpoises looping along beside the boat.

They landed in Manila harbor and Duke Mann put himself in charge of loading their gear aboard their vehicles. Cavite Beach was going to be their first stop, but when they got to it they discovered that all their liquor was missing. So Duke and Steve Paris and Molly Diamond went back to see if it was still on the dock where the freighter had unloaded. They came back with the liquor that evening and the surfers had a wild party by way of celebration. Boardman passed out when he tried to chugalug a pint of whiskey. Maggie Huntington sat on Neeley's chest and pulled his beard to open his mouth and then poured in beer till he gagged on it. She laughed till her stomach hurt.

Some time during the evening, their transistor radio announced the death of Adavi Lomo, the Ethiopian delegate to the Asian-African Conference in Morocco half a year earlier. Adavi Lomo had apparently shot himself to death aboard his cabin cruiser, *African Freedom*. The news took Billings' heart like an icy hand, but he had continued with his clownish antics, howling along with the rest of them and banging out chords on his guitar for their inane songs.

A little later he'd heard Molly Diamond scream and seen her on the ground with Duke Mann standing over her.

"The *African Freedom*, that's the boat you went visiting...."

"You're imaging things," Mann said, and smashed his hand across her mouth. "You couldn't have seen me."

"My face, don't mark up my face," Molly Diamond had begged.

MANN had finally stopped and gone off and Billings had pranced out to the girl, banging away at his guitar, then settling down beside her and trying to paw her. But she had only twisted away from him, patted her bleeding mouth with a handkerchief and said, "I'm Duke's whore. Haven't I told you that often enough? I'm Duke's whore."

"Don't want to crowd old Duke," Billings said solemnly. "What's his is his. Don't want to crowd a good old pal like Duke."

But his mind was racing. The girl might just know something.

A year ago a Nigerian minister and his bodyguard were shot to death while they were sitting on a deserted beach taking in the sun. That assassination, too, had gone unsolved. And suddenly Billings remembered it, and he wondered, just wondered, if the Nigerian had been shot by surfers as they rode a wave into the beach. It was a crazy possibility. Nevertheless, a possibility.

Now Billings concentrated on the beating Duke had given Molly Diamond again. And after being banged around by Mann that way, she just might be coaxed into talking. But how, how to go about it? But before he could come up with anything, she made the lead for him, "I'm too tired to be nice now, honey. Besides, you know how Duke is at night, he's demanding. But early in the morning if you want, we could go off surfing together, before the others get up. What do you say?"

"A lovely idea," Billings said keeping his style gay and crazy. "You'll find old Dickie boy awake, alert and available."

He'd gone back and joined the party, leaving Molly to pat at her still-bleeding mouth. He stayed with the others, drinking and raising a rumpus, but as soon as he felt he could manage it, he faked passing out. The party went on a while longer and he saw Molly Diamond and Duke Mann get under a blanket together. But no one paid any attention to him and after a while he was able to doze off.

He was awake before sunup the next morning but pretended to still be asleep even when he saw Molly Diamond tiptoeing toward him carrying her board. She shook him, put her finger to her lips, and motioned him to follow her. He whispered, "Be right with you." Presently the two of them were walking along the beach carrying their boards with a red rim of the sun just coming up over the horizon. The girl looked fresh and pretty in a green bikini with a knitted catchall bag swinging from her wrist. She touched her mouth at one point though, and said, "It really hurts. Duke did that to me. That was wrong of him. He shouldn't have done that." She sounds sore, Billings thought. Is she about to spill something? "There's a wonderful cove about a mile along the beach here," the girl said. "We can surf there."

They continued walking and after a while the saucer-like shore of the cove appeared ahead of them, with a rowboat drawn up on the beach. "Probably belongs to some fisherman around here," Billings said. They approached the boat, saw there were a pair of oars inside, and then knowing he'd have to press things one way or the other, Billings said, "Molly, there's something I want to ask. I couldn't help seeing that Duke was slugging you last night. A nice kid like you, it doesn't seem right. You want to tell me about it?"

The girl said, "I'm awfully glad you asked me, Dickie boy. Yes, I do want to talk to you about it. But there's something I want to show you first." She reached into the bag swinging at her wrist, "Look. I thought you'd like to see."

She had pulled out a black revolver and held it aimed at his stomach. "Keep both hands on that board, honey," she said. Billings stood stiff as a statue. Molly said, "Duke slugging me around last night was for your eyes alone, government boy. I have to get up to Batagapan today and I didn't want you following me around. I decided you'd tail around after Duke if we could establish him as the villain, so that's what we did yesterday. Old Duke, your old pal Duke. Well, your old pal Duke had nothing to do with killing Adavi Lomo yesterday. I managed that one myself just like I've managed all the others. You'd be surprised how easy it is for a pretty, innocent-looking girl to get close enough to a man to kill him. And Duke bounced me around last night only because we knew you were tuning in. And don't think he didn't almost wet his pants doing it. Duke still carries a slug around in his rump from doing something I didn't want him to do one time."

BILLINGS' head was reeling. He hadn't figured it this way at all. Even now he could hardly take it in, although the girl's gun gave him no choice. Molly Diamond, the head of the terrorists!

Then he saw three figures walking toward them along the beach, carrying surf boards. Molly said, "You see, I decided I wanted Duke with me at Batagapan today. So that meant I didn't want you tailing *him* around either. Poor Dickie boy, we're arranging an accident for you, a surfing accident."

The surfers were close enough for him to see they were Duke Mann, Tex Neeley and Steve Paris. He said, "What the hell is it with you, Molly? What's pushing you into this crazy stuff?"

The girl said, "We're a supra-national organization, Dickie boy. We want Africa to go all Red and we know the way to do that is to keep everything down there disorganized, chaotic. We owe allegiance to no country ourselves, only an ideology. And don't think we're just a handful of kooks. There are hundreds of us, thousands of us." Her face was flushed now, her eyes blazing. "In fact, there are three of us right at the Conference, today. That's right, three delegates with time bombs in their briefcases. Bombs to blow that Conference from here to Mars and all that crap about African freedom right along with it. Time bombs, Dickie boy. Time bombs all set to go off just when your friend Adam Ross is making his Wilmeth Siki speech."

"You know about that, too, do you?" Billings grated.

"Sure, we know about that, Dickie boy," the girl jeered. "Can you guess how? Can you guess how we found out stupid Dick Billings is really clever Dick Billings? Or how we found out a Senegalese spellbinder named Wilmeth Siki is really a CBII agent named Adam Ross? Can you figure it out, Dickie boy, can you figure it out?"

She turned to the three figures trotting toward them and waved an impatient arm, "Hurry up, goddamn it, hurry up." She turned back to Billings. "We've got to move fast on this accident of yours, Dickie boy. Our delegates are going to go out for a smoke just before Adam Ross starts talking and we have to be there to pick them up. You understand, don't you, Dickie boy? You understand!" She shouted, "All right, Mann and Paris in the water. And don't take all day about it. Get him on the first run."

Neeley came up beside her, grinning. Mann and Paris paddled out on their boards. Molly Diamond flourished her gun hand. "All right, Dickie boy, go have your accident. Into the water. We'll cry sad tears when we tell the others about it. So sad, so sad. Very tragic, very tragic. Get going, Dickie boy, *into the water!*"

Billings stepped into the hissing surf, feeling it cool and invigorating against his ankles. Mann and Paris were out ahead of him, sitting on their boards and facing in toward the beach. He walked in up to his knees, up to his waist. "Keep going, Dickie boy!" the girl screamed, and he could hear Neeley's cackling laughter.

He went in up to his neck, treading water a little, and then he saw Mann turn his head to say something to Paris and both of them were up on their boards and flying toward him. A fantastic thought entered his head. "It's a perfect wave, a beautiful, beautiful wave." And then he saw Paris out ahead of Mann and figured he had a chance to avoid the first board, but they were spaced out in such a way that the second would be on him the moment he came up. A nice fix he was in.

Then he saw Paris bearing down on him, crouching, and Mann breaking behind him. Good surfers, those two, he realized. Fantastic control, deft as ice skaters. He felt as though he were looking straight up a mountain slope with Paris pouring down it straight at him. He pulled himself down into the water, felt the rush of Paris' board powering over him, tried to dart out to the side and came up to receive a blinding smash alongside the head as Mann's board cracked into him. A tide of frenzied visions washed across his brains, and he sank down underneath again feeling a confusion of arms and legs and straining bodies all over him. They were both on him, to finish him off, he realized dimly. It was just a matter of holding him under for a minute or two. His smashed head would certainly make it seem an accident, a man thrown off his board and killed when its steel-hard rail cracked him.

A numbing blackness began to seep into his brain. A violent, tearing

pain filled his chest. He thrashed about in maniacal fury, felt his hands brush a face, a neck. He summoned up all the strength left him and directed it into his fingers. Hands were at his hair and eyes. He hung on, working his hands, twisting, tearing. The blackness rolled thickly into his brain and he opened his hands and popped up to the surface. Mann was a couple of yards away from him, staring, then flicking his eyes toward the beach. Another body lobbed up slowly to the surface—Steve Paris, limp, his sightless eyes turning briefly up to the sky before he turned lazily over and sank back out of sight again.

MOLLY Diamond screamed something from the shore. He couldn't make out the words. But a bullet splatted into the water close by and Mann thrashed toward him. Dully, the pain in his head making it hard to focus, Billings pushed himself over on his back, spreading his arms and legs wide, then closing them as Mann swam into him. Hunching his head in tight to the other's face, he pulled in hard with his arms and pushed forward with his head and shoulders. They rolled in the water, turning over like some sort of great wounded beast, Mann clawing, grabbing, swinging his head in a desperate effort to escape the ram-like, butting violence Billings was doing to him. But his upper body was being relentlessly pressed back and his lower body pulled in, and there was a point where he could no longer stand the pain and tried to scream. But he was underwater then, and his lungs filled up and Billings fell heavily away from him with a roaring, waterfall sound in his head, then rose to the surface, muttering, "Oh, my God, enough is enough. I can't take any more."

Then the rowboat was putting out toward him. Neeley was rowing and Molly Diamond sat in the bow, the revolver held across her forearm. A bullet hit the water several yards to Billings' right and he went down and up, down and up, knowing he was a difficult target. The boat was getting closer. At last he could see the girl's face clearly, white and tense, her lips fixed like parallel razor blades. "Hold it still, you fool." Billings went under still again, and a violent concussion beat at his eardrums as a shot went into the water. Underwater, he swam directly toward the boat and another shot told him the girl could see him and was firing almost straight down, yet missing because of the deceiving refraction angle.

He pushed himself down still lower, passed into the shadow of the boat directly above him and rose to the surface on its other side, looking straight up and seeing the girl sitting high in the bow. He pushed hard and rose like a dolphin, with one arm straight above him. The clawing hand fastened into the girl's hair, and he fell back down again pulling her in with him. She came light as a doll and he held her at arm's length, gripping tighter as her hands rose to his wrist trying to pull it free. A pretty girl, he realized, even under those circumstances, her face turning black, and he yanked her down turning himself over her, and saw by her face that she was dead and then he rose to the surface for the last time, heaving himself up against the side of the boat and staring at Neeley. His voice was a rasp, his head bleeding from the great gash Mann's board had put in it, his eyes murderous. "I've killed three of them Neeley, and I'm going to kill you too if you make me."

The red-bearded man sank back from him, his lips trembling. Billings hauled himself into the boat and said, "All right, row us in." He looked around for Molly Diamond's gun and cursed to himself. The weapon had gone in the water with her.

Neely rowed in to the shore, got out at Billings' order, then started along the beach with the other behind him.

Ten minutes later they came in sight of the other surfers. "Keep going," Billings gritted. "I'm right behind you and I'll break your goddamn back if you try anything." He saw the others staring at him, Kelly Stevenson and Ed Taylor working on their boards, Leach,

Taber and Mavis Hunter rolling up their bedding, Maggie Huntington drinking a cup of coffee, then flinging it away and bounding to her feet, her hand darting into her sweatshirt and coming out with a revolver.

"Right at her," Billings shouted and pushed Neeley with his hand and ran along behind him with the wild-eyed girl enlarging quickly before him and all the others still staring as though thunderstruck.

"Don't shoot, baby," Neeley screamed. "It's me, don't shoot, don't shoot."

The girl got off one shot, then another. One went into the sand. The other went high in the air. Billings hurled Neeley forward and stormed in over him to club the girl down with his forearm and grab the gun out of her hand even before she hit the ground. She started to get back up, spitting and snarling like a cat, but he kicked her back down, the trembling Neeley crouching beside her.

He swung around on the others. "No time to explain. I'm with the CBII and I need one of you to drive the station wagon for me. Hundred miles an hour if it'll do it." They hesitated, looked blankly at one another. He snapped, "All right, Taylor, you're it."

"Geez, I don't know," Taylor said uncertainly.

"I said you're it!" Billings shouted, grabbing him by the arm and throwing him up against the station wagon. "Now, get in there and crank it up."

He dragged Neeley and Maggie Huntington up from the floor, hustled them into the wagon. "Get it going," he snapped at Taylor and the big vehicle started forward leaving Leach, Taber, Mavis Hunter and Kelley Stevenson standing on the beach, gaping. Billings hefted the gun he had taken from Maggie Huntington, then jammed it up against her neck. "There are going to be three delegates at this thing with time bombs in their briefcases," he said softly. "Who are they, Maggie? I want to know."

The girl's face went white and perspiration dotted her upper lip and her forehead, but she shook her head. "I don't know what you're talking about."

Neeley moaned. Billings said, "I'm going to use this gun, Maggie." He jerked his head at Neeley. "Ask him if I'm kidding."

"He'll do it, Maggie," the red-bearded man whimpered. "He killed Steve and Duke and Molly. He'd do it."

"That's right, Maggie," Billings said. "Now, why don't you be smart."

"No," the girl said with her face white as chalk. "No, no, no."

The gun went off. The girl screamed. Blood poured down from the trench Billings had gouged in the side of her neck. Billings' own face had gone white, but his eyes were steady as stones. "I don't like doing it, Maggie, but I'll do it again if I have to."

"No, no, no, no, no," the girl whispered. "No matter what, I won't tell you."

But Neeley was shaking all over his body and now his voice came out in a quavering croak. "It's not worth it, Maggie."

At last she said to Billings, "Three delegates from the Republic of the Sahara—Tuareg tribesmen." Neeley put his face in his hands, his shoulders shaking. The girl watched him for a few moments, her face showing nothing, her hand at her neck holding a wadded sweatshirt there in a futile effort to stop the flow of blood. At last she turned from Neeley and spoke to Billings, her voice silky, something close to a smile on her pretty face. "Would you like to know something else, Dickie boy? Would you like to know how we knew you were a CBII man? Would you like to know how we knew Adam Ross was worked into the Senegalese delegation as a man named Wilmeth Siki?"

"Tell him, Maggie," Neeley cackled, his bearded face nodding like a billy goat's. "That's something he ought to know."

"Mary Hazlitt, Dickie boy," Maggie said, laughing, poking her face forward till it was almost against his. "How does that one grab you, Dickie boy? Mary Hazlitt's our contact right in your office. *Your* Mary Hazlitt, Dickie boy, *your* Mary Hazlitt. How does that grab you?"

They reached the green expanse and surrounding tents of Batagapan while Adam Ross as Wilmeth Siki was speaking. A great crowd of security agents descended on them, but Cole was there to push his way through. Quickly, Billings told him the situation and Cole sped the agents onto the field to clear everyone off it. A handful of men moved in around the delegation from the Republic of the Sahara. Like water widening outward from where a stone had dropped in it, the delegations rushed out to all sides of the field leaving their briefcases behind, falling back with the agents ordering them back still farther, farther.

The seconds ticked by. No one spoke. The sun shone brightly down on the strange scene, the vacant field was dotted with folding chairs and brief cases. Cole said, "Dick, you're sure?" And with an incredible roar, a boom of avalanching power, the whole center of the field erupted upward, filling the air with dust and rock. The sound echoed, re-echoed, and minutes passed with the great dust cloud that had been raised thinning out slowly until finally men could see the great hole that had been torn into the ground where they'd been sitting. Only then did Billings push Maggie Huntington and Tex Neeley up to Cole and say,

"These people have something to tell you, Arthur, something about how they've been getting their information."

He walked away then, moving around knots of excitedly talking delegates, and Adam Ross came after him wearing his Senegalese robes and a fez. Ross said, "You look like a mess, Dick." He stopped when he saw the other's face, then stepped close to him, "What is it, Dick? You all right? You look sick. What is it?"

"I'm all right," Billings said wearily. "A little beat, that's all. Things happen. Things you don't figure on. They beat the hell out of you." *

Choosing between dying for nothing and killing for $120,000 really isn't very much of a choice, is it?

UNDERTAKER WHO TURNED OUT TO BE A MAFIA HITMAN

By ROLAND EMPEY

"GIVE him the best. Never mind the cost. We'll be around tomorrow night at eight for the viewing."

The two men had gotten out of a station wagon in front of the Capital Funeral Home. They had gone around to the back of the wagon and taken out a stretcher with something on it under a sheet. They had come up to the door and marched in past Doug Lewis, the undertaker, taking quick, short steps. They were wearing business suits too tight for their stocky bodies. Their faces were the flat-nosed, puffy-cheeked faces of second-rate club fighters. They laid the stretcher down on the table. Lewis pointed them to and gave him some more instructions.

"Do the job yourself. A little guy like that, you ain't going to need any help. You got anybody in the building here, send them home and tell them to stay there till you call them. He was a private guy and he wouldn't want a lot of people messing around with his remains."

The dead man was no more than five-two even in his cowboy boots. Nevertheless, it was clear he had been a person of importance and authority. You could see it in his face, the firm jaw, the narrowed grey eyes. Except for killing him, the bullet that went through his forehead hadn't done any damage. Nothing had come apart there. His big head with the mop of frontier-type grey hair was still in one piece.

Lewis said, "I understand. Leave it to me. By eight tomorrow night, I'll have him looking like he's re-Zulu way off in the African jungle."

The men nodded and started toward the door. Lewis came after them, making no sound in his rubber-soled shoes. He was a thin man in his mid-twenties. He had a pointed chin, a nose like a knife blade, and large, shiny eyes. He heard one of the men mutter, "Little Tex, Little Tex, it's the end of an era." And the other, "It better not be. We're out in the street selling bananas if it is."

They became aware of Lewis behind him. They swung around, crouching, their hands at their jacket pockets. Lewis said, "What he's wearing is all right? The checkered suit, the boots, the pearl-handled revolver stuck in his waistband? Then there's that little hole in his forehead. I'm supposed to tell the police about that."

"There's another two, three, five thousand in it for you if you don't, one of them said. "Name it. You got it. Didn't we tell you he was a private little guy. The clothes are all right. Everything about him is all right. We'll be back for the viewing tomorrow night."

They went out the door and Lewis went back to the corpse, whistling softly. His shiny eyes were actually gleaming. "The end of an era, huh," he said, talking to himself. "Little Tex and the end of an era. And no one's supposed to know about him being here except me, and what about me when I've finished working on him? Hmm, what about me when I've got him all ready for laying away?"

it open. What he saw there made him laugh out loud. "Talk about sentiment. Laying him away with a loaded gun."

He put the gun back and went into his office. A typewriter was open on the desk there. He sat down at it, slipped an envelope into it and began typing, "TO BE OPENED IN THE EVENT OF MY DEATH."

THE viewers were there promptly at eight the following evening. They arrived in a fleet of long, black cars, some 40 to 50 men and women, all expensively dressed and many of the men wearing dark glasses.

Lewis met them at the door. He was wearing a suit and tie of somber black and a mournful expression. "First room on your right, first room on your right," he kept murmuring as the mourners filed past him. "I'm sure you'll find him looking lovely and lively."

The principal mourners were a powerfully built man with a broad, expressionless face laced with old scars, and a slender young woman in a black mesh dress, her pink-nippled, hard-thrusting breasts straining the material. As they approached the little man in the box, the girl was sobbing and the man was growling. "It ain't like it's only you. Rhoda. It's tough on all of us. There won't never be another like him."

Lewis closed in on them several times, wanting to talk to the scar-faced man privately, but couldn't maneuver it. At one point he saw him take a thin, pale, chinless man aside and heard

"Undertaker Who Turned Out To Be a Mafia Hitman"
Written as Roland Empey
For Men Only, November 1976
Artist uncredited

"Just give me the money and I'll
do the job," I'd say, and I didn't
want to argue about it with
them.

      If it's narcotics money, some-
thing else happens. They look at
your arm. If they see a needle
mark there, they don't want you.
If you're hooked, you're vulnerable. **You don't trust money to a
junkie. You don't trust money to
anyone with hard needs. That's
one of the reasons I was in
demand.** There wasn't anything
I needed all that bad - booze,
women or anything else. There
wasn't anything I couldn't take
or leave alone, whichever way I
wanted it.

      The Feds have me down in
their book for eighteen killings. That agrees with my own
figures, but they ought to also
have it down there that I never killed anyone for fun and I
never made it take longer than
it had to. It was always business. It was never shooting them

"MY BLOODY LIFE AS A MAFIA BAG MAN"

WRITING AS ROLAND EMPEY

For Men Only, August 1974

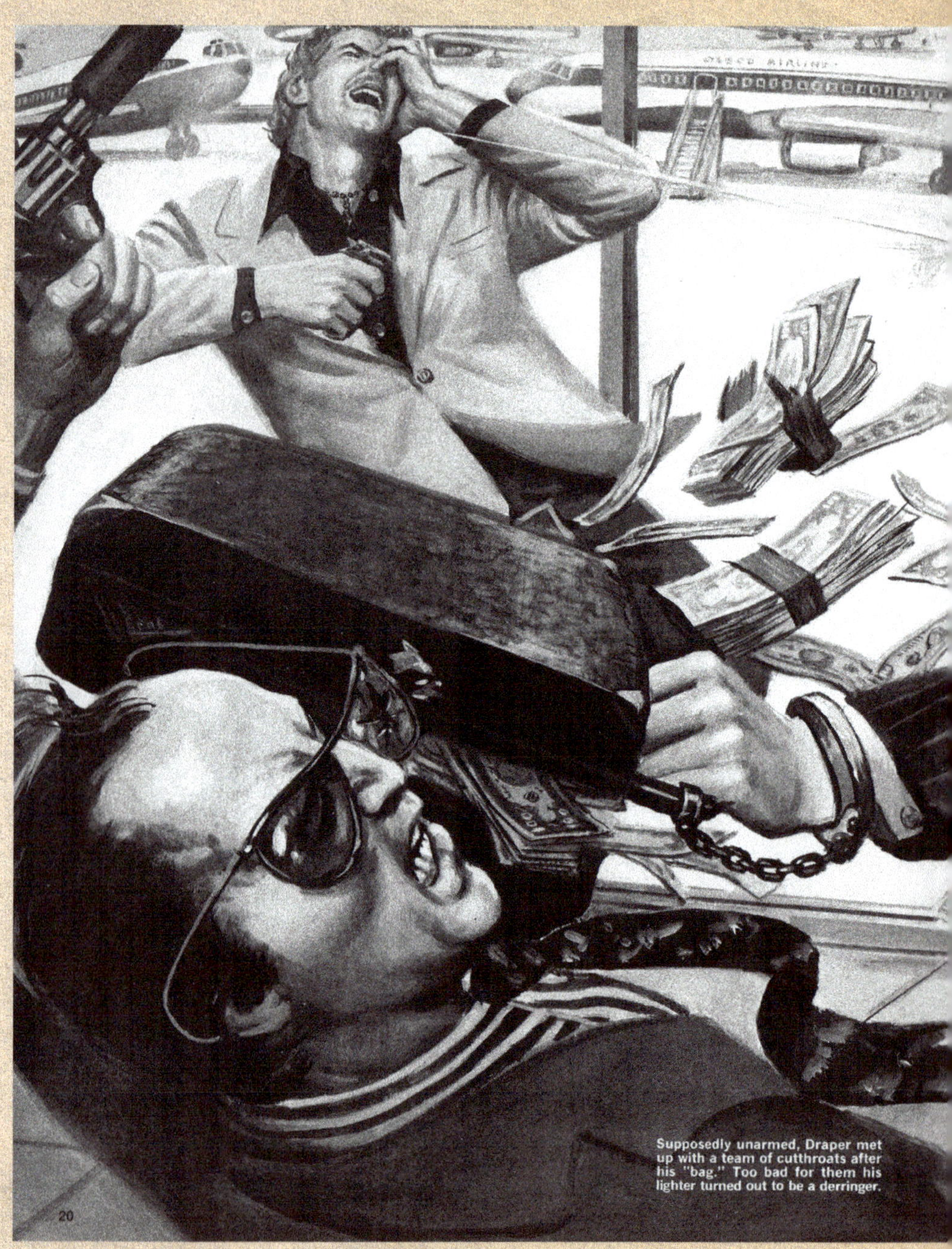

Supposedly unarmed, Draper met up with a team of cutthroats after his "bag." Too bad for them his lighter turned out to be a derringer.

"MY BLOODY LIFE AS A MAFIA BAG MAN"

...Ben Draper's 25 years of killing and running

WHEN Ben Draper was 17, a prostitute named Chickie Wells gave him fifty dollars to deliver her week's receipts to her Protector, a small-time pimp named Sonny Paris. When Paris learned a high school boy was going to be delivering his money, he arranged for a pair of knob-eared, brain-scrambled pugs to take it away from him. In that way he'd get the money Chickie Wells had sent him, then tell her it had never been delivered and force her to spit it up again.

Draper left Chickie Wells' place on a bicycle. He wore a shabby leather jacket and had a few packages in a wire basket on the handlebars, the idea being to make himself look like a run-of-the-mill delivery boy. He had the money, four hundred dollars in tens and twenties, wadded up in a side pocket of his trousers with a rubberband around it. His course took him about four miles down New York's west side from 77th Street to Greenwich Village.

The attempt to take the money was made from a grey coupe some four or five blocks from Draper's destination. The hoods

By BEN DRAPER (With Roland Empey)

ART BY SAMSON POLLEN

21

Illustration by Samson Pollen

WHEN Ben Draper was 17, a prostitute named Chickie Wells gave him fifty dollars to deliver her week's receipts to her Protector, a small-time pimp named Sonny Paris. When Paris learned a high school boy was going to be delivering his money, he arranged for a pair of knob-eared, brain-scrambled pugs to take it away from him. In that way he'd get the money Chickie Wells had sent him, then tell her it had never been delivered and force her to spit it up again.

Draper left Chickie Wells' place on a bicycle. He wore a shabby leather jacket and had a few packages in a wire basket on the handlebars, the idea being to make himself look like a run-of-the-mill delivery boy. He had the money, four hundred dollars in tens and twenties, wadded up in a side pocket of his trousers with a rubber band around it. His course took him about four miles down New York's West Side from 77th Street to Greenwich Village.

The attempt to take the money was made from a grey coupe some four or five blocks from Draper's destination. The hoods intended herding him up against the curb, bumping him off the bike onto the sidewalk there, and taking the money out of his pocket. But Draper had a rearview mirror mounted on his handlebars and saw them coming.

He watched them nearing him for four or five blocks, but waited until they were just a few yards behind him before making his move. Then he slid off the bike, picked it up by the seat and handlebars and threw it at their windshield, smashing the glass in all over them. The car went out of control, lunging up on the sidewalk and crashing half its length through the window of a supermarket.

Draper went the rest of the way to Sonny Paris' on foot, arriving just about the time he'd told Chickie Wells he'd get there. The incident tickled Sonny Paris. "Threw it right in their laps, did you?" He didn't even bother to deny it when Draper accused him of hiring the two hoods. Instead, he said, "You got the right attitude, kid. The mail must get through. I know all kinds of people that'll lay out big money for that kind of reliability. Let me go talk to some of them and see what we can line up for you. I got a feeling you just took your first step on the road to a great career."

It probably strains things a little to think of a bag man as having a "great career." But there's no other underworld skill that's valued so highly or that makes such harsh demands on an individual's capacity to dish out violence and also take it.

The bag man carries money. It's usually payoff money involving gambling, narcotics or prostitution. It's always cash and during the period of its transit, it's always "up for grabs." No one is recognized as having a legal claim to it. So anyone who can get his hands on it can call it his own. It's this aspect of the job that makes the bag man such a valued specialist.

"The first thing about a bag man is that he shouldn't call attention to himself," Ben Draper says as he looks back on twenty-five years of *carrying the mail.* "If you can stick the money in your pocket and ride it down on the subway without anyone spotting you, that's fine, that's great, that's the best you could do it. But you're not going to get to do it that easy too often.

"For one thing you're always going to be carrying too many bills to put in your pocket without looking like you got a brick there. Here, all you got to do is look at the arithmetic of it. A million dollars in thousands—that's a thousand thousands —that makes a stack seven inches high. All right, most times you're going to be carrying it in smaller bills, too, fifties and hundreds. So that means something to carry it in, a paper bag, a lunch box, a valise, an attaché case, one of those long boxes like for carrying flowers. It could be anything, but it's got to be something. So you can't sit there looking all that innocent. You got something in your hands and you got to be careful with it.

"But even more important than that, there's this. Nine times out of ten the people that are looking to grab the money know it's you that's carrying it. I mean, you're all in the same line of work. People know that's what I do. I'm not going to put on a beard and glasses and go sneaking past anyone. No, what's going to get me past people is having a .38 on me and everyone knowing I'll use it quicker than I'd sneeze. No thinking. No making up your mind. Someone looks at you a little cockeyed? Plug him. It's an instinct. Put it this way. They want to try taking the mail away from me? All right, that's their choice, but they know they could get themselves killed doing it. They know it's happened to eighteen of them already."

ALTHOUGH Draper puts it all in the present tense, his bag man days are probably behind him. He's currently in protective custody somewhere in Washington, D.C. and doing some "singing" for the Federal authorities. The situation came about because he was damaged in November of 1973 under conditions he considers highly suspicious. The gambler,

Artie Atkins, gave him a satchel of money to take from New York to someone in Denver, Colorado. But when Draper opened the bag to make a routine check of its contents, something inside it blew up in his face.

Although one eye was hanging out of his head and the flesh was coming off his face in shreds, he managed to get his .38 out and empty it into Atkins' head before the gambler could make it out the door. Then he left the building, stopped a cab by pointing his revolver at the driver, and had himself driven to a hospital. The police were just seconds behind him and asking him questions while he was on the operating table.

They didn't have to press him hard. Draper had already decided to cooperate. It was clear enough that he'd been marked for killing. He'd been around too long. He knew too much. There would be no dealing with those who wanted him done away with, particularly now that their first attempt had failed. The police were the only ones who could offer him any protection—the Federal Government, actually, since he'd functioned in an interstate way in most instances. But their protection was contingent on his "singing" for them.

So Draper made the deal. He'd "sing." They'd protect him. There's also another part to the deal, some "gravy." He wanted a tape recorder. He's got it in his mind to write a book. "Valachi did it. They wrote a book about Joe Gallo, didn't they? So why not me?" There didn't seem to be any reason not to let him have it.

And that's the way it is with Ben Draper these days. He's in a small apartment somewhere in Washington and there are at least two armed guards with him every minute of the day. They check his food. They go with him when he has to use the toilet. He's constantly being interrogated about his deliveries. How much? From whom? What for? To whom? They take him back and forth from the days he carried a few hundred dollars here or there for bedraggled whores to his "days of glory" as a trusted courier for thousand-dollar-a-chip gamblers and drug dealers moving vast sums of money across national borders and over oceans. "I been to Europe eight, nine times. I been in Cuba and South America. I been to Japan."

His interrogators know he's tricky, so they keep at him for long stretches of time, knowing they have an easier time with him when he's tired. It doesn't give him much time to himself, but when he has it he works on his book, hunching himself up to his mike and rasping into it—a chunky, balding man with a vacant eye socket and a face that looks as though someone ran over it with a well-sharpened lawn mower— "They took over two hundred fragments out of the goddamn thing."

He doesn't lack a sense of humor ("The only reason I'm folding

"MY BLOODY LIFE AS A MAFIA BAG MAN"

"I never worried about getting killed . . . about getting shot up . . . only about delivering the mail . . ." That was Draper's philosophy, and one that got him through 261 successful "deliveries" over 25 years. The one time he let his guard down, his rivals bombed his eye out!

my cards is, where do you find a broad to sack up with when you've got a kisser like this?") but he's absolutely serious about his book. He thinks he's led a fascinating life and he wants to tell the whole world all about it.

Some excerpts follow...

I NEVER thought about getting killed. I never thought about getting shot up. But attempts have been made. On my way out of Cuba once with a bundle of Mafia cash to be delivered in Miami, one of Castro's guerrillas tried to plug me. They found out how much money I had somehow, and Castro must have wanted it to help him stage the Revolution. Yet those things never bothered me. I didn't worry about them. The only thing I worried about was not delivering the mail. I'd have nightmares about people coming up and grinning at me and taking the satchel or the valise or whatever out from under my arm and the arm was numb so I couldn't move it and I couldn't stop them from doing it. I'd wake up and I'd be wet from sweating and it was a thing that happened a lot of times, that kind of dream. Not delivering the mail. It could make me puke just thinking about it. Maybe that's why I was so good at it. There wasn't anything I wouldn't do to make sure I did it.

TAKE THAT time in one of the big New York airports, with thousands of people around while it was going on.

I'd been in London for a couple of days to pick up some money to bring to New York. Now, this was investment money. This was a stockbroker named Fitz-Roberts investing a million two-hundred thousand in the operations of one of the big East Side drug rings.

There were some political guys involved. They were protecting the ring and it was their idea to let Fitz-Roberts in as a favor to him because he was doing some kind of favor to them over there.

All right, Fitz-Roberts got the money and he asked me what did I want to carry it in. I said just some kind of regular bag that they'd let me put under the seat instead of having to check it through. He found me something you could use for an overnight and then the two of us packed the money in it.

Fitz-Roberts looked at it sitting there in those nice, neat packs with a thick rubber band around each of them and he said, "How does it feel walking around with a bag in your hand knowing it's got a fortune in it?"

I said, "This trip, it's not the money I'm going to have on my mind. It's not having my gun."

I was going to be leaving from Heathrow and they were really checking you over careful there because they were worried about hijacking. There was no way I'd be able to sneak a gun past their metal detector, so I'd decided there was no point in trying. But it hurt, it hurt. You heard about people saying they felt naked without their gun. With me it was worse. With me it was like I didn't have a soul.

Fitz-Roberts looked worried. "Well, I hope there's something you'll be able to do if you run into trouble, Ben. That's an awful lot of money you've got there."

I said, "If anybody bothers me, I'm going to ask them real nice to go away. Maybe that will do it."

Sure there was something I was going to be able to do. But why tell him about it? How could I know if maybe he had some kind of double-crossing game in mind?

Well, I was right about them doing that careful check at Heathrow. Their detector even picked up my cigarette lighter, a big, shiny job I'd brought from New York. If they were opening your carry-on luggage, I would have had to turn around and figure some other way to get back across the pond. But they weren't doing that yet. They just put everything through the detector.

There was nothing to the trip. I sat next to some kid, twelve, thirteen or so, and talked baseball with him all the way back. I'm good for seeing two, three games a week right through the season and if I wasn't doing what I was doing, I'd rather be a ballplayer than anything else. Not that I was good enough, but the idea of eighty thousand people standing up and hollering while you're running around the bases—that gets to me. Williams, Mays, Aaron, Musial, DiMaggio, Mantle—I've seen them all forty, fifty times and the whole trip from

London to New York I was telling the kid about them and he was taking it all in with his mouth open like it was coming straight from God Almighty.

Well, we got to New York and the way they do it there is have you de-board through a kind of tunnel that goes direct from the plane to the terminal building, right into the waiting room of the line you're riding. What I always do is get off last, because if there's someone waiting for you that shouldn't be, he might get a little nervous when he don't see you right away and show himself before he wants to. And that's what happened this time. I could see two fellows moving around there looking like they lost something and I guess what they thought they lost was me.

I RECOGNIZED them right away. The Ronka brothers, Nick and Lester. That meant Marv had to be around there somewhere, too, because the three of them always worked together. I held back a little just outside the plane when I saw them there, and the stewardess who was telling us thanks for flying with them said, "Anything wrong, sir?" from behind me. I said, "No, it's just that I need a cigarette," and I got one out and stuck it in my mouth and got the lighter in my hand, but I didn't use it, yet. Then I said to the stewardess, "Now, I'm all right," and went down the tunnel into the waiting room.

The last of the passengers was just leaving it on the other side, so only Nick and Lester were there. But there was a lot of noise in the building from the other rooms and halls and everything and you could see people hurrying around past the glass doors. Neither Nick nor Lester was much for conversation. They just stepped up to me real close, Nick showing me a pistol with a silencer on it and Lester keeping a hand in his pocket so I'd know he had something there, too. Whatever talking they did, it was Nick that always did it. So this time he said, "Christ, it's like we hit you with your pants down, Ben. All right, give us the bag and then go look out the window there and at least you're out of it without losing your health."

I said, "Give me a minute to think about it. Let me light the cigarette."

Nick said, "Don't get cute, Ben. You're getting nervous? All right, light your cigarette, but hand the bag over while you're doing it and then walk over to that window."

I said, "All right, what the hell. Facts are facts," and lifted the cigarette lighter and, of course, it had a tiny derringer in it, and *whap! whap!* I'm putting two slugs into Nick from about six inches away and at the same time I'm swinging the bag at Lester, which isn't such a bad idea except that it opens up when I hit him and the money starts tumbling out of it.

The Ronkas work together all the time, but you wouldn't say what they had was an example of brotherly love. If that was it, Lester would probably have been down there trying to do something for Nick groaning his life away with blood pumping out of the two holes I'd put in his chest. But, no, what he was doing was grabbing for the money and all I had to do was get my hand in the back of his hair and smash his face down on the floor two, three, four, five times with the blood splashing out like his head was a paper bag full of it. Then I dropped him there, stuffed the money back in the bag, closed it up and walked out.

Some people had seen the end of it from outside the glass doors, but they just went scrambling back to get out of my way and I walked through them, saying, "Don't believe any of that. We're just practicing a scene from a movie we're making."

I took the escalator down to the main floor, saw the third brother, Marv, waiting at one of the exits and went over to him. The action was beginning by then, cops running in and a woman screaming somewhere, and I could see that Marv was all confused. Things weren't happening the way his brothers had told him they would. I said, "They're waiting for you back there, Marv. There's been a change in plans. They told me when I saw you I should tell you to go back to the waiting room so they can tell you what it is."

I delivered the money to Frenchy DePew, the head of the ring I was bringing it to, and of course he knew everything about it by then and he thought I handled it real good. "You got to be an awful cool cat to think of picking up the money at a time like that, Ben," he said. "We're going to throw in another twenty-five hundred for your doing it that good."

That was Frenchy in 1969. Four years later it was Frenchy that gave Artie Atkins ten thousand dollars to blow that bag up in my face.

So that's one thing about this business. You never know where you stand.

TWO HUNDRED and sixty-two deliveries over a stretch of 25 years. That's a little over ten a year. Nothing written down, but the whole thing's clear in my head. Each one's there with everything there is to know about it.

There's different things about each one though, depending on who you're working with. If it's money that's coming out of some prostitute's business, you can be sure she's going to want you to take your fee out in trade instead of real cash. But I never went for it.

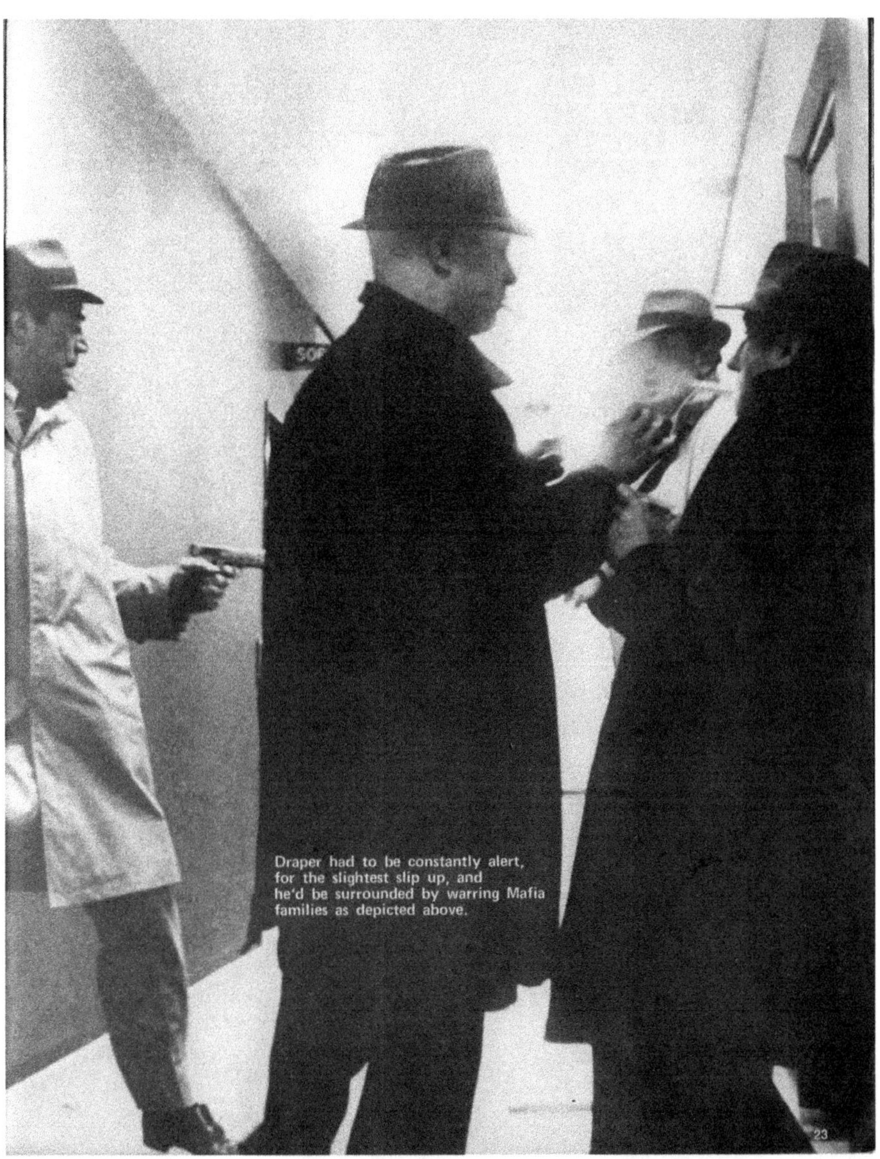

The gamblers want to cut you double or nothing for your fee. It can be a thousand, five thousand, it makes no difference to them. You get enough bag men who'll go for that one, but with them they're strictly in it for the money and they were ready to take the chance. With me I'm still not sure what I was in it for, but whatever it was the money was only part of it. So I never took them up on that bet. "Just give me the money and I'll do the job," I'd say, and I didn't want to argue about it with them.

If it's narcotics money, something else happens. They look at your arm. If they see a needle mark there, they don't want you. If you're hooked, you're vulnerable. You don't trust money to a junkie. You don't trust money to anyone with hard needs. That's one of the reasons I was in demand. There wasn't anything I needed all that bad—booze, women or anything else. There wasn't anything I couldn't take or leave alone, whichever way I wanted it.

The Feds have me down in their book for eighteen killings. That agrees with my own figures, but they ought to also have it down there that I never killed anyone for fun and I never made it take longer than it had to. It was always business. It was never shooting them up in arms and legs and all that first to keep them alive awhile, the way some of them do it. You do that if it's your idea of fun, but with me it was always business. The only one I would have ever done it to was Atkins and I didn't get a chance to. The eye was out of my head and he was trying to get out the door and all I could do was slam every slug I had into him someplace or other and then get out of there myself.

LIKE TRUMAN dropping the A-bomb on Hiroshima, I never lost any sleep over it. But there was one time if it had worked out different, it would have been all right with me. That was when I was with Heine Miller in 1971.

Heine ran all the Mafia's gambling on the East Coast from Boston down to Charleston, South Carolina. He got the players, he got the places where the games were held, and he got his own people to be the "house" out of the organization he was the head of. The Mafia put up the protection and Heine gave them a cut out of all his games. On an average week that came to about twelve thousand dollars, which added up to about six hundred thousand dollars a year.

It was my job to collect the weekly take from all Heine's games and deliver it to Vito Orlando in the back room of a barber shop on Atlantic Avenue in Brooklyn between four and five every Wednesday afternoon. But even more important than getting the money there was seeing that no one saw me doing it. The whole thing about the Mafia is that it's one link leading to another. You can't let the wrong people latch on at any point, because if they do, they've got too good a chance of moving up the ladder.

All right, I used to put in three days a week picking up the money from Heine's games doing the route by car, starting at Charleston and working all the way up to Boston and getting back to New York on a Wednesday morning and then going out to the barber shop by subway in the afternoon, dressed like a sailor and carrying the money in a duffel

bag. I was driving a good Buick and had it serviced at a place called
Tom and Willie's every Thursday afternoon. The one thing I couldn't
afford was a breakdown on the way. We were running on much too tight
a schedule for that. So the servicing was important and Tom and Willie
were good at what they did—both young guys, no more than twenty-
five, and always with a cheerful word for you and their prices were
okay, too.

I made this one trip where I had some time on my hands in
Baltimore and I picked up a girl in a bar and we had ourselves a pretty
good time in the back of the car. Now this was a girl with a lot of
passion, Naomi, and once she started getting steamed up it was all
sobbing and panting and "Benjy, keep doing it," and "don't let it stop,
Benjy," and Benjy this and Benjy that like she's going out of her skull.
She was so heavy, it was beginning to be a drag. I like things a little
more under control than that, so I dumped her as soon as I was able to.
Then I went ahead with the rest of my route, delivered the money to
Vito in the barber shop, and the next afternoon I put the car in Tom and
Willie's for the evening.

AT FOUR o'clock I went back to pick it up and Willie hands me my bill
and says in that cheerful way of his, "Just the oil change and lubrication,
Benjy. Everything else is okay." I paid him and we kidded around awhile
and then I went out of there without showing anything on my face
about what I was thinking. But I was thinking plenty, mainly that he'd
been calling me Ben for months and here suddenly it was Benjy right
after that crazy girl was doing it in the car in Baltimore.

So I drove the car to where I could look it over in private and it took
me only about ten minutes to find the bug they'd put in the padding of
the rear seat. It wasn't much bigger than the top of a milk bottle, small
enough so I could wrap it in my handkerchief. I did that and then drove
back to their place. It was past five by then and they were getting ready
to close up. Tom was doing something at the cash register and Willie
was coming out of the can wiping his hands on a paper towel. They
grinned when they saw me and Willie said, "Forget something?" and I
said, "No, but you did, I'm bringing it back to you."

I put the handkerchief on the counter and motioned for Tom to
open it up. He started to, but they both had to know what was inside
because suddenly they both started scuttling like mice, only there wasn't
room in there for them to get away. I got Tom by leaning straight over
the counter and firing down at the floor where he'd dropped and was
clawing at his coveralls for a gun he had in there. Willie managed to
get into the can, but I kicked the door open and kneed him down onto

the bowl and shot him sitting there with his mouth going, "No, no, for God's sake—" but no sound coming out, just his mouth making the words.

We had to do a lot of fast work after that, moving all Heine's games to different locations and abandoning the barber shop because we didn't know how much Tom and Willie had recorded. What we did know, though, was that they were Feds, and that killing them was the only thing I could have done with them. Still, of all the eighteen, they're the only two it would have been all right with me if it hadn't happened that way. They weren't bad guys. It was just that they were on the wrong side of the fence.

One more thing about Tom and Willie. For a couple of months after I killed them, they were the ones that were taking the money away from me every night in my dreams.

But that was only for a couple of months, and then it stopped. *

"The Caribbean Kingdom of Six-Foot Sarah Glad"
Male, September 1960
Illustration by Samson Pollen

She was staring at Roman intently now. "Some of us have
been here five weeks, eight
weeks. I myself have been here
for three months. It was because
of something I did to a major
who tried to force his attentions on me. He will walk bent
over for the rest of his life.
**Three months! Three months!
Do you know what that means
to a healthy woman with an
affectionate nature?"**
Roman said hesitantly, "I was
married the day before I went
into service. My wife, Rosalie,
and I were childhood sweethearts. We made a vow as I was
leaving that neither one of us
would ever fool around."
He stopped. The woman's hand was
working itself into his clothing. He said miserably, "We made
a vow," and then gasped. Her
hand was on his belly. That was
where he was most vulnerable.
It was as though he were nothing but bare, quivering nerves

"THEY CALL HIM FATHER ITALY"

— WRITING AS ROLAND EMPEY —

For Men Only, March 1975

TODAY THEY CALL HIM FATHER ITALY

By ROLAND EMPEY

ART BY EARL NOREM

MONTE *Rosa, Northern Italy, February, 19, 1943—*
"You there. Unite his hands and put him in."

It was said in Italian. Gregory Roman and the two men who had captured him had reached the stockade, a 7-foot-high barbed wire fence enclosing a desolate field. Grass had once grown there for horses to nibble on, but lack of care had dried it up. Now the hard ground was bare except where it was covered by patches of snow looking like crumpled parachutes in the darkness.

"Hurry up. It's freezing out. We want to go in and have a drink at the fire."

Roman's captors were getting impatient with the guard they had called to untie him. The guard had lost a leg in the Libyan campaign. He needed a shave. His uniform was dirty, shapeless, his overcoat dragging the ground. He limped over on a crutch from the sentrybox at the stockade gate, wiping his nose with a dirty rag and grumbling, "Do you know what you're doing? I've been in the army for twenty years and I can tell you it's never been done before."

"What else can we do   *(Continued on page 80)*

The people wept and tried to embrace Roman as eight of his favorite children bore him on the sedan through the town as they did each year he returned.

Illustration by Earl Norem

MONTE *Rosa, Northern Italy, February 19, 1943—*
"You there. Untie his hands and put him in."

It was said in Italian. Gregory Roman and the two men who had captured him had reached the stockade, a 7-foot-high barbed wire fence enclosing a desolate field. Grass had once grown there for horses to nibble on, but lack of care had dried it up. Now the hard ground was bare except where it was covered by patches of snow, looking like crumpled parachutes in the darkness.

"Hurry up. It's freezing out. We want to go in and have a drink at the fire."

Roman's captors were getting impatient with the guard they had called to untie him. The guard had lost a leg in the Libyan campaign. He needed a shave. His uniform was dirty, shapeless, his overcoat dragging the ground. He limped over on a crutch from the sentry box at the stockade gate, wiping his nose with a dirty rag and grumbling, "Do you know what you're doing? I've been in the army for twenty years and I can tell you it's never been done before."

"What else can we do with him?" the man who had introduced himself to Roman as "Count Fazio" demanded. "We can't have him in the castle with us, can we? What else can we do? There's nothing. All right, untie his hands and put him in there."

The guard limped around behind Roman. His breath was stale and sour on Roman's neck. He cut the rope holding his hands with a knife and pushed him toward the stockade. "Do you see the stable there? That's where you'll stay. Just go in and take a mattress."

The gate, which was of wood topped by barbed wire, swung closed behind Roman's back. He turned around to look at the men who captured him. They were smartly dressed in whipcord trousers, alpine caps and leather hunting coats. They flourished their rifles as Roman stared at them and the one who had given his name as Baron Orlando shouted, "Don't stand there like an idiot. Go inside where you'll be warm."

The guard limped back to his sentry box, muttering, "'Go inside where you'll be warm.' Do they have any idea what they're doing? Well, it will be warm enough for him in there, all right. There's no question about that. It will be warm enough for him."

Roman pushed his hands into his armpits to keep them warm and walked quickly toward the stable. He was a big man with a keg-like head and a prominent jaw, his face customarily wearing a wide, toothy grin, although at this moment it looked glum. He wore a US Army uniform with a Signal Corps patch and a Technician fifth-grade's stripes on the sleeve.

Roman came in at one end of the stable. The stalls were still there as they had been when the horses used them. Some straw had been scattered around on the ground, and also a number of limp mattresses. The only light came from a lantern hanging on a hook at the other end of the stable. From where he had come in, Roman could make out several forms gathered beneath it. He called down, "Hiya, fellows," but got no response. Too morose to follow up on it, he threw a mattress into a corner of a corner stall and stretched out on it, his arm across his eyes.

For some minutes he stayed like that, then became aware of feet scuffling toward him through the straw. He took his arm from his eyes and propped himself up on his elbows. Whoever was coming toward him was lighting his way with the lantern, swinging it low to the ground.

Roman said, "Hiya."

No answer.

He said uneasily, "Hiya, fellow."

The other reached him and stood there briefly, then suddenly sank down beside him. Roman stared, said, "Noooooo," then, "oh, my God," then, "they must have sent me to the wrong building."

The lantern's glow carved out of the darkness the fierce face of a young peasant woman, dark-eyed and with her black hair tumbling about her shoulders in a shaggy mane. She said, "This is the only building."

Roman said carefully, "Isn't that kind of unusual? Men and women together?"

The woman said, "Not men. Just one man. Just you."

Roman said, "Oh my God."

The woman said, "There is a village a few miles from here called San Dona di Camerino. In this village there are both rats and people of great nobility. The people of nobility are those that hate, despise and spit upon Mussolini." She shot her face close to Roman's and screeched. "We hate, we despise and we spit upon Mussolini." Roman drew back but thought better about wiping his face with his sleeve even though she had flecked him with her saliva.

"When the war began," she continued, "all the men of great nobility ran off to fight with the partisans. We women were not needed. Later, they told us, but not yet. It angered us, but what could we do? Then a company of the Fascist army arrived in San Dona di Camerino and was quartered in our homes. Now at last there was something we could do— sabotage. The rat poison in the lieutenant's soup. The explosive charge under the captain's outhouse. Putting dirt in the barrels of the soldiers' rifles so that they blew up when they were fired.

"But sometimes we are caught and then they send us up here to the stockade." She was staring at Roman intently now. "Some of us have been here five weeks, eight weeks. I myself have been here for three months. It was because of something I did to a major who tried to force his attentions on me. He will walk bent over for the rest of his life. Three months! Three months! Do you know what that means to a healthy woman with an affectionate nature?"

ROMAN said hesitantly, "I was married the day before I went into the service. My wife, Rosalie, and I were childhood sweethearts. We made a vow as I was leaving that neither one of us would ever fool around."

He stopped. The woman's hand was working itself into his clothing. He said miserably, "We made a vow," and then gasped. Her hand was on his belly. That was where he was most vulnerable. It was as though he were nothing but bare, quivering nerves there. He shouted, "I'm only human, Rosalie, I'm only human," and flung an arm up over the woman to sweep her in under him. She squirmed briefly, arranging herself for a good fit, then said, "Don't take all night, big boy." Three minutes later she wriggled out from under him and stood up, saying, "I'm Serafina," and returned to the other end of the stable.

Roman lay down on his back again with his arm over his eyes. Should he have held her off, even fought her off if that were necessary? What was the point in making a vow if you fell apart the first time a woman came into close range? Still, one relapse wouldn't necessarily put his marriage on the rocks. He'd put that one out of his mind and make sure it didn't happen again.

He was interrupted in these thoughts by a familiar sound—feet scuffling in the straw. Was Serafina coming back for something she had dropped, maybe an earring? He propped himself up on his elbows The lantern was coming toward him as earlier, swinging low to the ground. He said, "Drop something? I haven't seen anything."

The words turned to rocks in his mouth. The woman who had sunk to her knees beside him wasn't Serafina. This one had a round, pink-cheeked face and there were tears in her eyes. Roman said desperately,

"Miss, two wrongs don't make a right. I swore an oath to my wife."

But the weeping woman's hands were in his clothes and Serafina was shouting hoarsely, "The belly, Angelina, the belly." Then he was being stroked there, then kissed there, and then howling, "Rosalie, Rosalie, try to understand," and whirling a woman under him for the second time in ten minutes. And even as he did, the scuffling of feet in the straw began again and he made out others coming forward to get on line and wait their turn.

It had been two weeks earlier that Roman parachuted into the woods of Monte Rosa. The fighting in North Africa was coming to an end by then and the Allied High Command was readying the invasion of Italy. Saboteurs, spies and intelligence people of all sorts were being smuggled in to gather information. Roman was one of these. His specialty was drawing terrain maps.

Roman made his drop on the night of February 6, 1943. He carried a transmitter, a sending key, a code book, a gridded pad, a compass, a small shovel, a flashlight, and a supply of dehydrated food in cans and tin foil. He had memorized the call letters and frequency of the clandestine station he would contact, and the operator there had been equipped with gridded map sheets that conformed to his own so that the material he sent could be faithfully reproduced.

IT WAS a black night with no moon or stars to light the way. He got scratched a little tumbling through the trees, but managed to reach the ground without doing himself any serious damage. He quickly scraped a hole in the frozen ground with his shovel, stuffed the parachute in, and covered it up with dirt and rocks. Then he ate a chocolate bar, took a brief nap till sun-up, and then went to work.

For the next two weeks, Roman trudged up and down Monte Rosa mapping terrain features and transmitting them to his receiving station. It was dull work and he often wondered if it had any value. There had to be hundreds of others doing the same thing, but the invasion wasn't going to blanket all Italy. Maybe he'd just been given the job to justify the 66 bucks a month they were paying him.

He slept under bushes, in shallow caves and curled up against the trunks of trees. His food was the same canned crap day after day. He used cold creek water to shave with and scraped himself raw doing it. He saw other human beings every once in a while, a man in a little cart with a bedraggled horse pulling it, two girls striding along with baskets of freshly baked bread on their heads. But, of course, he couldn't talk to them. He had to keep out of sight. The only talking he did was with Rosalie and that put him under strain—"thinking about your great boobs, honey, thinking about your jugs—" It made it hard to work. It was almost a relief when he was finally captured.

It happened while he slept in thick weeds, dreaming of Rosalie's fingers tickling him under the chin and waking to find a rifle poking him there. A man of 50 or so in the expensive clothes of a gentleman hunter was at the other end of the gun, and another man of the same sort stood next to him, also armed. They introduced themselves quickly: "Count Fazio and Baron Orlando, victims of this cruel war." They had spoken in Italian, not expecting to be answered, and were startled to hear Roman speak it, too. "Gregory Roman, technician fifth grade, 32612802. That's all you'll get out of me."

They shrugged. "Why should we want even that? We'll hold you overnight with some others we've been asked to hold because we have the physical facilities for it, and tomorrow we'll bring you down to San Dona di Camerino where the army will ask you whatever questions they want to." They prodded him to his feet, tied his hands behind him, and started him on the long march to Count Fazio's castle. On the way, Baron Orlando said bitterly that he, too, had once had large holdings, but the Army had taken them over as a troop-training area, which was why he had moved in with the count.

Roman said, "Gregory Roman, technician fifth grade, 32612802. That's all you'll get out of me."

It was about 10 that night when Roman went into the stable. There were 11 women there and by two in the morning all were sleeping soundly and smiling in their sleep. It could probably be said that Roman was sleeping, too, but actually he was in some sort of stupor, his arms flung out to the sides and his eyes staring at the ceiling but seeing nothing.

The quiet in the stable was a godsend to the guards and the two noblemen. Every other night the women had cursed them for holding them there, screaming and howling. The men had flushed and shriveled under their obscene language and been unable to sleep themselves, but now every-thing was calm and serene. Count Fazio was so pleased, he phoned Colonel Gagliardi in San Dona di Camerino to ask if he could keep Roman another night. When he explained why, Colonel Gagliardi, who commanded all the troops quartered in San Dona di Camerino, was impressed—"You mean this one American serviced eleven women in one night?"

"Between the hours of ten and two," Count Fazio said. "We saw them extinguish the lantern."

"The most I ever heard of before was eight in six hours," Colonel

Gagliardi said. "He must be a gorilla. Tell me, do you think he could handle six more? We picked up six wild ones for derailing a troop train."

"Send them along," Count Fazio said confidently. "We'll put an extra potato in his soup tonight and he'll have them all singing sweet songs by morning."

So began Roman's incredible imprisonment. The six who derailed the train were followed a day later by four who blew up a field kitchen. Then in rapid-fire order, day by day, came eight more, three more, five more, two more, three more, nine more, four more, seven, eight more, and more after that, and still more after that. They crowded into the stable. They formed their lines. They came one by one to the young American lying gaunt and hollow-eyed on his flimsy mattress. From behind them came the muttered advice of those who had been there earlier, "the belly, the belly, it drives him wild in the belly." Then they were stroking him there, kissing him there, darting their tongues into his navel even as he sighed his feeble protests. "I'll have a breakdown. I'm only flesh and blood. What about my vow?" Then suddenly he was howling, "Rosalie, your husband is a weak, weak bastard," and whirling the woman of the moment under him. Two minutes later it was all over and she was murmuring her name in gratitude. *I'm Maria. I'm Theresa. I'm Celia. I'm Sophia. I'm Veronica. I'm Gina. I'm Silvia.*" And on and on, a whole telephone book full of names, a whole gallery of beaming, grateful faces.

They fed him as though he were a prize bull, depriving themselves to see that he had enough to keep his strength up. They kept him warm, kept him comfortable, saw to all his needs. The guards clung to the barbed wire fence like scarecrows tied there, maddened by their own needs, yet knowing better than to go inside. The women had guaranteed to tear them to shreds if they did. "He is all we need. He is a man for all times, a man for the ages." Even Count Fazio, Baron Orlando and Colonel Gagliardi looked grim as they stared across the cold, hard earth at the stable, knowing what went on there, knowing what never *stopped* going on there. They were all past their peak, but the situation was making difficulties for them.

"The man is a freak, some sort of a monster," Colonel Gagliardi said sourly, and the other two had to agree. It would be easier on all three of them if they could get him out of there, but the women would go berserk if they tried.

The number of prisoners reached a hundred, a hundred and fifty. The women of San Dona di Camerino were attacking the soldiers wherever they saw them. Their acts of sabotage were growing increasingly reckless. Anything to be sent up to the stockade. They reached two hundred. Then two hundred and fifty, three hundred. They covered the floor of the stable like bees on a honeycomb with the emaciated and glassy-eyed Roman in their center on a pile of mattresses four feet high. They fed him, held his head in their laps, crooned lullabies in his ears to help him sleep.

THE FIRST of the "big bellies" appeared and was immediately followed by others. The women floated about the stockade, patting themselves there and going, "Noooooo" at the agonized guards. The number of "big bellies" multiplied rapidly. A desperate Colonel Gagliardi tried to put the blame on Count Fazio and Baron Orlando. "How will we feed them? We're having a food shortage. My men are hunting rats. Why did you ever put that two-legged rabbit in there?"

"Why did you keep sending women up here?" Count Fazio said coldly. "You could have brought him down to your headquarters and treated him like a regular prisoner."

It was a pointless argument. Nature would take its own course regardless of who was to blame. One way or another, food would have to be found. 271 days after Roman's apprehension, the first of the "big bellies" gave birth to a baby boy. That same Serafina who had first enflamed him by stroking his belly. Minutes later another followed suit, and after that they came in a flood. There were 11 that first day, 8 a day later, 14 the day after that, then 9, then 6, then 4, then 12, and so forth, on and on, the women spreading themselves all over the stockade to nurse their children while the guards moaned and whimpered outside the fence and put their tongues to the barbs in utter futility.

"Will it never end?" Colonel Gagliardi gasped as the deluge showed no signs of letting up. "The man is a living reminder to us all that we're nothing but animals."

"Creatures of the caves and swamps," Baron Orlando nodded dully. "Frogs, pythons, amoeba. At the last count, which was taken half an hour ago, he was a father 304 times and there are still a number of big bellies there to be heard from."

It was a year after Roman's capture almost to the day that a 20-man team from the 18th American Airborne Cavalry parachuted down onto Monte Rosa. It was snowing heavily, which provided them with a perfect backdrop as they sailed down in their white camouflage suits. The men landed half a mile from Count Fazio's stockade and headed directly for it, having been told that there were prisoners of unknown description to be freed there. They had no difficulty with the guards there, most of them too listless to even look up as the raiders ran toward them. Some actually lay about in the snow like logs or piles of discarded clothing. Count Fazio and Baron Orlando were handled that easily, too. Their jauntiness of a year earlier had long since left them. They were dreary, dispirited. Their eyes were the eyes of men haunted by some unbearable vision.

With their prisoners secured, Sergeant Pete Williams led half a dozen men to the stable. A veteran of all the African fighting, Williams was known as a hard case, a man often picked to head up raiding parties in dangerous behind-the-lines areas. Warning his men to be silent, he ran quickly to an end of the stable and crouched there till they were all bunched around him. Then, nodding grimly, he said, "This does it," and hurled himself at the door, pounding it with his boot and gun butt. The door was no match at all for that assault, and in a matter of moments the raiders were crashing in through its splintered wreckage. But inside they came immediately to a skidding halt.

The entire enclosure seethed and steamed with humanity in a state of utter joy and contentment. Women chattered happily as they nursed, washed, fed and otherwise attended to their babies. The children cooed, cried, laughed, kissed, burped, wet themselves and their mothers, and turned loose their excretions with the rapidity of machine gunfire. The place smelled of milk and "do-do," and sheets (from Count Fazio's family treasure trove) hung on some 30 or 40 lines strung widthwise across the stable. Now, through these sheets, a figure approached the raiders, walking slowly and coming to a stop a few feet from them. For the men themselves, it was an awesome moment. In Williams' words:

"As soon as we saw him, we understood everything. The man was well over six feet tall, but he couldn't have weighed more than 80 pounds. Although we learned later that he was 24 years old, he came to us like an old man, shuffling his feet and peering at us as though he couldn't believe we were actually there. His voice was a weak croak—'American?'

"I said. 'Yes, we are, sir, and I see by your uniform that you are, too. May I ask your name, sir?'

"He thought a while as though he couldn't recall it, staring at me and staring through me. Then finally he said uncertainly, 'It used to be Roman. It used to be Gregory Roman. Technician fifth-grade Gregory Roman, 32612802. But in this place'—he gestured behind him, indicating everyone there, all those exuberantly happy women and the squealing, squalling children—'in this place, I am known as Father Italy.'"

EVERY year, a handful of middle-aged Americans returns to Europe to relive some event of World War II. They go to Aachen where they had

a leg blown off, or to Normandy where they carried a wounded buddy
to safety through a hail of German machine gunfire, or to Paris where
they spent 48 hours with a girl whose face and voice will haunt them all
the years of their lives. It's a ritual visit, a time for tears and alcohol, a
time of strong emotion.

Gregory Roman is one of those who makes that yearly pilgrimage.
A tall, well-built man of 52, Roman owns a transmission repair shop in
Brooklyn, out of which he makes, in his own words, "a very nice buck."
He has an attractive wife, Rosalie, two sons both married and doing
well in the moving van business, a house in the $50,000 range, and a
weekend fishing shack in Vermont. Life has been good to Roman and he
shows it in a firm handshake, a broad smile, a genial style that has made
him many friends.

Nevertheless, despite his open, easy manner, Roman is somewhat
secretive about his yearly pilgrimage to Italy. He began making it in
1947 and he hasn't missed one since. His wife, Rosalie, whom he married
before going into the service, doesn't exactly believe him when he says
of his trips, "Just some of the guys getting together. You know how it is
with old soldiers." She suspects he's hiding something, but life has been
so good for her with him, she's decided not to probe.

Whatever he is hiding, however, she's quite sure it's somehow
connected to that first year he was out of the service—the nightmares
in which he often groaned, "No, no, not tonight, just this one night, let
me in peace," and the fact that he was unable to carry out the husband's
traditional responsibilities to her during that entire period. Whenever
she tried to coax him, he shuddered and seemed on the verge of
having a fit. In time he came out of it, however, helped by her gentle
explorations which one night brought her hand and lips to his belly, a
part of his body she had never visited that way before. From that point
on, things turned around, and eventually they reached that plateau of
mutual happiness they had been living on ever since.

As for Roman and his yearly pilgrimage, he flies into Venice where a
car awaits him. He is driven from there into the mountains of northern
Italy, reaching the town of San Dona di Camerino in 10 hours. Here the
entire population throngs the streets to greet him. He is kissed, hugged,
wept over.

A sedan chair is produced. He takes his place in it. Eight stalwart
young men and women pick it up by its handles, and a procession
starts upward into the higher mountains. Everyone sings, dances, and
occasionally out of sheer exuberance, people will rush at Roman to fling
their arms about him, calling him "Papa." A number of times along the

way, the eight original bearers are replaced by others.

In time a grassy field is reached. A rusted, mangled barbed-wire fence encloses it. The collapsing remains of an old stable are inside. Everyone goes into the field and has a great feast, featuring great quantities of red wine. Roman is the central figure in all these joyous doings. The high point comes when 318 women approach him in a long winding line, each kissing him noisily on the mouth and murmuring her name, *"Serafina, Maria, Cecelia, Sofia—"* and so forth. Next come the 318 young men and women who call him, "Papa," and they, too, kiss and embrace him.

Finally, the entire assemblage toasts him in wine, hailing him as, "Father Italy, Father Italy, Father Italy." Then they will all return to San Dona di Camerino. From here the car brings him back to Venice. A few hours later, Rosalie meets him at Kennedy Airport.

"How was it this year?" she asks.

"The same as always," Roman shrugs. "What do you do with the guys? You have a couple of drinks. You shoot the bull. It's the same thing every year."

What else can he say? ✳

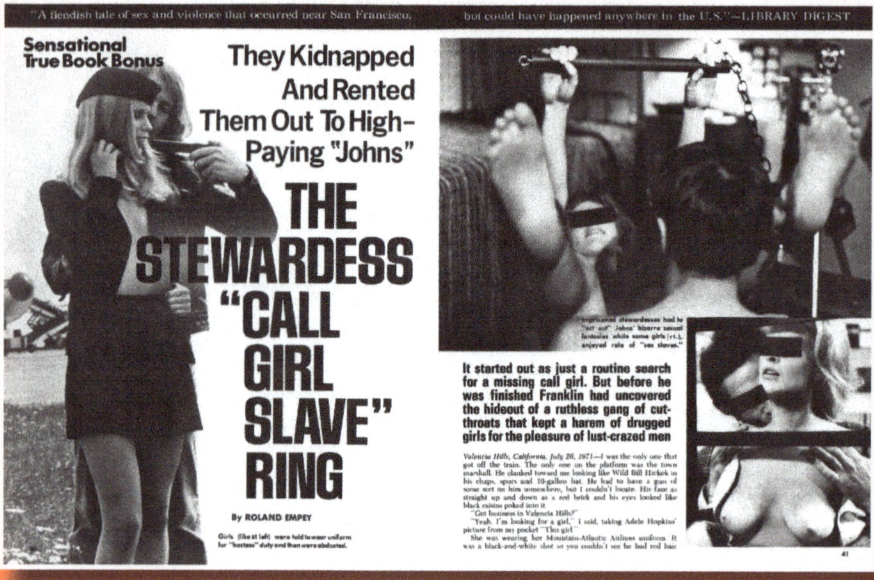
"A fiendish tale of sex and violence that occurred near San Francisco, but could have happened anywhere in the U.S."—LIBRARY DIGEST
Sensational True Book Bonus
They Kidnapped And Rented Them Out To High-Paying "Johns"
THE STEWARDESS "CALL GIRL SLAVE" RING
By ROLAND EMPEY
Girls (like at left) were told to wear uniform for "hostess" duty and then were abducted.
Implicated stewardesses had to "act out" Johns' bizarre sexual fantasies while some girls (rt.) enjoyed role of "sex slaves."
It started out as just a routine search for a missing call girl. But before he was finished Franklin had uncovered the hideout of a ruthless gang of cut-throats that kept a harem of drugged girls for the pleasure of lust-crazed men
41

Read
"Bar Room Girl Who Touched Off a Tribal War" (1966)
and
"The Stewardess 'Call Girl Slave' Ring" (1971)
in
WEASELS RIPPED MY FLESH!
Read
"Trapped in the Bayou's Pit of a Million Snakes" (1974)
in
I WATCHED THEM Eat Me Alive
THE MEN'S ADVENTURE LIBRARY

"When I got into writing
adventure stories, I was
having a good time. You just
went as far as you could. I
really think the idea was to
just have a lot of fun at what
you were doing, and you had to
know that what you were doing
was really pretty funny. I
enjoyed them right up until
the very end."

- W.K.

Editors' Acknowledgments

Thank you Jennifer Kaylin, Lucy Kaylin, Josh Alan Friedman, Bruce Jay Friedman, John Bowers, Rich Oberg, Mike Chomko, William Lampkin, and Jack Cullers at PulpFest, Christine and Malcolm Bell at Bookfellows, Tony Jacobs at Sideshow Books, Marc Campbell, Dave Coleman, Andrew Biscontini, Jason Cuadrado, Cormac Foster, Paul Silva, Scott Somerndike, Innes Weir, Doyle family, and all our friends in the Men's Adventure Magazines & Books group on Facebook.

With love and special thanks from Bob to Barbara Jo Butler Deis.

Robert Deis owns one of the world's largest collections of vintage men's adventure magazines (MAMs) published in the 1950s, 1960s, and 1970s. In 2009, he created a popular blog about the genre, **MensPulpMags.com**. A few years later, Bob and Wyatt Doyle of New Texture launched The Men's Adventure Library, a series of books that feature classic MAM pulp fiction stories and artwork. That series now includes nearly 20 lushly illustrated story anthologies and art books. In recent years, Bob and Wyatt have been featured speakers at PulpFest, and Bob was listed in the book *Who's Who In New Pulp*. Starting in 2021, Bob began working with Bill Cunningham, head of Pulp 2.0 Press, to publish a magazine that features MAM stories and artwork, called the *Men's Adventure Quarterly*. He has contributed articles about MAMs to various magazines and fanzines and also writes two blogs about famous quotations, **ThisDayinQuotes.com** and **QuoteCounterquote.com**. Bob lives near Key West, Florida with his wife BJ (who graciously tolerates his fascination with vintage MAMs), their three dogs, and four cats.

Wyatt Doyle is ringmaster of New Texture, and he edits and designs most releases. His own books include *Stop Requested* (illustrated by Stanley J. Zappa), *Dollar Halloween*, *I Need Real Tuxedo and a Top Hat!*, *Buty-Wave Is Now Closed Forever*, and *Jorge Amaya Doesn't Live Here Anymore*. A retrospective of his photography was presented by Gallery 30 South in Pasadena, CA. With Robert Deis, he edits The Men's Adventure Library series, exploring vintage pulp fiction, illustration art, and history. With Jimmy Angelina, he created *The Last Coloring Book* and *The Last Coloring Book on the Left*, as well as *Be Italian*. Together with Hal Glatzer and Norman von Holtzendorff, he produced *Things That Were Made for Love*, collecting the Jazz Age songsheet art of Sydney Leff. He assisted in the publication of Georgina Spelvin's memoir, *The Devil Made Me Do It*, and published Josh Alan Friedman's *Black Cracker* and *Tell the Truth Until They Bleed* via his Wyatt Doyle Books imprint. He administers the creative estate of Rev. Raymond Branch, and curates **RevBranch.com**. His screenplay with Jason Cuadrado, *I'm Here For You*, was produced as *Devil May Call*. A member of The Stanley J. Zappa Quartet, a recording, *The Stanley J. Zappa Quartet Plays for the Society of Women Engineers*, has been released.

> "*The blazing phosphorus whirled around the inside of the B-29 like a meteor gone berserk. Ricocheting off the curved roof of the plane, it bombarded Erwin with its searing heat...the putrid smell of scorched flesh filled the cabin... He fell backward, waving his arms, thrown off balance and dazed....*"

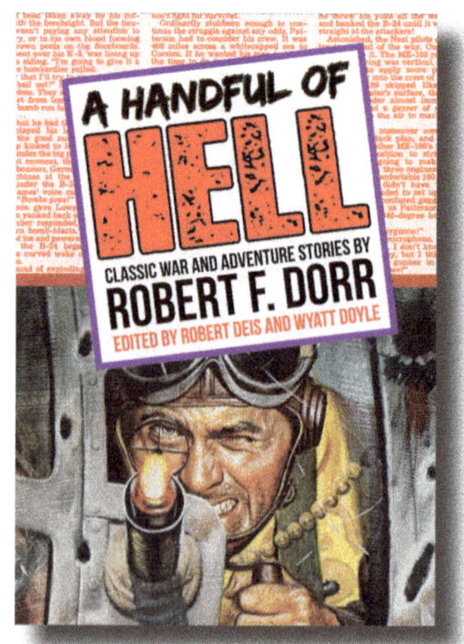

Aviator, diplomat, and historian, the prolific **Robert F. Dorr** was uniquely qualified to write for men's adventure magazines, bringing sweat-and-blood, nuts-and-bolts authenticity to his many stories of combat, adventure, and sacrifice. This white-hot collection showcases the very best of Dorr's tense, vintage tales of aerial conflict and boots-on-the-ground heroism.

PAPERBACK, EBOOK, AND DELUXE EDITION HARDCOVER WITH ALTERNATE COVER ART AND EXCLUSIVE CONTENT

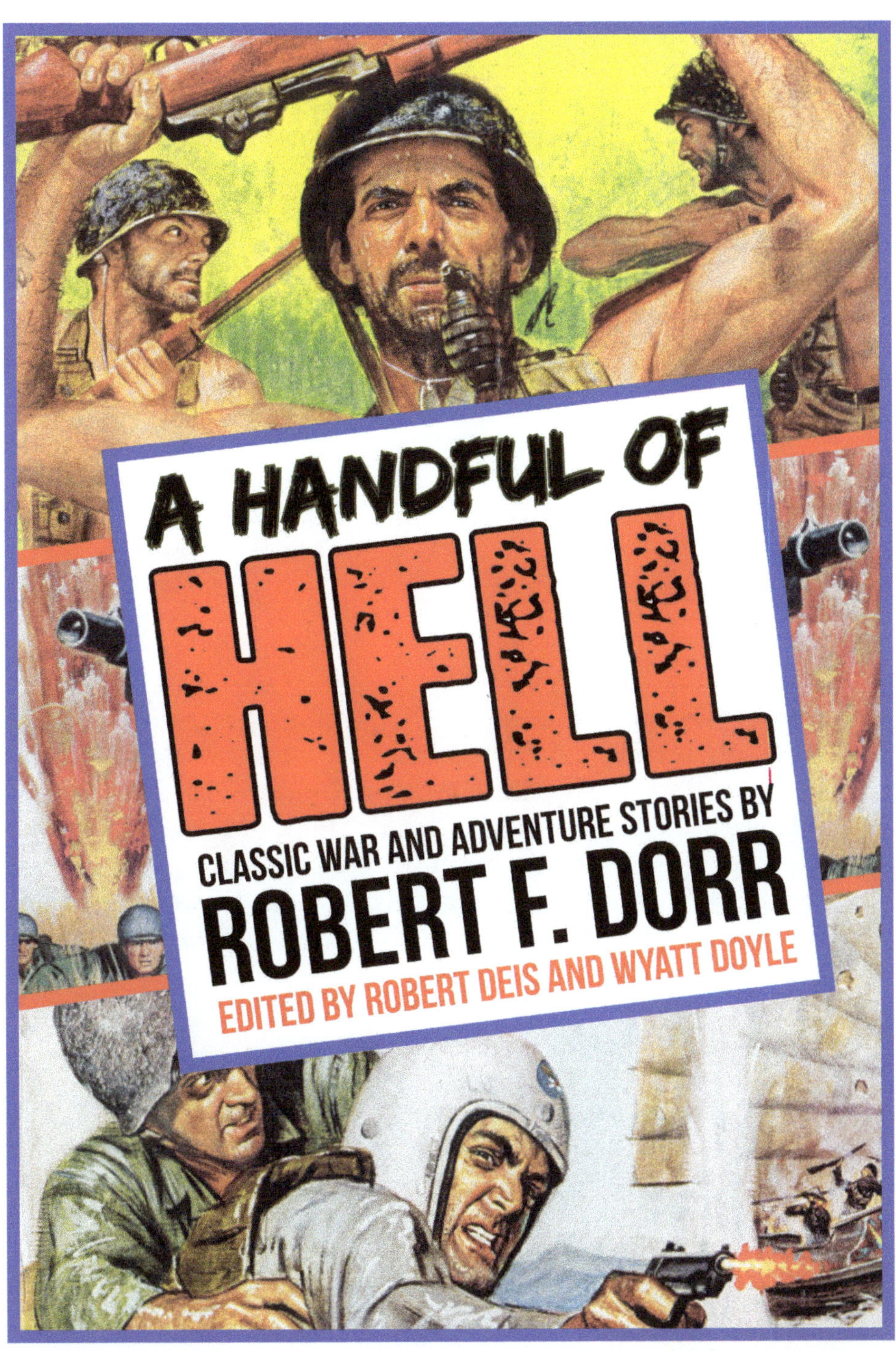

A HANDFUL OF HELL
CLASSIC WAR AND ADVENTURE STORIES BY
ROBERT F. DORR
EDITED BY ROBERT DEIS AND WYATT DOYLE
THE MEN'S ADVENTURE LIBRARY
MensPulpMags.com
new texture
WHERE THE ACTION IS!

THE MEN'S ADVENTURE LIBRARY

MANY TITLES AVAILABLE IN SOFTCOVER, EBOOK, AND DELUXE EXPANDED HARDCOVER EDITIONS

ROBERT DEIS AND WYATT DOYLE, SERIES EDITORS

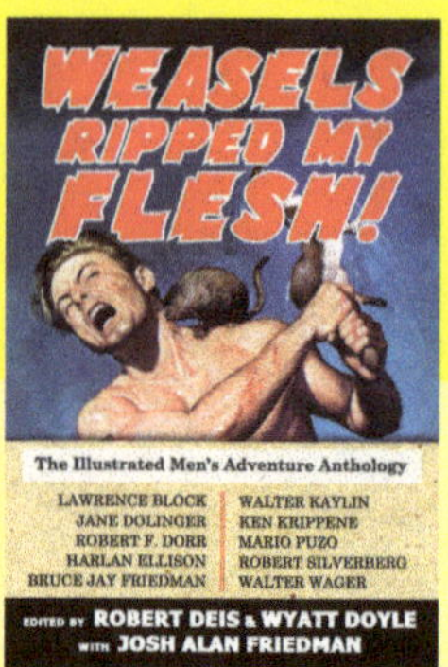

Weasels Ripped My Flesh!

With guest editor Josh Alan Friedman
Featuring Lawrence Block, Robert F. Dorr, Harlan Ellison, Bruce Jay Friedman, Walter Kaylin, Mario Puzo, Robert Silverberg *and more.*

From the jungles to the deserts to the mean city streets, the men's adventure magazines of the 1950s, '60s and '70s left no male fantasy or interest unexplored. War stories, exotic adventure yarns, (allegedly) true, first-hand accounts of white-knuckle clashes between man and beast, and spicy tales of sadistic frauleins and tropical queens hungry for companionship…plus salacious exposés of then-shocking subjects like free love, the Beat Generation, LSD, homosexuality, and the secret horniness hidden in calypso lyrics. This definitive guide to MAM fiction is your passport to a gonzo world where manly men fought small mammals bare-handed!

Atomic Werewolves and Man-Eating Plants: When MAMs Got Weird

Featuring Theodore Sturgeon, Manly Wade Wellman, Gardner Francis Fox, Gil Paust, Rick Rubin, HP Lovecraft, *and more*

Weird MAM tales of supernatural encounters, monstrous cryptids, vampirism, witchcraft, demonic death cults, killer robots, psychotic chicken butchers, and of course, atomic werewolves and man-eating plants!

Recommended by The Washington Post

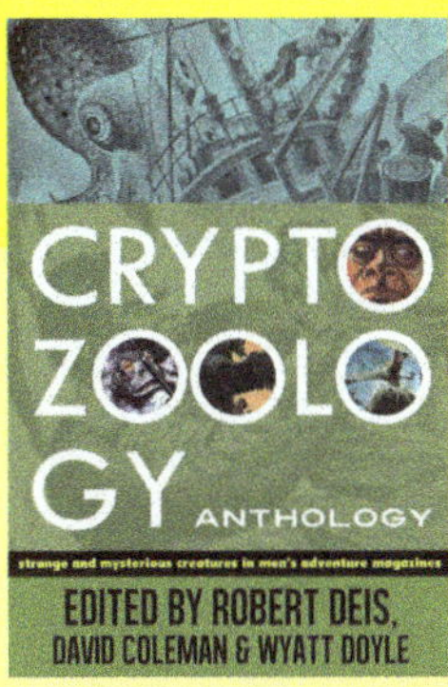

Cryptozoology Anthology
With guest editor David Coleman
Featuring Arthur C. Clarke, John Keel *and others*

When American men had questions about the Yeti, the Loch Ness Monster, Bigfoot, and other weird beasts from the strange world of cryptozoology, they found answers in the hard-hitting pages of men's adventure magazines. Here are samples of sensational period reporting and wild, "true" accounts of savage, fist-to-claw duels between man and Sasquatch, man and fishman, man and monster! Plus expert analysis by crypto authority **David Coleman**, cryptid-by-cryptid commentary, and much, much more. Don't leave civilization without it!

Recommended by The Washington Post

A Handful of Hell
Stories by Robert F. Dorr

Aviator, diplomat, and historian, Robert F. Dorr was uniquely qualified to write for men's adventure magazines, bringing sweat-and-blood, nuts-and-bolts authenticity to his stories of risk, combat, and sacrifice. Vivid, gripping tales of aerial conflict, battlefield heroism and action—some fact, some fiction, all adrenaline-fueled, white-knuckle adventure from one of the genre's greatest voices.

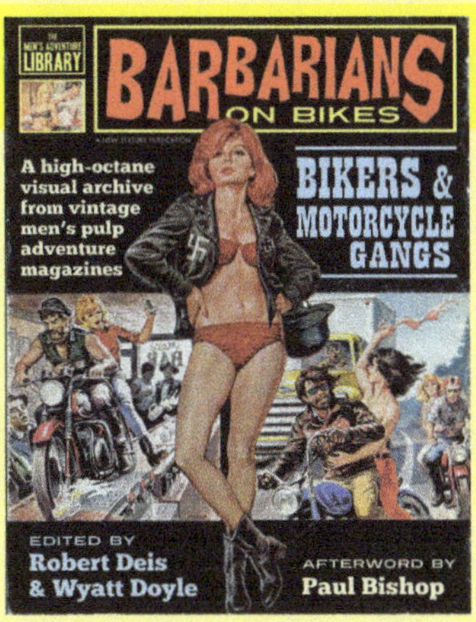

Barbarians on Bikes
Afterword by Paul Bishop

An oversized color collection compiling three decades of motorcycle-themed magazine covers and interior spreads from the 1950s through the 1970s, most unseen since their original publication. Biker illustration art at its most savage. A biker movie between covers, **Barbarians on Bikes** is big, bad, and untamed… Think you can handle the ride?

THE ART OF SAMSON POLLEN
Pollen's Women
Pollen's Action
Pollen in Print 1955–1959

A series of lush visual archives collecting some of artist Samson Pollen's most memorable pieces, selected from the hundreds of jaw-dropping illustrations he provided for men's adventure magazines (MAMs) from the 1950s through the 1970s. Pollen was equally celebrated for his abilities to effectively render action and movement, as well as his gift for painting beautiful and dangerous women. Illustrating work from authors like Mario Puzo, Martin Cruz Smith, Richard Stark (Donald Westlake), Norman Mailer, Ed McBain, Richard Wright, Don Pendleton, Erskine Caldwell, Walter Kaylin, and Robert F. Dorr, Pollen's immersive illustrations transported adventure-hungry readers from tropical jungles to brutal battlefields to raging seas and mean city streets. Samson Pollen painted it all—spectacularly. Yet almost none of these stunning illustrations have seen print since their original publication. Until now.

Both **Pollen's Women** and **Pollen's Action** are drawn from the artist's own exhaustive archives of his original artwork for MAMs, while **Pollen in Print 1955–1959** is the inaugural volume of a projected series presenting his artwork chronologically as it appeared in the magazines, allowing us to fill gaps in Pollen's archive and definitively chart the trajectory of a remarkable career.

All three big 11" x 8.5" horizontal volumes include the late artist's reminiscences and autobiographical comments.

Eva: Men's Adventure Supermodel
by Eva Lynd

Blonde Swedish countess Eva Lynd's multi-faceted career touches every aspect of 20th century popular culture. A model for leading illustration artists and top glamour and pin-up photographers of the era, she also appeared with some of the biggest names in entertainment on both the big and small screens. Eva shares her story in her own words and pictures. Includes artwork from pulp masters such as Norm Eastman, Al Rossi, Mike Ludlow, and James Bama.

One Man Army *by* Gil Cohen

Exploring the incomparable talent of Gil Cohen via the unique perspective he brought to the Mack Bolan universe as one of **The Executioner** series' most celebrated cover artists. **One Man Army** showcases Cohen's spectacular and original paintings for the bestselling action paperbacks, chronicling his seminal role in establishing the Bolan mythos for millions of dedicated readers worldwide.

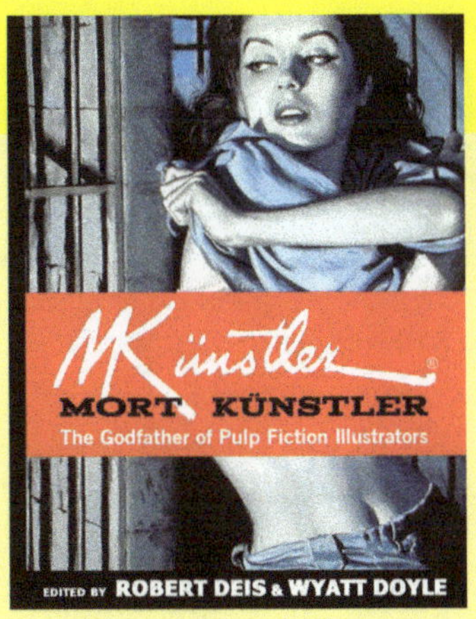

Mort Künstler: The Godfather of Pulp Fiction Illustrators

Celebrated for his ability to present large-scale action while never losing sight of essential details, **Mort Künstler** is a master of capturing conflict in paint—both its spectacle, and human cost. At last, here is a stunning selection of his finest pieces from the MAM era in this long awaited collection. A close study of an unequaled career, every page explodes with action, color, and artistry.

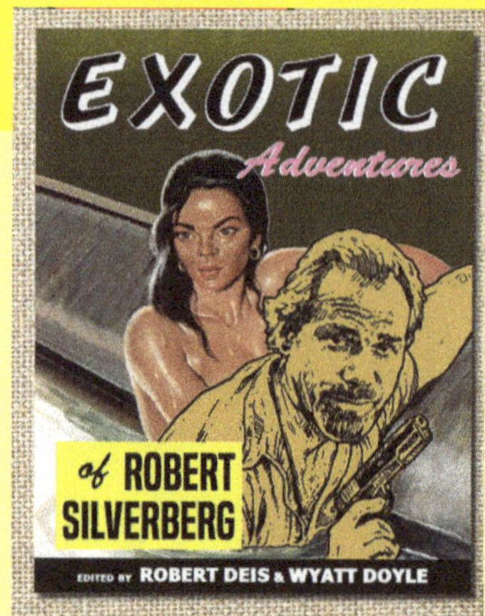

Exotic Adventures of Robert Silverberg

From safari to bordello, from smugglers' cove to opium den, Robert Silverberg's lost pulp exotica returns to print for the first time since its original 1950s publication, presented in bold new facsimile re-creations that look fresh off the newsstand, circa 1958. Strap in for fully illustrated globe-trotting adventures from the vivid imagination of one of speculative fiction's most honored talents, working incognito.

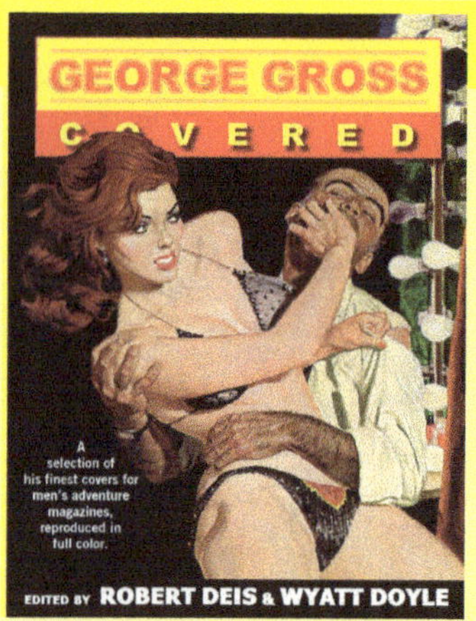

George Gross: Covered

A top artist for pulps, men's adventure magazines, and paperback covers, George Gross's artwork spans decades, and helped establish a visual vocabulary for action/adventure and hard-boiled fiction. A unique talent who led the way for generations of artists, his imagery continues to inspire and influence. Spotlighting dozens of his memorable covers, this full-color collection includes contributions by historian David Saunders and artist Mort Künstler.

The Naked and the Deadly
Stories by Lawrence Block

Spicy detective stories, international intrigue, and bedroom secrets… Before the bestsellers, Block cut his teeth on MAM fiction and nonfiction articles, collected here in their complete and uncut versions for the first time since their original publication. Includes a new introduction by the author.

Black Cracker, *an autobiographical novel by* Josh Alan Friedman

1962, flashpoint of the civil rights struggle. And young Josh is the lone white boy in a segregated grade school. An unflinching fun-house tour of a Long Island boyhood, and its now-forgotten poor Black shantytowns. Hilarious and heartbreaking.

Tell the Truth Until They Bleed, *by* Josh Alan Friedman

Up close and personal with important and unsung figures in blues and rock 'n' roll: the self-made, the self-serving, and the self-destructive. Illuminating parts of the music industry most don't talk about, this is show business without the showbiz.

Stop Requested, *stories by* Wyatt Doyle; *illus.* Stanley J. Zappa

"A series of rueful, witty and occasionally heartwrenching stories about riding the bus in LA. Doyle finds consequence in the inconsequential. He's Bukowski without the nasty streak. And he's real good. Highly recommended." —Marc Campbell, *Dangerous Minds*

---

nu luna, *a novel by* Andrew Biscontini

After 400 years of colonization, the moon is home to nearly a billion people, living in a crowded industrial police state on the verge of collapse. *nu luna* is a deeply personal matinee space adventure, spun through an improbably plausible future history. The future is beautiful and dangerous.

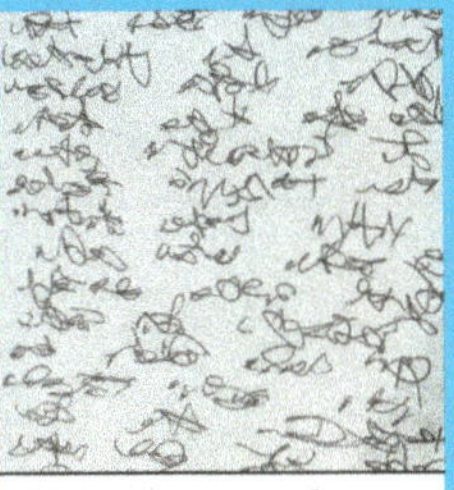

Teacher Tales, *a novel by* Richard Adelman

For 40 years, Mr. Kessler has kept his head down and not made waves. But new acquaintances and bad decisions in his final year before retirement bring his ordered world crashing down around him—tragically and hysterically. A smart and darkly comic novel.

A Day at the Beach, *a novel by* Richard Adelman

Atlantic City, summer of '63. A boy. A girl. And the other boy, who reluctantly pretends to date her to help his pal. A funny, nostalgic novel of young love, best friends, and poetry, capturing one 12-year-old's last great summer as a kid down the shore.

Nimrodia, *poems by* Eric Reymond

Visual art and ancient history are the starting point for most of the poems in this collection, as the modern world intersects with these domains again and again. Though language, culture, and time may divide us, these are also the forces that link us together.

Sub-Sub Librarian, Extracts on a, *poems by* Eric Reymond

The title poem imagines *Moby Dick*'s Sub-Sub Librarian experiencing transcendence and illumination through his wide readings. Additional poems find inspiration in texts as diverse as contemporary poetry, vocabulary quizzes, and course syllabi.

Things That Were Made for Love: The Songsheet Art of Sydney Leff
Wyatt Doyle, Hal Glatzer, Norman von Holtzendorff, *editors*

The first-ever songsheet art collection presenting the cream of the Jazz Age illustration artist's work on songsheet covers from 1924–1932. A gorgeous visual feast that playfully captures the moods, elegance, and style of an era.

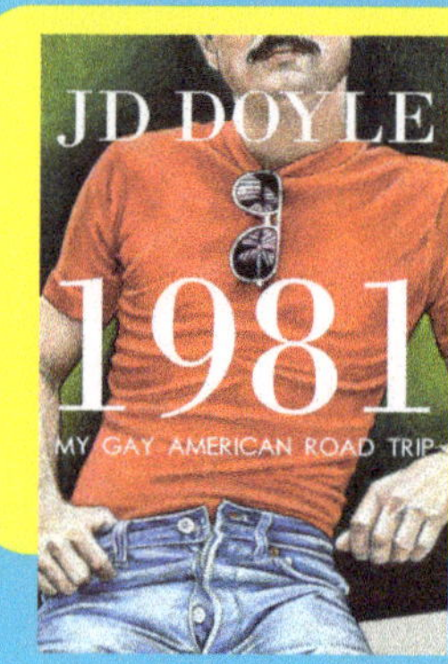

1981—My Gay American Road Trip
by JD Doyle

A playful, intimate, one-of-a-kind illustrated record of gay life, love, lust, and liberation post-Stonewall, in the heady days before the devastating crisis that would change everything.

#new texture Music

CD / DOWNLOAD

I've Got Heaven on My Mind
Reverend Raymond Branch

Sixty Goddammit Josh Alan

Jimmy Angelina s/t

Cursed Carolina

Continental / International
Jon E. Edwards

Map of the Moon s/t

Sing–Song Songs
Stanley J. Zappa

Free / Refuse
Hall, Skrowaczewski, Zappa

Live a Little
Manzappaczewski

The Stanley J. Zappa Quartet
**Plays for The Society
of Women Engineers**

Crossing Guards
Carter, Leffue, Sikora, Zappa

Turkey Bacon Donuts Bitches
MANZAP REBORN

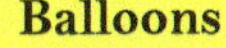

Balloons

Daniel Carter,
Nick Skrowaczewski,
Stanley J. Zappa

new texture